DELICIOUS

DELICIOUS

JAMI ALDEN

APHRODISIA

KENSINGTON PUBLISHING CORP.

http://www.kensingtonbooks.com

APHRODISIA BOOKS are published by

Kensington Publishing Corp.
850 Third Avenue
New York, NY 10022

ISBN: 0-7582-1532-0

First Kensington Trade Paperback Printing: November 2006

10 9 8 7 6 5 4 3 2 1

Printed in Mexico

To Monica and Nyree, for holding my hand every step of the way. You are amazing critique partners and even better friends.
And to Gajus, for your love, support, and unflagging faith in me and my dream. You'll always be my hero!

Chapter One

"How can you tell it's a scrotum?" Reggie turned the page sideways, then a full 180 degrees, then back to what she assumed was the original orientation.

"Well, there." Her sister, Natalie, traced a perfectly French-manicured nail along a blurry shape. "That's definitely a testicle. And right there"—she indicated a dark gray area at the top of the page—"I'm pretty sure that's his butt crack."

"I'm not seeing it."

The page had arrived in today's mail, shuffled in with junk mail, a PG&E bill, and her monthly issue of *Cooking Light*. The blurry black-and-white photocopy had just six words at the top: *Darling Reggie, these are Simply Delicious*. To add to the creep factor, the words were composed of magazine cutouts like psycho kidnapper serial killers always used in the Lifetime Channel's movie of the week.

"Yeah, but how long has it been since you've seen one?"

Reggie shot her sister a glare. "It may have been a while since I've had sex, but I think I could recognize a scrotum if it were in front of my face. Besides, there's no penis."

Natalie snatched the paper up. "Maybe his balls are the best part. Or maybe they're so massive, they obscure everything else."

"Gross! How does one even accomplish that?" Reggie's lip curled in revulsion.

"Well, I think if he put his leg over like this . . ." Natalie swung one thin, Blue Cult Jean–clad leg over the corner of Reggie's kitchen table. "And held his dick up like this . . ." She cupped her hand between her legs to demonstrate how a man might cup his penis up and out of the way of the photocopier glass. "I think you might get that angle."

Reggie looked at her sister, then back at the picture. She supposed, yes, if a man did decide to assault a hapless copier machine in such a fashion, such an image might result. This guy definitely had more ass to work with than Natalie. Not that that was a great achievement, since Natalie's skinny rump barely filled out the seat of her size two jeans.

Her admirer's butt, when smashed against the copier glass, left the impression of two hair-speckled pressed hams.

Since her cooking show, *Simply Delicious with Reggie Caldwell*, had become a big hit—for the Cuisine Network, anyway—she'd received all kinds of interesting fan mail. Everything from the mundane—recipe suggestions, self-published cookbooks fans hoped she would promote, general letters of admiration (and criticism, but she chose to ignore those)—to the slightly wacko.

That category included five marriage proposals, a handful of accusations from viewers claiming that she'd broken into their houses and stolen their grandmother's top-secret recipe for any number of dishes, and one offer of ten thousand dollars from a man who wanted to watch her smear pie all over her face.

But a lonely scrotum, that took the cake. She couldn't suppress a giggle as she imagined some guy, pants hanging off one ankle as he swung a leg over the unfortunate piece of office equipment. "This is great. Anyone can send flowers or chocolate, but a man willing to squash his nuts in the pursuit of great fan mail? This is even better than the guy with the pie fetish."

Natalie snickered. "Reminds me of the guy who wanted a pair of my panties after I did that douche commercial. Said he wanted to see if I was really as 'fresh' as I looked." Reggie made a sound of disgust as Natalie once again picked up the envelope the scrotum copy came in. Natalie's laughter stopped abruptly, and her perfectly waxed eyebrows compressed in a tight vee over the bridge of her nose.

"What's wrong?"

"I don't want to freak you out, but this wasn't sent through the network."

In an attempt to maintain her privacy, Reggie had all of her fan mail sent care of the network's New York offices, then forwarded either to her producer's office here in San Francisco or to her home address.

"This was sent directly to your home address. Whoever sent this knows where you live."

A cold little fist pinched somewhere around Reggie's small intestine. "But I'm not listed," she said, wincing at how stupid that sounded. Like that made a difference now.

She shook off the flutter of panic. So some oddball had figured out where she lived. Big deal. He was most likely as harmless as the rest of the other nutbars who wrote her. She shook her head, pushed back from the table, and went to the freezer to break off a square of dark Scharffenberger chocolate. "I don't think it's anything to worry about."

Natalie eyed the chocolate in her hand, her eyebrow raised skeptically. "Sure. That's exactly why you went straight for the chocolate pacifier. Remember, you're filming for the next two months straight."

Reggie rolled her eyes. She loved her sister, but sometimes she wondered how Natalie seemed to have infinite self-control over base urges like hunger and never succumbed to dreaded emotional eating. And Natalie never hesitated to remind Reggie that the camera added ten pounds. A not-so-subtle implication that Reggie's relatively slim size-eight figure looked positively elephantine when reduced to two dimensions.

At times like this she could barely restrain herself from shoving a dozen Krispy Kremes down her younger sister's size-two throat. Reggie defiantly broke off another square and devoured it with enough relish to give Natalie nightmares of cellulite and belly flab.

"If you cut carbs for the next few days, you should be fine," Natalie continued, "and you need to step up your cardio big time." Pausing, Natalie contemplated her own sinewy-looking arm, frowning as she pinched about a millimeter of extra skin. "As for that"—she looked meaningfully at the blotchy black-and-white photocopy—"I think you should do something about this guy."

Reggie poured a glass of water to chase the chocolate. "What am I supposed to do, Nat? Call the police and say I received a suspicious photocopy of genitalia in the mail? They have murders to solve."

Natalie combed her fingers through her waist-length, perfectly streaked, light brown hair. "Despite your attempts to stay private, some guy managed to find your address to send you a picture of his balls. Doesn't that freak you out just a little bit, considering you live here all by yourself? And it's not the most secure building in the world. Just yesterday your neighbor downstairs let me in and didn't even ask who I was."

"That's because he wants to get in your pants."

Natalie brightened, momentarily distracted. "Really?" She frowned again, refocusing on the subject at hand. "When I lived down in L.A., one of my friends"—she mentioned a well-known TV star—"had a stalker. It started out just like this. Letters, pictures, no big deal." She leaned forward intently, her dark blue gaze boring into Reggie's face. "Then one day she came home and her cat was hanging from the oak tree in her front yard." She sat back and nodded emphatically.

The chocolate curdled in Reggie's stomach as she imagined the unfortunate feline. But, she reminded herself, this was Natalie, with her flair for the dramatic and a tendency to embellish for effect. More likely, the actress had come home to find a squirrel had been hit in front of her driveway. "Good thing I don't have any pets." Rex, the ficus she'd barely managed to keep alive for the past five years, didn't count. "And my apartment doesn't have a yard."

Natalie's hands flew up in exasperation. "You have to take this seriously. Things like this start small, and then they escalate. I've seen it hundreds of times." She went on to list a handful of famous stars that had experienced stalker problems.

Considering the douche commercial and a couple of walk-on TV and movie rolls were the extent of her acting résumé, Reggie found it hard to believe that Natalie had ever, in fact, come within spitting distance of any of the women she named, much less discussed their personal security problems.

"This guy could come over any time he wants and catch you unaware," Natalie ranted. "Then what do you think will happen?"

"He'll take me to Kinko's?"

Natalie got up from the table and grabbed the telephone. "I'm calling the police. This way if anything else happens, at least they have a file started."

Reggie started to stop her, then thought better of it. Maybe Natalie was right. It *was* creepy to think that someone she didn't even know had gone to the trouble of tracking down her home address.

A prickle of unease raised the hairs on the back of Reggie's neck; she pushed away from the counter and yanked the blinds down over the kitchen sink. Then she went out into the living room and closed the blinds over her big bay window. She would enjoy her view of the Golden Gate Bridge some other day.

Then she snapped the blinds back up. What was up with that? No way was she going to let herself be intimidated by some freako who thought his balls were worth sharing. She had way too much going on to waste any thoughts worrying about this. Besides, didn't California have laws against this?

She walked back into the kitchen and cast the offending picture a scathing glance. As much as she hated to admit it, Natalie was right. The sooner she went to the police, the sooner they would nail this joker. Then he'd see it wasn't so funny, sending semiobscene material through the mail.

Natalie hung up. "They said we should come in to give a statement."

Reggie groaned. "I don't have time for this. My editor's going to kill me if I don't finish my draft of the side dish chapter." The first draft of her second cookbook was weeks overdue, and the fact that Natalie had sent the main dish chapter to the wrong editorial department last week hadn't helped matters.

Natalie rolled her eyes and held out Reggie's purse. "Oh, please. How long can it take you to write out a few stupid recipes?"

A lot harder than it is to mooch off my sister's charity while flitting from one fruitless audition to another. But Reggie kept quiet. It was her own stupid fault for hiring Natalie as her assistant rather than simply lending her money. It wasn't Natalie's fault she was borderline incompetent.

Forty-five minutes later, they were at the San Francisco Police Department providing a statement to the desk sergeant on duty. She was black, burly, and highly amused by the picture Reggie provided. "Honestly, what kinda man has to stoop to sending pictures of his stuff in the mail? No surprise he don't show no dick. Probably got a little itty bitty one." She held her thumb and forefinger about an inch apart to demonstrate.

Reggie couldn't help grinning in response. "That's exactly what I thought. I mean, what kind of guy humps a copier so he can send a love letter?"

"But, Sergeant Mulvaney, whoever sent it knows where Reggie lives," Natalie interjected. "Shouldn't that be cause for alarm?"

Sergeant Mulvaney tried her best to assume a serious expression. "Have you received anything of a similar nature?"

Reggie bit her lip. "Nothing like this, and never sent directly to my house." Suddenly the idea of the police diligently tracking down her prankster seemed a bit far-fetched.

"What about that guy with the pie fetish?" Natalie asked.

Sergeant Mulvaney looked quizzically at Reggie.

Reggie shook her head. "That was sent to the studio."

"Studio?"

"I host a cooking show."

Sergeant Mulvaney's big brown eyes got even bigger. "Ooh, girl, I knew I recognized your name! You're the one who does the easy recipes. You are so skinny in person!"

Reggie grinned and thanked her, resisting the urge to flash Natalie a smug look. Not everyone thought she was chunky.

Sergeant Mulvaney wasn't finished. "I made that chicken coated in the corn chips for a potluck, and it was such a hit. Except I mixed in some cayenne pepper to give it a little kick."

There was nothing Reggie loved to talk about more than food. "The cayenne is a great idea. Or if you wanted, you could even go with that new chipotle powder they have out now for a smokier flavor, and I've even mixed the chips with a little shredded parmesan, just to give it kind of a nacho taste—"

"Hello! I think we're getting a little off track here," Natalie said peevishly.

Reggie smiled sheepishly at the sergeant. "Well, uh, thanks for watching the show." Usually she loved being recognized. She loved talking to fans, sharing tips and ideas, hearing that she helped someone make a meal that his or her family loved. Good thing, since a huge part of her popularity was her approachability and reputation for fan-friendliness.

But she hated being recognized around Natalie. Natalie had clawed her way around Hollywood seeking fame and fortune for the past seven years, and suddenly in the last year both had fallen right into Reggie's lap.

Semi-fame, at least. Enough to make her feel guilty about

rubbing it in her baby sister's face. And a respectable fortune, especially now that her first cookbook had spent its twenty-second week on _The New York Times_ best-seller list and her agent had negotiated a ridiculous advance for her second cookbook.

An advance that might be revoked if she didn't get her butt in gear and finish the first draft. She should have known better than to agree to her editor's deadline of three months when she was simultaneously developing another cooking show.

Sergeant Mulvaney's glum look and tsking sounds brought her focus back to the issue at hand. "I'm real sorry, honey. We can dust this for fingerprints, but if there's no pattern and no threat of violence, there's not much we can do."

Reggie and Natalie slumped, defeated.

"But what about the antistalker laws?" Natalie protested.

The sergeant shook her head, the beads of her cornrows softly clicking. "Without anything to go on, there's not much we can do to catch him. And even if we could find him, without any threats of violence, we can't even press charges. My advice to you: Lock your doors, try to be more aware of your surroundings, and maybe enroll in a self-defense class."

They left after Sergeant Mulvaney confirmed she would start a file for the case. On the way home, Reggie dropped Natalie off for her audition for a local health club chain commercial.

Reggie wished her good luck, to which Natalie's only response was a grunt. Obviously, she was still ticked about having to deal with Reggie's fan encounter. "Nat," she called out to her sister's retreating back, "if you want, you can come in early to do my makeup tomorrow before the shoot. Then you can borrow my car to drive to your audition, okay?" Reggie breathed a sigh of relief at Nat's nearly imperceptible nod.

Inwardly, she cringed at her knee-jerk appeasement of her sister's temper. Wasn't it time she stopped feeling guilty for her own success? Hadn't she worked her ass off for the past four years since leaving her job as a successful CPA?

Shouldn't she be proud and impressed with her own success, since no one else in her family seemed inclined to be?

Still, her mother's voice echoed in her head. "Take care of Natalie, Reggie. You're her big sister, and you know you're the more sensible one."

By the time Reggie got home, all she wanted was to pour herself a glass of wine and settle down with a snack in front of the TV until she could slink off to bed at an astoundingly uncool hour. But not only was she way behind in getting recipes to her editor for her new book, with six weeks of location shoots starting in less than two weeks, this was her last chance to get the bulk of her already overdue manuscript done.

Deliberately bypassing the kitchen, she went directly to her office and flipped on her Sony Vaio. Call her a nerd, but after years of making do with a clunker of a laptop, she still loved the sound of the chimes that greeted her as she fired it up. It was her second gift to herself after her first book hit the nonfiction best-seller list, the first having been a move to a 1,500 square foot two-bedroom apartment in Pacific Heights. After living in a studio since graduating from college, she still found herself occasionally overwhelmed by all the space.

She quickly scanned through her e-mails. Predictably, Sharon, her editor, had e-mailed no less than three times, reminding Reggie that she'd promised to send the recipes for the last three chapters by the end of the week. Tyler, her PR manager, wrote to provide the details of a cooking demonstration and book signing she had scheduled for next week and asked again for her updated travel and shooting schedule so he could schedule appearances in the cities she planned to visit.

There was also a note from her mother, raving about the South Beach Diet and how it might help her butt look "less puffy" on TV.

Reggie shook her head. Her perfectionist mother had only two topics of conversation. One was about her weight. The other topic was about how she was wasting her life with this "cooking thing" and "little show" on a "no-name network" when she could be building a long and lucrative career as an accountant.

Virginia Caldwell was a rarity—a female senior partner at one of Boston's biggest law firms, and she'd expected her daughters to follow the path she blazed to some high-powered career. It had merely broken her heart when Reggie didn't go to law school and "settled" for a master's degree in finance.

When she'd quit her job as an accountant to pursue a career in food, it was nearly grounds for disownment.

Reggie hoped that with her next book on the way and another TV show about to go into production, her mother might finally realize that following her heart was the smartest business decision Reggie had ever made.

For now, she much preferred it when her mother focused on Reggie's big butt and not her so-called worthless career.

One would think that given how many hours Virginia worked, she wouldn't have time to wage a long-distance campaign to keep Reggie from letting her career go to her hips, butt, and thighs. But God forbid one of her daughters look less than perfect and reflect poorly on her.

Like Natalie, her mother knew to the decimal point the calorie amount of every bite of food she put in her mouth. As far as she could tell, both her mother and sister existed on a steady diet of dry lettuce, water, and black coffee. It was one of the few areas in which Natalie—whose aspirations of TV stardom were yet another source of maternal disappointment—and her mother found common ground.

She scrolled down, deleting offers to adjust her mortgage and increase her penis size. She came to one with the subject line:

You Look Lovely in Blue.

The creepy feeling stole over her again as she glanced down at her shirt, a slate-blue cowl-neck with long sleeves. It was probably just meaningless spam. Her finger hovered over the mouse, hesitant to click it open. Curiously, the "From" line was empty. She took a deep breath and opened it.

> Darling Reggie,
> You looked so lovely today, your blue shirt showing off the beauty of your neck, the glow of your skin, the lush roundness of your breasts. I love the way the afternoon sun brings out the reddish glints in your dark hair. You are breathtaking, and you don't even seem to be aware of it. It was all I could do to resist the urge to run up and claim you as my own. But for now, I think it's best I remain anonymous. I hope you enjoyed my token of affection. I hope someday soon you can experience them up close.
> I can't wait to taste your cherry pie.

He'd been watching her! Reggie jumped up and hurried through the apartment, closing and locking every window and drawing every curtain and blind. She sat back in front of the computer, taking deep breaths to calm the pounding of her heart. Mentally, she scrolled through her day, cataloging everywhere she'd been.

First, the studio this morning for filming. Maybe loverboy had seen her there. But no, she hadn't been outside, having gone directly from the parking garage into the building. It had to have been after, when she'd walked down to the Marina to window-shop and pick up groceries for dinner.

It is probably nothing.

But he knows where you live. He could be outside right now. She peered out of her office window, which looked out over the street. Nothing but regular evening traffic. No creepy degenerates staring up into her apartment. She pulled out the card Sergeant Mulvaney had given her and picked up the cordless phone. Then she paused. What could they do?

He hadn't threatened her, and his e-mail appeared to be un-traceable. Likely they'd just take another statement and add it to the file.

Her computer dinged, indicating another incoming e-mail. Sharon, her editor, again. Jeez, it was nine o'clock on the east coast. Didn't the woman ever stop?

She pressed her thumbs into her eye sockets and groaned. She didn't have time to waste going to the police for a most likely harmless fan. The demands of filming and promoting two shows and a book while writing another required all of her attention right now.

The familiar anxiety settled in her chest, threatening to cut off her air supply. Though she was grateful for her sudden and sometimes overwhelming success, lately she'd felt more and more pressure to keep her career on its unnaturally steep trajectory.

Her next TV show had to be a hit. Her upcoming book had to be a best-seller. Just because she'd been lucky enough to hit it big the first time didn't mean she was a proven com-modity. The network was taking a huge risk and spending a lot of money on *Simply Delicious, USA*, and she knew if she wasn't at the top of her game, there was always some other celebrity chef wannabe waiting in the wings to take her job.

She closed the offending e-mail with a definitive click. On the verge of ensuring she was more than a one-hit wonder, she simply didn't have time to be distracted by some weirdo who thought it would be fun to mess with her.

A branch rattled against her office window, sending her nearly to the ceiling. She picked up the phone.

Natalie answered on the second ring, and Reggie quickly filled her in on the e-mail.

The audition must have gone well, because Natalie made appropriate sounds of distress. "Did you call the police?"

"No, I don't want to bug them. But do you think you could spend the night tonight?" Reggie's fingers tensed around the phone as Natalie paused.

"Okay," Natalie said finally, "but it won't be until at least ten. I'm having dinner with that guy I met last week."

Reggie berated herself for being such a wuss. Did she really think this guy was going to break into her apartment, just because he'd sent her a picture of his scrotum? "Never mind. I don't want to ruin your night—"

Natalie cut her off with a laugh. "Look at it this way. You're saving me from potential stupidity, like sleeping with him on the first date."

Reggie hung up and clicked open the file for her cook-book. Thank god Natalie was coming over. Not that her underfed little sister could provide much extra protection, but she knew she'd sleep better knowing she wasn't alone.

After pulling together her notes for the side dish chapter, Reggie started on desserts. She pulled out a file of recent show scripts, disappointed that she'd done desserts for less than half the episodes. Not much of a dessert eater herself, she found those recipes the most challenging to develop. And telling her readers to enjoy a square of really good baking chocolate probably wouldn't cut it.

Maybe she could come up with yet another variation on a sundae.

She was typing out the ingredient list for "Hey, Your Peanut Butter's in My Chocolate Sundae" when the phone rang.

"I have the best idea!"

"Hey, Nat. How's the date?"

"He's a loser. But that's not why I called. I know how to deal with your problem. I can't believe I didn't think of it earlier."

Reggie cradled the phone between her neck and shoulder as she typed. "Yeah?"

"Remember my friend Adrienne from college? Now she's married to some hotshot investor guy and has gobs of money. Anyway, her brother was in the Special Forces."

"So?" Reggie said, only half listening.

"So now he's out of the military and is some kind of personal security guy, like a bodyguard."

Reggie rolled her eyes. "I'll admit things are a little weird, but I don't think this warrants me getting a full-time body-guard."

"He does other stuff, too, like figuring out how to make your apartment safer, teaching you self-defense things, stuff like that. A lot of people I knew in L.A. hired people for this."

"I don't have time—"

"I'll set it up. I'm your assistant, right? Let me assist."

Reggie barely managed to stifle a scoffing sound. She'd hired Natalie a month and a half ago to be her personal assistant, hoping to help her sister make rent more regularly since commercial acting jobs had proved few and far between. So far, Natalie's idea of "assisting" took the form of doing Reggie's makeup for television when she could drag herself out of bed at the ungodly hour of seven A.M., occasionally running personal errands for Reggie, but only if Natalie had something to do herself, and pissing off Reggie's PR manager, Tyler, by constantly entering incorrect information into Reggie's online calendar.

But hey, if Natalie was going to take it upon herself to hire Reggie a bodyguard, what better guarantee that it wouldn't get done?

Chapter Two

The following night, Reggie took Natalie out to dinner at her favorite Persian restaurant in the Marina, partly to thank her for staying over last night, and partly to gently confront her about her less than stellar assistant skills.

Reggie had to give Natalie credit, though. She had actually managed to call and schedule an appointment with Adrienne's brother, who was supposed to fly up from L.A. tomorrow afternoon for an initial consultation. She'd nearly choked when Natalie quoted her the fee, but as Natalie pointed out, it wasn't like she was living off leftovers from her private chef gigs anymore.

The restaurant was quiet for a Thursday night, for which Reggie was grateful. As much as she enjoyed interacting with fans, she didn't want any awkward interruptions as she had what would surely be a delicate conversation with her sister.

She fired her first salvo over the hummus appetizer. "Thanks again for scheduling the security thing." Lead with a compliment, proceed to the criticism. She paused, momentarily fascinated by the way Natalie carefully peeled apart her pita until it was a single ply, then applied a layer of hummus so thin it was barely visible to the naked eye. "Careful there. You might accidentally ingest a fat gram."

Natalie scowled.

Reggie scooped up a glob of hummus in the warm, soft

pita, humming in pleasure as the creamy, lemon-tinged spread hit her tongue. "I think it's great you took the initiative on that."

Natalie smiled and took a little bird bite of her pita sheet.

"But there are some other things that need improvement."

"Are you, like, micromanaging me?"

Reggie argued around another mouthful of pita. "I'm not micromanaging. I asked you a week and a half ago for my final travel schedule for the first week of shooting, and I still haven't seen it."

"I'll get it to you soon."

"Tomorrow, noon. Tyler needs my schedule so he can schedule some book signings while I'm on the road. He can't do that until he gets my travel and shooting schedule."

"But I have an audition."

"That's the other thing—last week you scheduled four cryptic appointments into my calendar that I can only conclude were your own auditions."

"It hasn't been that bad."

"Remember when you mailed my last two chapters to the wrong department? It took two weeks to track down that package." She placed the bread on her plate. "When you pull stuff like that, it makes me look unprofessional and incapable of handling my career. I know you think all of this just dropped in my lap, but I've worked my butt off to get where I am. I can't let your incompetence make me look bad."

"Fine." Natalie folded her thin arms over her chest.

"If you don't want to work for me, just say so. It's not like you'll hurt my feelings if you quit."

Natalie was silent for several seconds, her face compressed in a scowl as she traced designs in the hummus with the tines of her fork. "I can't quit. As much as I hate to take your charity, I need this job right now."

Reggie's reply was interrupted by the arrival of their entrées. Sighing, she saw that her waiter had gotten her order wrong, giving her the Chicken Kebab instead of the Chicken

Shawerma. She cursed herself for not ordering before her sister. Natalie's order for a Greek salad, no dressing, no cheese, no olives, and no onions had thrown the waiter, as happened at every restaurant. Invariably, whenever they went out, Natalie systematically stripped down a salad until she was left with a plate of dry lettuce, tomatoes, and the occasional cucumber. Waiters found this so confusing that any subsequent order placed was inevitably misunderstood.

Oh well, at least she liked kebabs.

"Well, well, well, if it isn't the Cuisine Network's big new star."

Reggie closed her eyes and sighed. Craig Ferguson, self-styled "Bad Boy" of the San Francisco restaurant scene, had arrived just in time to ruin her dinner.

Taking in his designer jeans, motorcycle boots, and black silk sweater that probably cost a month's rent, Reggie was astounded that she'd actually dated and thought herself in love with this man for over two years.

Oh, he was cute, with his dark blond hair styled with more hair product than she'd ever used in her lifetime and his blue-eyed, boyish good looks. And he could be funny and very, very charming as long as everything was going in his favor. But now that she'd had over a year and a half to distance herself from their relationship, she wondered how she'd missed his self-serving, self-absorbed core.

Reggie pasted a smile on her face and greeted him cordially. Craig had been the host of his own show on the Cuisine Network, but much to his dismay, production had been canceled about a year ago. Right when they had picked up *Simply Delicious* for a primetime slot.

The last thing she wanted was for someone to recognize them. Too late. Other diners were already whispering and nodding their heads in Craig's direction.

"I caught your show today," he said with a cheeky grin. "That thing you did with the tortilla wrap—nice. Have you started visiting trailer parks for inspiration?" He said it like he was kidding, but Reggie knew better. Even when they were dating, he'd never let Reggie forget that he was a chef, with a degree from the Cordon Bleu and several successful restaurants on his résumé.

Whereas she was a mere cook.

He'd never gotten over the fact that her simple, down-to-earth approach to cooking had proved infinitely more popular than his own all but unattainable haute cuisine approach.

Natalie bristled. "At least she doesn't expect people to spend thousands of dollars and half a day cooking up some truffle stew."

As much as she didn't want to see them get into it, Reggie's insides warmed at Natalie's staunch defense. So what if her sister was a flake and occasionally made unintentionally cruel remarks? Natalie was always first in line to defend her.

Craig hit Natalie with a scathing glare. "Ooh, that hurts, coming from someone who knows even less about food than your sister. How's that lettuce treating you, Nat?"

Reggie made a last-ditch attempt to keep Natalie and Craig from going after each other like rabid dogs. Later, she would wonder why she had bothered. Even when she and Craig were dating, Natalie and Craig had barely tolerated each other. "You guys, come on, can we not—"

Natalie interrupted, "You're just pissed because your show got canceled and your book tanked."

"Natalie, don't." Reggie said.

Craig leaned down and shook his finger in Natalie's face. "If your sister wants to cater to the fat housewives of America, that's fine, but when they want to learn from a real chef, they come to me."

Ouch. She'd put up with his pointed jabs as her success proved too much for his surprisingly fragile ego, figuring that if that was what he needed to make him feel better, so be it.

But denigrating her fans . . . that was below the belt, and she didn't have to put up with Craig's bad attitude and scathing sarcasm anymore.

Considering all the times she'd helped him out with his own show and pinch-hit as a sous-chef when he was short-handed, she deserved more respect than that. "My fans are not fat housewives. They're people like me who don't want to spend hours reducing sauce to make dinner every night."

Craig made a harsh scoffing sound. "Ride this wave as long as you can, because believe me, once people get sick of that perky chatty Cathy act of yours, you're through."

Reggie stood up and threw down her napkin, punching her finger into Craig's chest. "Oh yeah? If I'm such a flash in the pan, why am I leaving for New York in two weeks to start filming my new show? And why did I get a seven-figure advance on my next book? Just wait. This one is going to hit the *New York Times* list too."

She took unholy satisfaction in Craig's bewildered expression.

"New show?"

"*Simply Delicious, USA,*" Natalie chimed in. "Reggie's going to the biggest food cities in the country to bring regional specialties to your living room."

Reggie grinned down at her. "So you *have* read the promo materials."

Craig's expression reverted to its previous snarky state. "I can't wait to see your latest variation on the tuna casserole." He stalked off to a table in the back of the restaurant.

Reggie sat down and contemplated her suddenly unappetizing plate of food. Someone tapped her on the shoulder. A young woman, maybe twenty-five, wearing a tweed skirt, chocolate cashmere sweater, and knee-high boots smiled tentatively at her. "Hi, I'm sorry to disturb you, but I'm such a big fan."

So much for having an anonymous dinner. Reggie smiled and reached out to shake her hand.

"I don't care what that guy says, my friends and I think you're great. We even have monthly dinner parties based on your show."

Soon Reggie and the woman, who had introduced herself as Karen, were chatting like old friends, and even Natalie joined in the conversation, suggesting movies and music to go along with various dinner party themes. By the time Karen left, Reggie had almost forgotten Craig and his nasty attitude.

But Natalie wouldn't let her. "Craig is such an asshole," Natalie grumbled as they walked back to Reggie's apartment.

Reggie murmured in agreement, recognizing the familiar bitter taste she always had when she thought of Craig and how he'd slunk out of her life. "Yeah," she said, "you spend two years of your life trying to give them everything they want, and the second you take something for yourself . . ." she trailed off. She couldn't help Craig's bitterness and knew not to take it personally, but sometimes she wondered if maybe she were somehow better—nicer, prettier, kinder, more patient—he could have kept loving her in spite of her success.

It occurred to her for about a millisecond that Craig could be behind the notes. He was bitter, no doubt about it.

She dismissed the thought almost as quickly as it came. If Craig wanted to sabotage her career, he'd bad-mouth her in the open.

As Natalie dropped Reggie at her door, she reminded Reggie of their appointment tomorrow with Adrienne's brother. For the first time since Natalie had suggested it, Reggie didn't dread meeting her new security consultant.

At three forty-five the following afternoon, Reggie was pacing around her kitchen, fidgeting with utensils and glancing at the door every two seconds. "Are you sure he said three?"

Natalie grabbed Reggie's wrist so she could see her watch. "He had a meeting this morning and was going to catch a one o'clock flight from L.A., and in case of traffic we made the appointment for three."

Reggie opened the refrigerator for the millionth time, hoping something delicious would suddenly materialize.

Natalie rattled her magazine page in exasperation. "God, would you just settle down?"

"Nat, I have so much work to get done, and now this joker has wasted almost an hour of my time. I knew this was a bad idea"

"Why don't you go write or something?"

Reggie started pulling items out of the pantry and re-arranging them by food category. Veggies on the third shelf down, right side. Soups in the middle on the same shelf. Cereal on top, along with other grain products. "I can't focus if I know I'm about to be interrupted." Despite what Natalie thought, recipes didn't just spring fully formed from her head. Rather, they existed as scraps of notes and inexact measurements that she had to translate into easy-to-follow directions, and then add spirited commentary about the in-spiration for each dish.

As much as she loved it, sometimes the writing process was absolutely mind-numbing.

She was busily wiping down the counters when a knock fi-nally sounded at the door. "Can you get that?" God, she must be PMSing or something. It wasn't like her to be this crabby, even under these circumstances. Lots of her television appearances required a hurry up and wait mentality, and she'd forced herself to overcome her natural tendency to leap from one task into another. Until this precise moment, she thought she'd adapted pretty well.

"I'm very sorry I'm late," a masculine voice rumbled from the entryway. Low, deep, with the barest hint of a Southern accent. "I hope you got my message."

A gasp from Natalie. "Oh no! I must have turned off my phone." Natalie invited him in, the click of her stiletto boots on Reggie's hardwood floors echoing up to the crown molding.

"You think someone may be stalking you?"

Something about that voice . . . familiar but escaping her reach. Like a subtle spice she couldn't taste but knew a recipe would be ruined without. . . .

"Actually it's my sister who has a problem. Reg! Adrienne's brother, Gabe, is here."

Gabe. No. It had to be a coincidence. The world couldn't possibly be that small.

Natalie gestured to the man in her living room. "Reggie, this is Gabe Bankovic, your personal security consultant."

Her first look at him froze the air in her lungs.

No way.

But there he was in her living room, looking every bit as big and darkly delicious as the last time she'd seen him nearly a year and a half ago.

Except then he'd been naked in a tangle of bedsheets, sleeping the exhausted sleep of a man who had spent the last several hours showing her all the ways he knew to bring a woman to a soul-screaming orgasm.

"Gina?" Her name flew out of Gabe's mouth before he had a chance to think about it.

The woman who had introduced herself as the client's sister shot him a puzzled look. "This is Reggie, my sister, the victim I guess you could say."

Gabe closed his eyes and prayed. But she was still there when he opened them. Yep, that was Gina, or Reggie as she called herself now, with the glossy shoulder-length brown hair, big Bambi brown eyes to match, and a wide red mouth that brought heat to his crotch just looking at it.

What were the fucking odds that she would be his only client?

Somewhere, someone was having a huge belly laugh at his expense.

He deliberately schooled his features into a neutral expression and offered her his hand to shake.

"It's nice to see you again," he said quietly. A single touch of her small, capable hand sent a jolt straight to his groin, and his head flooded with images of those slender, pale fingers tracing down his chest, digging short nails into his ass as he sank into her deep and hard. He forced himself to let go almost immediately, afraid if he held on for one more second he'd have her pinned to the couch and damn his professional reputation.

Natalie looked between them in puzzlement. "You two know each other?"

"Your sister and I met some time ago while we were both on vacation." There, that sounded nice and neutral.

Obviously not neutral enough. Natalie looked at her sister in open-mouthed astonishment. "Is this the guy who—"

Reggie cut her off with a look that would curdle milk.

Natalie pressed her lips together and slyly ran her eyes down every inch of his six-foot-three frame. "Small world."

Gabe wanted to howl like an angry baby. Under any other circumstances, he would have been overjoyed to see her again. First, he'd let her know how angry he was that she left without a word after showing him the most fun he'd ever had naked. Then he'd give her an itemized list off all the things she could do to apologize for sneaking out while he slept.

Steeling his resolve, he knew he had no choice but to put personal desires aside. No matter how badly he wanted to get his hands on that luscious ass beautifully displayed in tight black pants, there was no way in hell he was getting involved with another client.

"Why don't you start by walking me through what's happened so far?"

She licked her lips, the small gesture making it almost impossible for him not to lean over and suck her soft pink tongue into his mouth.

What was it about her that was so damned alluring? She wasn't the most beautiful woman he'd ever seen. Sure, she was attractive, in a wholesome, girl-next-door kind of way.

Except for her mouth. There was nothing wholesome about those full, succulent lips and how they'd felt sliding along his rock-hard dick.

But that wasn't enough to explain why merely looking at

her had him hard as a spike and seriously contemplating abandoning all his self-imposed rules against dating clients.

He glanced around her apartment, trying to focus on something, anything that might distract him from the memory of Reggie's lips and tongue tracing a moist path up his inner thigh.

Thankfully, she distracted him with a rundown of the correspondence she'd received thus far, while he attempted to view her with the same emotional detachment he would have for a sixty-year-old software CEO.

If he was going to get through this job with his sanity and professional credibility in tact, he had to keep his distance.

God knew he'd learned that the hard way.

Natalie held out the photocopy Reggie had received earlier that week.

It never ceased to amaze him, the workings of the male mind. Himself, he appreciated his own balls, but he'd never once considered that a woman might be impressed with a close-up shot.

Reggie's voice broke the silence. "Takes a lot of balls to send something like that."

Natalie groaned at the horrible pun while Reggie laughed at her own joke. Damn, she had a great smile. It was the first thing he had noticed about her in that restaurant in Maui. It was so wide it completely took over the bottom half of her face, suffusing it in unabashed delight. And when she turned it in his direction, he felt it like a goddamn force of nature.

Suddenly her living room with its big bay windows and overstuffed furniture was way too small. He had to get away from her, even for a few seconds. "Mind if I look around a little? I need to see what's involved for the alarm system we install."

Thankfully, the phone rang, so she didn't follow. He walked down the hall and did a quick tour of the office, making a mental note to ask Reggie to show him the suspicious e-mail.

The apartment suited her, or what little he knew of her,

anyway. Decorated in warm tones with splashes of bright color, it was warm, comfortable, and inviting. Just like the woman he'd met in that bar in Maui.

Business, Gabe. You're supposed to be looking for points of vulnerability. He noted that the office windows were large enough to allow a man to crawl through.

The bathroom was typical of an old San Francisco Victorian, with the shower, bath, and sink separate from a closet-size room that housed the toilet. The bathroom windows were small and high enough off the ground to pose a significant challenge to an intruder, but he'd make sure they were wired nonetheless.

He made a right and entered what could only be her bedroom. Like the rest of the apartment, it was comfortable, cozy, decorated in deep reds, midnight blues, and rich browns. Not a hint of pastel or a square of lace in sight.

It was the kind of room only a woman could put together—no guy had that many throw pillows—but it wasn't so feminine as to send him running for the closest sports bar. The king-size sleigh bed with its dark red down comforter and oversize pillows elicited all kinds of images of him and Reggie, naked in a sweaty tangle making damn good use of every inch of mattress space.

Shaking his head before he got too carried away, he moved to the window. He ran his fingers along the sides and tested the all but useless latch. She was on the second story, but anyone could sneak a ladder around through the alley and climb right up here. That was, if this stalker of hers was as determined as her sister seemed to think.

This was exactly the type of job he hated. Grunt work. Half the time these celebrities so overestimated their own importance to their fans that they overreacted to what amounted to nothing more than inappropriate fan mail. Disconcerting as it was to receive, more often than not there was no threat behind it.

His gut told him Reggie wasn't a woman with an overinflated ego, but his gut had been so wrong recently, he'd all but stopped giving it credit.

Just because he knew exactly what the silky skin of Reggie's inner thighs tasted like, just because the look on her face as she came had saturated his dreams for the past year and a half, didn't mean he knew a damn thing about her character.

He went into the bathroom and splashed cold water on his face, wishing he had an ice pack to shove down the front of his pants.

Once again, he cursed the ridiculous coincidence that had landed him here in San Francisco, less than twenty feet from the woman who'd made him come so hard he'd nearly had a stroke.

What he really wanted—needed, actually—was a full-scale corporate security consulting job, or even work that involved protecting high-level executives. That was where the real money was, and it would only take a few referrals to bring him a steady stream of business.

Unfortunately, since a romantic entanglement with his last high-profile celebrity client had nearly annihilated his career as a security specialist, business had barely built to a trickle. As his assistant-cum-adopted mother Marjorie reminded him almost hourly, he was in no position to turn down any work, even if it meant walking little old ladies across the street for a dollar each.

He stared at himself in the mirror, finger-combing his hair and straightening his tie. So what if his new client was the sweetly sexy woman he hadn't been able to get out of his head for over a year? He had bills to pay and a professional reputation to rebuild. No matter how badly he wanted to get back into Reggie Caldwell's pants, he had no choice but to get this job done as quickly, thoroughly, and *professionally* as possible.

Chapter Three

R eggie perched on the couch and pretended to read a
magazine as she waited for Gabe to finish his inspection.
Her leg jiggled nervously as she anxiously watched for him
down the hall.

"You never told me you gave him a fake name. That's so
dirty and un-Reggie-like," Natalie whispered, settled on the
couch next to her and wearing an expression that screamed,
"Dish, girlfriend!"

"Can we talk about this later?" As Natalie knew very well,
her one-night stand had been rather dirty and un-Reggie-like.

But Craig's dumping her a week before their trip to a beautiful Hawaiian resort had left her bruised. And when an astoundingly gorgeous hunk of male flesh had approached her,
of all people, she hadn't been able to quell the urge to be
someone else. Someone seductive. Someone who had wild
one-night stands with big, dark, dangerous-looking men and
left them in the morning without saying good-bye.

Even though the last thing she'd wanted to do was leave.
But that was what you did with a one-night stand, right? At
least that was what she'd thought at the time.

But that hadn't kept her from second-guessing herself a
million and one times in the past several months. What if
she'd left her phone number? Her e-mail? Her real name, for
starters?

Eighteen months ago, she'd told herself anonymity was the best course of action. Besides, it wasn't like Gabe had indicated any desire to take it beyond one night of lust-filled fun. And with *Simply Delicious* about to start production, it wasn't like she'd had time to start a long-distance romance.

She'd accepted their encounter for what it was, a meaningless vacation fling with a gorgeous, dangerous-looking stranger.

Who would ever believe he'd show up a year and a half later in her living room?

Her face was so hot with embarrassment she could fry an egg on her forehead.

This was just her luck. The one time she'd done something crazy and out of character, it came back to haunt her in the form of a six-foot-three, impossibly hot bodyguard who, judging from his standoffishness, clearly had no interest in renewing their acquaintance.

Natalie didn't give up. "But he's the one, right? The guy you told me about?"

"Yes," Reggie hissed, kicking herself for giving Natalie even the sketchiest of details about her vacation fling. Trust Natalie, who could be flakier than phyllo dough about most details, to have a mind like a steel trap when it came to anything concerning a hot guy. She heard heavy footsteps coming down the hall. "Now, will you shut up?"

Natalie shot off the couch and offered her seat to Gabe, who refused in favor of the leather club chair positioned a good five feet away.

Talk about an ego boost.

Natalie moved behind his chair and raked his wide shoulders with an exaggerated leer. "He's so hot," she mouthed.

No kidding. Tall, at least a few inches over six feet, and brawny, he exuded the same barely restrained physical power she'd noticed the first time she saw him, across the restaurant at the Grand Wailea.

And his face, which had haunted her for over a year. Not

pretty at all, and not boyishly good-looking like Craig either. His face was strong, with a square jaw, high, slashing cheek-bones, and dark, deep-set eyes.

The only concessions to softness were his hair, which she remembered sliding like silk against her skin, and his mouth. His lower lip was lush, fuller than the top, which curved into an almost cupid's bow shape. His chin negated its potential femininity, jutting out in a sharp, squared-off edge.

Just remembering the firm, tender touch of those lips on her made her so hot she feared smoke might billow out of her waistband.

She resisted the urge to fan herself and stretched her lips into a friendly smile. "So what can we do about my admirer?"

Gabe ran a big, long-fingered hand through his hair. Dark brown and slightly wavy, it was cut much shorter than she remembered. Instead of waving back from his forehead, it lay close to his skull, betraying none of its tendency to curl. He fixed her with his dark, intense gaze, and she had a vivid flashback of him, buried deep inside her, eyes simmering with lust as he commanded her in his dark, smoky voice to look at him while she came.

To her absolute mortification, a tiny, strangled moan lodged somewhere in the back of her throat. She tried to cover it up with a coughing fit, but judging by her sister's smirk, she had fooled no one.

A flash of heat appeared—just for a millisecond—in his sable eyes. But it was enough to spark an encouraging flutter between her thighs.

But it was gone almost as it appeared, and he was once again one hundred percent business.

"Can you think of anyone who might be upset with you, out to get you in some way?" He pulled out a little notepad and silver plate ballpoint pen.

"Not off the top of my head. I've received some strange things from fans—letters, e-mails, gifts. Marriage proposals, less honorable requests, but nothing like this. And until the picture and the e-mail, everything was always forwarded through Max's office or from Tyler."

"Max and Tyler?"

"Max is my producer, and Tyler is my PR manager."

"So they would have access to your personal information."

"It couldn't possibly be either of them. First of all, I'm pretty sure Max is gay."

Gabe quirked a thick dark eyebrow. "Pretty sure?"

"He lives in Noe Valley, spitting distance from the Castro. He's forty, never been married, and he's the only reason my on-screen wardrobe is even moderately hip. And Tyler—"

"Tyler gets more ass than a toilet seat," Natalie snapped. "I can't imagine the man risking his precious equipment in a copier machine, since it might leave him incapable of satisfying the female population of San Francisco."

Gabe made another note, quirking his full, firm mouth in that adorable half smile of his. Reggie barely suppressed an adolescent sigh. "I'll want to talk to them, anyway. Maybe they can point to someone. Whoever is contacting you, he or she has access to your personal information."

"What about Craig?" Natalie asked. "He still hasn't forgiven you for stealing his show." Natalie made little air quotes around the stealing part.

Gabe looked at Reggie expectantly. "Craig?"

"My ex."

"You stole his show?"

"It's stupid, really. I was helping him with a cooking demo, and I guess I sort of took over."

"Reggie can talk a lot while she's doing something else," Natalie interjected.

Gabe smiled as though at a joke only he knew. Her cheeks burned as she wondered which of the many things she'd said during sex he might be remembering.

"I didn't know, but Craig had invited Max to the demo.

Max has developed other shows for the Cuisine Network, and Craig was hoping to work with him. I did my usual thing, kept up the chatter and asked Craig questions so he could show off. After the demo, Max called me and we came up with the idea for *Simply Delicious*."

"So it's possible he wants to get revenge, shake you up a little."

Reggie shook her head. "We broke up over a year ago. Why would he wait until now?"

"Because you're a much bigger star now," Natalie said, scowling, "at least in your little Cuisine Network world. And you have a new show. He has to be pissed about that."

"But he didn't know about that until last night. Besides, Craig is too egotistical to stay anonymous."

Gabe asked for Craig's last name and said he would check him but conceded, "With all the Internet search tools available, it's ridiculously easy for someone to procure private information. Is your real name the same as your professional name?"

Reggie nodded.

"That makes it much easier for people to look you up." He looked at her pointedly. "What is your full name, anyway?"

"Regina Jane Caldwell," she said quietly.

"Ah, Regina. That explains it."

Natalie perked up instantly. "The Gina thing, you mean? I don't know why she—"

Natalie mercifully was interrupted by the strange techno ring of her cell phone. Within minutes she was rushing out the door, muttering about a callback.

"Don't forget to send my travel schedule to Tyler!"

Natalie answered with a vague wave as she rushed out the door.

An awkward silence fell. Uncharacteristically tongue-tied, Reggie looked at Gabe with what she hoped was a semicomposed expression. She took several deep, calming breaths in an attempt to keep her hormones from spiking out of control. Bad idea, she thought, as she caught the citrus and sandalwood scent of his cologne.

She wondered what he would do if she loosened his tie and ran her tongue along the tan skin of his throat.

"Wow, so this is a strange coincidence, huh?" Reggie cursed her fair complexion as she blushed for what had to be the fiftieth time since Gabe had arrived. Great, she made it sound like they'd met each other at a cocktail party instead of spending several hours twisted naked around each other. "I have to admit I always wondered about you after I left."

She didn't realize how badly she wanted him to say that he, too, had thought about her since their one night until she was met with deafening silence. He tugged at his tie and cleared his throat.

Reggie winced at the carefully blank expression in his eyes.

"I was hoping to avoid any awkwardness, but at least we have this out in the open." His voice held all the emotion of Data from *Star Trek*. "We have a strict company policy about getting personally involved with clients. I've found that doing so inhibits my ability to do my job well and puts them at risk. So I'm hoping we can put our past encounter aside and keep our relationship on a strictly professional level."

Well, that settled that. "Of course," she said tightly. "I apologize if I made you uncomfortable."

A brief nod was his only reply. Did the guy have no social skills? The least he could do was reassure her that there were no hard feelings, especially when she was about to spontaneously combust with embarrassment.

Gabe flipped his notebook closed. "Okay, so I'll check these guys out over the weekend—quietly, of course. I try to interfere as little as possible in my clients' day-to-day lives. I'll also schedule for the security system to be installed sometime this weekend."

He stood to leave. "I'll also want to get a sense of your schedule next week, see if there is someone you see every day that might be behind this." He pulled out a card and wrote something on the back. "This is a cell number for emergencies only. I can't stress that enough. I only give it to clients in special cases, and if it rings, I assume you're in immediate danger. If you need to reach me, please use my main cell number."

Though he did his best to maintain an unemotional, robot-like exterior, it was obvious he wanted to get the hell out of there.

Reggie closed the door after him and slumped down against it. How was she supposed to deal with having him around for the next God knew how many days?

She looked at the clock. Five-fifteen. Her book deadline rode like a monkey on her back, but after the afternoon's events, she needed a little sustenance.

Reggie rifled through her pantry and refrigerator, nearly crying in relief when she found all the makings for home-made mac n' cheese.

She cranked up the stereo, hoping the blare of classic rock would help blot out the sound of Gabe's voice, so cold and emotionless as he told her it was company policy not to get involved with clients. While it made sense, it still stung.

Obviously he viewed their time together as a one-night stand, never to be repeated, no matter that fate had seen fit to throw them together. She stirred her roux with more vigor than necessary, sloshing milk all over the place. It wasn't as though she hadn't felt the very same way, so why was she so upset?

Because, she admitted as she moved her wooden spoon through the slowly thickening sauce, when the guy who had provided endless fantasy material for the past year had unexpectedly shown up in her living room, she couldn't help but indulge in the hope that maybe she'd end up naked with him again soon.

Yet it was hard to reconcile the quietly intense, infinitely passionate lover with the cold, aloof man who'd just left.

She shook her head as she drained the macaroni. Just goes to show, just because you know all the spots on a man's body that elicit an immediate erection, doesn't mean you actually know him as a person.

Funny, she'd never felt an iota of shame about her one and only one-night stand in Hawaii. But now the thought that she'd let such an unemotional jerk do all those . . . things to her gave her a slightly sick feeling.

"Doesn't matter," she said to her empty kitchen. "I don't need to be friends with the guy just because I slept with him. He'll be gone in a few days, and then I'll never have to see him again."

Reggie laughed mirthlessly at all the times over the past year she'd wondered if things would have been different if she hadn't snuck out without a word. Let herself fantasize that if she'd only left her phone number, her e-mail, Gabe would have tracked her down.

Obviously he hadn't felt the same connection, hadn't wondered if maybe their casual romp could have turned into something real. If nothing else, today had ensured that she'd no longer entertain naive illusions about the one she left behind.

The high trill and bumping backbeat of Natalie's cell phone pierced the quiet of the hallway where thirty other actresses pored over their scripts, trying to come up with the perfect inflection that would make a viewer run out and buy a comfort fit bra.

The casting director's assistant, or Attila, as Natalie had mentally dubbed her, shot her a dirty look. Geez, she knew her ring was obnoxious, but so were all of the others included in her new Nokia.

One of the other actresses shot her a sideways glance and nodded at something on the wall above Natalie's head: PLEASE TURN CELL PHONES OFF.

Crap.

Natalie glanced down at the display. Reggie. Double crap. She knew exactly why Reggie was calling. Natalie still hadn't gotten her travel schedule over to Tyler. Everything was good to go, but she hadn't had a chance to type it up yet. She planned to go over to Reggie's right after her audition to borrow her computer and e-mail Tightass Tyler the info he needed.

Her thumb hovered over the power button. But she had promised Reggie that she would get her act together. And as much as she hated to admit it, Reggie was saving her ass out of the goodness of her heart, because God knew, her strategy of moving up to San Francisco to be a bigger fish in a smaller pond had certainly backfired.

At this point, her mercy job as Reggie's assistant was the only thing keeping her decently housed and clothed.

"Hi, Reg. I'll have the schedule over to Tyler tonight."

Natalie only half heard Reggie's protests as she realized that Attila was stomping in her direction, clipboard clutched to the front of her perfectly pressed white shirt.

"Excuse me," she said, "if you're going to take a call, you have to go outside."

Natalie raised a finger in the universal "give me a minute" signal.

"You have to leave," Attila insisted.

Natalie pressed her thumb over the tiny mouthpiece so Reggie couldn't hear. She was already irritated at Natalie's tendency to drop anything and everything in favor of an audition. "But I'll lose my place in line." She'd already waited over an hour, and the open call was first come first serve for only the next forty-five minutes. No way she'd get in if she had to hop back in at the end. Natalie's eyes darted around the room in search of a sympathetic face.

Attila's glare was uncompromising. "And don't think you can get someone to hold your place."

"Are you listening, Natalie? You already flaked on my makeup this morning—which I managed with your cheat sheets, so thanks for that. But believe it or not, I hired you because I actually need help."

She was so tempted to hang up on Reggie she could taste it. But she could only push the flaky younger sister thing so far. Gathering up her purse, she shot a sneer at Attila that would have done a thirteen-year-old proud and stomped down the hallway.

A rush of cool fall air hit her face as she stepped out onto Battery Street and let Reggie end her tirade.

Hoping to shift her sister's focus and satisfy her own curiosity, she asked, "So what happened with hot Gabe the bodyguard after I left?"

"Nothing," Reggie said with uncharacteristic curtness. "Even if he was interested in picking up where we left off— which he's obviously not—he made it very clear that he has a strict policy against dating his clients."

Natalie winced in sympathy.

"When he came over to install the security system, he could have been a turnip for all the emotion he showed. Speaking of which, I need to give you the code."

Natalie fished out a lip pencil and scribbled the six-digit code on the back of her hand. "Too bad. He doesn't sound anything like you described him." As she remembered, Reggie had giggled like a teenager and given her disappointingly sparse details about her night of acrobatic sex with Gabe, but cold was definitely not a word she had used. "Why did you tell him your name is Gina, anyway?"

"Stupid impulse. I gotta go. We're about to start the second taping and gorgeous Gabe is supposed to be here to watch. Oh God, I hope I don't accidentally call him that to his face. Tyler will be here later if you want to stop by this afternoon."

The line went dead, and Natalie trotted down the street to grab the bus. If she typed fast, she should be able to get the schedule ready in plenty of time to swing by the studio. She spared a fleeting thought for the lost commercial opportunity. Not that she wanted to flit around in one of those ugly geriatric-looking bras, but still, a paycheck's a paycheck.

She sighed and slumped down on her seat, ignoring the investment banker type who kept leering at her over his paper. Definitely not her type—slightly puffy in the face and neck, a sure indicator that under the fine tailoring of his suit, he was all white skin and flabby man boobs.

The woman next to her was flipping through a magazine. She nudged Natalie in the arm. "That Reggie Caldwell. Don't you just love her?"

Natalie looked down at a two-page spread of her sister's giant grin as she hovered over a big plate of sandwiches dripping with cheese. She felt like a knot of yarn was caught in her throat. "Yeah, she's great," she managed to croak. She wondered what the lady would say if she pointed out that for all the teeth and crinkling eyes, Reggie was faking that smile better than a porn star fakes an orgasm. Ten to one odds Reggie had been suppressing the urge to vomit when that photo was taken.

The cheesy sandwich? Reggie wouldn't touch it with a ten-foot pole because it was made with yellow American, which Reggie considered an abomination.

Not that it ever stopped her from using it in a recipe if she thought viewers would like it.

Natalie sighed and once again did her best to stifle the evil resentment that threatened to rear its ugly head whenever Natalie was reminded of Reggie's sudden fame and success.

She was happy for Reggie. She really was. But she'd be a hell of a lot happier if she, Natalie, were still the more recognizable of the two. Even if it did mean Natalie was recognized from her frolic on a beach, expounding on the wonders of douche.

She let herself into Reggie's apartment, helping herself to a diet soda on her way to Reggie's office. Her stomach grumbled, all but begging for solid sustenance. She hadn't eaten anything all day on the off chance that the casting director would want to see how she looked in her bra, and now she was starving. She dug through Reggie's refrigerator and liberated a bag of baby carrots.

One good thing about Reggie's cooking—she always started out with healthy stuff. The key was to get your hands on it before Reggie doused it with oil, butter, or non-American cheese.

A thought occurred to her as she flipped on Reggie's computer. Why couldn't she have her own show on the Cuisine Network? She had as much, if not more, screen presence than Reggie. Of course, she didn't cook, but so what? There were lots of shows that employed a sidekick whose sole purpose seemed to be to ask questions so the hotshot chef could highlight his amazing skills.

Maybe she could do a healthy focus show, where they cooked low-fat, low-calorie dishes, and Natalie could serve as an example of what viewers could look like if they stopped shoving so much food into their heads. As she keyed in Reggie's travel information, she planned it all out. She'd pitch it to Reggie's producer, Max, who had developed several shows for the Cuisine Network. He was always looking for new ideas and fresh talent.

Too bad Max was most likely gay. Not that Natalie ever succumbed to the casting couch—she wasn't that desperate for douche and cat food commercials—but she wasn't above using her sex appeal to push a guy in the direction of giving her what she wanted.

No matter. Max would have to be blind not to see the potential. And by the time she headed for the studio, she not only had a printed copy of Reggie's itinerary for the next six weeks, she had a one-page proposal, complete with sample recipes. Hopefully whatever chef they found could help jazz up the titles a little bit. Lettuce with lemon juice probably wouldn't fly.

* * *

He'd put it off as long as he could. Gabe checked his watch. He needed to get to the studio before they finished taping for the day so he could get a feel for the people she worked around, see what security, if any, was in place during a busy taping session.

At least he wouldn't be alone with her. He'd almost lost it on Saturday, after the guy from the alarm company left and he'd walked Reggie around the apartment to show her what was wired and how it worked. If he closed his eyes, he could still smell her, clean shampoo and something else that smelled a whole lot like cinnamon buns.

It was all he could do to resist the urge to bend down and take a bite out of her buns.

Now that train of thought will get you in trouble.

Four days later, and he was still reeling from his unexpected reunion with his hot little Hawaii fling. The woman he hadn't been able to get out of his mind after all this time. He was ashamed to admit it, but it still stung, the way she had snuck out on him without so much as a a see you later.

Now, why's that, jackass? Did you think you'd get her number and try to make a romance out of it? Aren't you forgetting that you only fucked her in the first place to forget the last client you were stupid enough to get involved with? You know, the one who dropped you like a poisonous snake and all but ruined your career. Keep your distance, Randy Andy. You can get laid when you're off the job.

Resolve bolstered, Gabe entered the building and made his way to the studio, making a mental note that the guard at the security desk didn't ask for ID or call to make sure it was okay to send him up.

They were almost finished setting up for the next episode when Gabe walked in. Wrestling his expression into one of calm detachment, he greeted her with a silent wave. She gave him a tight smile and refocused on her conversation.

The tall, thin man had to be Max, the producer. He was

probably in his early forties, and he wore a lavender fitted button-down shirt with black slacks, his leather belt sporting a brushed silver buckle. His hair was tousled just so.

But Max is gay. Natalie's assertion echoed in his brain. Personally, his gaydar wasn't particularly refined, so he figured he'd have to take her word for it.

Still, there was something about the way Max stood, a little too close to Reggie, even if he was reading a script over her shoulder. Reggie didn't seem to notice anything odd about it at all.

Probably nothing, but he didn't like the way Max invaded her personal space.

Reggie marked something down on the script and handed it back to Max, then waved her hand in Gabe's direction. Max walked up and introduced himself just as Natalie and a big blond guy in a suit walked in, bickering fiercely in loud whispers.

"I apologized for forgetting the book signing in Dallas, okay? I'll fix the schedule," Natalie said through clenched teeth.

"How hard is it to maintain one woman's schedule? Your sister pays me a lot of money to help set these things up."

"I keep up with her schedule, Tyler. That one event just slipped my mind."

Ah, so this was Tyler, the PR agent. Gabe had done background checks on both him and Max over the weekend, neither of which had uncovered anything of note.

Tyler wasn't exactly what he'd expected. He hadn't worked with too many publicists—Marly Chase's toady had been his first up-close encounter—but he generally thought them to be a pretty smarmy bunch.

Tyler looked okay. Gabe supposed he could charm the pants off anyone with his Ken-doll looks and sharp suit. But instead of gracing Gabe with the expected slick smile, Tyler's expression was serious as he looked him in the eye and shook his hand.

"You're watching out for Reggie. Glad to hear it."

Tyler's handshake was firmer than necessary. Gabe knew when he was being sized up. But why? Did Tyler have a more than professional interest in his client? Not that Gabe could blame him if he did since he was doing his damnedest to deny the very same thing. But was Tyler's interest just a normal red-blooded response to an attractive woman, or was it something more sinister?

"Quiet on the set."

"Don't make a sound or Max will rip you a new one," Natalie whispered. "They do these shows live to tape, and it's a huge pain if they have to stop."

His eyes were drawn to Reggie, standing behind the counter of her kitchen set. She wore a bright green sweater that made her eyes sparkle. Or maybe it was the extra mascara she wore. He'd never seen her with that much makeup on—more than he generally liked on women, not that they ever asked. But he had to admit she looked sexy, even a little glamorous with that sinful mouth of hers glossed to a juicy shine.

Tactical error, looking at her mouth. It reminded him of how lush and soft it had felt on various parts of his body, especially the hot, aching tip of his cock—

"And rolling!"

Jesus, he hadn't had an unexpected hard-on since high school. Fortunately, no one noticed that he'd popped a woody, as everyone was focused on Reggie as she sprang into action.

Her smile was bright and animated as she walked out from behind the camera. "Hey there everyone. Welcome to *Simply Delicious*. I'm Reggie Caldwell. Today I'm going to show you a steak dinner so easy even the most kitchen-phobic person can put it together. And as always, it will be simply delicious."

And she was off. Gabe was astounded at her ability to keep up a nonstop stream of chatter. She spoke as though she had a couple of friends in the kitchen, seamlessly integrating all the necessary instructions and food facts as she worked. Gabe was struck anew by her enthusiasm and energy, the same vibrancy that had attracted him to her in the first place. And he was endlessly tormented by the memory of how she focused all that energy and enthusiasm during sex.

Nothing seemed to throw her off her game. At one point she dropped a mushroom she was chopping. Without missing a beat, she giggled and said, "Oops, I guess that's for the dog. I don't have a dog now, unfortunately, but when I was growing up we had a golden retriever who was like a living vacuum . . ." And so it went for another twenty minutes or so.

Once she had the meal plated up and gave wine suggestions, she sat down at the little kitchen table on the set. She took a sip of red wine and said, "As you know, this is the time during the week when we like to take a call from a viewer. Today we have a call from . . ." She squinted at the teleprompter. "I can't tell who we have a call from because I can't seem to read the screen. Go ahead, caller."

"Hello, Reggie." The hairs on the back of Gabe's neck stood on end. There was something about that voice, like it was disguised to sound deeper and raspier than it really was. Gabe wasn't the only one who noticed. Reggie had stiffened almost imperceptibly, her smile now tight around the corners, a hint of worry in her big brown eyes.

Nevertheless, she kept her composure. "Hello, caller. What's your question?"

"I want to know, Reggie, what you'll have as an accompaniment when you suck my cock."

Her eyes went wide, and for a moment everyone froze as she simply stared at the camera. "Well, caller, I personally prefer my cock unadorned, so I'm afraid I can't help you. Do we have another call perhaps?"

Chapter Four

The set erupted in pandemonium as the director screamed at the cameraman to stop rolling while Natalie and Tyler ran up to Reggie all talking at once and asking if she was all right.

"Everyone, calm down!" Gabe's booming voice quieted the chaos to a low din, and he pushed through the crowd surrounding her. "No one leave."

Gabe's wrapped his hand around her upper arm, the heat of his fingertips burning through the thin knit of her cobalt blue sweater.

He tugged gently as he spoke to Max, Natalie, and Tyler. "Will you excuse us please? I need to talk to Reggie in private."

Natalie opened her mouth to protest and Reggie quickly shook her head. Though his iron grip wasn't painful, she was guessing by the vein subtly pulsing at his jaw that he wasn't in the mood to hear arguments.

The man was furious, though he was visibly trying to hide it. But Reggie could feel the rage vibrating in that powerful body and sensed that he was nanoseconds away from blowing like a land mine.

He calmly steered her through the studio, out the door, and into the hall.

"Do you know that your nostrils flare when you're angry?"

She hadn't meant to say that, and wished she hadn't when the fires of hell ignited in his eyes.

But just for a split second. Gabe ran a big hand down his face, pausing to pinch his nose, as though to remind his nostrils to behave, and the cool, impassive mask was back in place. But a mean vein stood out in stark relief on the right side of his forehead.

He spoke in a cool, calm voice that was almost scarier for the simmering rage she heard underneath. "Reggie, I don't think you're taking this seriously." He positioned her against the wall, blocking her in with the solid mass of his chest. Somehow she knew he was barely restraining himself from lifting her off the ground and shaking her. But he kept it so well hidden that to any passersby they would look like two people having a quiet, if intense, conversation.

She tried to concentrate on what he was saying, something about how the stalker's threats were escalating, but when he stood this close she could smell the faint soap and clean laundry scent that clung to him, and under that, his own personal aroma, one that made her want to bury her nose in the open collar of his shirt. Which reminded her she probably smelled of cooked meat and garlicky mushroom sauce.

Finally, his words sank in and irritation replaced the feeling of surrealism that had overtaken her when she'd first heard the call. "What was I supposed to do? Gasp and faint and let him know he bothered me?"

"How about tell him not to call you anymore? Or tell him you've filed a police report and they're on his tail? When you respond with a smart remark like you did, when you engage with him, in any way, he may take that as encouragement." His fists clenched and unclenched several times as though he were contemplating wrapping them around her throat. Finally, he took a deep, cleansing breath. "You have to protect yourself, Reggie."

"Isn't that what I hired you for?"

The corners of his lips pulled tight and he frowned down

at her. He raised a finger and pressed it into her chest with just enough pressure to push her flat against the wall. As he pulled his hand away, his knuckles barely brushed the inside curve of her breast. She grimaced, trying to convince herself that her suddenly tight nipples were due to the air-conditioning.

"Yeah, that is what you hired me for." His Southern accent emerged from hiding with each syllable. "Your safety is my job, and I take my job very seriously. When you pull shit like this, you make my work a whole lot harder."

God, if she hadn't been paying an arm and a leg for his services, this fierce protector thing would have been a total turn-on. She nodded, though she wasn't sure what her response was supposed to be.

She got a little queasy as the reality of what had happened hit her. She'd been so shocked at first, then irritated at Gabe, that it was just now hitting her that someone, someone close to her, was making these phone calls, sending her these notes.

Mentally, she shook herself. It was ridiculous to panic at this point. After all, the sum total of her stalker's activities was a close-up shot of his balls, an e-mail describing what she wore, and a phone call. Sure, they were creepy. But he hadn't threatened violence of any kind, and he didn't seem inclined to introduce himself in person. Overreacting at this point would gain her nothing. "It was a harmless phone call, and no one was hurt. I really don't see what the big deal is." Just saying the words calmed her.

He shook his head, scowling. She made one last attempt to diffuse his visibly building temper. "Okay, okay." She held up both palms. "I promise, next time a pervert calls, I will not engage in conversation about his genitalia, all right?" She glanced at the clock over his shoulder. "Now, if you don't mind, Max is probably frothing at the mouth to finish that last shot."

Gabe opened his mouth as though to say something, but was interrupted as Natalie and Tyler came trotting down the hall, both talking a mile a minute.

Gabe let out a frustrated sigh and started back toward the studio. "I'm going back in to talk to everyone, see if they saw anything. Then we'll go file a police report."

Reggie groaned as she remembered what a great success that had been last time. Tyler put a comforting hand on her shoulder. "He seems to know what he's doing," he murmured. Natalie nodded in agreement.

Reggie shook her head. "I don't know. I think he's making me paranoid. Maybe we're making a bigger deal out of this than it really is." And on top of that, she'd barely slept the past two nights, unable to escape sexy, sweaty, lust-filled dreams starring Gabe in all his naked splendor. It had been a miracle that she'd been able to get through today's shooting without any major tape-stopping errors. "Thank God he's leaving in a couple of days."

Natalie and Tyler exchanged concerned looks. "Reggie, you really need to be careful," Natalie started.

But Reggie had made up her mind. "This is all just a joke, some guy's idea of a juvenile prank. Today's call is probably going to end up on Howard Stern or Crank Yankers sometime soon."

Natalie didn't look convinced. "As a single woman you still need to be careful," she said stubbornly. "And don't be so selfish. What would I do if anything happened to you?"

"Yeah, Natalie might lose her meal ticket," Tyler said, earning him a punch in the arm from Natalie.

Reggie gave Tyler an admonishing look and led the way back to the studio. Inevitably, her gaze was drawn to Gabe, in intense conversation with one of the cameramen. His shoulders strained the seams of his sport coat, and his coffee-colored hair looked like he'd run frustrated fingers through it a few hundred times.

A fluttery heat settled somewhere around her middle. Damned traitorous hormones.

Max flitted up, long, slender hands waving in the air. "Reggie, sweetie, I hate to do this to you, but if you're not too distraught, we really need to do that last shot. We'll just skip the phone call this week."

"No problem." They quickly strategized on a quick tip segment to fill three minutes of tape, and the crew quickly moved to set up the shot. They'd been here since eight in the morning, and the crew was no doubt restless to get home. Reggie sat still while Natalie touched up her makeup and hair and did her best to compose herself. She was a professional, and it would take more than a prank call and a hot bodyguard to distract her.

Or so she thought, until she looked up and caught Gabe's stare, just as she was explaining to viewers how they could test the doneness of steak by using their hands.

His heavy-lidded gaze was hot, hungry, and not the least bit indifferent.

Reggie's brain turned off midsentence, and she gaped like a grouper for several seconds before the director yelled, "Cut!"

Max shook his head in exasperation as they reset. But when she fumbled a second time he let his annoyance show. "Reggie, do you need a little time to pull yourself together?"

Reggie shook her head. "I'm really sorry, guys," she said to the crew. "It's just been so long since I've been propositioned, I got a little flustered." Tension broke as everyone laughed. Even Gabe couldn't hide the little half smile that quirked his lips up and to the right.

Reggie finally got it on the third try. Gabe came over, his manner aloof, and Reggie was convinced she'd hallucinated the earlier flare of heat she'd seen in his eyes. Her Gabe-inflamed libido obviously was making her see things.

"I'll take you home. I don't think it's good for you to go alone."

"Did you find out anything?"

He shook his head, his mouth tight with frustration. "No one came in or out during the taping, the switchboard operator didn't receive an incoming call."

"Then how—"

"Don't know yet. But I have a buddy who can help us figure it out."

He didn't say more as Tyler and Natalie approached. "Here." Natalie fished around in her oversize bag. She frowned, then dug deeper. "That's weird. I know I printed out two copies of your schedule. Anyway, Tyler has your schedule starting next week"—Tyler waved the aforementioned packet—"and your copy is on your computer at home."

Reggie murmured her thanks and glanced at her watch. "Yikes. We need to get going if we're going to make it on time."

"On time for what?" Gabe asked.

"Just a demo and a book signing. My publisher wants me to do one last push on my current book before the new one comes out in six months. Of course, I still have to finish it . . ." She broke off at Gabe's frown.

"How many people will be there?"

Tyler shrugged. "A hundred. Hundred fifty. Not too big."

"And no security, am I right?" Gabe looked at Reggie reproachfully, as though she had purposely neglected to tell him.

"This isn't a crowd that gets out of control. Reggie's fans aren't exactly a rowdy lot."

"Yeah, and I bet you never pegged her fans as sexual deviants before," Gabe said, "but she's managed to attract one, one who can easily get to her at an event like this."

Tyler conceded Gabe's point with a nod.

"He's right," Natalie said, turning to address Gabe. "You should come with us."

"Hello, since it's my money we're using, do I not get a say in this?" Reggie couldn't believe them—planning her life like she had nothing to say about it. "Gabe already put in my security system, and now his work is done." She smiled up at Gabe to find him frowning down at her. Big surprise. "Not that our little reunion hasn't been enjoyable, but I don't think a phone call merits my own personal bodyguard." Simply having Gabe in the same city with her was driving her to distraction. The sooner she got away from him, the sooner she could regain her sanity.

Natalie continued as though Reggie hadn't spoken. "Reggie has to be at Whole Foods on California Street at six. Can you give her a ride?"

"Didn't anyone hear what I said?" Reggie snapped.

Natalie rolled her eyes. "Reggie, don't blow this off just because . . ." Her gaze darted to Gabe.

Reggie stared hard at Natalie. For once in her life, Natalie got the clue and didn't elaborate. "Besides," Natalie continued, "maybe we can spin this to your advantage. Stalkers always generate publicity."

Reggie fully expected Tyler to tell Natalie she didn't know what she was talking about. Instead, he looked impressed. "Natalie's right. If we let the word get out that you're having enough trouble to hire a bodyguard, it could generate additional buzz."

Gabe shook his head, his face showing mild disgust as he looked at the three of them. "Any publicity is good publicity?" he asked snidely.

Fine. Let him be judgmental. "Okay, I give in—for now. Tyler, you do whatever you think is best. Nat, I'll talk to you tomorrow." She headed for the corner where she'd left her coat, Gabe hot on her heels.

When they got to her car he took her keys out of her hand without a word, his disapproval palpable as he drove in complete silence.

"I don't see what's wrong with trying to see the good in this situation," Reggie said, compelled beyond reason to defend herself to this man who obviously didn't care about her personal motivations.

"It just seems a little sick, using a guy who's threatening you to try to get your name out there."

"He hasn't exactly threatened me yet. And you make it sound so sleazy. It's just business."

"But the way you're acting, it's almost like you think it's a good thing this pervert is bugging you." Even in the dim light of the car, Reggie could tell he was white knuckling the steering wheel.

"Of course it's not a good thing. But if some creep is going to bother me, why not make the best of it?"

"As long as it gets your name out there, right?" There was no mistaking the snide tone now.

Reggie sniffed and looked out the window. "I prefer to think of it as making lemons into lemonade."

On the way to Whole Foods, Gabe called the police, who said they would send someone to question the crew first thing in the morning. As expected, though, the chances of identifying her stalker from a brief phone call weren't good.

As they navigated rush hour traffic, Reggie made a valiant attempt at civil conversation.

"Have you seen your sister since you've been here?" Reggie knew from Natalie that Gabe's sister Adrienne and her husband had a place not too far from hers in Pacific Heights.

"Yeah, I've been staying at her place."

"Is she your only sister?"

"Nope."

Nothing. No further elaboration.

Was this really the same guy she'd met in Maui? Whereas there he'd been quiet but charismatic, now he seemed determined to come off as an unfriendly, emotionless shell.

She had a sudden, vivid flashback to him sitting across from her in that bar. His easy smile, the way he'd looked at her like everything she said was fascinating. Sure, he was kind of quiet, but at least he'd been engaged in the conversation.

And later . . . things he'd whispered to her in the dark, praising the smoothness of her skin, the way she tasted, the way it felt to be buried deep inside her. He'd had no trouble carrying the conversation then.

She'd shared the most sexually intense experience of her life with him. Could he really be so indifferent?

Before she could dwell too much on that, Gabe parked the car and they made their way to where the demo area was set up. While Reggie got wired for her microphone and checked that all the ingredients for the recipes were there, Gabe circled the seating area looking big, tough, and very out of place.

His military background was evident even in civilian clothing, in the way he held himself with an air of quiet authority, as though he'd be more at home in a green T-shirt and fatigues. Still, his powerful frame was perfectly offset by the tailored business clothes, even if he did look in danger of popping a seam if he flexed too hard.

Tyler showed up to make sure Reggie's books were prominently displayed and ready to purchase before she started the demo. Natalie arrived shortly thereafter and insisted on adding another layer of blusher and gloss.

"It's not like I'm on camera," Reggie protested.

"You don't want to look washed out, do you?" Natalie stood back to admire her handiwork. "Not bad. Good choice on the pants. They make you look thinner."

Reggie had chosen her chocolate brown, boot-cut slacks primarily for comfort, but she took Natalie's backhanded compliment in stride.

Tyler reappeared, apparently satisfied that no one would miss the opportunity to buy Reggie's book. "Is Gabe here?" he asked, looking around.

Reggie fussed with her ingredients, arranging the bowls of precut vegetables and spices in order of use. "Mr. Personality? He's over there." Reggie pointed with her chin across the room where he stood, arms folded across his chest, legs slightly spread in a power stance. His eyes constantly tracked her and the people around her. Irritated as she was by her irrational ongoing attraction to him, she had to admit she got a nice feeling of security knowing that he'd never let her out of his sight.

She managed to ignore Gabe as she got into her groove. As she showed the crowd of nearly two hundred how to make chicken vegetable curry, Thai basil salad, and coconut sorbet sundaes, she couldn't have been happier. This was what she loved, performing for a crowd, imparting her love of food to them, seeing them smile and hearing their sounds of pleasure as they sampled the food. The hour flew by as she told stories and answered questions from the audience.

She was struck, as she was so often these days, at how lucky she was to have found success doing something she truly loved.

She caught a glimpse of Gabe out of the corner of her eye. Now if only her personal life could be so fulfilling.

Gabe stood behind Reggie, not so close as to be intrusive, but close enough so he could get a good look at everyone who approached. So far he hadn't seen anyone who would fit the profile of a stalker. However, he'd learned as a member of the U.S. Army's elite Delta Force not to put too much stock in appearances. That innocent-looking granny walking through the marketplace could easily be concealing a bomb underneath her berka.

Nevertheless, the crowd here tonight was hardly a suspicious-looking group—about ninety percent women, ranging in age from early twenties to early seventies, and only a few men. But most of the men appeared to have been dragged along by their wives, and all of them were milling off to the side. Fortunately, the event organizers had been kind enough to provide complimentary wine and cheese so the guys had something to do.

Gabe relaxed by degrees as Reggie signed the last book. He tried not to stare at her, but failed miserably. He never should have taken this job. As soon as he'd recognized her sexy smile and big brown eyes, he should have referred her to another security specialist in one breath and asked her out to dinner in the next.

And then what? With the sad state of his bank account, he'd be able to take her to Taco Bell.

Suck it up, Bankovic. Most times life doesn't go the way

you want. Instead of mooning over her and whining over what he couldn't have, he should be grateful she hired him, happy he was able to cover his bills and help Marjorie out with her rent for another month.

But this was a bad situation. Reggie fucked with his equilibrium, no doubt about it. It took extreme effort on his part to keep his emotions from boiling over on a daily basis, and every second with Reggie threatened his hard-won control.

She captivated him. It sounded completely hokey and ridiculous in his own head, but there was no other word for it. Watching her on the set the other day and watching her tonight, smiling and laughing, it was easy to see that she was delighted with what she was doing. And he wasn't the only one, the rest of the crowd smiled along with her.

That, combined with the intensely erotic dreams he'd suffered through for the past four nights, made Reggie Caldwell a very dangerous woman indeed.

So caught up in remembering the hot, sweet feel of Reggie writhing under him in that bed in Hawaii, Gabe didn't notice Tyler standing beside him until the other man spoke. "She's really good, isn't she?"

Gabe prayed that his face showed none of his lustful yearning as he glanced at the other man, then back at Reggie, who was talking to a woman in her twenties as though they were old friends.

"Fans absolutely love her, men and women, which is unusual for a woman as attractive as Reggie."

Gabe turned back to Tyler, confused. "What do you mean?"

Tyler shrugged. "Who understands why it happens, but as a rule, women viewers don't like the thin, attractive female hosts. It's like they're resentful, or don't believe they eat their own food."

"That's why it's good she's a little big," Natalie said. "She looks like she probably eats enough."

Gabe glared down at Natalie. Before he could stop himself, he said, "Reggie's not big. She has an awesome body."

Natalie's eyebrows shot up, and her eyes got a speculative look. "So you've been studying it?"

Heat flooded Gabe's face and he was grateful for his olive complexion. "I haven't been studying—"

Natalie interrupted, "Oh, that's right. You have, shall we say, intimate knowledge of Reggie's body."

"What do you mean by that?" Tyler's indignant interruption was all that saved Natalie from being strangled.

"Didn't Reggie tell you?" Natalie blinked up at Tyler innocently, but her mouth held a sarcastic twist. "She and Gabe met when she went to Hawaii . . ." She let her voice trail off suggestively.

Tyler's Ken-doll face was a grim mask as he stared at Gabe with angry blue eyes. "You and Reggie were involved?"

Before Gabe could answer, Natalie laid a hand on Tyler's arm in mock sympathy. "Poor Tyler. You've been trying for so long to get into Reggie's pants—"

"I have not—"

"It's okay to admit you're jealous," Natalie taunted.

Gabe struggled to keep his professional objectivity as he took another look at Tyler, doing his utmost to suppress a sudden upswell of territorial impulses. He'd taken his cue from Reggie and Natalie, and even his own instincts didn't lead him to believe that Tyler was responsible for the harassment. But maybe the culprit had been right here close by all along.

"Jesus Christ, Natalie," Tyler said, obviously struggling to keep his tone low. "Yes, I'll admit I find your sister attractive, but rather than risk our professional relationship, I decided not to pursue it. Thank you for embarrassing us all." He offered a sheepish smile. "Besides, Reggie wasn't interested or I might have been more inclined to do something about it."

Gabe studied Tyler's body language for several moments. Though slightly embarrassed and uncomfortable, Tyler didn't appear to be hiding anything. Tyler might have harbored an attraction to Reggie, but Gabe's gut said Tyler wasn't his guy. But he would keep an eye on him just in case.

Stiffening under Gabe's intense scrutiny, Tyler muttered, "Don't worry, Gabe. I'm not going to poach on your claim."

So much for keeping his personal feelings under wraps. Still, he did his best to regain his composure and set the record straight. "I'm not in a position to make any claims."

He turned back to the crowd, back to where Reggie had been chatting with a fan just a few feet away.

Except she was no longer there.

Frantic, Gabe scanned the crowd. Lots of people were mingling and chatting, sipping wine. No Reggie. Where the fuck was she? He'd taken his eyes off her for half a minute, and now she'd disappeared.

He plowed through the crowd, muttering apologies as he knocked against wineglasses and stepped on feet. Great, while he'd been focusing on her hot ass one minute and then assuring Tyler and Natalie he didn't want a one-way ticket to Reggie's pants the next, she'd managed to slip off alone.

It was exactly as he had feared. Once again, he failed to maintain a professional distance, and it compromised his ability to do his job. He asked the organizer if she'd seen Reggie and choked down panic when she said no.

He started moving through the store, scanning down each aisle, growing more anxious every second that the slimeball bothering her had shown up tonight, had somehow pulled her away from the crowd.

He was supposed to be the professional, the one in control of the situation. He took every client seriously. But Reggie was different. He would never forgive himself if his carelessness got her hurt.

Suddenly, there she was. He skidded to a stop, relief, quickly surpassed by fury, sweeping through him. Reggie was standing in the middle of the ethnic foods aisle, talking with a nice-looking lady in her fifties, expounding on the wonders of fish sauce.

She'd nearly given him a fucking heart attack, and here she was blithely talking about fish sauce.

Without thinking, he walked up and grabbed her arm. He barely held his voice to a reasonable volume as he said, "Don't ever wander off like that again."

The woman gave him an uneasy look and took a few steps back.

Some still semi-rational part acknowledged the image he presented. A big gorilla of a guy walking up and manhandling a much smaller woman. But he was too angry, both at himself and her, to really give a shit.

"Gabe, do you mind? I was having a conversation with—" Reggie smiled beseechingly at the woman. "I'm sorry, remind me of your name?"

"Miriam," the woman replied with an uneasy smile. Clearly, she expected Gabe to start smashing things at any moment.

Reggie nodded and tried to pull her arm out of Gabe's grip. He didn't give an inch. "Miriam wanted to know about the fish sauce I put in the curry I made." She turned back to Miriam as though Gabe didn't have his hand wrapped all the way around her bicep. "So like I was saying, if you can't find this, you can use soy sauce."

Miriam nodded eagerly.

"I'm sorry, Miriam, but Reggie really has to go." Careful not to hurt her, Gabe all but lifted her off the ground and yanked her down the aisle. Miriam watched their progress with an expression of horror.

Reggie struggled violently against his hold. "Let go of me, you big yeti."

Yeti? Even through his haze of anger, he had to give her points for originality.

He pulled her back over to the demo area where the last of the crowd was lingering. All conversation stopped as Gabe hauled her past without a word and asked the event organizer if they could use her office to talk.

He pulled her inside the tiny closet-like room and slammed the door shut behind them.

"How dare you do that? How dare you manhandle me at a public appearance, make me look like a fool."

"Do you not understand the kind of danger you could be in, Reggie? First mouthing off to the caller, and then wandering off like this."

"Do you understand that I have an image to uphold with my fans? I have a reputation for being approachable. Don't talk to me like I'm a four-year-old."

"Don't act like one then, goddammit!" he boomed.

"She was a nice lady who wanted to know more about Asian condiments. I seriously doubt she was planning on dragging me off to a dark corner to assault me."

In a much quieter voice, he said, "But anyone else could have seen you go off by yourself with her. It's late. The store is virtually empty. Miriam wouldn't have been much defense if someone had tried to grab you."

She raised her chin stubbornly. "The only one grabbing me tonight was you."

He sighed raggedly and dragged his hands through his hair. God save him from women who refused to see reason. "Reggie, if you don't take your safety seriously, how can you expect me to?"

Her eyes narrowed and her glossy mouth pursed. He didn't know what he wanted to do worse, turn her over his knee and spank her, or kiss the living hell out of her. For starters.

"Pull over here, please." Reggie uncrossed her arms long enough to indicate the convenience store on the corner.

"Why?"

"Because I need to pick something up, that's why." She was still mightily irritated at his earlier treatment of her at Whole Foods. It was bad enough that he had talked to her as though she had all the mental capabilities of a slow child, but making her look bad in front of fans, that was way out of bounds.

The only consolation was that after tonight, she never had to see him again. Which made her unaccountably sad, considering what a class-A jerk he'd turned out to be.

"Why didn't you get it at the other store?"

Now she had to answer to him? "Because they don't carry what I want at Whole Foods, not that it's your business." He slowed and she reached for the door handle, only to be met by the electronic lock engaging.

"Let me park and walk in with you."

She blew a frustrated breath up toward her bangs. "Can't you wait on the corner? You can see me fine from here." Was it too much to ask for a few moments of privacy so she could go score some Hostess Ding Dongs? If she had to spend one more second in this close proximity, she was afraid she would literally jump out of her skin.

He shot her a "you're crazy" look and pulled around the block to park.

For once she didn't feel compelled to keep up a stream of friendly chatter, determined to give Gabe the silent treatment he seemed to crave. He held her arm stiffly, barely touching her with his fingertips as he walked beside her. No doubt he was in as big a rush to get away from her as she was from him.

So she took her time perusing the junk food aisle, picking up and replacing snack foods with apparent deliberation.

The toe of his oxford beat out an impatient rhythm. "How long does it take to pick out a Twinkie?" he finally muttered.

"I'm looking for the one with the best expiration date," she said, studying the label of a Snowball.

Peering over her shoulder, he snapped, "What, December 2008 isn't far enough in the future for you?"

A snappy comeback was forming on her lips when Gabe suddenly stiffened, shifting her subtly but firmly behind him. "Let's go," he whispered tightly.

"I still need to get my Ding Dong," she protested.

"We'll stop somewhere else. I don't like the looks of that guy."

Reggie angled her head to see whom Gabe was looking at. A skinny guy in a windbreaker and tattered jeans was loitering over by the magazine rack, shifting uneasily from one foot to the other, his hand repeatedly touching the small of his back.

Sure, he looked a little strung out, a slightly unusual sight in this relatively upscale part of San Francisco, but not unheard of. Even if he was high, Reggie imagined he'd come in for cigarettes, a snack, or even a beer to take the edge off whatever he was on. Clearly, Gabe took himself and his job way too seriously, seeing goblins around every corner.

Rolling her eyes, she grabbed a pack of Ding Dongs. Yanking her arm from Gabe's hold, she stalked up to the cash register.

"Get down!"

Reggie barely registered Gabe's roar before his full two hundred plus pounds hit her with all the finesse of a linebacker on Super Bowl Sunday. Before she could grunt in protest, he rolled off her, his body a blur of motion as his long legs swept out, knocking the junkie to the floor.

Something clattered down the magazine aisle. A gun, Reggie realized to her horror.

By the time she tore her shocked gaze from the weapon, Gabe had the guy's arm twisted into an obviously painful—judging from the guy's screams—hold, while his knee was planted in the middle of the junkie's skinny back.

Barely breathing hard, Gabe calmly instructed the cashier to call the police.

Chapter Five

"Come on, Reggie, you can't tell me that you didn't think it was a little sexy, the way Gabe took that guy down." Natalie was perched on the corner of Reggie's bed, watching her pack for her six-week stint on the road filming her new show.

Reggie threw another pair of running shorts into her monstrously oversized wheelie bag. "Honestly, it was a little scary. Don't get me wrong. I'm glad he saved me from getting mugged and the store from being robbed, but he's definitely overqualified for what I need. Besides," she continued, shoving another pair of boots to the bottom of her bag, "you should have seen the way he embarrassed me in front of that poor woman at Whole Foods. Between that and the news coverage the robbery attempt received, people are going to think I habitually surround myself with thugs."

"I still don't think you should have fired him."

"I didn't fire him, Natalie. I told him his services would no longer be needed. Which would be true anyway since I'm leaving tomorrow." And she'd been polite about it. After they'd arrived at her apartment, she'd calmly thanked him for protecting her from the gun-wielding drug addict and written him a check.

"What if you need his help again?"

Reggie blew out a scoffing breath. "Doubtful. And even if I did, I still think Gabe is overqualified for what I need." When she'd met him in Hawaii, Reggie had sensed an air of intensity, danger even, surrounding Gabe. But last night, he'd gone from mildly irritating to absolutely lethal in a matter of seconds. She had no doubt that if he'd been inclined, he could have killed that guy with his bare hands. As sexy as she found Gabe, she feared the reality of him was more than she was capable of handling. She should thank her lucky stars that he had no interest in getting involved.

So why had she spent the past two days trying to come up with an excuse to call him again?

"Besides," Reggie continued, "I'll be gone for six weeks. Plenty of time for Mr. Balls to forget about me and set his sights on some other victim."

"He can still watch your show."

"But he can't get to me."

"Bullshit," Natalie said, then paused to study the sweater Reggie had just thrown into her suitcase. "You're not taking that sweater."

"Why not?"

"I thought the idea was to take mostly stuff you can wear on camera."

"Yeah?" Reggie added a slate-blue cotton/lycra button-down and yet another pair of black pants to the mix.

"Reg, a thick wool cable-knit sweater will make you look like a burly fishwife on camera. Take it out."

Reggie rolled her eyes, but took the sweater out. As much as Natalie's comments about her size needled, more often than not she was right. Natalie rarely said anything deliberately cruel or insulting, but she had no qualms about reminding Reggie that despite her size-eight figure, she was far from camera ready. "I don't know why it matters," she grumbled, even as she put the sweater away. "Don't you remember how popular *Two Fat Ladies* was? I bet they never worried about the camera adding ten pounds."

"True. But they were also never asked to do a shoot for *Men's Only* either."

Great. In addition to her book edits that she'd have to squeeze in on the road, now she had to worry about finding time to exercise too.

Reggie grimaced, wondering how she'd ever let Natalie and Tyler talk her into the photo shoot for the notoriously provocative men's magazine. Especially since it was scheduled toward the end of her shooting schedule. She never ate well or kept up her exercise routine on the road, and by the time they get to L.A. for the much dreaded photo shoot, she'd no doubt be bloated and flabby.

Reggie hadn't been particularly open to the idea of a sexy photo layout, but Natalie and Tyler had joined forces to gang up on her. Tyler because it would expose her (no pun intended) to a potentially new audience of noncooking males who might tune in just to look at her, and Natalie because to her, an appearance in *Men's Only* was the ultimate validation that a woman was hot.

Natalie took a swig of her diet soda. "Lucky for you they have airbrushing."

"Gee, thanks."

Oblivious to her sarcasm, Natalie stayed mercifully silent as her attention fixed on the *E! True Hollywood Story* on in the background. But like Reggie, Natalie couldn't stop talking for long. "I still think you should try to call Gabe before you leave. You never know—"

"Natalie, could you drop it, please?" Reggie flipped her suitcase closed and yanked on the zipper. "I don't want to talk about him anymore. He's a classic example of a guy who's great in the sack but an asshole in real life."

She wasn't entirely sure that was true. She'd spent time— okay, not a ton of time, but time—with him before they'd made it back to his room in Hawaii. She'd found him charming; quiet, but courteous, with a wry sense of humor that snuck up on you. The kind of guy you really listened to because when he spoke, it was for good reason. And the things he'd said to her, especially in bed . . . He'd made her feel like the sexiest, hottest woman in the world.

Clearly his charm was something he turned on only when he wanted to lure unsuspecting girls like herself into his den of sin. Otherwise, she imagined being in a relationship with him would be like dating the Terminator.

She tugged again on the zipper, still stuck at the halfway mark. She grunted, leaning onto it. No dice. "Nat, get up here." Natalie obligingly balanced on the lid of the suitcase, bearing down as though that could lend her greater weight. "Dammit," Reggie strained, wincing as the zipper cut into the flesh of her finger. "We need greater mass. Trade places."

With Reggie sitting on the suitcase, Natalie had it zipped in seconds. Hah. Sometimes being heavier was an advantage.

"Anyway, as I was saying," Reggie continued, hands on hips, as she wondered how in the hell she was going to close her suitcase by herself after tomorrow, "Gabe is clearly an example of why you don't try to make a relationship out of a vacation fling. I'll admit, when he first showed up, I wouldn't have minded another round."

"You'd have to be crazy not to. The man is smokin'. So big and brawny and . . . *big*."

Reggie willed the telltale flush out of her cheeks as she remembered exactly how beautifully, deliciously, *powerfully* big Gabe was. Everywhere. "Irrelevant. And when I come back in six weeks, I'll have forgotten that pervy stalkers and rude, impersonal bodyguards like Gabe ever existed."

By the end of the first day of shooting, Reggie was exhausted. She'd spent almost the entire day on her feet, filming a segment on the street foods of New York. Between shots she tried to find a quiet spot to sit and work on her book, without appreciable success. Which meant she would have to work on it now, instead of crawling into bed with a good glass of red wine and the remote.

She was packing up her laptop and getting ready to head back to the hotel when one of the crew members approached her with an envelope. She thanked him and started to slip it into her briefcase.

"The guy said you should read it immediately. It sounded urgent."

"What guy?"

The cameraman looked around, his expression growing confused. "He was right there." He pointed to the busy street corner where thousands of New Yorkers were fighting pedestrian traffic in their quest to get home.

Frowning, she studied the envelope. Nothing was written on the outside and it wasn't sealed. She pulled out a single sheet of paper, her blood icing over when she saw the familiar cut-and-paste magazine letters.

> *Darling Reggie,*
> *I hope you're enjoying New York. The weather is so lovely this time of year. Looking forward to seeing you soon.*

Reggie almost laughed at the note's friendly, casual tone. If it weren't printed in psycho serial killer cutouts, it would have been like any note any of her friends or colleagues might have sent.

And, of course, there was a picture copied on the bottom. Not a scrotum or any other body part, thank goodness. Rather, this was of a lingerie model in a kneeling pose, hands behind her as her back arched her voluptuous lace-clad breasts toward the camera. But the model's face was superimposed with a picture of Reggie's own, taken from a recent article in *Good Housekeeping*.

"What's that?" Reggie jumped a foot as Carrie, her producer, seemed to appear out of nowhere. Carrie had wild red hair, her petite, wiry frame draped in baggy khakis and an oversize canvas coat. Her wild red hair practically shot sparks of intensity.

Frowning, Reggie muttered, "I wonder how he found me."

Carrie's bright green eyes turned almost feral. "What do you mean, he found you."

Normally, Reggie liked her new producer's intense, take no bullshit style, but sometimes the woman downright scared her. Trying to laugh it off, Reggie said, "It's nothing really. Before I left San Francisco, I received some strange communication from a fan."

"A stalker? And now he's followed you all the way to New York?"

"I don't know if you can really call him a stalker."

"This is not good."

"Carrie, I'm perfectly safe, I promise."

Carrie's breath exploded in a harsh laugh. "It's not you I'm worried about. If this guy knows where we're shooting, do you have any idea how he could mess up production?"

Reggie embarrassedly admitted the thought hadn't even occurred to her.

"I'm going to have to talk to the VPs about this. I don't even know if we can get a replacement in time." Carrie seemed to be talking more to herself than to Reggie.

"Replacement?" The mere suggestion sent Reggie into a panic. "You can't replace me. It's *Simply Delicious, USA,* and I'm *Simply Delicious,*" she said, her voice rising hysterically.

Carrie shook her head, sending her wild mane of red curls in every direction. "No offense, Reggie, but you're an unknown quantity. You have no location experience, no experience in handling guests. The network is taking a huge chance with you on this, and they won't support you if you prove to be a liability."

Desperate now, Reggie grabbed the other woman's hand.

"Carrie, you don't have to go to the network with this. I'm sure it's nothing, just a few harmless notes."

"Reggie, I like you, a lot, but this isn't personal," Carrie said quietly. "My butt's on the line too. You think if we mess this up, they'll ever let me out of the studio again? I'm really sorry but—"

"What if we hired security?" She was grasping at straws now, she knew.

"This show already has one of the highest per-show costs of anything Cuisine Network has ever done. They'll never go for it."

Gabe's face flashed in her head. "What if I paid for it myself?"

Carrie started to shake her head.

"I know a guy, he used to be in the army Special Forces. Trust me, nothing gets past him." When Carrie remained silent, Reggie plundered on, "It's the best solution. You'll never be able to find another host without delaying production. And think how much it will cost to get another name with this short notice."

Carrie's lips pursed as she thought it over. "Are you sure you can get him for the full six weeks, with overlap if the schedule slips?"

"Positive," she said, crossing her fingers and praying that it was true.

"This is Gabe. What's the problem?"

"Gabe, it's Reggie."

His adrenaline level, which had spiked at the first ring of his emergency line, surged another notch. He gripped the phone, willing himself to calm down. It wouldn't do her any good if he lost his cool, no matter how the thought of her in danger freaked the hell out of him. "What happened?"

"I'm so glad you answered."

He began pacing anxiously around his sister's living room,

his phone clenched in a death grip in his right hand. "Are you in any danger?"

"Me? I'm fine. I have a proposition for you, though."

"I thought I made it clear you're only supposed to call this number if you're in immediate, physical danger."

"Oh, right, sorry." Her voice was blithely chipper on the other line. He wished he could reach through the phone and strangle her. Or bend her over his knee for a spanking . . . "I was wondering if I could hire you for the next six weeks."

Gabe plopped down on the couch, stunned. Now this was an odd turn of events, especially considering the last time they spoke. Oh, she'd tried to be as cordial as possible as she told him firmly that she'd no longer be needing his services. But there was no escaping the aura of fear, mixed with a little revulsion as she said it.

On top of her irritation over embarrassing her in front of a fan, it had visibly freaked her out to see him take down that guy in the convenience store. If that scared her, she'd die if she ever found out about the things he'd done in the name of defending his country.

That night, their client relationship had been permanently terminated, and he'd had no illusions that she ever wanted to see him again.

Which made her phone call even more puzzling.

She spoke without taking a breath for a full five minutes, explaining about the note she'd received, Carrie's reaction, and most importantly—to her, apparently—the fact that she was in danger of losing her job as host of this show. "I can't let that happen, Gabe," she repeated over and over. "I can't lose this job, and I will if you don't agree to this."

Gabe shook his head in disbelief. It seemed to have gone completely over her head that whoever her admirer was, he knew her every move and had obviously taken the time to track her all the way across the country. He should take this job, because Lord knew this woman needed a keeper. "I have to think about it, check my calendar," he lied, knowing full well the next several months were wide open.

"Please, Gabe, I have to give them an answer tonight."

A month and a half on the road, in close proximity to Reggie Caldwell. Responsible for guarding her body from danger. Her curvy, succulent, bound to drive him insane body. He was crazy to even consider it.

Then he remembered his assistant's message from earlier this afternoon. Marjorie's landlord had stopped by again today, threatening eviction if she didn't pay the six months' back rent she owed. She'd stuck by him all this time, accepting whatever payment he could scrape together. Letting her get kicked out of her apartment was no way to repay her loyalty. "I'm going to need payment up front for the first few weeks." Heat crept up his neck as he issued the demand. He didn't know why, since this was a simple business transaction, but demanding money from a woman he'd slept with didn't sit right. But he couldn't see that he had any other choice.

Knowing he was going to regret it, he said, "Okay, where do I need to be?"

He wrote down the name of the restaurant in Boston where she'd be filming the next morning and glanced at the clock. With luck, he could still make a red-eye.

In the meantime, he told her to switch hotel rooms and have Natalie rebook all of her future reservations.

"Don't you think that's being a little paranoid?" Reggie protested. "All he did was send me a doctored picture from a Victoria's Secret catalog."

He gritted his teeth, anticipating several weeks in alternating states of sexual lust and frustration as Reggie questioned every single decision. "Listen, Reggie," he bit out, "if I'm going to help you, we have to do things my way. I don't care if this guy is sending you Hallmark cards with little kitties on them, we take every communication seriously. If I work for you, your safety is my number-one priority, and everything I do is to further that goal. So if I tell you to change hotels, you change hotels. Got that?"

"Yes, sir." He could practically hear her sarcastic salute over the phone.

"Good. Now that's settled, I'll see you in the morning."

Gabe showed up at Gianni's Trattoria shortly before noon the next day. Reggie was still irritated by his high-handed treatment over the phone last night. Clearly, the man had control issues. Still, he was currently her only guarantee of keeping this job, so she mustered up a wave and an approximation of a friendly smile.

Gabe responded with a brief, impersonal nod.

Reggie turned her attention back to this segment's guest, Gianni Carposi, a plump exuberant Italian man in his mid-forties. Gianni was funny, flamboyant, and harmlessly flirtatious.

Still, the shoot wasn't without its hiccups, as Reggie struggled to get into the groove and accustom herself to sharing screen time with another person. Gianni was boisterous and talkative in his own right, and they found themselves talking over each other more often than not. Judging from her pinched look and the way she dug her thumbs into her temples, Carrie wasn't overly impressed with Reggie's performance.

It didn't help that Reggie had barely slept the night before. Even though she had faith in the room's deadbolt, she found herself jumping at every ping of the air conditioner, every muffled footfall outside her room. Damn Gabe and his contagious paranoia. After only a few hours of sleep, Reggie woke up feeling like crap and looking worse.

Natalie had offered a quick over-the-phone consult on how to cover up under-eye puffiness and circles. Reggie had swallowed her embarrassment and purchased a small tube of Preparation H from the airport newsstand before she boarded her flight.

She had to admit, in a pinch the ass cream worked. Now if only her on-camera persona could be so easily perked up.

They took a break a few hours later, and Reggie, Gianni, and the crew took the opportunity to snack on the handmade gnocchi with Gorgonzola sauce they had made. She waved Gabe over from his position in the back of the kitchen. Thanking him for coming on such short notice, she made the only available peace offering at hand. "Come have some food."

He shook his hand, holding up a palm in refusal. "I'm fine."

Reggie rolled her eyes and grabbed a small plate and a fork, piling on a small helping of gnocchi. His expression was resigned as she approached. "You must be starving. Just have a little."

"Reggie, it's not your responsibility to feed me. I carry plenty of food with me."

She scanned him in puzzlement. From what she could tell, he carried only a small briefcase, nothing big enough to hold enough food to keep a man of his size running.

He pulled something out of the pocket of his sport coat. Reggie took it and turned it over until she could read the label. "Are you kidding me? I have homemade gnocchi for you, and you're refusing it in favor of Power Bars?"

A tiny vein throbbed at the corner of his jaw. "I prefer not to take meals with my clients," he said quietly so no one else could hear. "It brings a personal element to the working relationship that I'm not comfortable with."

So this was how he wanted to live the next six weeks of their lives? Struggling to tamp down her frustration, she waved the fork in front of his face as though feeding a toddler. "Yummy, yummy, open wide." She pressed the fork against Gabe's lips. "Come on. Just a bite. It's really good."

Narrowing his eyes in a look that promised future retribution, he opened his mouth. Reggie slid the fork between his lips, mesmerized by the sight of their full firmness closing over the tines. A sudden image flashed behind her eyes, a vivid memory of his full, firm lips closing over her nipple, his tongue darting out to flick the delicate skin of her breast.

Maybe feeding him was *not* such a good idea.

She started to speak, then cleared her throat at its sudden dryness. She tried again. "Now that wasn't so hard, was it?"

Gabe's expression was inscrutable as he wordlessly took the plate from her grasp and quickly polished off the gnocchi. "Happy?"

"Yes, I'd hate to have that argument in front of my parents tonight."

Gabe looked up from his empty plate, his eyebrows raised.

"We're having dinner with them in an hour. And I'd eat up if I were you. I didn't inherit my cooking talent from my mom."

After a quick stop at the hotel to clean up, they drove out to Newton, the affluent suburb outside of Boston where Reggie had grown up. Gabe parked the rental car in front of a two-story Cape Cod. In the dark, all he could tell was that the house was painted a light color with darker shutters on the windows. A rambling porch empty of furniture spanned the front of the house and a wide expanse of lawn sloped down toward the street.

He reached for the door handle, but Reggie's hand shot out and grabbed him by the forearm. "Wait," she said, flipping down the lighted visor mirror. She pulled out a powder compact and a tube of something and proceeded to pat and rub at a spot on her right cheekbone. "Do I look okay?" she turned to face him. "All the makeup I've been wearing is making me break out."

Gabe leaned in for a closer look. Granted, the dim light of the rented Ford Escort didn't show every detail, but from what he could see, she looked perfect. Her dark eyes looked huge against her pale skin, her rounded cheeks glowed with color, and her sexy plump mouth looked perfectly suckable, shiny pink with a gloss that gave off a faint, fruity aroma. As for the skin she seemed so worried about, it was as smooth and fine grained as a child's. "You have the nicest skin I've ever seen on a woman," he said, immediately wishing he could bite back the reply.

Her eyes widened in surprise, and her lips parted in that infectious smile of hers. "Really?" she asked in surprised delight.

He swallowed convulsively, an electric pulse rocking his system as he remembered vividly how silky smooth her skin was . . . everywhere. "Yep. From what I can tell, you hardly need makeup."

She looked back in the mirror. "Trust me, my mother will notice every flaw."

Finally, she shoved the makeup back in her purse. Once they got to the door, Reggie gave it a quick rap and squared her shoulders as though girding herself for battle.

The door flew open and a tall, jovial-looking man with Reggie's big brown eyes and a masculine version of her upturned nose greeted them.

"Daddy," she squealed, throwing her arms around him. Her father hugged her hard, lifting her up off her feet.

"Reggie, I've been so worried. We saw that thing on the news about you and you haven't returned our calls."

"Dad, it's fine, really. In fact, this is Gabe." She turned to introduce him. "Gabe is a security consultant I've hired to travel with me."

Gabe held out his hand and introduced himself.

"John Caldwell." He stepped back and motioned them into the foyer. "A bodyguard? Is it as dangerous as that?"

"As yet, no," Gabe said, "but you never—"

"It's just a safety precaution, Daddy." Reggie waved dismissively. "Mostly the network bigwigs wanting to protect their investment. Don't worry about it."

John led them into the living room, motioning them to sit on the couch in front of a platter of vegetables and dip.

"Where's Mom?" Reggie asked.

"Kitchen." John indicated the direction with his thumb.

Gabe wasn't sure, but he thought father and daughter shared a grimace.

"What's this about the news?" Gabe asked, reaching for a celery stick and dipping it in the dip. Reggie gave him a funny look and shook her head. Gabe ignored her, waiting for John's answer.

"It was on *Good Morning America* this morning. 'Celebrity chef has a ravenous fan.' "

Reggie sat back with a sigh. "Tyler didn't waste any time. Gabe, you might not want to—"

Too late. He'd already taken the first bite of the celery and dip. After the first chew he realized it was not so much the taste, but rather the texture, that was truly abominable. Where he had expected something creamy and savory, his mouth was instead filled with a grainy, lumpy mixture that reminded him of ranch-flavored gelatin.

Reggie's hand covered her mouth, but he could see the telltale shaking of her shoulders as she laughed.

John watched him in sympathy. "My wife doesn't share Reggie's cooking skills."

His voice broke off abruptly at the swift tap tap of heels striking the highly polished hardwood floors.

Reggie's mother was about Reggie's height, with the same thick dark hair, but that was where the resemblance ended. Where Reggie's body was sweetly curved, her mother was bone thin, giving a glimpse of what Natalie might look like in her late fifties.

And damn, Natalie better have a donut soon, because the future wasn't pretty.

It wasn't that she was unattractive. But her face had a tight, drawn look to it, her skin stretched so taut her cheekbones looked like they might slice through at any moment. Her dark eyes had none of Reggie's luster, sunken in her skull, eyebrows pulled up into an unnaturally surprised curve by plastic surgery.

Reggie stood and greeted her mother, hugging her with

none of the warm affection she'd shown her father. No wonder, since Reggie risked busting her mother's ribs if she squeezed too hard.

She released Reggie and turned to Gabe. He took her proffered hand gently, aware of the birdlike fragility of every bone. "Virginia Caldwell," she said in an upper-crust Bostonian accent.

"Gabe Bankovic."

She raised her eyebrow. "How very . . . ethnic."

Gabe released her hand and gave her a tight smile. "It's Croatian."

"Mom, Gabe is a security consultant who's traveling with me."

Virginia shuddered dramatically under her cashmere cardigan. "Oh, yes, that nastiness. Your father and I saw it on the news this morning. I can't believe you didn't tell us, Regina."

Reggie seemed to shrink under her mother's censorious gaze. She nibbled listlessly at a naked carrot. "I didn't want you to worry."

Virginia shook her head and held the bowl of vile dip up to Reggie. "Reggie, you must try the dip." Reggie reluctantly dipped her carrot into the gelatinous white goo, extracting about a milliliter. She crunched down on her carrot, admirably concealing her disgust.

Virginia turned to Gabe with a sly smile. "I keep telling her, you don't have to cook with all that fat to make it taste good. That dip is made with tofu and fat-free mayonnaise, and I bet you couldn't taste the difference."

"Ah, tofu. That would explain the texture."

Virginia went on to extol the virtues of tofu as a substitute for everything from hot dogs to whipped cream. Reggie had sucked down her third glass of cabernet by the time Virginia led them to the dinner table.

Dinner wasn't any better than the appetizer. "Here, Gabe, let me give you the biggest piece." Virginia placed a miniscule piece of sad-looking white fish adorned with a tired smattering of herbs. Then she heaped on a pile of green beans that, he realized when he tasted them, were flavored only with lemon juice.

He thought back wistfully to the rich, cheese-laden gnocchi Reggie had fed him earlier.

Reggie poked listlessly at her fish, taking tiny bites between sessions of arranging and rearranging her food. Gabe made a mental note to hook her up with a Power Bar later. Or if they were lucky, they'd pass a Taco Bell on the way back to the hotel.

"I hope you don't mind our simple fare," Virginia continued. "As you can see," she cast a sidelong gaze at her husband, "my husband's side of the family is prone to heaviness. Poor Reggie didn't inherit my slender genes."

Genes??!! Anyone would look like a starvation victim on this diet.

He was surprised when Reggie didn't come back at her mother with a snappy remark, or tease her about her own lack of cooking skills. Instead, Reggie seemed oddly diminished as she sat at the table, answering all of her parents' questions without her usual vivacity.

Her father seemed to understand and tried to keep the conversation light and insubstantial, focusing on Reggie's new show and asking about her new cookbook.

"You're going to regret it if you keep cooking that way, using all that butter and oil," Virginia sighed.

"Mother, studies have shown that olive oil is very good for your heart, and almost everything I make is healthy."

Virginia piously chewed on her unadorned fish, then smiled ruefully. "After the example I set for you girls, I can't believe you've ended up doing work that's so menial. Gabe, do you know that I went to Harvard Law school when the girls were babies? I nearly killed myself, first to get my degree, then to make partner, and what do I end up with? One daughter who gives up a successful accounting career to be a cook, of all things, and another who humiliates me by hawking feminine hygiene products." Virginia's laugh trilled shrilly through the dining room.

Gabe froze, fork halfway to his mouth as he glanced uncomfortably at Reggie and her father. John's cheeks were red, and his lips were pursed as though he'd learned after many long, hard years of marriage not to bother arguing with his wife.

Reggie's face was purple as she stabbed murderously at her green beans. "Menial? Mom, who are we, the Kennedys? What, a best-selling book and two TV shows aren't enough for you?"

Virginia chewed silently for a moment, then murmured, "We'll see how long this success lasts. Considering you're not even a professional chef, there's only so far you can go."

Reggie threw down her fork, sputtering as she got sucked into what was obviously a long-running argument between mother and daughter. "Only so far? Mom, how would you even know? Look at Martha Stewart—"

Virginia cut her off, "Yes, let's look at Martha, with her stint in federal prison."

Gabe winced. Reggie refilled her wineglass.

Reggie leaned her head back against the headrest, watching the flicker of streetlights play off Gabe's cheekbones and jaw. A faint shadow of beard darkened his jaw, giving his features a rough cast. She could easily imagine him in the desert somewhere, hefting a big gun as he warded off enemy fire.

She closed her eyes, but that made her head spin. She really should have stopped before that last glass of wine. Maybe if she sucked down a bottle of water before she went to bed, tomorrow wouldn't be too much of a nightmare. She rolled her head back in Gabe's direction. "Thanks for driving."

White teeth flashed in the darkness of the car. "The way you were pounding the wine, I don't think I had much choice."

Reggie grimaced, then repeated the gesture, noting with interest how rubbery her lips felt. "Sorry," she said again. "It's my mom. She makes me crazy."

"I can see why."

"I just wish, for once, she'd acknowledge what I've accomplished. All she sees is that her daughter has lowered herself to cooking fattening food for other people."

He momentarily took his eyes off the road and regarded her thoughtfully. Even in her inebriated state, she felt his gaze as though he were trailing his fingers down her body.

"I guess you didn't get your love of cooking from her."

"No way. Tonight's dinner was a perfect example of what my mom served on a regular basis. I learned to love food because of Maria Detaglia." She smiled as she remembered going over to Maria's house after school, how amazing smells permeated the air. "Maria was my best friend in grade school."

"Her mom cooked?"

"Her mom, her dad, her grandma, aunts, uncles, everyone. Maria's dad, Joe, is this big, burly Italian guy, and her mom is this tiny little woman he met on his tour in Vietnam. I don't know if you know this, but the Vietnamese have an amazing culinary tradition. By the time we were eight, Maria and I were helping her mom make Bo Luc Lac and helping her dad make Bragiole on the weekends. Eating at her house was like seeing in color after living in black and white." She fiddled with the radio, punching several buttons until she found an alternative station she liked. "I wanted to go to culinary school right out of high school, but my mom wouldn't hear of it. And now she gives me a hard time about my lack of professional schooling." She shook her head. "There is no pleasing that woman," she said almost to herself. "What about your mom? Is she a good cook?"

"She's a great cook—she and my sisters. Probably the reason I don't cook myself, they were always chasing me away. And my grandma—she came over from Croatia when I was twelve and lived with us until she died—she used to make Prsurate; it's kind of like a Croatian donut."

"You should learn to cook. I remember the first meal I cooked for myself when I went away for college. Rosemary lemon chicken with mashed potatoes." She looked over at him, smiling softly in the darkness. "Maybe I'll teach you to cook. Kind of like a bonus plan."

"Maybe."

"Trust me. Cooking a meal is a guaranteed ticket into a woman's pants."

He glanced over, his eyebrow raised sardonically. "I seem to do okay on my own."

Reggie knew the heat in her cheeks was not just from the wine. "Yeah, I guess you do."

They were silent for the rest of the ride. Reggie stared out the window, and Gabe smiled when he heard her soft snore. He didn't know what had brought on his uncharacteristic inquisitiveness. But even though he'd vowed to keep his distance, the more time he spent with Reggie Caldwell, the more he wanted to know about her.

Meeting her mother explained a lot, especially Reggie's drive, her seeming desperation to keep her TV hosting gig at all costs. That she loved what she did was obvious, but professional recognition was obviously vital as well. Anything to get her mother's elusive approval.

He could relate. Ever since he'd had to retire from the Special Forces, when a bullet shattered his left femur, he'd felt the need to prove himself, to show he could make a difference even if he was no longer able to serve active duty. Unwilling to settle for a desk job, he'd moved into the private sector, eager to put his skills to use at his friend's security company.

It had been great while it lasted. Instead of putting himself in danger ridding the world of terrorists, he spent his days installing and testing high-tech security systems and making sure his clients stayed out of harm's way. Some days he'd missed the intensity of being out on a mission. But most of the time, he enjoyed making a lot more money with a hell of a lot less risk.

And he'd lost it all over another client with big eyes and a seemingly sweet manner. He jerked upright at the swift reminder that he couldn't let himself fall for Reggie, no matter how attractive he found her.

Unfortunately, his body, exhausted from travel and work, wasn't inclined to listen, instead wallowing in memories of how the woman asleep in the passenger seat had felt naked against him, arching her breasts into his chest as she rode him like a rodeo queen that night in Maui.

Tugging at his fly, he shifted in his seat so his hard-on wasn't quite so restricted. The way things were going, by the end of six weeks, he was going to have a case of blue balls for the medical books.

Reggie woke up as they pulled up to the valet. When they got to their suite, Gabe set up the foldout couch while Reggie went for the shower. He closed his eyes, listening to the sound of water running, imagining what she would do if he went in there, took off his clothes, and grabbed the soap from her hands. He could almost feel her pale, smooth breasts with their dark rose nipples, slippery with soap as he cupped and massaged them in his hands. He'd pull her against him, back to front, so he could run his palms all over her tits, down her belly to that dark, luscious triangle of her sex where he'd find her plump and juicy like a ripe peach.

She'd grind her delicious ass against his rock-hard cock, teasing him and urging him on as he slid his fingers up and down her slit, dipping and teasing until she was begging him to make her come. Then he'd slide into her unforgettably tight pussy, shove so deep inside her she'd feel him at the back of her throat . . .

"Gabe? Are you okay?"

Reggie stood about five feet away, dressed in a pair of leopard-print pajama bottoms and a stretchy red shirt with two cats that read, FUNNY CATS IN HATS. Her face was scrubbed clean of makeup, and her damp hair tumbled around her shoulders. He wanted to suck a bruise onto the pale flesh of her neck. "I'm fine."

"You had a funny look on your face. Bathroom's all yours. I'll see you in the morning." She closed the door to her bedroom with a soft "good night."

Gabe unbuttoned his shirt and grabbed some extra pillows from the closet. As he walked back to the bed, something on the floor caught the corner of his eye. Tossing the pillows on his bed, he walked over to pick it up.

Reggie's bra. He fingered the silky ice blue fabric. Against all better judgment, he lifted it to his face and inhaled. The scent of warm cinnamon buns and creamy naked skin almost brought him to his knees.

To think, she was just one door away. The woman whose succulent body and sassy mouth he hadn't been able to get out of his mind. Worse, by the way she looked at him when she thought he didn't know, he knew she'd take him up on it.

Reggie shifted restlessly on the bed. Despite the wine at dinner, she was too wired to sleep. She'd hoped the hot shower would help her wind down. But as she'd rubbed her own soapy hands over her wet skin, she'd found herself wishing Gabe would ignore his professional code of ethics and walk through that door and join her. Flustered, she'd finished with a quick, cold rinse and made a beeline for the bedroom before she did something stupid. Like try to jump him.

She flipped over on her back, trying to ignore the awareness that made every nerve ending tingle. She could feel him through the paper thin walls, his heat, his masculinity, surging over her, overwhelming her with memories of the single, sultry night they'd shared.

As though with a will of its own, her hand trailed down her belly, lifting the hem of her pajama top so she could feel her own smooth skin. She remembered Gabe's callused fingertips sliding over her, drifting up her ribcage to capture the soft weight of her breasts. His dark, fathomless eyes had flared with heat as he'd pulled her dress off her shoulders, revealing her to his gaze.

"Your nipples are the same gorgeous pink as your lips," he murmured, sucking and licking one into his mouth. His thumb slid inside the lace edge of her panties, brushing over her clit in a matching rhythm. "I wonder what color these beautiful lips are." His thumb traced the dripping seam of her sex, teasing the entrance of her body with shallow thrusts of his fingers.

Reggie's thumb and forefinger pinched at her own nipple as wet heat pooled between her legs. God, it had been so long since she had been touched, since she had been fucked. Her other hand slid into her panties, fingers sliding into her damp, swollen folds. Her clit was a firm, throbbing bud, dying for the touch of the man sleeping on the couch less than twenty feet away.

Her breath hissed at the first touch of her sensitive skin, and she nearly came at the first brush of her finger. But as much as she needed the release, she wanted to slow down, savor it. It was pathetic, masturbating while the man she craved was so close by, but she couldn't face another rejection. So for the first time since Gabe had reappeared in her life, she allowed herself to relive every look, every touch, every stroke.

He gazed down at her as she lay sprawled on the bed, eyes gleaming in the dim light. "Damn, darlin', you're about the sweetest piece I've ever seen." His drawl thickened with every syllable. "But I'll never forgive myself if I don't treat you properly."

From what she could tell, there was nothing "proper" about their behavior, but she wasn't about to argue as he started dropping soft moist kisses down her neck and across her collarbones.

She twined her fingers in his hair, tugging insistently until his mouth hovered over her rock hard nipple. The harsh, hungry sound he made as his lips pulled firmly sent a jolt of heat straight to her pussy. The hot, rigid length of his cock burned against her inner thigh, and she squirmed in anticipation of feeling his thick length buried inside her.

"Sweet thing, you taste so good I hardly know where to start." He lavished attention on her breasts, alternating almost rough sucking with gentle, teasing lashes of his tongue. *Oh God, she wanted—needed to—feel that skillful tongue on her pussy.* Tugging at his hair, she guided his head down her belly.

"You read my mind." He landed a wet, sucking kiss just below her belly button and slid her panties down her legs. *"Mm, you smell like peaches."* With a purely male sound of satisfaction he stroked his thumbs against her plump lips, spreading her wide for his hungry mouth.

Reggie circled her clit with her middle finger, wishing it was Gabe's tongue flicking against the turgid flesh.

She nearly came at the first touch of his tongue, lapping at her clit before slipping down to probe her drenched slit.

She dipped her finger inside her throbbing pussy, imagining it was his thick cock pressing deep.

He soaked the plump head of his cock in her juices, stretching her wide as he sank into her with one powerful stroke. "Honey, you're so tight and sweet," he moaned, increasing the pace of his thrusts as she hitched her legs over his hips, opening herself more fully. "Your pussy feels so good, squeezing me like a tight little fist."

No one had ever talked to her like this, in such graphic terms, and she would have been embarrassed if she hadn't been so turned on. Sharp moans erupted from her chest in tandem with his thrusts. He reared up and grabbed her hips, driving into her in a hard, circling rhythm that made her thrash against the sheets and claw at the slick skin of his back.

Her fingers stilled on her clit as she sought to hold her orgasm at bay, just for a few more seconds. She wanted to draw it out, relive the memory of him fucking her deep and hard for just a little longer.

He stilled his thrusts, watching her with hot, dark eyes as he traced his thumb against her lower lip, pressing it inside her mouth for her to suck. Then he settled that moist thumb in the slick folds of her pussy, right where they were joined. He held himself deep, impossibly deep inside her, grinding as his thumb circled and pressed against her throbbing clit.

"Open your eyes, Gina." A long slow slide, a stroke of his thumb. "Open your eyes and look at me when you come."

Her finger increased the pressure on her clit, every nerve pulsing as she imagined him watching her again. Her eyes drifted closed and she bit her lip against the cry working its way up her throat. She was coming, but it wasn't enough, it wasn't the same without his thick cock driving inside her.

But unless Gabe walked through the door, it would have to do. As the last tremors of her climax receded, she rolled to her stomach, willing herself to sleep.

Gabe had nearly drifted off when the soft noise penetrated the haze of near sleep. He slipped off the couch and padded toward Reggie's door. There it was again, a soft, high sound, a hitch of her breath carrying through the thin plywood door. His cock went instantly hard as he remembered her making a similar sound, only louder, when he had sucked her clit into his mouth for the first time.

Easy there, big boy, he admonished his cock, *she's most likely having a bad dream.* But her door had only been closed for about five minutes, hardly enough time to go into REM sleep and dream. He put his palm against the door, applying the lightest of pressures. It opened a few inches.

Moonlight spilled over the bed, and Gabe nearly fell to his knees at the sight that greeted him. Reggie's eyes were closed, her teeth clamped down on her lower lip as she fought to stifle the little sounds working their way out of her throat. One hand had disappeared up her shirt, the other down the front of her pajama bottoms, and from the way she was squirming around, she was showing herself a very good time.

He held his breath, afraid he'd groan if he let it out. He wanted to dive on the bed, strip off her clothes and replace her hands with his own. Her movements stopped, and he froze, half afraid, half hoping she'd realized he was watching. Then she'd beckon him over to the bed, spread her legs wide to show him how wet she'd made herself, all in preparation for the real thing.

Then she started again, her hand moving in sure, deliberate strokes. She arched up into her hand, fucking herself with a steady rhythm, his cock pulsed a matching beat. His fingers itched to feel her soft, slick flesh, to feel the tight, muscular grip of her pussy closing around him like she couldn't get enough. She uttered a stifled cry and stiffened, and his heart pounded in his ears. He was so hard he hurt, wanting with every cell in his body to join her in that bed, to see if fucking her could possibly be as good as he remembered.

Instead he watched her get herself off. Her body relaxed in post-orgasmic satiation. Gabe knew he should move, should walk away before she saw him standing in the doorway. Instead he stared, cock aching, as though willing her to open her eyes. If she turned those big brown eyes on him, he had no faith in his ability to practice self-restraint. He'd be a dead man.

His stomach curled in anticipation as she shifted to make herself more comfortable. Instead of turning toward the door, she rolled onto her stomach without opening her eyes, completely oblivious to his presence in the doorway.

Muttering a vicious curse, he slunk back to the foldout couch, his hand wrapped around his aching cock. He flopped back on the foldout bed, wincing as a metal bar nearly severed his spine through the flimsy excuse for a mattress. He'd thought the training he'd gone through for Special Forces was hard. But tailing Reggie Caldwell without touching her was going to be the longest month and a half of his life.

Chapter Six

Biddy Lee Hughes gave new meaning to the term *Guest from Hell.*

Miss Biddy Lee was the owner and operator of Biddy Lee's Teahouse, a restaurant in Savannah, Georgia, that dated back to the Civil War. And from the looks of her, so did Miss Biddy Lee herself. While she might yet hold the secrets to perfect buttermilk biscuits in her little blue-tinted head, her short-term memory had pooped out somewhere circa 1989.

At first everything had seemed fine. By the time Reggie and Gabe arrived, the crew was set up and ready to go. Biddy's rinse and set curls were picture perfect, and she smiled up at Reggie with a pearly white set of dentures.

The trouble started when they started preparing Biddy's special family recipe for Shrimp and Grits. Reggie asked her how the recipe came about. What started as a story about the shrimping boats turned into a half-hour-long, rambling story about how Biddy didn't like crackers in her soup. Meanwhile, she'd only managed to chop half an onion and the butter had burned.

Carrie pulled her aside. "Reggie, you're going to have to take over."

A little flutter of panic bloomed in her belly. "But I don't know the recipe!" Though all recipes from the show needed to be tested and verified by the Cuisine Network kitchens before being posted on the show's Web site, Biddy Lee's assistant had been adamant about not giving it out ahead of time. As a result, beyond the basic ingredients spread out before her, Reggie had only the vaguest idea of how they were all put together.

Carrie gave an impatient shake of her wild red mane. "This happens sometimes. That's why we need a strong host to carry the show. You'll have to wing it."

Reggie closed her eyes and said a little prayer. She was a strong enough host to save the segment from a crappy guest, dammit. Wasn't grits the American South's version of polenta? She'd made that a thousand times.

That in mind, Reggie started putting the ingredients in the Dutch oven heating on the stove top. Every so often Biddy Lee would ask her who she was, and Reggie would ask her what she should do with whatever ingredient was at hand.

But then, in the middle of it all, Biddy Lee wandered off. Reggie turned her back to stir the pot, and Biddy Lee walked out of the kitchen, into the dining room, and promptly asked one of the waiters to bring her a glass of sweet tea.

When Carrie tried to coax her back into the kitchen, Biddy Lee cheerfully claimed to have no idea what she was talking about, and that it was time for her lunch. That it was five o'clock in the evening seemed to make no difference.

Now Reggie slumped in a chair that one of the crew had thoughtfully provided. A glass of sparkling water appeared in front of her. Icy, fizzy water adorned with lime never looked so delicious.

"You looked like you could use it." Gabe's low, velvety voice washed over her like a balm. Her shoulders relaxed infinitesimally. "I would have brought you a beer, but I figure you need your wits about you."

Reggie gulped gratefully at the cold drink. "This is perfect. Thank you."

He crouched next to her chair. "It's getting late."

Reggie looked at her watch and groaned. There was no way they were going to make their flight to Memphis. "I better call Natalie."

"Does this sort of thing happen often?" Gabe asked.

Reggie shrugged. "Hell if I know. I've only ever been in the studio." She never thought she would miss the close confines and controlled environment of the *Simply Delicious* set so desperately. "I feel bad for Jeremy, though."

Jeremy, the line producer who had booked Miss Biddy, was busy getting a new asshole torn by Carrie. "How could you not have realized she was senile when you talked to her?" Carrie's small, wiry body vibrated with fury.

"Her assistant said she was a local celebrity, one of the best-known cooks in the region," Jeremy protested.

"So you never talked to Biddy Lee herself?"

"No, but—"

"Of course her assistant is going to say she's wonderful. She wants the free publicity for the restaurant. From now on, you talk to the talent first, and at least make sure they're mentally capable of filming a segment."

Jeremy hung his head, his shoulders slumped in defeat.

Somehow they got through the rest of the shoot. After a snack, Biddy Lee was moderately more lucid, and with Reggie's guidance they managed to come up with a finished dish that would suffice for the "ta-dah!" shot at the end.

And Gabe, bless his heart, ate his share without protest and proclaimed it the best Shrimp and Grits he'd ever tasted.

Natalie went over Reggie's schedule one last time with Tyler. She stole a glance at the clock. She'd been here for forty-five minutes already. How many times did they need to review it?

It was ridiculous that she could feel claustrophobic in his office. Tyler had a spacious work/living loft in South Beach, and his huge windows provided a glorious view of the Bay

Bridge. But still she felt short of breath, crowded by him even in the large room, his spicy cologne permeating every breath she took.

"For the fourth time, yes, you can book a signing in Dallas at seven P.M. Why do we have to keep going over this?" She hated the snappish tone in her voice. But even though she and Tyler had settled into a moderately friendly working relationship, she always felt on edge around him.

"Because I need to make sure I have Reggie's most up-to-date schedule before I confirm appearances," he explained patiently.

"All I've changed are the hotel bookings—"

"Which I still need," Tyler interrupted.

Natalie ran a frustrated hand through her hair. How was she supposed to explain tactfully that Gabe had instructed her not to give Reggie's hotel information to anyone, including Tyler? Her cell phone rang. "It's Reggie, gotta take it."

Reggie told her about the Miss Biddy Lee catastrophe and their subsequent delay. "I'll get you on a later flight," Natalie said. "How was mom?" She winced as Reggie relayed their dinner conversation. "Nothing ever changes. You're a fat loser and I'm a stupid loser. Speaking of which, are you working out? Remember, the photo shoot is a little over a month away."

She said good-bye and hung up, startled when she met Tyler's icy blue glare. "What?"

He merely shook his head, saying nothing.

Great. Now he thought she was a jealous bitch, compelled to put her sister down because of her own insecurities. Sadly, he wasn't far from the truth. She tried to stop herself, she really did, but she couldn't seem to keep herself from making sly digs at Reggie's expense. Reggie, with her affable good humor, always laughed it off. Natalie convinced herself that Reggie knew she was joking. Besides, it wasn't like Natalie didn't get her own fair share of criticism from her mother and the endless stream of casting directors.

And while Tyler seemed to appreciate her sometimes cutting sense of humor, clearly her remarks about Reggie made her look petty and mean-spirited. No wonder she seemed to be the only woman in San Francisco he didn't bother to look at twice.

Needing to escape his suffocating presence, she said, "Can we wrap this up? I have another meeting to get to." For some reason she felt compelled to redeem herself. "I'm going to meet with Max to pitch my own show for the Cuisine Network." See, she had no reason to be jealous of Reggie, because soon she'd have a show of her own.

He couldn't keep the stunned disbelief off his face. "You? Doing a food show?" He didn't even bother to choke back a laugh. "What are you going to talk about? The many virtues of Diet Coke?"

Natalie tightened a grip around her can of said soft drink. Usually she enjoyed their teasing banter, but that hit a little too close to home.

Shaking his head, Tyler continued, "I don't know if you realize this, but the most popular women on Cuisine Network are the ones who actually look like they eat."

"What about Reggie?"

Tyler shook his head. "As you so kindly point out to her at every opportunity, while Reggie is relatively thin in real life, on TV she looks like a normal, healthy weight woman. And she's attractive enough to draw in the minority of male viewers."

"I bet guys would like me," Natalie retorted, knowing she sounded pathetic.

"Maybe," he conceded, his voice laced with doubt.

She sat back with a frown. What did Tyler know, anyway? Max liked her idea well enough to take a meeting with her. He wouldn't bother if he didn't think it was at least worth a shot.

She pushed herself back from the desk and gathered up the papers. "I'm meeting Max at Reggie's apartment in half an hour. I'll call you later to give you any schedule updates."

As she reached for the doorknob he called out to her. She turned, surprised to see a faintly uncomfortable expression on Tyler's face. "Uh, I just wanted to say good work getting that contact's name at *Good Morning America*." He laced and unlaced his fingers. "We never would have gotten Reggie's story covered if we hadn't been able to call him directly."

As she walked out to where she'd parked Reggie's car, she tried to convince herself that it wasn't Tyler's compliment that had raised her mood a good ten degrees.

The little bitch was trying to hide from him. He'd nearly trashed his house the other night when he found out his message hadn't reached her in Boston. She wasn't where she was supposed to be, and he had no way to find out without causing suspicion. She must have changed hotels. No doubt at the behest of that big goon she had shadowing her like a faithful rottweiler.

Her bodyguard, she said. But he knew different. The gorilla wanted her. But Gabe would never know what a woman like Reggie needed. Not like he did.

Once he found her, he'd convince her of that. And soon he'd pay her a personal visit, to show his darling Reggie how very devoted he was.

"What do you mean there's no new reservation?" Reggie leaned over the check-in counter, hoping the woman would suddenly realize her mistake.

"I'm sorry, ma'am, but you missed your earlier flight to Memphis and I have no updated reservation for you."

Reggie put her head down on the counter. It was already nine o'clock, she'd been up since six, and after wrangling Miss Biddy Lee all day, she was so tired she wanted to cry. "Dammit, I knew I should have done this myself, or at least checked in with Natalie." But her cell phone had gone dead, and in the rush to pack up and get to the airport Reggie had decided to put her faith in her sister and for once give her the benefit of the doubt.

More fool she.

"What's the next possible flight to Memphis we can get on?" Gabe asked, his Southern accent thickening like honey as he laid on the charm. "Reggie here has an important meeting tomorrow morning and it's real important that she get a good night's sleep." He smiled beseechingly at Wanda, who looked momentarily shell-shocked at the surprising sweetness of his smile.

She frowned at the screen. "I have seats available on a flight at eleven tonight . . ." She looked up from her screen and studied Reggie for a moment. "I know you, you're on TV! My granddaughter loves your show! She comes over and plays Reggie Caldwell in my kitchen. Leaves a heck of a mess, but sometimes her concoctions are actually edible."

Reggie immediately perked up, returning the woman's delighted smile. "I started cooking when I was a kid too. How old is your granddaughter?"

Gabe's foot began to tap. Reggie grabbed his hand and gave it a warning squeeze.

"She's twelve. And it's so nice to see her watching your program rather than all that other trash that's on TV. I know this is an imposition, but would you mind signing something for me?"

Reggie reached for the pen and paper, then thought better of it. "I have a better idea." She grabbed her wallet and handed Gabe a couple of bills. "Gabe, can you go over to that bookstore and see if they have a copy of my book?"

"I can't leave you alone."

The eager light faded in Wanda's eyes. "Don't worry about—"

Reggie turned to Gabe and dropped her voice to a low whisper. "If we're nice to Wanda I bet we'll get on an earlier flight."

Gabe dutifully headed for the bookstore, which was only about ten feet away, grumbling under his breath. Sure enough, by the time he got back with the book, Wanda had booked them two first-class seats on a flight leaving in a half hour.

Reggie wrote a quick inscription and autographed the book, and they took off for the security checkpoint.

They settled into their seats, and Reggie eagerly accepted her complimentary glass of champagne and hot towel. "I've never ridden first class before," she confided, luxuriating in the leg room in front of her seat. "It really is different up here. Is this your first time too?"

"No."

Frustrated by his lack of communication, Reggie continued to prod, "With another client?"

He grunted something that sounded like "yeah" and settled back against the headrest with a yawn. "Mind if I sleep? That foldout couch about killed me last night."

"Of course not." Reggie looked around the plane. "I doubt anything can happen to me here. Why didn't you say anything about the bed?"

He peered at her through one eye. "What would you have done about it?"

"We could trade off sometimes so you can have the real bed once in a while." Or you could have shared that great big lonely king size with me, she thought naughtily.

"Reggie, you're paying me. I'm your employee. You're not obligated to give up your bed."

She grimaced at the harsh reminder that while she might entertain fantasies about slathering him with dark chocolate and licking him clean, to him, she was just another client, one he wanted to have as little personal interaction with as possible.

Tired but unable to fall asleep, Reggie accepted another free drink—this time a very nice glass of merlot—and a light snack. She fired up her laptop and set to work transcribing another pile of scribbles to send to her editor.

Every so often she snuck a glance at Gabe. His hard features softened in sleep, his soft, sensual lips slightly parted. He looked almost cute, if a guy who was six-foot three and probably outweighed her by a hundred pounds of solid muscle could be described as such.

She unbuckled her seatbelt and stood, back to the seat in front of her, as she tried to squeeze past him into the aisle. But Gabe's legs were sprawled out in front of him, blocking her way. She carefully lifted one leg up, stepped over his outstretched thigh, and was about to lift the other when Gabe's hand shot out and locked around her forearm. Yanked off balance, Reggie fell forward, bracing her other hand against the muscled wall of his chest so she didn't collapse on top of him.

Blinking sleepily, he sat up straight, eyes going from unfocused to acutely aware in a matter of seconds. "Where are you going?"

"The bathroom?"

His grip on her arm gentled, but he didn't let go. Heat washed through her as she became excruciatingly aware of the intimacy of their position. She stood in front of him, one leg between his. If she sat, she'd be straddling his left thigh. Seated, he would only have to pull her forward a few inches to press his lips to hers.

She wondered if he really was completely awake, as his calloused thumb traced tiny circles on the tender skin of her inner arm, sending liquid pulses from her forearm straight to the tips of her breasts. Sneaking a quick glance down, she confirmed that sure enough, her nipples were peaked like diamonds against the thin blue knit of her sweater.

Reggie licked her lips nervously and tugged at his grip. "I have to go . . ."

As though suddenly becoming aware that he held her, he quickly jerked his hand away. He scooted his legs back, clearing her path so she could get into the aisle.

It took a few minutes in the bathroom and a couple of cold

wet paper towels to her face for Reggie to regain a tentative hold on her composure.

She didn't look at him for the rest of the flight and tried to focus on her work. Hopefully, this next round of recipes and notes, which she planned to e-mail off tonight from the hotel, would keep her editor busy for at least a few days.

But when they got to the hotel, e-mailing was the least of their problems.

Not only had Natalie not rescheduled their flight, she had also forgotten to call the hotel to confirm a late check-in. Reggie and Gabe's adjoining rooms had been given up to two gentlemen in town for a footwear conference. Attendees of the same conference had filled up all the rooms of the hotel but one, a smoking room on the first floor with one queen-size bed.

"Ma'am, I'm very sorry," the desk manager, who looked like he was about eighteen, said. "But we have nothing. I'd be happy to call around to other hotels to see . . ."

Embarrassingly, Reggie felt the unmistakable sting of tears burning at the back of her eyes. She looked at Gabe, standing stoically a few feet behind her, his face void of any expression.

She looked at the clock behind the manager's head, releasing a shaky sigh. It was already after eleven. At this rate she'd never get to sleep, and, as Natalie so kindly reminded her, she desperately needed to squeeze in a workout tomorrow morning.

"Do you have a cot or something I could sleep on?"

Ten minutes later, Reggie and Gabe dragged their suitcases into the room, followed by a bellboy who wheeled in a cot folded up like a big bed taco.

As the bellboy unfolded the cot, it became evident that there was no way in hell Gabe could possibly fit his massive frame on it. "I'll take the cot," Reggie said.

Gabe's expression was grim. "You shouldn't have to sleep in the cot. I'm your—"

"Employee. I know," she snapped. God she was exhausted, physically and emotionally, and the last thing she wanted to do right then was argue with a stubborn male. Hefting her briefcase onto the miniscule desk provided, she said, "Gabe, the way I see it, you have two choices. You can sleep in the bed alone, or you can share it with me. But it was my assistant's fault the reservation got screwed up, and if anyone's sleeping on the cot, it's me."

He looked skeptically at the double bed.

Foolishly, she was a little miffed that he didn't even seem to consider the possibility.

She pressed the power button of her laptop so hard she nearly jammed her finger. Gabe was thankfully quiet for a few moments, and she heard rustling sounds behind her as he sorted through his suitcase.

"Why don't you hire a real assistant?" he asked after several minutes. His voice was truly inquisitive, with none of the irritation she would have expected from a man forced to suffer along with her for Natalie's mistake.

Sighing, Reggie turned in the uncomfortable wooden desk chair. Gabe had removed his sport coat and laid it neatly across the bed. He'd also unbuttoned a few more buttons of his shirt, offering a teasing glimpse of tanned chest and soft brown curls. The already tiny room reduced in size by several square feet.

She forced her gaze to his face, which wasn't much better for her concentration. His short hair was rumpled, as though he'd run his fingers through it. Exhaustion made his already deep-set eyes even heavier lidded, and the way he stared at her made her feel like she was melting into a pool of hot fudge.

Embarrassed, she realized she'd forgotten his question. "What?"

Thankfully, Gabe didn't seem to notice the party happening in her pants. "Why don't you hire a real assistant, someone who can really help you?"

Compelled to defend her sister, Reggie muttered, "Natalie helps me. Sometimes she just forgets details, isn't as careful as she should be."

"I think your life would be easier if you got someone who was a professional. I know I wouldn't survive without my assistant, Marjorie."

Reggie could just imagine Marjorie. Probably blonde, stacked, and loved taking dictation. No, scratch that. "I bet with your policy of no on-the-job nooky, Marjorie's a real battle-ax."

Gabe chuckled and sat down on the edge of the bed to take off his shoes. "She looks very good for a woman of fifty-odd years."

She didn't bother to examine her feelings of relief that his assistant was an older, maternal type. "Natalie's had a hard time getting work lately, and I thought this would be a good way of helping her out without giving her handouts." When he shook his head, she said, "You said you have sisters. Wouldn't you help them out if they needed it?"

"Of course I'd help them. But I would never involve a family member in my professional life. It's like getting involved with clients. It doesn't make good business sense."

"Why can't business and personal mix?" As soon as the question left her mouth, she realized she wasn't talking about hiring her sister.

Several emotions flashed across his face. Frustration, maybe even a little regret, among them. And finally, resolve, which took its form in the cool, impersonal mask Reggie was beginning to despise. "Some people don't have a problem blurring the lines. Me, I need nice, tidy borders. Black and white, and nothing in between. It's the way I work."

He gathered up a pile of clothes and closed himself in the bathroom. Seconds later, she heard the water running and turned her attention back to her computer screen.

By the time he emerged from the bathroom, a scented,

steamy cloud in his wake, Reggie was ready to forward all her notes to her editor.

She unplugged the cord from the phone and into her modem, and clicked on her ISP icon. An ominous gray box appeared, naming an error of some sort. In short, her modem didn't work. She unplugged and replugged the cord, growing more frustrated by the second.

Muttering and swearing, she dug around her computer bag for a floppy disk, shoving it into the drive with more force than necessary. Could nothing about this trip be easy?

As though to make up for yesterday, the next two days of shooting were a breeze, even though they started out a little rocky when Reggie tried to sneak off for a workout. Ignoring her protests that she could make it to the gym and back by herself, Gabe insisted on going with her.

Great. As if Gabe needed another reason to stay away from her, now he had the added bonus of watching her huff and puff her way through the treadmill workout Natalie had designed. The one that ended with her beet red and sucking air like an emphysema patient.

Gabe, the jerk, set his treadmill at a sprightly seven-minute-mile pace and barely broke a sweat. He then proceeded to bench more than her body weight with no apparent effort, while she struggled through a set of bicep curls.

"You'll get better results if you lower the weight slowly," he observed.

"It's a miracle I'm doing this at all," she snarled. "I don't need commentary from the peanut gallery."

"Ooh, someone's grumpy in the morning," he teased. "Not much of an exerciser?" He commenced on a set of shoulder presses that made the veins pop out in sharp relief against his biceps.

Funny, she'd never paid much heed to other guy's muscles, but with Gabe she had an almost overwhelming urge to sink her teeth into that firm, rippling swell. She did another set, grunting in an oh-so-feminine fashion as she lowered the weight slowly this time. "It's not that I don't like exercise," she said, taking several gulps from her water bottle. "I hate exercising like this. Running on a hamster wheel, lifting and lowering weights in some barren, airless room. I'd rather run outside."

Gabe nodded. "Good to know. Maybe today while you're shooting I can call the hotels in the other cities and have them map out some safe running routes."

Reggie was taken aback. When was the last time someone had actually listened to a personal desire of hers and done something about it? That Gabe, who tried so hard to keep himself at a distance, would even bother touched her more than she wanted to admit. "Thank you," she said earnestly, "that would be really great."

He laid back down on the bench with a massive-looking dumbbell in each hand. "Not a problem," he said, blowing out a breath as he brought his hands together above his chest, "I hate running inside too. It'll make my life easier."

Of course. He wasn't doing it just for her. It served his purposes too. Typical.

After they showered and packed up, Reggie made a quick stop to the hotel business center to e-mail her notes to her editor. Then they were off to the shoot at a hole in the wall barbecue joint where Reggie learned how to make the best ribs she'd ever tasted in her life.

Gabe seemed to have eased up a bit on his stoic, keep-his-distance attitude. He wasn't exactly easygoing, but he talked, or rather listened while she talked, amiably on their hour-long flight from Memphis to New Orleans. At least it was less like talking to a brick wall and more like talking to the Gabe she had met what seemed a lifetime ago.

To make up for her colossal fumble the day before, Natalie had booked them in a hotel room that could have served as a permanent residence. Not only did the suite boast two decently appointed bedrooms, it also had a kitchenette complete with a mini-fridge, microwave, and two-burner stove.

Not that Reggie planned to do any cooking, but at least she'd be able to make her own coffee.

Even the shoot was a breeze. The local crew was professional and polished, and her guest, himself a veteran of numerous TV appearances, was an absolute dream to work with. After the shoot, Gabe devoured his share of the leftovers without a word of protest.

Afterward they all went to Beaudine's on Bourbon, a famous restaurant owned by Georgia Beaudine. Georgia, with her Southern charm and down-home manner, was host of one of the most successful Cuisine Network shows in the history of the network. Along with her restaurant and best-selling cookbooks, she'd just signed a deal to develop a signature brand of cookware for a major retailer. Reggie felt like she was about to meet the Queen of England.

As she and Gabe rode in the cab to meet the rest of the group, she fidgeted with her purse, ridiculously nervous at the thought of meeting one of her idols.

"I don't see what there is to be worried about," Gabe said, as she checked her lipstick for the five hundredth time.

"Don't you know who this woman is?"

"Reggie, until you hired me, I'd never even heard of the Cuisine Network."

Reggie shook her head in irritation. "Hasn't there ever been someone you really wanted to meet, where making an impression was important?"

"Of course," Gabe replied, shocking her by leaning over and giving her a reassuring squeeze on her knee. "But just be yourself, and I'm sure she'll like you fine. And if she doesn't, well, fuck her."

A surprised laugh burst from her chest, but surprisingly, Gabe's coarse advice went a long way in calming her nerves.

Unfortunately, when they got to Beaudine's, Sentinel Gabe was back in full effect. "I'll be over there." He indicated a corner across from their table. "I can see the entrance from there."

"You're kidding, right?"

"No, it's not appropriate for me to eat with you when I should be watching the place."

"Is there a problem?" Reggie turned to face Georgia Beaudine, who wore the sunny smile that made *Georgia's Southern Kitchen* so popular.

She'd deal with Gabe's obstinacy later.

Reggie introduced herself and Georgia gave her a low, hearty laugh. "Of course I know who you are, darlin'. I can hardly get away from your face."

Georgia signaled a waiter over and ordered bourbon on the rocks while Reggie ordered a dirty vodka martini for herself. "I know this sounds corny," Reggie said, "but I'm such a big fan." She found herself basking in Georgia's wide smile and bright blue eyes. Even though physically they couldn't have been more different, something about Georgia with her warm, friendly manner and easygoing style reminded her of Mrs. Detaglia.

"The feeling's mutual, darlin'," she replied, accepting her drink from the waiter and taking a big gulp. "And let me just tell you something." She leaned in as though to impart great wisdom. "Other people like to take jabs at self-taught folks like you and me, and you just have to ignore it. They're just pissed off that they ain't gettin' the same airtime. I'll tell you something else, too, and don't take it the wrong way." She took another sip of her drink. "You're real hot now, and that's great. But at some point the next Reggie Caldwell is gonna come around and push you off your little throne."

Reggie sipped at her drink, not entirely sure where this was going. Was Georgia trying to reassure her or insult her?

"So what you gotta do is cram in as much as you can while you're hot, get your name out there and make all the money you can. Then, after a few years, you can open your own place if you want and live off your book royalties."

Reggie nodded in fervent agreement. "That's what I'm trying to do, with this show and my next book. I'm hoping other things will come out of it before the well totally dries up."

Georgia winked at her and wrapped a motherly arm around her shoulders. "Don't worry, honey, you still got at least a few more years in you."

Reggie smiled, but still a kernel of anxiety settled in the pit of her stomach. The truth was, she wasn't sure how much runway she had left. What if *Simply Delicious, USA* didn't get enough viewers? What if her next book bombed?

What if Craig was right? That she was just a flash in the pan who would be back cooking for wealthy, socially overwhelmed Bay Area housewives in no time flat?

"Now who's this handsome devil I see with you?" Georgia looked expectantly at Gabe.

"Gabe Bankovic," he said, stepping forward and offering his hand. "I work for Reggie."

"Now how come none of my employees look like this?"

Gabe's expression stayed politely impassive, but Reggie saw that the tips of his ears burned a bright crimson.

"Gabe's actually a security consultant, kind of like a bodyguard," Reggie explained. "I had some . . . trouble with a fan."

"Darlin', if you ever get tired of hanging out with cute young things, you can guard my body any time."

The maître d' came up and whispered something to Georgia, who politely excused herself. Reggie couldn't wait to get a look at the menu, but her good humor at meeting Georgia Beaudine quickly fled as Gabe once again refused to sit with her and her crew. "What's the big deal?" Reggie asked. "Do you actually think someone's going to come into a crowded restaurant to harass me?"

A muscle ticked in Gabe's jaw as he put his hands on his hips and stared down at her. "Why can't you trust me to do what you hired me to do?"

Reggie raised her chin another few notches, infuriated by

his attempt to physically intimidate her. "Why do you feel the need to embarrass me?"

"Embarrass you?"

"It's bad enough I have some goon shadowing me, but when you refuse to act like a social human being, it makes me look bad." She winced, hating how much that made her sound like a prima donna.

"God forbid the big goon threatens your precious public image," he bit out.

"I don't understand why you're making such a big deal out of it! It's not like we've even heard from scrotum boy in the past few days."

"Then maybe you don't need me. Maybe I should go home."

"Maybe. But before you go, you're going to sit down and have dinner with us like a normal human being."

Gabe couldn't decide what irritated him more: being goaded into lashing out at her, or not sticking to his guns about not eating dinner with the group. He didn't want to sit down like they were all friends. The whole situation felt too friendly, too intimate. It was appallingly easy to forget that she was a client, and not a date.

In spite of himself, Gabe was being drawn inexorably into Reggie's web. And the hell of it was, she wasn't even trying to lay one. He simply found her smile, her laugh—not to mention her deliciously curved body—almost irresistible. For the hundredth time since he'd arrived in Boston, he cursed himself for getting into this impossible situation.

But he couldn't just abandon her as he'd so foolishly threatened. So, instead, he sat down next to her, shared dinner with the rest of the crew, and though he hated to admit it, had a damn good time.

He knew Reggie enjoyed food, and it was a surprising pleasure to watch her eat. Unlike a lot of the women he had dated, she didn't pick at her food or nibble at a salad. Her eyes lit up when she read the menu, her voice thick with anticipation as she said the ingredients out loud. "Listen to this," she said, licking her lips. Lust fired in his groin and he couldn't help but stare at her mouth as she pronounced each ingredient. He generally viewed food as a necessity, something he put in his body to keep it functioning. Never in a million years would he have imagined that risotto with mushrooms could sound so erotic.

He prayed Reggie had the good sense to lock her bedroom door tonight. The way he was feeling right now, he had serious doubts about his level of self-restraint.

When they got back to the hotel, Reggie was smiling blurrily, no doubt a result of the martini and red wine she'd consumed with dinner.

He started for his room, but she grabbed his hand. "Stay up and watch TV with me," she said, trying to pull him over to the couch. "I bet we can get them to send us up a bottle of wine."

Did she even realize what she was offering? Her smile was tipsy and guileless, but surely she knew, even in her somewhat inebriated state, that if he joined her on the couch, there would be no TV watching happening. God, he wished he could just throw caution to the wind and take her up on it.

For a moment, he nearly caved. She was different from Marly. She treated the crew like old pals; she gave her sister a job even though the woman was more trouble than she was worth. She even put up with his constant rebuffs without turning into an icy bitch.

Then rationality took over as he remembered flashbulbs, base insults, the feel of facial cartilage crunching under his fists. Followed by the threat of lawsuits, the embarrassment to himself and his colleagues, the humiliation of being fired for the first time in his life.

He couldn't risk going through that again. Not even for Reggie.

"Come on, sit down," she urged, clicking on the remote and patting the cushion next to her.

He gently tugged his hand from her grip and backed away. "I should really go to bed."

Her lower lip pouted deliciously, begging him to lean down and take it between his teeth. "Party pooper." She sullenly flopped back against the couch. Then she clicked off the TV and stood up too. "I guess it is kind of late."

They both retired to their rooms, and Gabe had removed his shirt and was about to unzip his pants when he heard her call out his name.

He flung open her door, finding her pointing stiffly at something on the bed. She had changed into a tank top and loose cotton pants, and the bare skin of her arms prickled with goose bumps in the otherwise warm room.

Gabe looked at the bed where she indicated, spying a scrap of fabric among the busy flower print of the bedspread. "What is it?"

"I went to get in bed, and th-that was on my pillow."

Gabe knelt on the bed and gingerly picked up the fabric between two fingers. As he held it up he realized he held a pair of black thong panties adorned with a viscous white fluid.

Unthinkingly, he put a comforting hand on her shoulder and pulled her out of the room. "It's okay." He lifted it up for closer examination.

Peering over his shoulder, she whispered, "How could he have gotten in here? No one else knows we're here except for Natalie." Grimacing as Gabe held the underwear up to the light, she said, "Are you sure you should be touching that? Shouldn't we call the police?"

A familiar aroma teased his nose. Frowning, Gabe lifted the panties toward his face.

"Oh my God, what are you—" Reggie's revulsion-filled outburst ended with a gagging noise.

Gabe sniffed once, twice, and again just to be sure. "Cinnamon."

"What?"

"This isn't semen. I think it might be lotion, or maybe hair conditioner." He sniffed a third time, wrinkling his nose. "It smells kinda like . . . cinnamon."

"Cinnamon buns," Reggie mumbled.

"What?" Gabe asked.

"My lotion. It's called cinnamon buns. It smells like, well, cinnamon buns."

"At least we know he didn't jerk off into your panties." Gabe sighed. "Is it possible that your lotion spilled in your suitcase and got on your underwear?"

Reggie's dark eyebrows snapped together in a frown, and she folded her arms tightly around her chest. "No, it wasn't there when I left for dinner, and I always keep my toiletries separate from my clothes to prevent spills." She rubbed a tired hand over her eyes. "But I don't know, we move around so much, packing and repacking . . ." She sighed and walked out of the room.

Gabe looked at the delicate scrap of fabric dangling off his fingers and thoughts of her juicy ass framed in stretchy black lace careened across his brain. He dropped the thing like it was covered in cyanide and willed his erection to take a breather.

He found Reggie in the kitchenette pouring herself a glass of water. Her hand trembled, causing little waves to ripple through the liquid. "I'm becoming completely paranoid," she laughed shakily. "A guy sends me a couple of notes and weird e-mails, and I have him sneaking into my hotel room to frolic in my underwear. I'm worse than Carrie with her doomsday scenarios about him closing down production." She shook her head and took a long drink. Her eyes met his, huge and dark with wariness. "You don't think he was in here, do you?"

Gabe didn't know what to believe. On the one hand, toiletry spills were common enough. On the other hand, it was certainly odd that it would have landed only on a pair of sexy panties, and that they would in turn end up on her pillow. This whole situation was like nothing he'd ever seen. Most stalkers didn't keep themselves hidden. They wanted their victims to know who they were, because in their deluded brains they actually thought their victims would return whatever twisted version of love they felt.

Something wasn't right about this whole situation. He could feel it in his gut.

Then again, his gut had also told him Marly Chase had really cared for him, and look where that had gotten him.

Reggie lifted a shaky hand to her face, brushing her hair back in a nervous gesture. "I can't believe I'm letting this get to me. It's all so surreal and strange, the idea of having a stalker. Why me? What makes me so interesting that a stalker would even notice me, much less follow me?" She was trying to convince herself that it was nothing, that she was blowing the whole thing out of proportion. "And how could he even know where I am? Nobody knows where I am but you and Natalie."

"Maybe Natalie inadvertently gave someone your schedule."

Reggie sighed and leaned her head back to stare at the ceiling. "She's so scatterbrained sometimes, I suppose it's possible. But who would care? Who do I know who would bother to do this? I'm just an average girl who likes to cook." Her voice cracked and she looked at him helplessly.

Unable to stop himself, he stepped toward her, until he could just feel the soft press of her breasts against the bare skin of his chest. He wrapped his arms around her, pulling her head into the shelter of his chest. With a relieved sounding sigh, she fell into his embrace, leaning fully against him as her arms went around his back.

Her hot breath wafted against his already heated skin, and he became excruciatingly aware of his colossal mistake. Even as a spike of desire hit him straight in the groin, he couldn't bring himself to pull away.

His hand came up to cup her cheek, and for a few seconds he could do nothing but stare at the soft curves of her lovely face. "Reggie, you are anything but average."

Her gaze was unwavering, uncertain as it locked on his. She nervously licked her lips. Gabe chased its path with the pad of his thumb.

With that, logic fled, and the tenuous hold on his control snapped.

Cupping her face in his hands, he crushed his mouth down on hers, thrusting his tongue into her mouth with no preamble, no finesse whatsoever. The wine hot taste of her tongue rushed through him, his cock immediately going ramrod stiff. He backed her against the counter, his knees bending slightly as he rocked his erection against the giving softness of her belly.

She emitted a soft, surprised cry against his tongue, her hands running frantically down his back and sides, digging her short nails into the muscles along his spine.

He squeezed her ass, groaning as the firm, lush flesh spilled over his palms. One hand came up to knead her breast, rubbing, pinching at her nipple hard enough to wring a sharp cry from her throat.

His other hand snaked around, pressed flat against her belly, then lower to cup her between her legs. He tugged the strap of her tank top down her shoulder, exposing her breast to his eyes and his lips. He pressed the heel of his hand against her mound, and even through the twin layers of underwear and pajamas, he could feel the wetness already drenching her sex. Groaning, he bent and sucked her nipple into his mouth, pulling hard as he shoved his hand down the front of her pants.

Her plump, juicy pussy wept against his hand, and for a second he was afraid he was going to come in his pants like some fucking thirteen-year-old.

Reggie didn't help matters, her busy little hands deftly unfastening his belt and trousers. Her hot palm slid inside the waistband of his boxers, nearly bringing him to his knees as her soft palm pressed against the burning flesh of his rock-hard cock.

Cupping her ass in his palms, he lifted her off the floor and set her on the kitchenette table, swiftly stripping her of her tank top and yanking off her pants and underwear.

Then she lay naked before him, spread out like a gourmet feast. Cheeks flushed, mouth bruised, hair tousled, she looked like a raunchy porn fantasy of the girl next door gone bad. The deep pink folds of her sex winked at him through her dark curls, the hot little bud of her clit peeking out, begging to be stroked and sucked.

Lust powered him forward, his motions almost frantic as the voice in his head warning him to stop faded in the wake of pure unbridled need. Aching with the need to taste her, he sank to his knees, roughly shoving her thighs apart as he buried his face against her. Wildly, he plunged inside, savoring her salty sweet taste, his tongue licking along her tight passage and emerging to circle hotly around her clit. "God, Reggie, you taste better than anything I've ever known."

Her hands fisted in his hair in response, hips bucking against his face. Shaking, chest heaving like he'd run a fast mile, Gabe stood up, shoving his pants and boxers off his hips in the same movement. Pressing his palms on the pliant skin of her inner thighs, he spread her wide. He gripped himself in one hand as he guided himself to her dripping core, soaking the head of his cock in her juices as he shook with the effort not to explode.

With one firm, unrestrained thrust he shoved inside, wringing a surprised cry from her throat. For a millisecond he paused, afraid in his wildness that he'd hurt her. He rained soft, soothing kisses across her cheeks and suddenly, unbelievably, she was coming, clenching and shaking around him as she gripped his ass hard, grinding against him like she wanted to swallow him whole.

He threw his head back, squeezing his eyes shut at the almost unbearable heat and tightness. So good, so perfect, a million times better than he remembered. She gripped him hard, rippling and kneading around him with the force of her orgasm. Realizing he had no reason to hold back, he began to thrust slick, unrestrained, deep strokes as she took every hard inch of him. She thrashed beneath him all the while, moaning and clawing at him in a frenzy of need.

Nothing had ever felt this good. No woman was this tight, this hot, this slick, this wild as she clenched around him.

Suddenly, she stiffened, her mouth open on a silent scream as she peaked again. His cock swelled another inch, his balls tightening as the force of his orgasm built at the base of his spine.

One tiny, still functioning brain cell whispered that maybe the reason she felt so fucking good around him was because he had completely ignored the need for a condom.

He moved faster, harder, toes curling as waves of a bone-shattering release ripped through his guts. That same functioning brain cell prompted him to pull out just in time, his cock throbbing and jerking against the soft skin of her belly as he soaked her with the force of his release.

Shaking, his arms gave out under his weight and he collapsed on top of her, resting his forehead against hers.

Eyes drowsy with satiation, Reggie threaded her fingers through his hair and captured his mouth, a purr of satisfaction vibrating through her entire body.

Gabe pulled away, released his grip on her hips, and rested his cheek on the table beside her head. "Son of a bitch."

Chapter Seven

The languid warmth coursing through Reggie's veins abruptly froze at Gabe's soft swear.

His softly whispered "Son of a bitch" was not a curse of satisfaction.

Proving her point, he hastily levered himself off her. Without meeting her gaze, he quickly dragged his trousers back up his hips and zipped them with a quick jerk of his hand.

Reggie propped herself up on her elbows, trying to regain enough of her faculties to reach for her own clothes. If she put any weight on her legs right now, she feared they'd buckle beneath her.

Still not looking at her, Gabe went to the sink and wet a dishtowel, tossing it in her general direction. By some miracle she managed to catch it, then used it to wipe up the tacky remnants of semen off her belly. At least he'd had the decency to use warm water.

She heaved herself the rest of the way up and snagged her tank top and pajama bottoms off the floor. Leaning against the table for support, she drew them on with trembling hands.

Once she was decently covered, Gabe turned from the sink to face her, focusing his gaze somewhere past her ear.

"Reggie, that was extremely unprofessional and inappropriate. I can't tell you how sorry I am about what just happened."

"You're sorry?" She felt like a tight fist had invaded her

abdomen and was busy twisting her small intestine. "That's all you have to say?"

"I know anything I say will be insufficient."

Unbelievable. Ten seconds ago he'd been grunting and straining over her like a man fresh out of prison, and now he was as cold and impersonal as the guy who did her dry cleaning! Scratch that—at least the dry cleaner always smiled and said thank you.

"And if you want to terminate our contract, I completely understand."

She snapped. "This is great. You attack me like a raging ball of testosterone, and now you want to abandon me?" A psycho-sounding cackle erupted from her throat. "Sorry, buddy. I still need you around to make sure I keep my job." A knot the size of a grapefruit lodged at the back of her throat, and she knew if she didn't get away from him right then, she'd burst into tears.

She stomped over to her bedroom and slammed the door so hard the walls shuddered. Reggie flung herself down on the green and gold printed bedspread and punched the pillow.

Gabe had slept with her and unhesitatingly rejected her. But what had she expected?

She should have stopped him, should have realized that for him, sex was nothing more than a good way to release tension after a particularly stressful few days. But from the second he touched her, any thought of pushing him away had fled as every drop of blood abruptly headed south.

And who could blame her? She'd been walking around in state of arousal from the moment he'd reappeared in her apartment. All it took was a tiny stick of dry tinder to make her burst into flame. And Gabe, well, he had a nice big log.

She slumped down on the bed and buried her face in her hands. God, maybe he was right. Maybe she should have fired him. But did she really want another man, a stranger at that, following her around and tracking her every move?

On the other hand, did she really want to spend the next, oh God, four weeks in agony over a man who drove her hormones berserk, but who was determined to avoid her like the plague? And when he did finally succumb to his oh-so-human urges, he looked like he wanted to flay himself and stroll around in a hair shirt for the next month.

A soft knock interrupted her moping. She squelched the urge to tell him to get lost. Thanks to her big mouth, she was stuck with Gabe for quite a while, and the sooner they made peace, the better. "Come in."

Gabe entered warily, as though he expected her to be waiting in a corner to pounce. He folded his arms over his chest, his mouth pressed in a tight line. Difficult to believe that same mouth had been pressed ravenously between her legs not ten minutes ago.

Reggie squeezed her eyes shut and forced herself not to think about it.

As he moved closer to the bed, the scent of his skin teased her nostrils—his own hot, musky, soap smell, entwined with the sharp tang of pure sex.

She jumped up off the bed before she lunged at him and started clawing at his pants and raised her eyebrows in what she hoped was an imperious manner. "Was there something else?"

He paused, pressing and unpressing his lips as though trying to find the right words.

Reggie braced herself for more insults.

"We, uh, we didn't . . ." he stopped again.

Reggie stared at him expectantly, enjoying his discomfort.

His cheeks puffed as he blew out a breath. "We didn't use anything." Another pause. "Birth control-wise."

Reggie's face went hot as a habanero. "B-but you pulled out."

Though his eyes were blank and impersonal, he couldn't stop the streaks of red that appeared across his cheekbones.

"I know. But I also thought you should know that I get tested regularly, and I'm clean."

Hot embarrassment flooded her as she realized what an ignorant teenager she'd sounded like. Of course disease was an issue. She'd grown up in the eighties, prided herself on being relatively smart and sexually aware. She looked up. Gabe was staring at her expectantly. Then she realized he was looking for the same reassurance.

"I had a full workup six months ago, and since you're the last person I slept with, I know I'm still fine."

For a split second, surprise and an emotion Reggie wouldn't dare call pleasure illuminated his face. Then he nodded curtly and turned to go.

As soon as he closed the door behind him she flopped back on the bed. Why in the hell had she told him that?

Now he would think she was so desperate, hard up, that of course she would jump at the chance to screw his brains out with the slightest provocation.

Obviously, that was true, as evidenced by her embarrassingly immediate orgasm earlier, which had taken her completely by surprise. As had the second one mere minutes later.

Well, there was nothing to be done for it but to take Gabe's lead and just pretend it never happened. She rolled off the bed and ripped back the covers. Praying, in futility, for a decent night's sleep, she climbed into bed.

She snapped off the lights and stared up at the darkness. If nothing else, the tenuous friendship they'd formed over the past few days would make their time together more bearable. If they could regain that, surely she could tolerate his presence for the next several weeks.

Gabe watched Reggie as she finished up shooting in and around New Orleans the next morning. Even with the unmistakable signs of exhaustion lining her face, she managed to appear vibrant for the cameras.

He couldn't help the smug sense of satisfaction he got from knowing she'd slept as poorly as he. All night he'd struggled with the urge to slip into her room, climb into bed, and slide into her tight, willing body.

Far from taking the edge off the desire that had ridden him from the first moment he'd seen her again, last night's tussle in the kitchenette had only made him want her more.

In Hawaii, he'd gotten the sense that he'd only touched on the surface of her deep and giving sexuality. But when she'd snuck off without a word, he'd resolved to be satisfied with the small taste circumstances had allowed.

But now he knew what a little hellcat lurked under that wholesome exterior. All that energy and heat she possessed permeated every facet of her life. Including sex. He got hard just thinking about how she'd gone off like a rocket at the mere feel of him inside her. This morning he'd had to jerk off like a goddamned teenager when he felt the heat of the shower sting his back where she'd raked her nails across the skin.

And now, as he watched her bite into a beignet, he unconsciously licked his lips as he remembered the tiny bite mark he'd discovered on his shoulder this morning in the mirror. He'd been so fucking hot for her, he hadn't even felt her teeth sink in with enough pressure to leave two tiny, crescent-shaped bruises.

He'd barely spoken to her all morning, deciding the best move was to keep as much distance as possible. He did his best to ignore the tight wad of guilt lodged in his chest. He knew he was handling this badly. She deserved better, another apology and moderately civil behavior at least, but he didn't know what else to do. It wasn't like he could avoid her, and he was afraid any attempt at conversation would be a slippery slope. If he wasn't careful, the next thing he knew, he'd be ripping her clothes off and going down on her right in front of the crew.

His emotions, which he fought so hard to keep under con-

trol, rode way too close to the surface when it came to
Reggie, and they were searching for any tiny crack to spill
out. And it scared the hell out of him. Last night, against all
better judgment and good sense, he literally hadn't been able
to stop himself from having her. Craving for her had superseded control to the point where he'd been past caring, even
though he knew the risks involved in letting Reggie be anything other than a client.

Now, doing damage control was his main priority. The
only way to prevent future slipups was to remain ruthlessly
distant, uninvolved on any personal level.

Finally, the shoot wrapped and Reggie made her way over.
Fumbling through her bag, she pulled out a sheet of paper
with her flight information on it. "Let's see, where are we
going today," she said in a singsong voice. "Aha! Dallas."
She looked up at Gabe. "Don't you have family in Dallas?"

He nodded coolly. "My parents and one of my sisters and
her husband."

"I have a great idea!" She clapped her hands and looked
up at him with a huge grin, and he couldn't ignore the curl of
warmth twisting in his belly. "Why don't you call your family and invite them to watch some of the shooting. Then they
can join us at the Fort Worth Stock Yards for dinner."

"I don't think so."

"Why not? Is it too short notice?"

Why couldn't she just take a hint? Pulling her aside so the
rest of the crew couldn't hear, he said, "Reggie, while I appreciate the gesture, I'm here to work. We're not buddies,
and I don't want you to do me or my family any special favors."

Reggie jerked her head back and stared at him. His heart
twisted at the flicker of hurt that flashed in her eyes, the faint
tremble in her soft lips as she pursed them.

Then, eyes narrowing, she said, "Do you have a pen?"

Confused, Gabe pulled one out of the inside pocket of his
sport coat. Mouth tight, Reggie flipped over her itinerary

printout and began to write, reading aloud as she did so, loud enough that her producer and cameraman looked over with interest. "Note to self: Never try to do anything nice for Gabe again because he is an asshole." She dotted the period with a flourish and folded up the paper. Blinking innocently up at him, she said, "Can you remind me to have Natalie program that into my Palm Pilot so I get a daily reminder?"

Gabe had to bite the insides of his cheeks to keep from laughing. He wished he didn't like her so damned much.

Reggie's cell phone trilled. Glancing at the screen, she said, "Speak of the devil."

Gabe listened as she told Natalie about last night's events, leaving out the part about how he'd attacked her like a Neanderthal.

"Sure, go ahead and tell everyone. I don't care. Maybe I'll get my face in *Us Weekly.*"

It bothered Gabe that they would exploit the possibility, however far-fetched, that Reggie's stalker had followed her all the way to New Orleans to generate publicity. Could Natalie have inadvertently leaked information about Reggie's schedule? What if her stalker actually had been in their hotel room? It was a long shot, but Gabe couldn't suppress the ugly suspicion that the threat was real, more real than Reggie was willing to admit to herself.

And Natalie's carelessness could be placing Reggie in harm's way. "Let me talk to her," he said, reaching for the phone.

Natalie nodded as Tyler passed her a note to remind Reggie about the book signing he'd scheduled in Austin at the beginning of next week.

"Oh, hi, Gabe."

Tyler frowned across the desk at her greeting.

Ever since screwing everything up in Memphis, Natalie had been busting her ass to prove to Reggie and Tyler that she was capable of being Reggie's assistant. So far she was doing a damn good job, if she did say so herself. So she was wholly unprepared for Gabe's assault.

"Natalie, I don't need to remind you not to share Reggie's hotel information with anyone, do I?" Gabe asked, his voice dripping with acid-laced condescension.

Natalie held the phone away from her ear for a second. She heard a brief scuffle on the other end as Reggie tried to get the phone back from Gabe. "I haven't told anyone, just like you said."

"It's possible this guy found out where Reggie and I were last night. Reggie didn't tell anyone. I sure as hell didn't. So that leaves you. What, are you and Tyler scheming to set her up to get more publicity?"

"I would never endanger my sister." Though she had, with Tyler's encouragement, leaked information about the stalker to the press, and with great success if she did say so herself. Still, the implication that she'd willingly place her sister in danger cut her to the core.

Suddenly, embarrassingly, her throat closed up with an on-slaught of tears. Obviously, the entire world saw her as either a huge fuckup or an idiotic mercenary who had no regard for anyone else, including her own sister.

She let Tyler tug the phone out of her hand without looking up. Great. Now he and Gabe could talk about what a parasitic loser she was. At least Max had promised to give her show idea consideration after their meeting the other day at Reggie's.

"I don't know who you think you are, Bankovic, but you have no call to talk to Natalie like that."

Natalie nearly fell off her chair as Tyler continued, "She's been doing a damn good job, and she wouldn't leak informa-tion that would put Reggie in danger." He was silent a mo-ment as he listened to Gabe's reply, then, "I was the one who called *People*, okay, so get off Natalie's back." Another pause. "Yeah, well, that's my job, buddy. We all work for Reggie, in-cluding you."

He stabbed at the End button and shoved the phone back at Natalie. "Reggie should fire that asshole. He was way out of line."

But Natalie suddenly felt like Gabe was right. "He takes his job seriously. Besides, I think he still has a thing for Reggie." Like the rest of the world. Suddenly, Natalie felt excruciatingly sorry for herself. *Look at you,* she thought scornfully, *twenty-six years old and nothing but a glorified gopher living off your sister's charity so you can pay rent on that rathole you call an apartment.* Maybe she should go home, grab a box of Krispy Kremes, and have herself a full-blown pity party.

Tyler came over to her side of the desk and squatted next to her chair. Handing her a tissue, he awkwardly patted her shoulder. Natalie turned to face him, knowing that her tear-ravaged face looked like the wrath of God. He, of course, looked perfect, the epitome of a Nordic god. This close she could see the tiny golden hairs sprouting on his chin where he'd missed a spot shaving. That tiny crack in his Ken-doll perfection was oddly comforting. His blue eyes, which never regarded her with more than casual friendliness, were deep and warm with what looked like real concern. "You've been doing a great job lately, so don't let him upset you."

Natalie sniffled, wishing with everything she was worth that she could lay her head on his big, cotton-clad shoulder. But he stood up and looked at his watch. "Speaking of which, I need to wrap this up." He waggled his eyebrows mischievously. "I have a lunch date with that hot little lawyer who works across the street."

For some reason she chose not to examine, that made her want to cry even harder.

If Gabe wanted the silent treatment, Reggie had no problem giving it to him. Bad enough that he'd refused her olive branch—the last she would ever offer, guaranteed—then he'd had the gall to insult her sister.

Before they went to the airport, they stopped at an Internet café so Reggie could check her e-mail and send off another round of notes to her editor. About halfway through the list of nearly fifty messages was one from "Your One and Only," with the subject line: **Black lace and cream.**

Though the address was unfamiliar, she knew instantly who sent it. She called out to Gabe, who sat across the room from her at the only other available terminal.

"It's from him," she said, indicating the message with her mouse.

Gabe pulled up a chair and clicked on the message.

> Darling Reggie,
> Why do you persist in hiding from me? Don't you know by now I will find you, no matter where you go? All that matters is you, darling Reggie, and I won't stop until we can be together.
> I trust that by now you've received my latest token. Though I wanted to leave something more personal behind, I decided it best that I wait to give it to you in person, when the time is right.
> Thinking of you always.

Chapter Eight

Cold shock iced Reggie's limbs as reality hit her. Whoever was sending the creepy notes really *was* following her. He knew her every move, and he had actually broken into her hotel room the night before. Now he was talking about being together. Was this the escalation that Gabe was talking about?

"I'll be damned. He really was there," Gabe muttered.

Reggie shook her head, denial welling in her chest. "I can't believe it. I thought I was overreacting."

"I want to send this to a friend of mine. He was in the forces with me and has his own security company now. He's an expert at finding electronic trails."

Reggie sat quietly while Gabe left his friend a message and forwarded her e-mail. But she still had several messages to go through, so Reggie sat back down for the next hour and did her best to focus on the work at hand and not obsess over how the stalker had gotten access to her hotel information and worse, their hotel room.

One bright spot was an e-mail from her editor, saying that she loved the previous chapters and that since the *Good Morning America* story aired, sales of her last book had climbed a full ten percent. She didn't know why having a rabid fan made her books more appealing, but she'd take any good news she could get at this point.

With that in mind, she made a mental note to call Max

about ratings for *Simply Delicious*. Maybe they'd received a boost too.

The next few days passed in a blur as they traveled all over Texas. Reggie immersed herself in work, and much to her editor's delight, made a decent dent in the work required for her next book.

On set was a little hairier. Though she did her best not to let it get to her, she couldn't shake the uneasy feeling that had settled like a heavy cloak around her shoulders. She'd tried to convince herself that the stalker was harmless, that everyone else was overreacting, but what if he really meant her harm? And while Gabe's presence went a long way in making her feel safer, memories of his warm, wet mouth sliding over her skin tortured her every time she so much as looked at him.

As a result, she knew she was coming off as flat and distracted on-screen, but couldn't seem to do anything about it.

After the director demanded a fifth take on an intro shot one afternoon in San Antonio, Carrie pulled her aside once again. "Reggie, I know you've got a lot on your mind lately, but you have got to pull it together. The last two days have taken twice as long as they should have, and I hate to say it, but it's pretty much all your fault."

As a rule, Reggie liked the shoot-from-the-hip, pull-no-punches style of the petite, dynamic producer. But not when she was on the receiving end of her sharp tongue.

Taking a few deep breaths, Reggie raised her face to the warm fall Texas sun as though she could absorb its energy through her pores. In the past few days, her usually boundless energy had abandoned her, leaving her listless, disconnected, and even a little depressed.

She snuck a glance over at G.I. Gabe, looking cool and composed, even as the sun beat down on his light wool sport coat. In his dark sunglasses, the sunlight playing off the sharp bones of his face and that sinfully voluptuous mouth, he looked like a Hollywood fantasy of a tough but sexy protector.

What she needed to do was take a page from Gabe's book. Be a stickler about not letting personal matters interfere with work. Besides, while her fans might love her because she seemed so down to earth and approachable, she didn't think she wanted to be everyone's friend if it meant some people might take it as an invitation to break into her room and soil her underwear drawer.

The rest of the day went better. She managed to do the rest of the shoot with minimal takes, and they all piled into mini-vans to be shuttled off to Austin.

Thankfully, they were spending two nights in Austin with no early calls, and Reggie was hoping for a chance to rest and rejuvenate. She collapsed in her bed that night, looking forward to a long, leisurely sleep.

Gabe apparently had other ideas.

"Hey, wake up."

Reggie rolled over and squinted at him, then at the clock. She pulled the pillow over her head and snuggled deeper under the comforter to ward off the air-conditioned chill.

Gabe ripped back the comforter and plucked the pillow from her grasp. "Come on, lazy, we're going for a run."

"It's only six-fifteen." Her gaze momentarily locked on his muscular, hair-dusted thighs displayed quite nicely by his nylon running shorts. She closed her eyes again. The last thing she needed was to start the day horny.

"It's the best time of day," he cajoled, reaching down to tug on her arm. He looked adorable, short hair tousled, eyes still a little sleepy, smile teasing the corners of his lips. "Besides, by the time you finish your coffee ritual, it'll be after seven."

She sat up, resenting how good he looked when she probably had a bed crease the size of the Grand Canyon running down her cheek. "I don't have to be at the restaurant until ten," she grumbled.

Gabe started rifling through her suitcase, pulled out a pair of shorts, jog bra, socks, and a T-shirt, then threw them at her. "That gives us time for a good, long run. And I'm going to teach you some self-defense moves."

"Self-defense moves?" Her feet were on the floor and she thought about standing up.

"After having the guy break into your hotel room, even you have to start taking him seriously." He left her to get dressed.

Forty minutes later, her caffeine needs met, Reggie trotted off after Gabe. Within ten minutes they reached the jogging trail that ran alongside the city's Town Lake.

It took only a few minutes for the beauty of the early morning light glinting off the lake to lift her spirits. Soon she found it impossible to keep up the icy indifference of the past couple of days and was chatting with Gabe about anything and everything. When he remarked she might run faster if she didn't talk so much, Reggie couldn't bring herself to take offense.

They ran in silence for a little over forty-five minutes, Gabe slowing his pace considerably to match hers. She'd tried once in their travels to encourage him to go as fast as he wanted. He'd given her his "you're an idiot" glare and informed her he'd never jeopardize her safety like that.

They passed a grassy clearing and Gabe pulled her off the trail.

"Is this the part where I get to beat you up?" she asked. She plopped on the grass, damp blades tickling the backs of her thighs as she took the opportunity to stretch.

"You can try," he said with a slight grin as he assumed a defensive stance, feet braced wide on the grassy earth. "First, let's go over the basics. You should never try to overpower a man, even if he's smaller than you. There are, however, several points of vulnerability you can go for."

"Oh wait, I know this," she said, her mind rifling through its extensive pop culture database. "Something, instep, nose, and groin, right?"

"Have you been reading up?" he grinned.

She bent one knee into a hurdler's stretch and folded over her straight leg. "Nope. But I've seen *Miss Congeniality* a hundred times." She widened her legs into a straddle and bent her nose toward the grass. When she looked up, Gabe was staring at her with a slightly dazed expression. She widened her legs another few inches. His face flushed a darker shade of red, and it wasn't from the slowly rising Texas heat.

He cleared his throat and seemed to shake himself a little, disappointing Reggie with how quickly he regained control. "You forgot solar plexus. Now, if you want to get up, we can do a little practice run. You jog across the field, and I'll act like I'm attacking you from behind."

Reggie rolled to her feet and started to jog. "How is this supposed to work if I know you're coming?"

Her only answer was heavy footfalls in the grass behind her. Funny how even though she knew it was Gabe and knew he was harmless, relatively speaking, her adrenaline still picked up and she instinctively broke into a sprint. He caught her easily, one thickly muscled arm wrapping around her waist as his other hand engulfed the lower half of her face. "What are you gonna do now, little girl," he whispered menacingly in her ear.

Thrashing, she kicked at his legs and clawed at his arms, all to no avail. After several seconds, he eased his hold on her waist and uncovered her mouth. Holding her like this, his chest was plastered against her back and she could feel his hair-roughened legs brushing against hers. His scent invaded her brain, clean sweat and soap that made her want to turn around and lick every salty drop from his body.

So wrapped up in her fantasy of giving him a tongue bath, she barely heard what he was saying.

"Focus. Try to stay calm so you can locate points of vulnerability, and save your energy to land blows that count." She nodded, trying to ignore the way his hand splayed across her belly in a casual, yet intimate hold. He stiffened, every sinew tensing as he, too, became aware of how closely he was holding her. There was no denying the stirring pressure against her lower back as he carefully set her away from him. His voice, when he spoke, sounded like he'd swallowed ground glass. "Let's try that again."

This time when he caught her, she ignored the delicious feel of him rubbing against her and focused on channeling all of the past two weeks' frustration into incapacitating blows. While she couldn't get to his knee, she landed a blow on his instep that made him howl, leaving his groin vulnerable to attack.

But even in her frustrated state, she couldn't bring herself to do it. Call her an idiotic optimist, but she couldn't help but hope she'd have occasion to use that part again soon, and she didn't want it in any way incapacitated.

"Good job," he said, wincing slightly as he put weight on his right foot. "We'll work more on that, but for today I want to stop before I break any bones."

They set off back to the hotel, and as they rounded the corner of the last block, Gabe slanted her a sly, boyish look. "Race you."

He was off like a rocket. After putting her heart into it for about ten yards, Reggie realized it was much more entertaining to watch the tight muscles of his ass flex as he sprinted down the street.

"What about never leaving me to danger?" she said mock-testily when she caught up.

He grinned down at her, sweat beading in sexy trickles down his face as he caught his breath. "Best defense of all. If you're running fast, who's gonna catch you?"

Winded, legs heavy from exertion, Reggie felt better than she had since New Orleans. Though she had protested at first, the run left her energetic and rejuvenated, and she had to admit a greater feeling of empowerment and security now that she had at least a passing familiarity with some self-defense moves.

Within half an hour she was showered and dressed in one

of her many pairs of black pants and a cobalt blue knit top with little lacings along the sides. She took extra care with her makeup, apprehensive about how she'd look next to today's guest.

With good reason. As they arrived at Peliroja's, the restaurant where they were filming today, Reggie saw that Katrina Garrett was as beautiful as she remembered. About ten feet tall, mile-long legs, boobs out to here, and a waist so small Reggie suspected she'd had a couple of ribs removed, the striking redhead strode across the elegant dining room to meet them. She held out her hand to Reggie and shook it in a firm, confident grip. "So good to see you. Rosie, isn't it?"

Reggie's eyes squinted as she struggled to maintain her smile. Katrina was still gorgeous, and apparently still a bitch. Reggie knew the slight was intentional. She'd met Katrina once before at a Cuisine Network function—Katrina's show was set to debut early next year—but even if Katrina didn't remember her name from that, she'd been well briefed on Reggie and the show when they'd scheduled this segment.

When Carrie had suggested the idea of bringing together two of Cuisine Network's sexiest (Carrie's word, not Reggie's) female chefs and doing a little cross-promotion, Reggie had inwardly balked at the idea. But knowing full well she wasn't yet big enough to argue every little misgiving, she'd agreed to Carrie's idea.

Now, noting the undisguised feminine interest in Katrina's eyes as she turned her gaze to Gabe, Reggie wished she'd exercised a little veto power.

With a warm, unmistakably suggestive smile, Katrina introduced herself to Gabe.

Gabe introduced himself, quickly explaining his presence.

Katrina's laugh tinkled up to the ceiling. In her high-heeled, hand-tooled cowboy boots, she could almost look Gabe in the eye. Moving infinitesimally closer, she spared Reggie a quick glance. "That's right. I heard about the stalker situation." She turned to Reggie with a saccharinely sympathetic smile. "Amazing, isn't it, how some people will obsess over just about anyone."

Reggie chewed on the inside of her cheeks to prevent herself from lashing back. Katrina wanted to play queen bee? Fine. She was not going to lower herself by engaging in a catfight. "Thanks again for letting us film a segment here. Hopefully the show will be good publicity."

Katrina finally released Gabe's hand and tossed her glorious auburn mane over her shoulder. "Not that we need it. We're booked solid for months. I wish I could return the favor and have you on my show, but I'm only visiting other chefs who have four-star restaurants. Speaking of which, are you and Craig Ferguson still an item?"

Reggie feared her cheek muscles would start spasming at the force of her strained smile as she shook her head. "No, we broke up over a year ago, actually. I'm sure he'd be more than happy to appear on your show. Now, I thought before we started, it would be a good idea to go over the recipes again."

As unobtrusively as possible, Reggie steered Katrina back to the kitchen and away from Gabe. Once in the kitchen, setting up the shots, Reggie's good mood from the morning deflated. With her skin-tight jeans hugging her tiny, firm ass and exotic good looks, Katrina made Reggie feel about as attractive as a pile of mud. How could a woman work in a restaurant and still have a body like that?

Brushing off Reggie's attempts to go over the talking points, Katrina assured her rehearsal of any sort was not needed. "So what's with muscles there?" Katrina said, nodding her head in the general direction of the dining room where Gabe waited. "Is he really a bodyguard, or just paid companionship?"

Reggie wasn't sure on whose behalf she should be more insulted: her own, for the insinuation that she had to pay for companionship, or Gabe's, for the insinuation that he was the sort of man who would allow his companionship to be paid for.

"I have a man sneaking into my hotel rooms to frolic in my panty drawer," she explained, unable to keep the testiness from her tone. "Why do you think he's here?"

The shoot, at least in Reggie's mind, went downhill from there. Not that they made any major flubs—in fact, they got almost everything done in one take. The issue was that Katrina didn't hesitate to get in her subtle digs at every opportunity. Like when she told Reggie how to cut an onion as though Reggie were a particularly slow five-year-old. Or when she explained that she was making a chiffonade of the basil, and maybe Reggie didn't realize that since she never went to cooking school.

All little reminders that she, Katrina the Amazon goddess, was an award-winning graduate of the Cordon Bleu, whereas Reggie's lack of education left her unqualified to run a hot-dog stand.

By the end of the day, Reggie actually missed Biddy Lee Hughes.

When they wrapped, Reggie lingered in the kitchen. Trapped in the presence of perfection, Reggie hadn't been able to bring herself to eat. Now starving, she shoveled in several bites of roasted quail with poblano chile reduction. Katrina charged out the yin yang for her "Tex-Mex fare with a nouveau twist," but damned if it didn't taste like a rather anemic plate of good old mole poblano. Tyler was right. Good PR could turn manure to gold.

She left the rest to the crew, determined to get some really good tacos before her book signing tonight.

She emerged from the kitchen, the sight before her threatening to send the quail spewing all over Katrina's bright white tablecloths. Katrina and Gabe were seated at a table in the otherwise empty bar, sipping what looked like margaritas. Christ, the man wouldn't even have a glass of wine with her and here he was boozing it up with the whore of Babylon. Gabe smiled and laughed at whatever Katrina said, and in that moment she was vividly reminded of the man she'd met that night in Hawaii, with his dark, intense gaze and sexy, lopsided smile. Except now both were focused on someone else.

She got to the table just in time to hear Katrina say, "So if you're not busy later, I'd love to show you more of Austin."

Before Gabe could answer, Reggie interrupted, "Unfortunately, I pay Gabe very well for his time, and tonight he has to go with me to a book signing."

Katrina's eyes lit up. "Oh, where?"

Gabe told her the name of the bookstore.

"I'll join you! Nothing like having a local celebrity there to help draw a crowd."

And Katrina made good on her word. But instead of meeting and greeting the fans, she kept herself planted next to Gabe the entire evening. On several occasions Reggie caught her leaning in and whispering something in his ear. Though he wasn't obviously flirting back, he sure as hell wasn't giving Katrina the aloof impersonal vibe he strove for with Reggie.

As Reggie smiled and penned a message for yet another fan, she wondered what would happen if she leapt across the room and stabbed Katrina, *Bourne Identity* style, with her ballpoint pen. Except she'd aim for her boob instead of her hand.

After most of the crowd had dissipated, a younger man approached the table. He was cute, in an executive kind of way. He had pretty green eyes and a great smile. She couldn't help responding to it with one of her own.

"So, whom do I make this out to?" she asked, looking up at him through her lashes. Definitely attractive, and definitely more her regular speed than Gabe ever was.

"Make it out to Trey," he replied. As she signed the book he leaned over, close enough that Reggie caught a subtle whiff of his cologne. "I actually owe you for saving my ass with dinner a couple of months ago."

"Don't tell me," she said with the tiniest stab of disappointment, "you pissed off your girlfriend and made her my patented 'I'm sorry' menu."

"Worse," he chuckled. "I was out of town for my mom's birthday, and I forgot to call her, send a card, anything. But I made her one of your recipes off the show Web site, and all was forgiven."

"You can always tell a guy's a good catch when he treats his mother well." She looked up and gave him a quick wink, then a teasing frown. "Unless, of course, he still lives with her."

Trey laughed, and without asking he pulled up a chair next to her. "No way. I live in San Francisco. I'm in town on business. My mom lives up in Mill Valley. That's about twenty minutes away."

Hmm. Gabe wasn't the only one who could find a little companionship on the road. "I know where that is. I live in Pacific Heights."

He gave a sincerely delighted, ego-boosting smile. "I had no idea you were a local girl. I live in the Marina."

They were quickly absorbed in conversation, discussing favorite restaurants and hangouts in the city. Suddenly, Trey cut off midsentence. Reggie didn't need to look behind her. She felt Gabe's overwhelming, ominous presence like a physical force.

Spinning in her chair, she looked up.

She could see why Trey looked so nervous. Gabe's deep-set eyes were like chips of black ice stabbing down at them. His thick arms were crossed over his chest, and even in his work uniform of dress slacks and a sport coat, he looked dangerously uncivilized.

"I'm sorry to interrupt this," a dark undercurrent of rage throbbing in his voice, "but Miss Caldwell has to get up early tomorrow."

A bald-faced lie, but something told Reggie that arguing with Gabe at this point would not give her the results she wanted. Still, the night wasn't a total loss. She stood and offered her hand to Trey, who glanced apprehensively at Gabe before accepting it. Pretending Gabe wasn't hovering over them like a medieval ogre, she smiled and said, "I really enjoyed meeting you, Trey. Why don't you give me your card, and maybe I'll call you when I get back to San Francisco?"

Still looking uncertain, Trey handed her the card, and she made a big show of tucking it in her wallet so it wouldn't get lost.

Without a word to Katrina or anyone else, Gabe pulled her out of the bookstore and barely got a block before his simmering rage exploded into a high boil. Backing her into the dark doorway of a store, he hissed, "Are you completely naive or just incredibly stupid?" Before Reggie could form a comeback, he continued, "After everything that's happened in the last few days, I thought you were taking this more seriously. But either your short-term memory is shot, or you lack the capacity to apply knowledge to other situations."

Pushing futilely at his chest, Reggie yelled, "I don't know what your problem is. I was just talking to a nice guy while you were busy burying your face in that glamazon's cleavage."

"You weren't just talking to him. You practically drew him a map to your apartment." He affected a high, singsong falsetto. "Oh, I live in Pacific Heights. I eat at Belelnut all the time. I get my coffee at exactly eight oh two every morning at the Starbucks on Lombard Street. If you pass my apartment at precisely seven oh two you can catch me coming out of the shower."

"It was nothing like that," she snapped, swatting him across the chest. Deep down, she knew he was right, that she'd let her little fit of jealousy override common sense. But with images of Gabe's head bent attentively toward Katrina seething in her brain, she wasn't willing to concede just yet. "Besides, you said the stalker is someone who knows me. I've never met Trey before."

"How do you know? How many people do you meet every goddamned day of your life? Forget your show—you talk to everyone. How can you be sure you never met him in

San Francisco? Maybe he's been following you around. Maybe he works for the network and has access to your schedule."

He plowed his hands through his hair as though he wanted to tear out every strand. "And even though he's probably not the guy, that's not the point. The point is you're a celebrity. Like it or not, people assume they have a relationship with you, whether you know it or not. When you go batting your eyelashes and shaking that sweet ass in front of every guy you meet, the crazier ones are going to get ideas!"

Though she couldn't tell for certain in the dim streetlight, Reggie thought maybe Gabe's face had turned purple. "Are you saying I *asked* for the guy to stalk me?" Still royally pissed, she didn't allow herself to be distracted by Gabe's "sweet ass" comment.

Gabe let out a frustrated sigh. "Reggie, I'm not blaming you. But it's not safe for you to make eyes at every guy you meet and give him detailed directions to your bedroom."

Stepping back, he let her out of the alcove and started down the block to their hotel.

"I don't do that with every guy," Reggie called. "Just the cute ones."

Gabe looked like he was about to argue further, then snapped his mouth shut, apparently thinking better of it. He walked her back to the hotel, saying nothing but a gruff "good night" as he dropped her at her door. Two seconds later, the door to his adjoining room slammed with enough force to rattle the mirror over her dresser.

Reggie tried to work on her book, but she was too irritated and distracted by Gabe's overreaction to concentrate. Flopping back down on the bed, she called Natalie.

When her sister answered, Reggie quickly filled her in on the details of the past few days, including Katrina's shameless flirting and Gabe's behavior tonight.

"I don't know how I can stand him for another month, Natalie," she sighed. "One minute I think we've settled into some workable relationship, and the next it's like we're walking on eggshells. He's getting to be more of a distraction than the stalker."

"Poor Gabe," Natalie laughed. "He wants you so bad he can taste it, but he's trying so hard to maintain a professional distance." She said the last so derisively Reggie could practically hear her eyes rolling.

I wish. "I don't think that's the problem," Reggie sighed, aimlessly flipping through the channels. "Besides, he wasn't exactly fighting Katrina off, if you know what I mean." The image of them sharing margaritas was still seared in her memory.

"That redheaded cowgirl slut?" Natalie scoffed. "Trust me, Reggie. I could tell by the way he looked at you. He remembers exactly how good it was in Hawaii, and he wants it again. Bad. I'm surprised he hasn't succumbed to temptation already."

A sudden image popped into Reggie's head, of her, coming her brains out on the flimsy kitchenette table in New Orleans as Gabe heaved and growled above her. Followed by an equally vivid image of how he'd coolly apologized, as though he'd accidentally dented her car or something.

Natalie was still talking. Like Reggie, once she got on a roll, she didn't let up until she was sure she'd made her point. "As far as the guy goes tonight, Gabe was jealous. It's so obvious."

"I don't think so, Natalie." No matter how bad she wanted it to be true. "You saw the way he treated that woman in San Francisco. Tonight was the same."

"That night you disappeared. Were you ever out of his sight tonight?"

"No."

"You were in view, totally within his protection at all times. There was no need to pull you away from the guy, except that Gabe couldn't stand the sight of you flirting with someone else."

"Did I not mention that Katrina was practically giving him a lap dance at this point?"

Natalie made a scoffing sound on the other end. "And yet he still kept a close enough eye and ear on you to come running over when he thought you were getting too cozy. Trust me, Reggie. I only had to be in the room with you two for five minutes to see he's still into you, big time. All he needs is the proper encouragement to break his stupid rules."

Maybe Natalie was right, Reggie thought as she hung up. Gabe had, after all, practically attacked her the other night. It wasn't as though she'd been the instigator. Obviously there was some attraction there.

But then the coldness afterward . . . maybe he was one of those guys who could casually fuck a woman and turn off the passion as soon as he was through. And maybe the other night had been about stress relief, with no more meaning for him than if he'd gone out for a jog. It wasn't like their "relationship" in Hawaii had engendered any big commitments.

Then again . . .

Sometimes, like this morning, she did catch him looking at her.

Digging through her suitcase, Reggie pulled out her favorite Ella Moss top and cutest, most flattering pair of Lucky Brand jeans.

Maybe she'd get lucky tonight.

She did a quick makeup check, twisted her hair up into a clip, and grabbed her key. Shifting nervously from one booted foot to the other, she rapped lightly on Gabe's door. Maybe if she was really lucky, he'd answer it shirtless.

"What?"

Reggie stepped back at the gruff, abrupt greeting.

Unfortunately, he still wore a blue cotton button-down, but a couple of buttons were undone. That vee of exposed tan skin was nearly her undoing.

Remembering what she was there about, Reggie smiled up

at him. "I didn't eat much today and I'm starving, so I wanted to know if maybe you wanted to go downstairs and grab a bite to eat with me." At his uncomfortable frown, she quickly added, "No big deal, just keep me company since I'm going crazy cooped up in my room." *And I'm wondering if, in fact, you want to jump my bones.*

Gabe shifted from foot to foot, not responding. God, he looked sexy. His short, dark hair was ruffled, as though he'd run his fingers through it. His surprisingly sensuous mouth was slightly pink and a little swollen. He almost looked like he was wearing . . . lip gloss?

"Uh, Reggie," he stammered, "I don't, uh, this isn't . . ."

Her stomach cramped and started an abrupt slide to somewhere around her ankles even before the slender, feminine hand appeared to slide up the firm muscle of Gabe's chest.

An involuntary gasp escaped her lips as Katrina Garrett's curly red head appeared over Gabe's shoulder. "I'm sorry, Reggie, but Gabe is ordering in tonight."

A smug smile glossed in rosy pink decorated Katrina's beautiful face.

It occurred to Reggie that she could pull rank. As Gabe's temporary employer, she would be within her rights to demand that he boot Katrina out and accompany her wherever she damned well pleased. But she feared if she had to look at him across a plate of food, she'd either throw up or burst into tears. Or both.

She swallowed heavily and self-consciously tucked her hair behind her ear. She stretched her lips into a semblance of a smile. "Whoops, didn't realize you had company, Gabe. I guess I'll just do room service as well." She prayed they didn't notice how her voice cracked at the end.

Gabe reached out, guilt and irritation warring on his face. "Reggie . . ."

She stepped back, nearly falling on her ass in her impractical stiletto boots. Holding up her hand, she said, "Really,

Gabe, no big deal. You've been stuck with me all this time. You deserve a night of"—she gulped down the bile burning the back of her throat—"recreation."

Hurrying back to her room before she humiliated herself further, she closed her door and slumped against it. God, what an idiot. Jealous? Hah! She should have known better than to listen to Natalie. Like her track record was indicative of any deep knowledge about men!

She started to take off her boots, preparing to change into sweats, then thought better of it. She couldn't bear to spend another moment in this room, staring at the TV and torturing herself thinking about what Gabe was doing to Katrina on the other side of the wall. Picking up the phone, she quickly dialed Carrie, who agreed to swing by her room and join her in the bar downstairs for a couple of drinks. At least downstairs she'd have no chance of overhearing something that might make her sick, and maybe a couple of cocktails would take the edge off the sharp ache that pinched the center of her chest.

Chapter Nine

"I'm not kidding, Katrina, you have to leave." Gabe rounded on her as he shut the door, his annoyance at Katrina for having followed him now compounded by the unwanted guilt he felt at hurting Reggie.

The pushy bitch lounged on the bed and pouted in a manner she no doubt thought very seductive. Gabe was reminded of a temperamental three-year-old. "Come on, Gabe, we were just starting to have fun."

"Fun? I don't know about other guys you date, Katrina, but I don't consider being followed to my hotel room and orally raped much 'fun.'"

Katrina sat up then, insulted. "Orally raped? What the hell's wrong with you, anyway? Most men would be flattered."

Gabe shook his head. Katrina had showed up fifteen minutes ago, having tailed him and Reggie back to the hotel and followed him stealthily up to his room. He cursed his distracted stupidity. If he hadn't been so distracted by the idea of Reggie flirting with Joe Banker at the book signing, he would have known they were being followed. But as usual, Reggie fucked with his instincts and made his radar go haywire.

When he'd answered the door, Katrina hadn't waited for an invitation before shoving him inside and attacking him like a cat in heat. Before he could react, she had his shirt half off and her tongue halfway down his throat.

For some asinine reason, he'd thought to spare her pride rather than throwing her out bodily on her skinny jean-clad ass.

Unfortunately, she seemed convinced that if she just stayed where she was, Gabe would give in and fuck her.

But now that she'd seen fit to rub Reggie's nose in their supposed liaison, the gloves were off. "I don't get it," he said, shaking his head, struggling to keep his temper under control, "if a guy did this to you, you'd be calling security and pressing charges. But because you're a woman, I'm supposed to be flattered? You're in my room and I don't want you here, Katrina." And now he'd inadvertently hurt Reggie's feelings *again*. He tried to convince himself it didn't matter, but he couldn't banish the image of Reggie's hurt brown eyes and soft, trembling mouth. Helpless rage surged in his chest at the thought of how she must be feeling right now, thinking that he'd invited Katrina up to his room.

Some of his temper must have shown in his face, because Katrina's expression took on a vaguely alarmed cast. Sidling warily off the bed, she kept an eye on him as she gathered up her purse and finally—thankfully!—headed for the door.

She reached for the doorknob, tossing a glare over her shoulder. "Your loss."

The door clicked shut and he threw the deadbolt for good measure, rolling his eyes at her cockiness. Another time, another place, he might have banged Katrina out of sheer boredom.

But not now. The fact was, his dick got hard for just one hot little chef these days, and unfortunately, he'd vowed to keep his hands—and any other interested body parts—off of her.

Maybe he should call Reggie, take her up on that offer to go grab a drink and a bite, explain what really happened with Katrina. Sure, he'd vowed to keep his distance, especially after what happened in New Orleans, but wasn't it in both their best interests to maintain a positive professional relationship?

After all, he couldn't let her believe he picked up women on the road and took them back to the hotel room she was paying for. She might badmouth him to other potential clients. Letting her continue to think badly of him would be way more unprofessional than joining her for a drink.

He dialed her room, frowning as her phone went into the hotel messaging system. Maybe she was in the shower. He waited ten minutes, impatiently performing twenty complete circuits of the hotel cable's eighty available channels before calling her again.

Still no answer. He tried her cell, which dumped him into voicemail. Either she was avoiding his calls, or she couldn't get to the phone to answer it.

Grabbing the key cards off the dresser, he stepped out into the hall and knocked on her door. When she still didn't answer, he knocked harder, calling her name, a knot tightening in his belly. He looked down at the other key card in his hand. Her room key. If she was inside and avoiding him, she'd be hugely pissed at the invasion of her privacy.

Cold sweat trickled down his spine as it occurred to him how easy it had been for Katrina to follow him, how easy it had been for her to come straight to his room with no interference from hotel security.

How easy it had been for the stalker to break into their room in New Orleans.

He'd risk her wrath.

After another sharp rap he slid the card into the lock and slowly opened her door. "Reggie?"

Poking his head through the door, he suddenly wished he'd brought his Glock 9mm. But with the heavier security measures on airlines these days, it was too much of a pain in the ass unless a client was under appreciable physical threat. So his trusty Glock was locked in its case back in his apartment in L.A.

He crept into the room, swiftly taking in every possible hiding place. Nothing. He stopped, listening for a betraying breath, Reggie's voice, muffled behind a hand or a gag. Silence. He checked the bathroom, dark with its door slightly ajar.

Reggie's room was completely empty.

"Fuck!" His curse echoed off the walls as he loosened his choke hold on the temper he fought so hard to keep under control. He nearly punched a hole in the wall before he got himself calmed down.

His father's decades' old advice rang in his head: "Son, when you get hot, you get stupid. You've got to keep your anger under control and let your brain get to work."

Gabe took several deep, calming breaths, just as his father had taught him. As his molten temper cooled, so did his panic. His roiling emotions settled to a more reasonable level, and finally ceded control to his logic.

He had a pretty good idea where Reggie was.

Two minutes later, he stepped off the elevator into the lobby.

Bingo.

There she was, cute as hell, seated at the bar chatting with Carrie and a well-dressed couple in their forties. Laughing and talking, hands waving as she emphasized some point. She giggled as she sloshed a little of her martini on her sleeve. By the flush on her cheeks, he guessed it wasn't her first.

His temper, just barely under control, threatened to flare to life again. He stifled it. At least she'd had the good sense not to leave her room alone, but Carrie wasn't exactly what he'd call a protective presence. And he had to acknowledge his part. It was his carelessness, after all, that had allowed Katrina to get the jump on him. And he shouldn't have let her leave when she saw Katrina in his room, should have explained at once instead of getting stunned speechless by the laser beam of guilt that shot out from her big, hurt-filled brown eyes.

She was so engrossed in her conversation she didn't even notice when he braced his hip on the stool next to her. He waited politely for her to finish her story, something about how when she was little her mother would only let her eat the middle of the pumpkin pie at Thanksgiving, claiming the crust was too fattening. "To this day," Reggie said with a chuckle, "the crust is my favorite part of the pie."

"I'll have to e-mail you the recipe for my grandma's pie crust," the woman said. "Lard and all, it's the flakiest, most tender crust you'll ever taste."

Gabe waved off the bartender's inquisitive look and gently tapped Reggie on the shoulder. Her head snapped around and she visibly braced herself for his usual tirade.

Keeping his tone quiet and polite, he asked, "Reggie, can I speak to you for a moment?"

Her eyes narrowed almost imperceptibly and she took a slow, deliberate bite of her olive. "If you hadn't noticed, I'm having a nice conversation here. Besides, aren't you otherwise . . . occupied?" She scanned the room over his shoulder, obviously looking for Katrina.

He set his jaw and reminded himself to stay calm, stay focused, so he could have a reasonable conversation with Reggie and give her the apology she deserved. "That's what I want to talk about. Do you want to have this conversation here, or can we go somewhere quieter?"

She stared at him for several seconds as Carrie and her new best friends looked on curiously. Finally, she slid off the stool and grabbed her purse. "Will you excuse me? My *friend* and I need to have a quick chat."

Gabe took her arm carefully and steered her to the bank of elevators across the lobby. The second the doors shut she whirled on him. "You are unbelievable, you know that?" Dark eyes sparkling with anger and hurt, she poked him in the chest for emphasis. "You yell at me for a little harmless flirting, and then you have the nerve to invite that, that *skank* up to your room! You feed me this line about not getting personally involved with your clients, but I guess that doesn't rule out banging a random woman on the road as long as I'm safely tucked in my room."

"Reggie, first of all, I would never, as you put it, bang some random woman on the road when my first priority is your safety. I didn't invite Katrina up to my room, she followed me." He moved closer as he mounted his defense, until mere inches separated them. Reggie's chin lifted, mutinous. Clearly, she didn't believe a word.

Irritation danced on the edge of anger. One thing he wasn't was a liar, and it infuriated him to no end that this woman in particular would think so. "At the risk of repeating myself, I take my job very seriously. And just as I don't get involved with my clients, I don't allow myself to get distracted by any other offers, regardless of how tempting."

Reggie pointed her finger triumphantly. "Aha! So you at least admit you were tempted."

"Not by Katrina—"

"You know what I think?" Her cheeks flushed with anger, eyes glaring daggers. "I think"—she poked him in the chest, hard—"that this whole hands off clients is a load of crap. I think it's a convenient excuse because you don't have the balls"—another sharp poke—"to tell me to my face that you're not interested."

That last poke did it. He'd spent the past several weeks in a state of semi to full arousal, trying to get the taste of her out of his mouth, her spicy, cinnamon bun scent out of his nostrils, and now she had the gall to accuse him of having no balls!

The last shred of sanity fled, overwhelmed by the scent of her, the heat emanating off her angry skin, the frustrated lust that had only multiplied after their wild coupling in New Orleans.

Grasping her ass in his hands, he jerked her hard against him. "I've got balls, all right, and right now they're so blue they look like two smurfs on a sausage." He met her shocked gaze and rubbed his painfully hard erection against the giving softness of her belly. "Feel that? Still think I'm not interested?" His breath came in hot pants as he bent down to capture her mouth in a rough, tongue-thrusting kiss. "Did it feel like I wasn't interested in New Orleans, Reggie?" he growled against her cheek, biting into the plump flesh. "When I had my tongue buried in your pussy, when I fucked you deep and hard?"

Reggie moaned, rubbing against him as she fisted her hands in his hair and jerked his mouth to hers.

He sighed into her parted lips, making helpless sounds of need as his tongue sank into the sleek recesses of her mouth. He shoved her against the wall of the elevator car and feasted on her mouth as his fingers pressed into the voluptuous curves of her hips. Christ, this was insane, but he couldn't fight it anymore. He was too turned on, too attracted to everything about her, to continue pushing her away.

A soft ding echoed in the elevator and a discreet "ahem" momentarily jolted Gabe out of his lust-filled haze. Lifting his head, he saw a middle-aged man standing in the open doorway of the elevator. With a sheepish grin, Gabe pushed away from Reggie, pulling her against him to hide the tented front of his trousers. It took an eternity to get to the eighteenth floor, but finally he had his door unlocked and Reggie in his room and in his arms.

Bracing her against the wall, he bent his knees so his aching cock lined up with the notch in her thighs, feeling the heat of her response as it radiated through the fabric of their clothing. As ravenous as he was for her, he wanted to take this slow, to savor every square inch of her creamy skin, linger over all the spots guaranteed to get her off like a rocket, and discover some new ones.

He wrapped one hand around her throat, stroking the tendons and the tender skin of her earlobe. He slid the other under the silky fabric of her blouse, flattening it against the hot skin of her belly, inching up until his fingers just brushed the underside of her breasts.

God, he couldn't get enough of her mouth. Spicy and tasting faintly of vodka, her tongue rubbed against his. Her lips were full and succulent, like some exotic, delicious fruit he could feast on forever and never be sated.

She sucked on his tongue and he feared his cock would bust through his zipper. Her palm slid down the front of his pants and she grasped him, groaning in satisfaction as she measured the length and breadth of him.

Then, inexplicably, she was shoving against his shoulders. "No, stop," she panted, tearing her mouth from his.

Gabe bent to stifle her protests with a kiss, but she turned her head away. He licked and nipped her earlobe instead.

"I can't do this," Reggie panted, ducking out from under his arm and putting a good five feet between them. Her lips were swollen and bruised from his mouth, the delicate skin around her mouth abraded from his beard. That, combined with the still dreamy look in her eye, gave her the look of a woman eagerly awaiting a good, long fuck.

So why was she stopping?

"You may be able to turn off your emotions like a faucet, but I can't." She closed her eyes and swallowed hard. "I'm not that tough, Gabe. When you sleep with me and then treat me like I'm barely an acquaintance, it hurts too much."

Something cracked in his chest. He didn't know what the hell was going on inside him, didn't know what to tell her. But he knew he had to have her. He wanted her more than any woman he'd ever known, he liked everything about her, and the knowledge that he'd hurt her twisted in his gut. As logic tried to remind him of his last, disastrous relationship with a client, his gut told him to grab on to this woman and never let her go. Later, he might curse his foolishness, but right now he'd face any consequences just to get inside her again.

* * *

This had to be a dream. Gabe, the man who tried his damnedest to be a robot, was surely not tugging her blouse slowly but surely up her torso as he grinned his wickedly sexy grin. She grabbed his hands, stopping their progress north.

"Trust me, Reggie," he whispered, so close she could feel the hot puff of his breath caressing her face.

She wanted to, God knew she wanted to. He kissed her then, gently, coaxing her mouth open, as though now that he knew her concerns, he was willing to take as long as he needed to convince her.

Not that it would take much effort. She sighed into his mouth, tracing his soft inner lips with the tip of her tongue, luxuriating in the delicious rasp of his beard against her fingertips. Her sex wept and throbbed inside her jeans. All he'd done was kiss her and already she was dripping.

He drew back, cupping her face in his big calloused hands. "You're so beautiful," he whispered, and kissed her so gently tears stung her closed eyelids.

She couldn't put her finger on it, but something about this time was different. This wasn't the guy from Hawaii who wanted a simple night of great sex with no strings, nor was he the out-of-control sex maniac from last week. It was different, *he* was different.

Everything in his touch, his kiss, told her he knew exactly where he was, exactly who he was with, and exactly what he was doing. And that he had no desire to be anywhere else.

Tracing the sharp contours of his cheekbones, she opened to the luscious penetration of his tongue. "Are you sure?" she whispered between kisses. "I don't want to wake up tomorrow and have you acting all cold and distant again like you don't know me and there's nothing between us."

"Reggie," he whispered, "shut up." He pressed his forefinger against her lips.

She couldn't resist. Closing her eyes, she sucked the digit

inside her mouth, flicking the tip with her tongue. When he groaned she released it with a smile. Any lingering misgivings retreated in the face of white-hot need.

Electricity trickled down her spine as he unfastened the clip holding her hair up and threaded his fingers in the heavy strands. His hands slid to her waist, then back up, snagging her blouse along the way. This time she let him pull it up over her head.

Her own hands flicked open the buttons of his shirt and pushed it off his gorgeous broad shoulders. Really, the man should be an underwear model if he ever got tired of being a bodyguard. His torso was tanned golden bronze, highlighting his bulging pecs and the rippling muscles of his abs. Dark hair dusted his chest, converging in a silky trail that disappeared seductively below his waistband. Several scars nicked his torso, souvenirs of the dangerous life he'd led.

He tugged impatiently as the cuffs snagged on his wrists, then pulled her hard against him and made short work of her bra. "Mmm, I love the feel of you naked against me," he whispered, rubbing his chest luxuriously against her breasts. His hands traced down her back, and he pressed his wet, open mouth to her bare shoulder. "Your skin is so unbelievably soft."

The contrast of hot, smooth skin and the crisp abrasion of his chest hair sent sparks of sensation straight from her nipples to her groin. She was swollen and wet, chafing against the heavy fabric of her jeans.

Gabe scooped her up in his arms and walked the few steps to the bed, laying her back with a soft kiss to her belly. "I can't wait to get inside you."

She smiled.

He must have noticed, because he paused. "What?"

"Did you know that when you get turned on, your accent gets more pronounced?"

The heat in his dark gaze sent shivers pulsing through her.

He settled his knees on either side of her hips and toyed with the snap of her jeans. "Is that so?"

She wriggled beneath him and ran her hands along the smooth sides of his torso. "Yeah. When you get angry too." She licked her lips with a sly, catlike smile. "Problem is, it always makes me think of sex. With you. So now I get turned on whenever you get mad too."

He unfastened her jeans and slid his palm in the front of her panties. Arching her back, she moaned as his middle finger slid between her plump lips, flicking the sensitive bud of her clit. "That sounds kinda kinky," he said, exaggerating his drawl. "And here I took you for a nice girl."

"Oh, I'll be really nice if you keep doing that."

His smile faded as he palmed her sex, dipping his middle finger into her slippery wetness. He leaned down and took her mouth in a hungry, thrusting kiss, then abruptly levered off her. Grabbing each leg in turn, he pushed up her pant legs and stripped her of her boots and socks. He paused for a moment, contemplating one spike-heeled Jimmy Choo with a naughty half smile. "Someday, sweet thing, I want you to cook me dinner wearing just these."

Reggie stretched luxuriantly, feeling the heat of his gaze on every naked inch of skin. "That doesn't sound very sanitary."

He cocked his head as though considering that for a moment. "I'll let you wear a hairnet."

Reggie giggled as he stripped her of jeans and panties, then lifted her up the bed, until she rested against the oversize down-filled pillows. Then he turned and walked to the bathroom.

She levered herself up on her elbows. "Where do you think you're going?"

He glanced back over his shoulder. "Supply run."

She grinned and eased back against the pillows. Rummaging noises came from the bathroom and he emerged moments later, triumphantly brandishing a handful of foil wrappers.

Her eyebrow cocked as she shot him a speculative gaze. "Now if you were so dead set on keeping your distance from me, what are you doing carrying condoms around?"

He smiled sheepishly, his cheeks blazing with telltale color. "I suppose the road to hell is paved with good intentions. And as my grandpa always said, you gotta be prepared to take the heat." He placed the condoms on the bedside table.

Her eyebrows raised another notch when she counted a half dozen. "Feeling energetic?"

"Ohhh, you have no idea what you're in for, sweet thing."

He flipped open the tab of his slacks and Reggie licked her lips as every nerve stood up and sang in anticipation. The throbbing between her legs increased in pace as he stood over her, rippling muscles gleaming in the lamplight.

She couldn't keep from staring at his big, long-fingered hands at his fly, at the huge, cylindrical shape of his cock fighting the confines of wool gabardine.

Her tongue swept her bottom lip again.

To her frustration, instead of taking off his pants, he stood there, unmoving. She looked up and met his laughing, lust-filled gaze. "Reggie, darlin', you keep lookin' at me like that and I'm not liable to last long."

Sitting up, she pressed herself against him and pushed his hands out of the way. "I haven't exactly demonstrated amazing staying power with you." Unable to resist the temptation, she leaned forward and nipped the taut skin of his belly as she jerked his zipper down and shoved his pants and boxers down off his hips. Grasping his surging cock in her fist, Reggie traced her tongue along the rigid curves of his abdomen, eliciting a soft rumble from his chest.

With a teasing smile, she eased up on her knees and rubbed the engorged heart-shaped head against the silky skin of her breasts. A pearly drop of pre-come oozed out of the tip, and she drew his cock to trace around her nipple until the dark pink bud was shiny and wet.

"You are askin' for all kinds of trouble," he growled in his sexy Southern drawl. Her pussy fluttered and clenched as his hands covered her breasts, plumping and squeezing the soft flesh around the steely length of his cock.

He held himself still, quivering with the effort to hold back. She couldn't resist the temptation and bent her head to swirl her tongue around the silky tip. "Baby, I don't know if that is such a good idea." He swore softly as she traced her tongue along the vein that ran down its side, stroking and kneading him in her fist as her other hand fingered and teased his balls.

Her lips closed once again over the thick head of his cock, her tongue swirling against the sensitive ridge of flesh on the underside. She slid her mouth down, taking as much of him as she could into her mouth, then released him millimeter by millimeter, tongue following in a teasing path. His hands twined in her hair, strong fingers kneaded at her scalp as they guided her with firm but gentle pressure to take him deeper, until she could feel him pressing against the back of her throat.

She moaned around him as one of his hands stole down to pinch her nipple, sending a shock of heat through her abdomen. She'd never been so turned on performing oral sex, but his soft groans of pleasure and whispered encouragement made her feel almost as though she were sharing his pleasure along with him.

She looked up to find him watching her and released him for a second, shooting him a naughty smile as her lips closed over him once again. Watched him watch her as her lips lovingly devoured his pulsing cock.

"You have the sexiest mouth I've ever seen," he said through clenched teeth. Groaning, he reached for one of the condoms and pressed it into her hand. "Suit me up, darlin'."

With shaky hands, Reggie ripped open the condom wrapper and tried to remember the tips from her freshman dorm safe-sex workshop, the only other time she'd put a condom on anything. Back then it had been a banana, not nearly so distracting—or impressive—as Gabe's gorgeous erection. She couldn't help it. She had to give him one more kiss. His breath hissed out on a soft curse as her lips closed over him, her tongue savoring his heady, salty taste.

Then she slowly, carefully, rolled the condom down his oh-so-majestic length.

Breathing hard, Gabe flopped back against the pillows and pulled her on top of him. "You drive me absolutely fuckin' crazy," he rasped.

The thick hardness of his erection prodded the pliant flesh of her buttocks. Her knees fell wide over his hips, and she reached down to guide him into position. Bracing her hands against his chest, she savored the long, thick slide of him, toes curling as he sank as deep as he could go.

They moaned in unison as she began to move, leisurely strokes up and down that he met with a rocking counter-rhythm. He watched her through slitted eyes as his hands and fingers traced down her back, stroked and pinched her nipples, grazed her legs, teased the sensitive crack of her ass.

Reggie threw her head back, moaning as his fingers circled the plump bud of her clit. She ground against him, holding him deep inside her as her pussy pulsed and clenched around him. "Oh God, I'm coming already," she whimpered, swallowing him as deep as she could. He leaned up and captured her nipple in his mouth, sucking hard, flicking with his tongue until the sensation of his fingers and tongue on her and his cock throbbing inside her became unbearable.

Gabe struggled to hold himself in check as Reggie shuddered and spasmed around him. Her brow furrowed and her gorgeous lips parted as she sobbed in orgasm. Spent, she sank down against his chest. He kissed her flushed face, tasting the salty tang of sweat. Her heart pounded so hard he felt it vibrating throughout his entire body. He arched helplessly as the last shudders of her climax stroked him, nearly sending him over the edge.

He rolled so he was on top, bracing his weight on his elbows as his hands cupped her face. Her dreamy, satisfied look threatened to send him into overdrive. Holding himself motionless inside her, he bent and tasted her mouth, savoring her as she drew his tongue into her mouth.

Of their own accord, his hips began a slow thrusting, rocking inside her hard and deep. Her cinnamon and sex scent intoxicated him as he curled his fingers in her hair. She seemed to imprint him everywhere. Skin on skin, mouth on mouth. And deep inside, where she held him so sweet and wet and tight.

He swallowed her shuddery moans in his mouth and gave her his own as he strained against her, never wanting this to end.

For the first time since he'd discovered what an orgasm was, he didn't want to come. Didn't want this to end. Didn't want to lose this feeling of being deep inside Reggie, her arms and legs wrapped around him like she would never let go.

She cried out, high and soft around his tongue, and he felt the firm, helpless contractions as she came again. This time he couldn't stop himself as firm pressure built at the base of his spine. Head thrown back, teeth bared, his orgasm bore down on him with surprising, gut-wrenching intensity. He was momentarily blinded, his vision awash in color as his whole body trembled and throbbed with the force of it.

He collapsed against her, so spent he couldn't move for several seconds. Rolling to the side, he cradled her against his chest and placed a soft kiss against her tousled hair, smiling at her sleepy, contented sigh. He tilted her chin up to meet his kiss, fighting the surge of emotions suddenly roiling in his chest.

He cursed his loss of control even as he savored her soft warmth nestled against him. He fought the urge to close himself off, to run and hide from Reggie and the surging, overwhelming emotions that left him shaking and vulnerable. All his life he'd struggled to keep himself under control. As a kid, he'd been easily carried away and paid the price for it by getting teased for being a crybaby, and when he was older, getting in trouble for kicking someone's ass, regardless of how much a bully might deserve it.

His father, a career military man, had taught him the importance of controlling his emotions, channeling them into work and other appropriate outlets. Gabe's own years in the military, particularly as a member of the elite Delta Force squad, had required an immense level of self-discipline. Now, at the age of thirty-two, his head shouldn't be struggling to impose its will over his heart. Or any other sundry body parts.

But the incident with Marly Chase and the paparazzi had reminded him that he was still susceptible, that he had to remain vigilant. He thought he'd wrestled himself back under control.

Until he'd stepped into Reggie Caldwell's apartment three weeks ago. Though he'd fought it, his head lost the battle the second he laid eyes on her. Now he was raw and exposed, every irrational impulse surging for the surface.

She shifted in his hold, and he realized his arm was locked around her so tight she probably couldn't breathe. Loosening his grip, he looked down into her sleepy brown eyes, full of anxiety she couldn't quite hide.

Her tongue came out to lick her lips and he chased its path with the pad of his thumb. Her voice was husky when she spoke, "What are you thinking?"

A thousand replies rushed through his brain, none of them appropriate. Anything he could think of would either expose the chaos roiling in his head or would come out sounding glib and cheesy. And his feelings for her ran way too deep for him to feign nonchalance. The realization of just how much he cared made him swallow convulsively.

At his continued silence Reggie propped herself up onto his chest. "Never mind. That's a stupid question anyway. It's one of those chick questions girls ask when they can't think of anything to say, and they don't really want to hear the answer anyway."

She was on a roll, chattering nervously with no sign of stopping. "Because the truth is, at a time like this, guys are usually thinking something dumb, like whether they missed *SportsCenter*, or that they need to pee. Or something you don't want to know, like how your ass didn't look that big clothed, or how long she's going to want to cuddle before she'll shut up and go to sleep so he can sneak out without an uncomfortable good-bye."

He cut her off the only way guaranteed to shut her up, flipping her neatly under him and covering her mouth with his. He didn't let up until he was certain she was dazed and, for the moment, speechless. A condition that didn't last long.

Feeling his semihard cock surge against her belly, Reggie grinned and squirmed lasciviously against him. "Bet I know what you're thinking *now.*"

Laughing, he bent and nipped the top of her breast. "Darlin', the spirit is willing, but the flesh isn't eighteen anymore. You need to give me at least another five minutes."

Another kiss and he gently pulled away to go to the bathroom where he got rid of the condom and attempted to compose himself. He eased back into bed beside her, struck by how *right* this felt, climbing into bed with her and pulling her close. Holy shit, he was in big trouble.

"Are you upset?" She idly stroked his chest, next to where her cheek rested. "About breaking your own rules, I mean?"

He sighed, wishing they could both just let it go, enjoy the night without unpacking all of his baggage. "I'm a by-the-book guy because I had to learn to be. I used to react emotionally to every situation, but when I was in Special Forces, I had to learn to distance myself. If any one of us went off half-cocked and broke the rules, there'd be a cluster fuck." He shifted, shoving his arm up under his head.

She pushed up on her elbows, her forehead wrinkling. "But you have to let your emotions get involved sometime."

"Not when it comes to work. If I let emotions take over, I lose control of the situation. I might do something stupid, or worse, put you in danger." He paused, carefully weighing his next words. Truthfully, he had no desire to ruin the moment by dredging up memories of his past stupidity. On the other hand, Reggie deserved to know the truth of why he had fought so hard to keep her at arm's length. "The last time I let my emotions get involved, I almost ruined everything."

Reggie tensed. Now she'd finally gotten him talking, maybe she'd rather he shut up. But what could he confess that would be so awful?

"Remember when we met in Hawaii, you mentioned Marly Chase was staying at the resort?"

"Uh-huh," she nodded warily.

"I was there as her bodyguard."

She was afraid she knew where this was going. "And let me guess, you were sleeping with her too."

His "yep" was barely audible.

Her stomach sank as she vividly remembered Marly Chase, stretched out on a lounger at the Grand Wailea in Maui, her taut, lean physique tanned a gorgeous golden bronze. Then she remembered her own curvy figure encased in a one-piece as she huddled under an umbrella to shade her fair skin from the fierce Hawaiian sun. She'd actually gotten naked in front of a guy who'd dated some perfect, hot, centerfold-worthy actress. If only she had one of those memory erasers from *Men in Black* to permanently delete the image of her naked white ass from his mind.

As revelations went, sleeping with a woman who was widely considered to have one of the best bodies on television wasn't the worst thing he could have admitted, but it sucked pretty hard just the same. She rolled over onto the free pillow and pulled the covers up to her chin.

He snuggled against her, ignoring the hint.

"So before Marly this was a regular thing for you, banging

your clients, providing any extra services they might desire?"
She knew she sounded bitchy but couldn't stop herself, hating the idea that she might be yet another in a line of faceless
women that he forgot as soon as he issued the last invoice.

"No, dammit." That genuinely pissed him off, judging
from the sudden flare in his dark eyes. "I didn't sleep with my
clients before that. Granted, they were mostly men, or wives
of men I was protecting, but that's beside the point."

"So Marly was too tempting to resist?"

He hooked his arm around her waist and propped up on
his other elbow. "She's an attractive woman; she came on
strong, and I fell for it. Honestly, I think she was a little
bored and wanted to entertain herself by slumming with the
help."

She snorted. "Whatever. Like you don't know you're gorgeous."

That sidetracked him. "Gorgeous? Yeah?"

More gorgeous than any guy she'd seen in real life, but she
wasn't about to admit that now. "I suppose it's impossible to
say no when the world's most perfect ass is swinging in your
face," she said sourly.

"Hey now." She held herself stiff as he rolled on top of her,
pinned her in place, and forced her chin up to meet his gaze.
"She may have looked good on a magazine cover, but in person she was all bones and abnormally large boobs. And
when it came down to sex . . ."

Reggie wasn't sure she wanted to hear this.

He whispered conspiratorially, "It was like fucking a
cricket."

A reluctant smile stretched her face. "So what was the appeal, then?" she prodded.

He released an exasperated sigh. "I don't know. I guess I
was taken in by her needy little-girl act and I liked feeling like
a hero." His gaze softened and he kissed her with a sweetness
that had warmth blooming in her chest and tears stinging her
eyes. "I got a little starstruck, that's all."

She wondered how his feelings for her compared, but stopped herself from digging deeper. It wasn't fair to try to pin him down when her own emotions were in a royal tangle.

She had no right to be jealous of any of his women, past or future, when she wasn't sure herself exactly what she wanted from him. She liked Gabe a lot, no question about it, and the sex was beyond anything she'd ever imagined. But that didn't mean they were any closer to having something real than they'd been that one night in Hawaii. Once the stalker stopped, well, stalking, Gabe would go back to his life in Los Angeles. As for her, she was so busy she didn't have time to pursue a relationship with a guy who lived down the street, much less one who lived in another city.

She shoved the thought from her mind, unwilling to let reality invade and ruin what was left of her postorgasmic glow. "So what happened to make you so dead set against getting personally involved?"

Gabe struggled with how to explain the fact that he'd beat the crap out of someone without making himself sound like a ruthless thug preying on some wimpy photographer. As he'd learned in high school, no matter what you saw in the movies, girls generally weren't impressed by guys who got into fistfights with any regularity. His stomach twisted as he remembered Reggie's look of shocked horror when he'd subdued the junkie in the convenience store.

"You don't have to tell me if you don't want," she whispered.

The temptation to seize her offer of an out was so strong he could taste it. But he didn't succumb. He'd been an asshole to her for the past several weeks, running hot and cold as he struggled to push her away. She deserved to know the truth, even if it did change her opinion of him.

"After I got out of the forces, a good friend of mine, Malcolm, who was in my unit, hired me to work at his security firm. He runs a high-end group, has a lot of corporate clients, some overseas contracts, and a handful of celebrities. I thought I was hot shit, even though the job was basically grunt work, nothing strategic about it. But it was high profile, and he gave it to me because I clean up good and for the most part can blend in."

Reggie snorted.

"What?"

"Blend in? Are you kidding? You may as well have 'badass' tattooed across your forehead. No matter how much you clean up, you still look barely civilized." She nuzzled against his chest and continued, "The first time I saw you, I thought you looked dangerous, a little scary."

"When you met me, I was dangerous, given what had happened. A couple nights before, Marly and I were out in Lahaina having dinner. We'd been keeping it quiet, not letting on that there was anything going on beyond a professional relationship." Though she'd protested vehemently to the contrary, Gabe knew that Marly hadn't wanted to sully her good-girl image by letting it be known she was sleeping with the hired help. But he'd let it go, since he'd known it could be potentially bad publicity for his friend's company. He'd stupidly thought he'd had the whole situation under control, unaware that it was about to blow up spectacularly in his face. And even though he couldn't deny he was mostly at fault in the ensuing debacle, it bothered him still that Marly could so easily fool the world with her wholesome, girl-next-door image when, in reality, she was a calculating, self-centered media whore.

His fingers tangled idly in Reggie's thick dark hair. "Now that I look back on it, I think the idea of sneaking around was more appealing than anything."

"I'm sure that's not true."

"She'd had a few glasses of wine at dinner and got a little loopy, and as we were leaving the restaurant she started kissing me." Reggie tensed in his arms, and he stroked a soothing hand down her back. "She didn't kiss near as well as you, sweet thing." He reached down and squeezed the soft curve of her ass for extra reassurance. "Out of nowhere this guy jumps out and starts taking our picture, and pretty soon a crowd is gathering. Marly pushed me away, but the photographer started taunting her, saying really evil, disgusting stuff, trying to get a rise out of her for more photos."

He paused, then shook his head against the pillow. "I lost it. I completely lost my shit, like I haven't since high school. I didn't act like a bodyguard, I acted like a boyfriend defending his girlfriend's honor. I grabbed the guy and started punching him, and by the time I stopped his nose was broken and his camera was in twelve pieces."

"Sounds like he deserved it."

"Whether he did or not, he still threatened to sue Marly, who, in turn, threatened to sue my company. In the end, Marly twisted the whole thing in the press to make it sound like I'd gone off unprovoked, and Malcolm had to pay the guy a hefty chunk of change to convince him not to press charges."

"And you got hung out to dry," Reggie said quietly.

"I don't blame Malcolm for firing me. I would have done the same. It was unprofessional to sleep with a client to begin with, and I was bad for the company image and a liability. He still refers clients to me, but if they dig deep enough in the background check they always find out."

She rolled to the side, propping up on one elbow as she reached out to stroke his hair. "Lucky for you Natalie's not thorough enough to run a background check."

He frowned. "Normally, I'd lay into both of you for being so careless, but in this case I suppose it's worked to my advantage."

She raised her eyebrow in mock-offense. "You suppose?"

He grinned as she tugged on a tuft of hair in punishment. Rolling over until he was pressed more firmly against her, he sank his fingers into the plush curve of her hip. Her eyelids drooped and her low purr of satisfaction vibrated all the way down to his groin.

Her face was so close he could see every individual eyelash and the greenish gold flecks in her brown eyes. When he spoke, his lips brushed hers. "So you're not upset that you unwittingly hired someone with a reputation as a brutal thug?"

Her palm was warm against his cheek. "Like I said, it sounds like the guy deserved it, and maybe if he sees a brutal thug shadowing me, scrotum boy will think twice before he makes good on his threats to confront me in person."

"A lot of people would still be afraid to trust me."

Silently, she studied him for a moment. "Whatever you did, it was because your instincts told you it was the right thing. And despite how you see it, I don't think you ever completely lost control."

"No?"

"All you did was break his nose, right? Look at you"—she reached down and squeezed his biceps for emphasis—"you could have maimed him, killed him if you really let loose. All you did was fire a warning shot over his bow."

"I should never have hit him in the first place."

"But I doubt he would have gotten the message to shut up and leave you alone any other way."

Gabe had to concede that point.

Her tongue came out to moisten her lips, officially moving him from the recovery stage to rarin' to fuckin' go in a millisecond. "The most important thing is I know you would never hurt *me*, no matter how mad you got, and if this all ends with you giving my stalker a concussion, or worse, I see that as a bonus."

"Bloodthirsty little thing, aren't you?" He buried his face in the curve of her neck, nipping and licking at the soft skin until she squealed.

Something inside him untwisted a little. He would never let himself off the hook, never forgive himself for his loss of control and the clusterfuck that had ensued. But Reggie's soft words of trust got to him. Scary how quickly she'd pierced the armor he worked so hard to maintain. Scary how much her opinion of him mattered.

Warning bells pinged in the back of his head. After everything he'd been through, was he about to repeat past mistakes? His gut told him Reggie was nothing like Marly. Reggie would never use him and leave him hanging out to dry. Then again, his instincts had convinced him that Marly had actually cared about him, but in the end she'd placed all the blame on him and used the situation to generate publicity and make herself look like the victim.

All he knew for sure right now was that Reggie was warm and soft and perfect in his arms. In that, at least, his head and his heart were in firm agreement.

Chapter Ten

Reggie awoke several hours later to the sound of Gabe snoring. He lay on his back, one arm stretched up over his head. They'd fallen asleep with the lights on, and in the lamplight she studied his face. Hard jaw, bristling with stubble, framing his unaccountably sensuous mouth. His lips were slightly parted, a soft rumble vibrating up his throat with every breath.

She smiled, slightly resisting the urge to nuzzle him awake and have her way with him again. But only because she was aware of a second, more pressing need.

Sidling over to the side of the bed, she swung her feet to the floor. Just as she rose, Gabe's hand shot out and locked around her forearm.

"Where are you going?" For a guy emerging from what looked like a deep, peaceful sleep, his voice was remarkably clear.

"Um, bathroom?"

For a minute Gabe looked as though he was about to deny permission, but he released her wrist and said grudgingly, "Okay."

While in the bathroom, she took the liberty of borrowing his toothbrush and tried to avoid glimpsing herself in the mirror. Unlike Gabe, her middle of the night look was not drop-dead sexy, proved by the brief glimpse she'd caught in the harsh overhead bathroom light.

Once again she remembered Marly Chase, sleek, tawny, and perfect in her electric blue bikini. Gabe had intimate knowledge of that perfection. While his cricket comment was reassuring, Reggie still wished she'd forgone the many hand-fuls of nuts she'd consumed earlier at the bar.

She rinsed her mouth, carefully keeping her eyes averted from the mirror until the bathroom light was off.

Gabe watched her from the bed as she walked across the room, a smile playing around the corners of his lips. The heat of his gaze hit her like a physical caress, and she knew with-out looking that her belly was flushed, her nipples were deep pink and swollen as though he'd traced them with his tongue. A creamy throbbing pulsed between her legs, and just like that she wanted him again.

She slid into bed next to him—snapping off the light this time—and marveled at her seeming insatiability. Sure, she'd always liked sex, once she'd gotten past the awkward first few times and figured out what she liked and how to effec-tively communicate those preferences to her partner.

A hot shiver ran through her as Gabe slid his arm around her waist and pulled her firmly back against him. With him, her body didn't discriminate. It liked everything he did.

Case in point: the way he was rubbing his cock against her ass, lifting her top leg slightly so he could thrust gently against the already wet folds of her pussy. Normally she didn't like it from behind, but here she was, squirming against him and reaching between her legs to press his cock more firmly against her slick center.

"I thought you were gonna sneak out on me again," he rumbled, nipping and licking at her earlobe.

She shuddered and ground back against him. "Again?"

His thumb feathered across her beaded nipple. "Like you did in Hawaii." He pinched her, sending a jolt of sensation rocketing between her legs. "When I woke up to find you gone, I spent half the next day trying to find you."

That gave her pause. She stilled his hand on her breast and craned her neck around on the pillow. With the lights out and the drapes closed, she could barely make out his features. "You did?" When he didn't answer, she continued, "I assumed that was standard procedure after a one-night stand. Not that I'd ever had one, but it seemed the easiest way to avoid an awkward scene in the morning, and that way I couldn't terrify you with my bedhead."

His chest shook against her back, and it took her a few seconds to realize he was laughing at her. He kissed her, laughing even as he did, and cupped his hand intimately over her naked hip. "When I woke up to find you gone, I wished I'd had the chance to know you better."

The thought that he'd wanted more that night sent a curl of warmth through her chest, and now she wondered what might have happened if she'd been brave enough to stay the night, or leave him a note, anything but sneak off the way she had.

All regrets fled as his big hands took on a life of their own as they mapped the curves of her body, touching her everywhere. The inky darkness was like a deep well of lust, where she could only feel.

He slid his knee between her thighs, urging them to part as his hand flattened against her belly. A shuddery moan escaped her throat as she felt him there again, sliding against her, covering himself with her hot juices.

"Do you have any idea how hard it's been for me to keep my hands off you?"

Groaning, she reached down between her legs, teasing the thick head of his cock with her fingers. "I have a pretty good idea."

"I don't think so." He caught her hand in his, closing her fingers around his shaft. "All I have to do is look at you and

I get hard." He thrust himself against her to demonstrate. "I've already come twice tonight, but you barely touch me and I'm ready to go again."

Whimpering, she guided his cock until it rested against her clit, rasping the oversensitized bud every time he moved. "It's the same for me," she gasped, squirming against the insufficient caress. Her body clenched and throbbed, reacting instinctively to his primitive, possessive hold.

His fingers parted her pussy lips, two fingers coming to rest on either side of her throbbing clit. "Is it?" he whispered, his fingers closing against her in a delicate kneading motion that sent bolts of sensation through her core, yet wasn't nearly enough to drive her over the edge. "Right now, are you already thinking of the next time you'll fuck me? Thinking of all the places you want to touch and taste, but know you won't get to because you know you have to have me inside you right now?" He reached over her toward the bedside table and she moaned in anticipation at the sound of foil ripping.

"Please," she whispered as he removed his hand from between her thighs. "Please don't stop . . ." Her protest melted into a moan as he gripped her leg, drawing it up toward her chest as he buried himself to the hilt in one sleek stroke.

His ragged sigh wafted across her cheek. "Christ." Sounds of sex echoed in the darkness, flesh sliding against flesh, low murmurs and groans as he held himself deep inside her, grinding firmly against her ass, fingers pinching her nipples and dipping into the wetness where they were joined.

Her orgasm built slowly, coiling in her belly until it was a tight knot tingling at the base of her womb. Slow, shuddering contractions shook her, the waves of her climax pulsing up her spine, down her limbs until every inch of her skin tingled with it.

She came back to herself to find Gabe hard as granite inside her, shaking now as he drove into her in quick, shallow thrusts. She reached down, cupping his balls, drawn tight with his impending orgasm. He gave a choked cry as she pressed her finger firmly against the base of his sac, simultaneously squeezing him inside.

His cock jumped and pulsed, her name an oath against her neck as he came. He rained lazy kisses across her shoulder, his chest heaving as he slipped from her body.

He rolled over onto his back and cuddled her close, tipping her face up for a kiss. Lips smacking, he said, "Did you brush your teeth?"

Busted. "I used your toothbrush. I figured since our mouths have pretty much been everywhere else, it wasn't such a big deal. You don't mind, do you? I didn't want to scare you off with my morning breath."

Sighing, he cuddled her close in a way that made her feel unbelievably cherished. "Trust me, darlin'. Right now I can't think of a damn thing that could chase me away."

Reggie was still smiling at that when she fell asleep.

That smile was on Reggie's face when she woke up the next morning and it remained throughout the short flight to Santa Fe. Though she'd had almost no sleep, energy coursed through her, enabling her to get an astounding amount of work done on the plane. She was still way behind on her book (as Sharon reminded her in multiple daily calls), but at least she was getting some traction.

Reggie marveled at the stark beauty as Gabe drove the hour from the airport in Albuquerque to Santa Fe. "I never realized how beautiful it is here," she murmured as she took in stunning rock formations and, off in the distance, the pine-covered tops of the Sangre de Cristo Mountains.

"You should see it in the summertime," Gabe said, tilting his chin up to the blindingly blue sky. "Every afternoon you get these big purple thunderheads, and if you're really lucky, a lightning storm over the desert."

Reggie turned to him in surprise. "You've been here before? How come you never mentioned it?"

"It's not in my nature to offer up personal details to my clients," he grinned. "And since we've gotten more personal, we haven't spent a whole helluva lot of time talking."

Her whole body blushed as she vividly recalled how they'd been spending their time. She asked him again when he'd been to New Mexico.

"We lived here for a few years when I was about eight or so, before we moved to North Carolina."

Since for once he actually seemed inclined to talk about himself, Reggie drilled him with questions about his childhood, learning that he moved six times by the age of eleven and had lived in such exotic locales as Alaska and Hawaii. Then, at eighteen, he'd started his own career in the army and had been stationed all over the world.

"Wasn't it hard, moving around that much? Leaving your friends all the time?"

He shrugged, big broad shoulders rippling under the cotton of his shirt. "Sure. I think that's part of the reason so many military guys get married so young. If you have a family, you have a guaranteed connection with at least one other person. And when you're stationed overseas, you always have someone to come back to."

"Were you ever married?" She immediately clamped her lips shut, as though she could call back the question.

He gave a shocked laugh. "Hell no."

"You have something against it?" Now why did the thought of him as a commitment phobe make her feel like her intestines had morphed into a den of snakes? She'd had sex with him exactly three times (well, seven actual times, but on three separate occasions), and it wasn't as though she was picking out china patterns, regardless of what that little apron-wearing bitch in the back of her brain who was building a three-bedroom ranch house surrounded by a perfect picket fence had to say about it.

"No, I'm not against marriage," he said defensively. "I just wasn't ready for it myself. Besides, I saw how hard it was on my mom, raising four kids, getting them and herself settled only to have to move again. Then when I joined the Special Forces, it was even worse. We go overseas, and the guys who are married can't even tell their wives where they're going, or when they'll be back for sure. Or if they'll be back at all, given how dangerous most of the shit was."

Reggie shivered a little, thinking about the scars that decorated Gabe's body—the slash across his back, the palm-sized starburst on his right thigh. Weird to think that the man sitting across from her had been to the most dangerous parts of the world, that he had actually been shot. How many times had he flirted with death?

God, what he must think of her trivial fears about a perverted fan.

After they'd checked into their hotel, Reggie met briefly with Carrie to review the shoot for the next day. Afterward, she and Gabe went out and gorged themselves on what Reggie declared to be the world's best enchiladas.

The next morning, Gabe forced her out into the crisp fall air for a brisk run. Though she grumbled nearly the entire way, she figured she'd better work off those enchiladas.

And he made up for his drill sergeant demeanor by giving Reggie possibly the best shower she'd ever had in her entire thirty years.

By the time they got to the plaza to film the segment's introduction, Reggie was grinning like a fool. They walked to where the crew was setting up. Carrie looked up and cocked her head. A knowing smirk spread across her face.

Reggie's cheeks heated as she tried to ignore the sly glances of the rest of the crew. Just what she needed, the entire set speculating about her sex life.

"Reggie, we're ready whenever you are," Carrie snapped impatiently.

Flustered, she took her position in front of the row of vendors selling their wares in Santa Fe's central plaza. Gabe stood off to the side; his gaze was cool and businesslike as he continuously scanned the crowd, barely sparing her a glance.

Why did she find it so irritating, his ability to completely shut off and go into work mode, when she could barely keep herself focused on smiling for the camera?

"Reggie, hello!" Carrie snapped.

Reggie realized that she'd managed to completely miss her cue.

Mentally kicking herself, she tried to completely ignore the gorgeous man hovering in her peripheral vision and tried again. "Today we're in Santa Fe, home to some of the nation's hottest restaurants." Her gaze flicked inexorably in Gabe's direction, just in time to catch him smiling at her. "No wonder, since it's also home to some of the chookin' hot— dammit!" She smacked her head and looked down at the cobblestones that lined the plaza. "Can we try that again?"

She flubbed the next take, and the next. Carrie shot her an irritated look as she moved Gabe out of her line of vision, shooting Reggie a very pointed look.

For the next two hours Reggie did her best to ignore Gabe as they changed locations to a restaurant for the afternoon shoot. Once she met the chef and they did a quick run-through of the recipe, she settled herself into a corner and pulled out her laptop.

She felt a prickle of irritation as Gabe seated himself two tables away. She scolded herself. Having him act like her boyfriend on set wouldn't go very far in solidifying her reputation as a professional. And it was best if he kept his distance so she could get some work done. Gabe was proving to be too much of a distraction already, and she needed to figure out how to remain productive while suffering from hormone overload.

Finally, they were ready to shoot. As the guest chef cooked, Reggie chattered nonstop about all the different spices used in the chef's Navajo Indian–influenced recipes.

As she and the chef prepared green chile stew, he offered

her tastes of the house's special chile sauces. She took the proffered spoon, closing her eyes in ecstasy as a potent combination of chiles and spices exploded across her tongue. When she opened them, her gaze locked with Gabe's as he stood frozen behind the camera, watching her lick her lips with a look so full of lust her mind momentarily went blank.

Mindlessly, she reached for another spoonful of sauce to buy some time.

"Now, be careful. That last one's a bit hot," the chef cautioned.

Once again there was an explosion of flavor in her mouth, but not the kind she expected.

Her eyebrows shot up to her hairline. "That's got a kick to it," she squeaked, desperately clinging to her composure, but the habanero chile sauce was more than even her seasoned palate could handle.

Her mouth felt like it had been doused with napalm. Sweat beaded on her brow and under her eyes as she flushed beet red and tears streamed down her face.

The set erupted in chaos as the director yelled "Cut," and the chef apologized profusely and fumbled for water.

Without hesitation, Gabe shoved a path through to Reggie. With one hand he grabbed a fistful of flour tortillas as he wrapped his arm around her. "It's okay, honey, just eat this. It'll soak up all the oil." Jerking his head up, he barked, "Will somebody get us some fucking milk?"

A tall glass of milk appeared, which Reggie finished in three gulps. Sighing in relief, she melted against his chest as he pressed a kiss to the top of her head. "Better now?"

They both realized their audience at the same moment. The crew stared at them, obviously shocked to see this supposedly big, tough, unreachable bodyguard treating his client in a manner that could only be described as tender.

Reggie turned to the crew as though nothing was out of the ordinary. "Shall we try that again, this time without the habaneros?"

* * *

Somehow Reggie managed to get through the rest of the shoot without a hitch, and did a damn good job, if she did say so herself.

As they were wrapping, Gabe pulled her aside. "About earlier. I didn't even think how it would look. I, uh, just kind of reacted." Which he looked damned displeased about if the grim set of his face was anything to go by.

"It's no big deal, really."

He glanced around. "Are you sure? One of the sound guys keeps smirking and giving me a thumbs-up. And right now Carrie's glaring like she wishes she was Cyclops and could burn a giant hole through your back."

Exactly what she'd been trying to avoid, but there was nothing to be done for it now. "They were bound to figure it out sooner or later. In fact, the way set gossip works, they probably thought we were sleeping together all along."

Yet another reason she should strive to follow Gabe's example of professionalism.

But now the cat was out of the bag, or the horse was out of the barn, or some other animal analogy. "No use getting upset about it now. As long as I don't interfere with shooting, let them gossip all they want. Although we probably will want to refrain from French kissing or groping in full view."

His full lips quirked in that half smile that made her belly dip. "I'll do my best, but you prove damn tempting sometimes."

"Just sometimes?"

"Reggie," Carrie snapped. Gabe was right. She was pissed.

Reggie was relieved to learn her behavior was not the main source of her producer's irritation. Rather, it was a last-minute scheduling conflict with their guest in Seattle, meaning their shoot would have to be delayed several days, or they would have to scramble for another guest.

"But we were scheduled to have a short break between

Seattle and L.A.," Reggie pointed out, "so it won't have a domino effect on the rest of the shoot."

"No," Carrie snapped, "but it means I have to rebook the local crew and reschedule all of the establishing shots. And we have to rebook all of the travel arrangements, and that will cost money . . ." She dug her fingers into her wild mane of red hair.

Not knowing what else to say, Reggie tried to console her. "I'm sure everything will be fine."

"It will, but listen, Reggie, we can't have any more delays or screwups."

Reggie frowned. What did she mean by that? Sure, she'd had a couple of off days and had flubbed a few lines here and there, but it wasn't as though she delayed shooting with her diva-like antics.

"All I'm saying is," Carrie leaned closer and lowered her voice, "don't let your little romance with Thor the wonder-schlong over there become a problem."

"It's not—it won't," Reggie protested.

Carrie gave her a "bullshit" look. "This morning you could barely keep your tongue in your mouth, you were so busy drooling. You proceeded to fuck up your lines and eat a mouthful of hot chili that Luis specifically warned you away from."

"He did? All he said was it had a kick."

"Before we filmed that part, he said you shouldn't eat it. But instead of messing up the shot when you reached for it, he decided to go with it. Result? You end up on the gag reel, and now we're an hour overschedule and paying the crew extra for it."

Carrie stared hard at her for a moment, and then her demeanor softened. "I'm not trying to be a bitch here. But you know how competitive this business is. If you get any reputation whatsoever about being unprofessional or difficult to work with, it can kill any chances you have at getting more shows. You are hugely popular with viewers, but you're not at the point yet where you can do whatever you want and get away with it."

If anyone had told her when the Cuisine Network first picked up *Simply Delicious* that the world of food television was so cutthroat and competitive, she would have laughed her butt off. But a scant year later, boy did she know better.

Carrie echoed her thoughts. "There's always another Reggie Caldwell waiting in the wings, someone cuter, younger, funnier. Not to mention cheaper."

Reggie nodded resignedly. Carrie didn't tell her anything she didn't already know. But to have her lay it all out made Reggie feel like she had climbed a very tall mountain, only to have the clouds lift and find that what she thought was the summit was, in fact, just a plateau, with the summit still thousands of feet away.

Mentally, she kicked herself for being so resentful. Wasn't this exactly what she always wanted? A successful career doing what she loved? And no one ever said maintaining and growing that level of success would ever be easy. For the time being, it required almost all of her energy and concentration, and it meant giving up almost all personal time.

Involuntarily, her gaze drifted over to Gabe, who was talking on the phone over by the steam table. At what point could she ease off enough to regain some semblance of a life?

"Thanks for being up front with me," she told Carrie.

"You're doing a good job, Reggie, and you're great to work with. But you need to do what you can to make sure that doesn't change." Carrie punched a number into her cell phone and stalked off to rearrange the Seattle shooting schedule.

"Everything okay?" She could feel the warmth of Gabe's body as he came up behind her. Suddenly exhausted, she fought the urge to lean back against him. No more PDA today.

She nodded and told him about the schedule change.

"What do we do for the next five days?" he asked.

"Go back to San Francisco, I guess." But even though she should meet with Max and have more than a five-minute conversation with Tyler, the last thing she wanted to do was go home.

Ignoring the voice that warned she should use the next few days to catch up on her writing, she acted on impulse. She'd fallen in love with Santa Fe, and from the time she'd arrived had been trying to figure out when she could get back for a longer visit. Why not stay? And five days with Gabe with no location shoots . . . Her head spun at the possibilities.

"Or we could stay here," she said, absolutely failing in her attempt to sound like she didn't care one way or another. "I'd love to explore a little more, and we could spend some time together without having to worry about getting on a plane or driving to the next location. What do you think?"

Her gut clenched at his continued silence. This was too fast, trying to rope him into a romantic getaway when they'd been dating, if you could even call it that, for all of forty-eight hours.

"Are you sure?" he asked finally.

Typical Reggie, she cursed herself, jumping in with both feet without thinking it through. Despite all of his romantic skill in the bedroom, he hadn't said anything about wanting an actual relationship. She swallowed hard, terrified she was about to humiliate herself by crying in front of him.

"Because I think," he murmured, "that if I'm left in a hotel with you for five days with nowhere to be, you're not gonna get a whole lot of exploring done."

Chapter Eleven

"I'm sorry I'm late!" Natalie trotted the last few feet to Reggie's door, no easy task in Reggie's four-inch Manolo Blahnik pumps. Max waited at the entrance of Reggie's building looking stylish as usual in a crimson button-front shirt with just enough spandex for it to be tastefully fitted. Paired with black jeans and Kenneth Cole uppers, he looked ready to hit the bars on Castro later that night.

To her relief, he didn't look annoyed that she was ten minutes late for their meeting. She quickly dialed in the key code that opened the front door. "I got caught in a meeting with Tyler. There's a problem with the Seattle shooting schedule, and he needs to figure out some logistics for a couple of appearances." She paused as it occurred to her that she wasn't supposed to tell anyone but Tyler the details of Reggie's schedule. But surely Max didn't count. Her boots echoed on the stairs as they hurried up to Reggie's floor.

"What's she doing?" Max asked.

"Tyler is trying to book her on a morning news show and the usual book signing and cooking demo will need to be rescheduled." She unlocked Reggie's apartment door and motioned Max inside as she quickly entered the alarm pass code. Even though she had the code memorized, she still broke into a bit of a sweat ever since the day two weeks ago when she'd inadvertently set off the alarm. She'd been struggling with a pile of dry cleaning and a box of books that had arrived for Reggie and must have weighed 500 pounds. She'd dashed the dry cleaning into the bedroom, figuring she could make it there and back with enough time to disarm.

Wrong.

It had been gratifying, though, to see how quickly the police had shown up. Not so gratifying was the phone call she got from Gabe after the security company alerted him to the false alarm.

Alarm safely disarmed, she motioned for Max to have a seat in the living room. But instead of sitting down, he wandered over to the huge window that offered a spectacular view of the Golden Gate Bridge. "This place is spectacular. And Reggie's decorated it so nicely," he said, nodding at the putty-colored sofa and love seat that Reggie had accessorized with cushions in rich tones of crimson and deep blue.

She wrinkled her nose. To Natalie's eye, Reggie's apartment reeked of Pottery Barn generic, but whatever. She fumbled in a bag for the neatly typed five-page proposal she'd produced for her new show concept, *The Skinny Squad with Natalie Caldwell*. "I did what you asked after our last meeting and wrote out a more detailed proposal along with a list of episode ideas."

Tension coiled in her shoulders as Max wandered aimlessly around the living room, inspecting the books, DVDs, and framed photos that adorned the bookcase that took up an entire wall.

"I didn't realize Reggie was such a *Star Wars* fan," he remarked, picking her special commemorative box set off the shelf.

What the hell? Was Max always this scattered? Reggie had never mentioned it before, but he even struck Natalie as a freak, and that was saying something. "She's kind of a closet science fiction nut." She tapped her papers on the coffee table in a very businesslike manner and tried to steer Max back to the topic at hand; namely, her and her TV show, which would save Cuisine Network viewers from the obesity sure to be caused by their other programming. "As I said, the show will focus on both food and fitness. And I thought at the end of every show, we can have a trainer come in and tell everyone exactly how much exercise they need to do to burn off whatever recipes we've presented that day! Like, if we make burritos, they'd have to run on a treadmill for an hour at a six-point-five-mile per hour pace!" She was rather proud that the knowledge accumulated from her seven-year subscriptions to magazines like *Shape* and *Fitness* finally had some practical applications.

Max smiled benignly. "Reggie had a schedule change, you say?"

Natalie's teeth clenched so hard she feared damaging her twenty-thousand-dollar veneers. "Yes, with the Seattle shoot. Now, as I was saying, I envision a set with a fully functional fitness area, so guest trainers can demonstrate workout moves." She used Reggie's kitchen to give Max an idea of the layout she envisioned and how they could set up free weights and cardio equipment. "It might have been easier to envision if we'd met at the studio."

"Meeting here was more convenient," he replied. "Besides, I think there's enough space for me to get an idea."

She looked up from her handout and met Max's stare. The baby hairs on her nape bristled. Sometimes she got an odd vibe from him. Nothing she could put her finger on, just an uneasy sense that maybe there was something about him they were all missing.

Like now, the way he was looking at her, his gaze flicking up and down her body like he was checking her out, but . . . not. Ninety nine percent of the time she would have sworn on a stack of bibles that Max was gay, but every once in a while he'd look at her, look at Reggie, and she wasn't sure what to think.

Then he smiled and he was the same old Max, good looking in his fastidious way, and she dismissed the creepy feeling. Obviously, Reggie's run-in with the stalker was making her paranoid.

"What's going on in Seattle?"

God, did he want a printout of Reggie's daily itinerary? She forced her tone to sweetness, and said, "There's been a delay, so they won't be shooting there until Thursday next week, instead of Monday through Wednesday. Like I said, it's not a big deal."

"So will she come back home? I'd really like to discuss her ideas for next season, and I can barely get her on the phone these days." He ran his hand across the soft fabric covering the window seat. "Sometimes it's so much easier to communicate in person."

Her cell phone chirped and she nearly growled. Yeah, these meetings are better in person, like the one you're supposed to be having with me right now! "I have to take this," she said when she saw Reggie's number on the display. She flashed Max an apologetic smile as she greeted her sister. Max mouthed the word *bathroom*? and she motioned him down the hall.

Five minutes later, Natalie hung up, trying to convince herself that the pit in her stomach was due to the fact that she'd only had diet soda and a piece of dry toast today.

In between rapid-fire requests to print out and mail drafts to her editor, follow up with Tyler on her appearances, and water her plants, Reggie had managed to relay with giddy enthusiasm the fact that she and Gabe were . . . something. Natalie wasn't totally clear on how they were defining themselves, but she was clear on two things. Mainly that the sex was phenomenal, and whatever it was, it wasn't casual, at least on Reggie's side.

Why Natalie felt so awful about it she didn't know. Maybe because lately, the only man who managed to capture her interest treated her with nothing more than casual friendliness.

She sighed. Not like her sister's news was any big surprise, given the way Gabe had circled Reggie like she was a big, juicy bone and he was a starving wolf.

Though based on what Reggie said, Gabe actually had a big, juicy bone.

Natalie hung up, wishing that someone, someone with gorgeous blue eyes and thick blond hair, might slaver over her for once.

Her phone went off again. Tyler. Had she inadvertently summoned him with her lascivious thoughts? "Oh hey, I just talked to Reggie. She and Gabe are staying in Santa Fe a few extra days," Natalie said after she answered.

"Are you okay? You sound upset?" he replied.

She closed her eyes and ignored the pulse of pleasure that shot through her at his display of concern. It meant nothing. Though they had an amicable working relationship, he'd given no signs of actually being attracted to her. Besides, she reminded herself for what felt like the millionth time this week, Tyler wasn't even her type, uptight, yuppie womanizer that he was. Though she had to concede that she'd hooked herself up with some real dogs in the past that could put Tyler's prowling ways to shame. She assured Tyler she was just distracted, as she was in the middle of a meeting with Max.

"Pitching your show?" he taunted.

Now that was the Tyler she knew and . . . she didn't even want to go there. She clung to the faint sarcasm in his tone, praying it would douse the spark of attraction she was foolish enough to feel. "Yes, and it's going fabulously," she singsonged and rang off.

Speaking of Max, what was taking him so long? She tiptoed down the hall, not wanting to disturb him if he was still in the bathroom, but still, he'd been in there a long time.

The bathroom door stood open. No Max.

From the office came the sound of feet and paper shuffling.

Max looked up with a bright, benign smile. "Sorry. This apartment is so cute I couldn't resist taking a look around."

Mentally, she rolled her eyes. Her chances at her own TV show seemed to be dwindling by the second. "Yeah, this is the office, where all the brilliance happens."

Max made himself at home in front of her computer, admiring the slick flat-panel display. "Nice. So that was Reggie on the phone?"

"She and Gabe decided to take a few days in Santa Fe."

"Ooh, right. The burly bodyguard. It's a shame Reggie feels the need to employ him."

"Her secret admirer has her a little freaked out. Besides," she said, unable to keep the spite from her tone, "I don't think Gabe's company is exactly a hardship."

Max's eyebrows raised. "Ah, how very Whitney Houston, Kevin Costner. How do you turn this thing on?"

"What?"

"The computer. I'm in the market, and I'd love to just have a look. I don't think Reggie would mind, do you?"

He stood so Natalie could sit in front of him. Sighing, she powered up and logged on to the computer. Was Max always this off focus when he worked? Maybe once she sated his curiosity he'd concentrate on the topic at hand.

She keyed in the password and pushed the chair back, startled to find Max standing so close behind her. Was he looking down her blouse?

Max stared at the screen. "Nice display. Great for graphics and watching videos, too, I imagine." He gasped. "Look at the time! I have a meeting in twenty minutes with the host of a home decorating show I'm developing." He started down the hall.

Natalie hurried after him. "But I haven't even gone over my menu plans yet. And we haven't even discussed a target date to shoot the pilot."

Max barely spared her a glance as he hurried out the door. "We'll set something up next week. And can you have your sister call me? I have another idea for her to do some local specials."

Natalie sank down on the couch. The printout she'd carefully prepared for Max lay abandoned on the coffee table. How could she be so stupid, thinking she actually had a shot at getting her own TV show? Max had been humoring her, stringing her along to be nice. Meanwhile, all he wanted was to produce more shows with her sister, the cash cow.

Reggie Reggie Reggie! God, she sounded like Jan Brady at her demented worst, jealous of her older sister and all her success in every facet of life. Wasn't it enough that Reggie got the hot TV show and the fat book contract?

Now she was off visiting fabulous places and having incredible sex with an amazingly hot guy to boot.

A small voice attempted to remind her of how hard Reggie worked, even while visiting said fabulous places, and that the aforementioned hot guy was around because another man sent Reggie pictures of his balls and broke into her hotel room.

But Natalie was too invested in feeling sorry for herself to pay the voice any heed.

Contrary to what he thought, Gabe was not, in fact, able to keep Reggie tied to the bed for the next five days.

Not that he didn't do his best to exhaust her. But she seemed to have boundless stores of energy for visiting Santa Fe's many art galleries and shopping in its many western-themed stores.

"I don't see why you need a shearling coat," he grumbled, as she modeled what had to be the tenth coat at a gigantic secondhand store she'd found. "It never gets below forty degrees where you live, and that thing looks ready for an arctic expedition."

Twirling and admiring herself in the mirror, she said, "It's not about need. It's about how cool this is."

Then it was off to the Georgia O'Keefe museum, and then the Cowgirl Hall of Fame for margaritas and barbecue.

Despite Reggie's attempt to make their time as vacation-like as possible, Gabe refused to let down his guard. She was recognized often, and they were hard-pressed to walk any-where without someone stopping her to say hi, exchange recipe tips, or tell her how much they enjoyed her show.

Reggie met each fan with an enthusiastic smile, eagerly shaking hands and sometimes, to Gabe's increasing fear and annoyance, offering hugs. He did what he could to keep them at bay, but even his most fearsome glare couldn't ward off her seemingly endless stream of fans.

"Can't you give it a rest?" Reggie whispered as Gabe stepped bodily in front of a woman before she had the chance to touch Reggie. "I'm sure all she wants is an autograph." Reggie peaked around his shoulder and took the woman's proffered pen and paper. The woman eyed Gabe warily.

Smart woman, he thought viciously.

"Reggie, you're killing me," he muttered under his breath.

"Can't you can the bodyguard act for one day?" she said after the woman left. Her dark eyebrows were set in an irritated frown as she looked up at him.

He rubbed his eyes tiredly. "What is it going to take to get through to you? You seem to think that since there hasn't been contact from the stalker in over a week and he hasn't threatened you physically, you can pretend he doesn't exist." Her nonchalant attitude toward her safety was enough to send him over the edge.

"I suppose you're right," she conceded sullenly. "But I wish for once we could just act like a regular couple."

Gabe did his best to indulge her—to a point. He refused to let up his guard, but later that night as they walked back to their hotel, Gabe stopped several times to steal a kiss. On their way, he even stopped to buy her a box of chocolate-covered strawberries he caught her eyeing.

Though he still kept his guard up, watching every moment for any potentially suspicious activity, their time still felt like a respite from the real world.

Tucking her hand in his, he picked up the pace, eager to get her back to the hotel.

Still, business came first, and as always he did a quick sweep of the room before motioning her inside. Once she was, he quickly flicked the deadbolt and pressed her up against the wall. Here, at least, he could let down his guard.

Reggie let out a soft "Mmmmmm," as he nibbled the tender flesh of her neck. He quickly divested her of her leather coat and led her over to the couch.

He released her for a moment to retrieve the strawberries and a bottle of champagne from the minibar.

He poured the champagne into two glasses and handed her one. "In here at least, we can try to act like two normal people who," his tongue tripped on the next word as she raised her eyebrows expectantly, "like each other. A lot."

His heart felt like it was busting open at her quivery little smile. He hoped his hand didn't shake as he lifted his glass of champagne to his mouth. Goddamn, but this woman got to him like no one ever had in his entire life.

From the second he'd spotted her across that bar in Hawaii, he'd sensed she'd be trouble. Now he was sure.

Unaware of the emotions rioting inside him, Reggie raised her own glass in a toast. "To liking each other. A lot," she said wryly.

Gabe grinned sheepishly. "I never claimed to be eloquent."

"Considering you barely speak, I should be grateful for what I get, huh?"

"Since you talk enough for the both of us, I figure why waste the effort?"

"Are you saying I talk too much?"

"No, but you do have a talent for holding conversations."

"Well, maybe you better shut me up." She tilted her sweetly rounded chin up pugnaciously.

He could take a hint. He threaded his fingers into the hair at her nape, gently tugging her head back for his kiss. His head filled with her sweet, spicy scent, and he teased her lips with light, delicate tastes.

She parted her lips and tried to lick inside his mouth, but

he kept his lips closed, savoring the hot, sliding caress on his sensitive flesh.

He brought a glass of champagne to her lips. "Open."

Her lips parted at his command, and he poured the frothy liquid into her mouth. He chased the sweet mouthful with his tongue, relishing the hot flavor of her mouth mixed with the cool bite of champagne.

Hands moving restlessly against his back, she tugged his shirt out of the waistband of his slacks. Her fingers traced a delicate path up and down his spine, sending shudders through him as the sensation shot directly to his groin.

He fought the urge to tear off her clothes and sink deep inside, ensuring immediate, immense gratification for them both. Instead, he focused on her soft mouth, the heat of her skin muted by the barrier of both their clothes, the sexy sounds of frustrated lust coming from her throat.

For longer than he wanted to remember, sex had been a means to an end. A way to scratch an itch or blow off steam. He never had a hard time finding it. Girls saw the uniform, the big muscles, and the sometimes scary look in his eyes and wanted to flirt with danger.

But they were always disappointed when all he wanted was a quick bang and a good night's sleep.

None of them aroused anything more than passing physical attraction.

But Reggie he wanted to kiss all over, memorize every patch of skin and its own unique taste. It scared the hell out of him, the intensity and intimacy he felt at her simplest touch.

Shaking, fighting to rein in the desire ripping through him, he pulled back and reached for a chocolate-covered strawberry. He held it to her lips, his erection hardening almost painfully as she closed her lips around it with a sly grin. She sucked and released the plump berry, her pink tongue flicking against the tip.

Still watching him, she slid her hand down to his crotch,

circling her thumb over the tip of his cock through his clothes.

Then, very deliberately, she bit the tip off the strawberry, chewing and swallowing with exaggerated relish.

With a half laugh half growl, he pushed her back against the couch, covering her mouth in a hot, devouring kiss that wiped the smug grin right off her face.

"I never realized I could get so turned on watching someone eat," he whispered, rubbing his face down the front of her shirt, mouthing her breasts through the soft knit fabric of her shirt.

A soft laugh exploded from her chest. "I guess that's better than wanting to watch me parade around in cheap lingerie." Her fingers tunneled into his hair, and he inched her shirt up, raining kisses on each smooth patch of flesh he uncovered. "But if we keep this up I'm going to get even fatter."

He froze, her shirt halfway up her chest.

"What?"

Sighing, he pulled her shirt over her head, pausing to trace the plump, lace-covered swells of her breasts. "Why do you do that?"

Muscles in her belly rippled as she tensed. "Do what?"

Rather than answering, he slipped off the couch, kneeling at her feet to pull off her boots and socks. Then he stripped off her pants, running his hands appreciatively up the smooth pale skin of her legs. "You are so damn sexy, and yet you always talk down about yourself."

"No, I don't."

"Just now you said you worried about getting fatter. Which implies you think you're already fat."

"When you consider most women on television look like Natalie, I am."

"Do you really want to look like that?" Gazing down at her, he couldn't imagine why. With her plump breasts, flat belly, and lushly curved hips, she was damn near perfect.

She sat up straighter on the couch, crossing her arms in

front of her. "I know it's vain and shallow, but I see myself on TV, and I worry that I look chubby. And then when my mom calls me and tells me my ass looks big on camera, or a reviewer refers to me as 'a healthy girl with a healthy appetite,' it's hard not to let it get to me." She uncrossed her arms and spread her hands over her bare thighs as though to hide them.

He couldn't have this.

Rising to his feet, he scooped her up off the couch and jostled her in his hold. "See how easy that was? You can't be that big."

She buried her head against his shoulder and laughed. "You're not exactly the average man, Conan."

He walked the few short steps to the bed and laid her gently against the pillows. "Uh uh," he scolded as she moved to get under the covers. And for good measure he snapped on the bedside lamp.

He hooked his shirt over his head and shucked his pants. Wearing only his boxers, he stood next to the bed, luxuriating in the heat of Reggie's appreciative gaze. "Reggie, honey, when I look at you, chubby is about the last word that comes to mind."

Settling down beside her, he swept his hand up her sweet thigh, over the flat plane of her belly, coming to rest over the plump flesh of her breast. He felt the ripples in her skin as he nibbled his way down her neck into the soft valley of her cleavage. "I think of words like creamy." His tongue swept under the lacy border of her bra. He pulled the cup down so he could suck the deep pink flesh of her nipple into his mouth. "Succulent."

He suckled harder, making her squirm. Tugging the other cup down, he lavished the same attention on the other breast.

He ran his tongue over the skin of her belly, tasting the faint dew of perspiration. "Silky."

His hands gripped her hips, urging her to turn over onto her belly. He knelt on either side of her torso and flipped open the catch of her bra before focusing his attention on the lush, lace-covered flesh of her ass.

He gripped a cheek in each palm. She jumped a little when he bent his head and gave each cheek a soft nip. "And this, Reggie, this is just luscious. Right here," he whispered, running his hands over the small of her back, just above the swell of her hips, "I think this is my favorite part of you. Your back dips in, and you have the sweetest dimples right here"—he bent his head to kiss first one, then the other—"and here."

Her back arched, her ass lifting in invitation. Dancing near the edge of his control, he slipped her panties down and pressed a hand between her thighs.

She was steamy hot, ready for him. He swallowed hard as her legs parted farther, showing him the smooth, glistening flesh of her pussy, practically begging him to come inside.

Unable to resist the temptation, he shoved his boxers down and dipped the tip of his cock against her hot core, squeezing his eyes shut at the almost unbearable pleasure.

He flipped her over onto her back. She stared up at him, brown eyes liquid with emotion. Carefully, he lowered himself over her and cradled his face in her hands. "You are so beautiful, Reggie, and you don't even see it."

Tears leaked from the corners of her eyes as she kissed him fiercely. "For a guy who claims not to be eloquent, you can pull it out when it really matters," she whispered unevenly. She kissed him again, marveling that a man so tough and scarred could be so tender. She'd never felt so beautiful, so desired as she did at that moment.

He feasted on her mouth, then pulled away to nibble at the tender flesh of her neck and shoulders. His lips blazed a path down her chest, pausing to tongue her nipples before sliding down her belly. He landed a wet, sucking kiss just below her belly button.

By the time he settled her knees over his shoulders, she was a quivering mass of nerve endings. "I love how soft you are right here," he whispered, his voice taut with lust as he gently sucked the soft flesh of her inner thigh.

Reggie twisted her hips up, urging his mouth closer, burning with anticipation of feeling that skilled tongue against her.

With a purely male sound of satisfaction, he stroked his thumbs against her plump lips, spreading her wide for his hungry mouth. "Right here, this is the tastiest spot of all."

She almost came at the first flickering touch. His tongue circled lazily around her clit, then slipped down to probe her drenched slit. He was silent, focused as he ate her hungrily, sucking and licking until her legs were literally shaking as she teetered on the edge of a bone-shaking release.

"Oh, oh, Gabe." Keening sounds erupted from her throat as his lips closed over the hard bud, sucking and stroking with the flat of his tongue. Her heels dug into the muscles of his back, hips arching off the bed as orgasmic shudders racked her from head to toe.

One more gentle kiss against her still-quivering flesh and he gently slid her legs down his arms and reached for a condom. Her breath hissed between her teeth as he rubbed the blunt head of his shaft against her still-pulsing flesh.

His fingers had a faint tremor as they traced down her cheek. "Don't you see it, Reggie?" he said, his voice almost reverent. "You're incredibly beautiful, in every way."

And as he slid deep inside her, his fierce dark eyes locked on hers, she almost believed him.

"My beautiful Reggie," he murmured as he moved inside her with deep, sure strokes. They wrestled and thrashed on the bed, slipping and sliding in a sweat-slicked tangle. Reggie lost count of the number of times she came, whispering nonsensical words of her own as she moaned and gripped him to her.

Finally, they ended up with him on top, Gabe gripping the headboard in one hand, bracing his weight with the other, and using the footboard for leverage. She loved watching him come, his face pulled tight, every muscle standing out in stark relief.

She held him fiercely, wondering if she'd ever get over the triumph of knowing that she, wholesome all-American girl that she was, could reduce a tough, sexy brute like Gabe to this.

Several minutes passed before either of them could move.

Reggie stared at the ceiling over Gabe's shoulder, tracing the pads of her fingers up and down the hot, slick skin of his back. A kernel of fear took root in her belly.

Damn Gabe.

He'd gone and made her fall in love with him.

Chapter Twelve

R eggie managed to shove the frightening realization aside for the next two days.

Almost.

Every so often—okay, every five minutes or so—she'd look up and catch sight of Gabe. He could be doing anything, smiling at her, casing the room with a cool, analytical gaze that missed nothing. Or even—and this was how she knew she had it bad—drinking coffee in his underwear. That's all it took, and she would go all melty inside in a way that she'd never done with any other guy in her life.

Worse, she had no idea how he felt about her. Well, that wasn't entirely true. She knew he liked her and especially liked having sex with her. But underneath she sensed he was still wary of getting too deeply involved, unwilling to look beyond what might happen after her stalker was caught and she no longer needed his services.

The only man she'd been close to in the past five years was Craig, who'd proved himself to be too emotionally fragile to handle her success when his own was waning.

Wasn't it just her luck to fall in love with another emotionally unavailable man?

Unlike Craig, Gabe didn't strike her as the type to be threatened by her career, but how would he react when she left for another extended location shoot or a multicity book tour? Were his emotions even remotely strong enough to foster that kind of commitment?

He reached over and grabbed her hand over the gear shift. Today they were headed for Taos to visit the Pueblo and go for a hike in the surrounding mountains.

God, she hoped so.

Gabe snuck glimpses at Reggie's profile as he drove, unnerved by her unusual silence. She'd been acting weird for the past two days.

Ever since she'd told him she loved him.

He'd tried to put it out of his head, telling himself that it didn't mean anything, said in the heat of the moment like that.

Did she even realize she'd said it?

Sometimes he even wondered if he'd really heard that hot, shaky whisper breathed into his ear as she came.

Each time they'd made love since, he prickled with anticipation, straining to hear it one more time.

So far, nothing.

And now she was silent and distracted.

Maybe she was embarrassed at having said it and was praying he hadn't even noticed.

Maybe she actually meant it, and she was in love with him and upset with him for not saying it back.

He didn't know what scared him more—that she might be in love with him, or that he wanted her to be.

Or that it was highly possible he was in love with her too.

Her high-pitched, obnoxious cell phone ring pierced the silence of their rented Escape.

"Natalie," she mouthed silently as she picked it up. "Oh crap," Reggie breathed.

Natalie obviously had screwed up, again.

"Call her back, tell her she'll have it by tomorrow," her voice was frantic now, and he could see the tension spreading up her neck like a sheet of ice. Oddly, she thanked Natalie profusely before hanging up.

"We have to go back. I can't believe what an idiot I am," she smacked her open palm against her forehead. "Didn't you hear me? We have to go back."

He gestured irritably at the two-lane mountain highway laden with blind curves and absent a decent shoulder. "I can't exactly turn around here. What's the hurry?"

Reggie shook her head. "I completely spaced on a deadline. I was supposed to send the first round of revisions back to Natalie yesterday so she could print them and Fedex them to Sharon."

She fumbled in her purse for a moment and pulled out her Palm Pilot. "It's right there, too, but I've been too busy running around with you to bother turning it on."

He stiffened. It wasn't as though he'd chained her to the bed or something. She could have caught up on work whenever she wanted, and damned if he would let her blame him for her choice to ignore work.

It's starting again, an evil voice in the back of his head taunted. *She's wrapped up in her career, and she'll drop you like yesterday's panties if she sees you as a threat.*

"I didn't mean that the way it sounded." Her hand, warm and small and strong, squeezed his thigh just above his knee. "I can't believe after the hard time I've given you about not relaxing, I'm the one who's ruining our plans. I'm sorry." She sighed and leaned her head back against the headrest. "But I can't afford to slow down at all right now."

He couldn't believe it, didn't want to believe it.

Damn that bitch.

She was his.

What was that thug still doing hanging around, anyway? In the past two weeks he had exercised admirable restraint. Even though he had piles of letters and pictures to send

Reggie, he'd resisted, hoping that if she could stop being scared of him, she'd send the big thug away.

And then he could prove to her that they were meant to be together.

As soon as he'd known where to find her, he'd come. Promising himself he would keep himself hidden. He just needed to see her. He missed seeing her.

Now he saw what a whore she was.

His lip curled in disgust. From across the street he had a clear view of them approaching the hotel, walking up the wide steps.

Hand in hand.

Then the big ape grabbed her and hauled her against him, manhandling her and slobbering all over.

Not that she seemed to care, the way she rubbed up against him like a bitch in heat.

All he wanted was to be with her, to have Reggie for his own.

His heart felt like someone was stabbing it with a red-hot poker. After everything he'd done for her, how could she betray him like this? She'd be nothing without him, and now she repaid him by breaking his heart.

He wanted to punish her for refusing his advances while acting the whore with that animal.

He wiped away the hot sting of tears. For now, he had to be patient, bide his time for a little longer. But someday, somehow, he would make her pay.

When they got back to the hotel, Reggie set herself up at the desk and fired up her laptop. She pulled out a sheaf of papers thick enough to keep her busy for the next week, as far as he could tell.

He took the opportunity to step outside to make a phone call.

Malcolm answered on the second ring. "This is Reed."

Malcolm Reed was the owner and CEO of Reed Security

Systems Inc., one of the fastest growing security companies on the west coast. He'd hired Gabe after his discharge, as soon as his doctors pronounced him physically ready for civilian work.

He'd also fired Gabe eighteen months later after the Marly Chase debacle.

Fortunately, Malcolm had seen no reason to end their close friendship, and Gabe had filled him in on all the details of Reggie's case when he asked Malcolm to investigate some of the stalker's earlier e-mails. That had been over two weeks ago, and Malcolm hadn't gotten back to him with any additional information.

"It's Gabe."

"Hey, man, how's babysitting the cook?"

He could imagine Malcolm, leaning back in his chair, size thirteen Alan Edmonds propped up on his cherry wood desk, the jacket of his $1,500 suit hung neatly from the coat rack, his chair angled so he could appreciate his twentieth floor view of downtown Los Angeles as he talked.

Malcolm had enough appreciation for the finer things to assure his clients that he ran a first-class operation, but enough Special Forces–instilled intensity and toughness to make them feel good about entrusting him with their personal or corporate security.

"Fine so far."

"Sorry I haven't been able to get back to you on those e-mails. We've been slammed. So, no escalation in contact?"

"No, in fact, no communication at all for the past week and a half."

"Sounds like your boy is losing interest."

Gabe wanted to think that. "I've never seen anything like this. No escalation, no attempts at personal confrontation, and now he's been inactive for nearly two weeks. If not for the break-in in New Orleans, I might be inclined to think it was all a prank that got a little out of hand."

Malcolm was silent for several moments, and Gabe could

practically hear his friend's brain churning. When Malcolm spoke, it was with great deliberation, as though he was choosing his words very carefully. "Maybe you're onto something. It wouldn't be the first time a celebrity faked a stalker."

"No," Gabe snapped. "That doesn't make any sense. Why would she spend all this money to hire me if it was a hoax?"

"You said yourself she needed security to keep her job. If she admits she faked everything, she looks like even more of a flake, which would no doubt piss off the network execs even more."

Gabe considered the possibility that Malcolm was right, but couldn't believe it. Reggie wasn't the type of person to stage an elaborate hoax, then go to great lengths to cover her tracks.

Would Natalie do something like this behind her sister's back? Maybe. But why? Though they were close, Natalie was jealous. But if jealousy was the motive, wouldn't she have stopped, rather than helped Reggie milk all the publicity she could out of the situation? And if it was to help Reggie, wouldn't Natalie have clued her in so as to avoid scaring her sister?

Her stalker was real. He was certain of it, despite the seed of doubt Malcolm attempted to sow. The stalker may be laying low, but he wasn't gone. Gabe's gut told him their guy was still out there, waiting, biding his time until he had the opportunity to get close.

"She wouldn't do that," Gabe said curtly. "In any case, I wanted to see if you could have Dave trace some more e-mails for me."

One thing that sucked about working on his own was he'd lost a network of experts. When he'd worked with Malcolm, he'd had a crack team of network security specialists who could track down the source of most e-mails and phone calls in the time it took him to go out for coffee.

Fortunately, his friendship with Malcolm and the rest of

the guys was strong enough that he could usually get them to help him out during their free time.

"How many?"

"A dozen or so. All from different Yahoo and Hotmail addresses—no ISP we could trace a subscriber back to."

"Hmmm" was Malcolm's only response. Then, "We're so bogged down we haven't even had time to get to that first batch you sent us. Dave can do it, but it may take a while. We've got a couple things cooking down here that will keep him busy for the next week at least. In the meantime, send me what you have."

Gabe thanked him. "Reggie's shooting in L.A. next week. Maybe you can stop by the set."

"As long as I have you on the phone, there's something else I want to talk to you about. I have a potential client in San Diego. They need someone to test evaluate their existing security system and manage any upgrades we feel are appropriate."

"I'm listening."

"We don't have the capacity to handle it right now. So I thought I could farm it out to you as a consultant."

His piquing interest was dampened somewhat by an unwanted shard of guilt. A month ago, he would have given his left nut to receive Malcolm's offer. Now, however . . .

Before Gabe could reply, Malcolm continued with his sales pitch. "The bullshit from last year has died down enough that I can start referring clients to you again. It might take another year, year and a half before I can hire you back full time, but until then I'd have enough to keep you busy. The only difference would be no health insurance or full-time employee benefits, but I'll pay you enough to cover the loss." He quoted an hourly rate nearly double that he was charging Reggie.

Part of Gabe wanted to pump his fist in triumph. This was exactly what he needed, not only to get his career back on track, but to prove himself worthy of the second chance his friend was so generously offering. But he couldn't stop thinking of Reggie, one room away, brow furrowed as she tapped away at her keyboard. How could he possibly leave her in potential danger?

"Normally I'd be jumping at an opportunity like this," he said, "but I signed a contract with Reggie that I don't feel comfortable breaking."

Not to mention the thought of leaving her alone and vulnerable made him sweat like a whore in church.

"I can refer a dozen guys who are qualified to babysit," Malcolm said dismissively. "Someone who can be on a plane tomorrow. You said yourself there hasn't been much activity."

"That doesn't mean he's gone away."

"Even if that's the case, you're wasting your time on these low-rent jobs, Gabe. I need someone with your skills to help me fill out my team."

"You didn't mind wasting me on babysitting before."

"I thought you could use the vacation. Stupid me. So what do you say?"

"I'll think about it."

"Make your decision by the time you get to L.A. I don't want to play hardball here, but if you can't do it I need to start looking for someone who can."

Malcolm's offer was a godsend, and he was an idiot for not jumping at it. Never in a million years did he expect Malcolm to hire him back, regardless of their long-standing friendship. You couldn't nearly ruin a guy's company that he'd built from the ground up and expect—no matter how close a friend he was—that he'd welcome you back with open arms.

What a clusterfuck. As long as Reggie was paying for his services, his business would stay solvent. Then what? Not to mention the fact that sleeping with the woman paying his bills was starting to leave a bad taste in his mouth.

Maybe he should take Malcolm's offer. He'd personally screen any replacement, make sure whomever Malcolm sent was more than qualified to keep Reggie safe.

But if he left her now, he had a really bad feeling he might never see her again. Oh sure, they'd try to meet up, schedules permitting. But as time passed and they went longer and longer without seeing each other, whatever they had would inevitably peter out. Like Reggie had said earlier, she couldn't afford to slow down at all right now. And he couldn't afford to follow her around like a faithful lapdog.

He let himself back into the room.

Reggie looked up and smiled, which sucked the breath from his lungs.

The semifunctioning logical part of his brain reminded him of his vow not to let emotional entanglements interfere with his career. He had a shot at getting his career back on track in a major way. Was he really going to blow it for the chance to get their relationship on more solid ground?

But the rest of him got physically ill at the idea of putting Reggie's safety in the hands of someone else.

As they taxied into SEA-TAC airport two days later, Reggie tried to convince herself that Gabe's mood was not actually worsening by the day.

She was projecting, that was all. She was stressed, so she thought she saw signs of stress in him as well.

But he *was* giving her the silent treatment.

At least she thought he was, but with Gabe, who could tell?

He was certainly as amorous as ever. She had a hickey on the inside of her left thigh to prove it.

Still, he was withholding something, something he'd started to let out before she'd had to cancel their plans to spend the day in Taos. She was afraid her obsessive attention to work had shoved it firmly back inside him and slammed the door.

And she wasn't helping matters. Ever since she'd discovered she was in love with him, she'd been skittish herself, afraid of coming on too strong and freaking him out. Normally she wouldn't be such a coward, but his manner the past few days hadn't exactly been approachable.

She tried to make small talk, her anxiety superseded by irritation as Gabe limited his response to grunted monosyllables.

By the time they got to their hotel room, she couldn't stand it anymore.

"Are you going to tell me what's wrong, or am I going to have to hone my telepathic skills?" she snapped, heaving her suitcase up on the bed.

"I don't know what you mean."

"Oh, come on. You've been acting weird the last couple of days; you barely said two words on the plane. You're distant. I'd say quiet, but you're always quiet. But this is a different quiet, like you're mad and keeping it from me."

His face bore the age-old exasperated expression all guys got when their girlfriends decided it was time for "the talk."

"I'm not upset—"

She barreled on before he could finish. "I know what's wrong. I know my schedule sucks."

"You think I'm sulking because you're busy? I know we're not some boyfriend and girlfriend on vacation here."

Ooh, there it was. The B word. She'd been hesitant to refer to Gabe that way, even in her head. But now that he'd brought it up. "How do you see us, Gabe?"

He froze, his hand halfway to the closet with his suit jacket. "What do you mean?"

She wanted to stomp her foot. Why did every semi-intelligent man become obtuse when it came to this topic? "I mean, I know that our circumstances aren't exactly normal, but how do you see us? How do you see me? Am I your girlfriend? Or am I a client who's enjoying some really great perks?"

His eyes narrowed and he at least had the grace to look insulted. "I don't think of myself as some gigolo, if that's what you mean." He finished hanging up his jacket and stalked toward her, his shoulders set in tense, irritated lines. Good. She'd take irritated over distant any day. "Why don't you tell me, Reggie? What *are* we doing here? Am I an entertaining way to pass the time on the road? What happens after you no longer need my services? Are you going to stuff a check in my shorts and send me on my way?"

She gasped, outraged. Did he actually think she was capable of using him like that? She started to tell him off but snapped her mouth shut when she caught his hard stare. Though he tried to keep it hidden behind his flat, dark stare, she could see the confusion, the vulnerability as he, too, wondered where they stood.

Taking a deep breath, she squared her shoulders. Someone had to be brave enough to take the first step. "You want to know how I feel?" Oh God, she was really going to do it. Blurt it all out, let him know where she stood and risk letting him trample her heart into a fine-grain powder. She gripped his hands, hoping he didn't notice the film of nervous sweat glazing them. "I really care about you, Gabe, and even though I have, like, zero time for a relationship, I want to see if we can make this work."

Her heart thudded in her brain and she was afraid she might stroke out in the face of his ongoing silence.

His dark eyes unreadable, he finally spoke, "There's something we need to talk about."

A sentence to make the hardiest woman's blood run cold. As she'd feared, she'd freaked him out by laying it all out there and telling him how much she cared, and now he wanted to get their relationship back to business before she completely lost her mind and fell in love with him.

Too late. The fact that she never said "I love you" was a minor consolation.

She nodded curtly and braced herself for the crushing blow.

"When we were in Santa Fe, I talked to my friend Malcolm."

At Reggie's confused frown he clarified, "My buddy who had to fire me."

She nodded again, still perplexed, wondering what Malcolm had to do with Gabe dumping her.

"He has a potential client for a high-level corporate security job that he can't take on right now. He wants me to fill in."

Afraid she already knew the answer, she asked, "When would it start?"

"The client wants to start as soon as possible, but he's given Malcolm until the end of the week to get back to him."

"I assume if you took this job more referrals would follow?"

"Malcolm said he could hire me back as a full-time consultant." He raked a hand through his hair, leaving it in thick, silky tufts. After a few moments, he said, "He can have someone to replace me immediately."

She wanted to hurl herself on the floor and wail like a two-year-old. Not fair, not fair! How dare reality intrude on her perfect situation. Stuck in close quarters with her fantasy vacation guy who actually turned out to be the kind of man she could fall in love with, with the opportunity to spend time with him in a way that simply wasn't possible with her currently jam-packed life.

If he left at the end of the week, she'd never see him again.

But she knew this was exactly the opportunity he needed to get his career back on track.

And since her stalker seemed to have gone AWOL, the need for twenty-four-hour protection was rapidly deteriorating. At this point, any rent-a-cop would no doubt placate Carrie and the network. She hardly needed someone as highly trained as Gabe.

Determined not to cry or lay him with a guilt trip, she tried to dispel the tension with an attempt at humor. "I guess the decision would be a lot harder if scrotum boy hadn't up and disappeared."

He gripped her hand where it fisted on the table. "I wouldn't even consider leaving if I didn't know that Malcolm would find someone just as good, if not better than me."

She smiled sadly. "We both know your skills as a bodyguard aren't really the issue here."

The lines on either side of his mouth deepened as he took her arm and walked her over to the couch. She sat next to him, unable to look at him for fear she'd burst into tears. "You've already broken one rule about work and personal relationships. I'm not going to ask you to sacrifice an opportunity like this so you can keep babysitting me."

And she sure as hell wasn't going to ask him based on whatever tenuous romantic attachment he might feel for her. God, being noble and self-sacrificing really sucked, especially considering what she really wanted to do was yell and scream that she'd hired Gabe first, and Malcolm could go find himself another security consultant.

Long, calloused fingers grazed her cheek. "No matter what happens, I want this to work too," he said. "I don't want to stop seeing you just because I stop working for you."

The words should have filled her with relief, but instead anxiety bloomed in her chest. How was that even possible? She wouldn't have a break in God knew how long, and until then she'd be lucky to see him once a week if he was willing and able to travel. Although there was one possibility . . . "What are you doing for Christmas?"

He sat back, confused. "I thought I would stay with my sister in San Francisco. Why?"

"It's the one week off I'll have until February, and I thought maybe . . ." She let her voice trail off, wondering if she was pushing too hard, too soon. He said he wanted to keep seeing her. He didn't say he was ready to commit to a major holiday.

"You want to bring me home for Christmas?" he asked warily.

"Good God no! I'd never subject you to my mother's

Christmas dinner." She cracked up at Gabe's heartfelt sigh of relief. "I was thinking more along the lines of just the two of us, holed up somewhere for the week."

His slow smile sent warmth cascading through her. "Maybe Maui, a return to the scene of the crime?" He waggled his brows lasciviously.

All tension melted from her face and she practically glowed. "Back to the Grand Wailea?"

"You in a bikini, me making sure every inch of you is thoroughly covered in sunscreen? Sounds like a very Merry Christmas to me."

Several hours later they emerged from their hotel room and found an Internet café close by so Reggie could send Natalie the latest revisions to print off and mail to Sharon and access any updates to her schedule in Los Angeles.

Though she was heartened by her discussion with Gabe, it was hard to ignore the cold weight of reality bearing down on their fledgling relationship. In a sick way, she was almost upset when she saw nothing disturbing or out of the ordinary in her e-mail box. If only her stalker would contact her again, she'd have a legitimate excuse to ask Gabe to stick around. She said as much in a whiny e-mail to Natalie.

Once the shoot started, Reggie was too busy to say two words to Gabe, but she remained, as always, intensely aware of his presence. It was hard to believe how intrusive he'd seemed at the beginning, especially now that the thought of not having him around to shadow her every move left a big, gaping hole in her chest.

Chapter Thirteen

Natalie opened the door to Tyler's knock. His cheeks were slightly flushed, his blond hair slightly disheveled from the blustery November wind whipping around San Francisco.

He looked better than he had a right to in a gray single-breasted suit and a French blue shirt that perfectly matched his eyes. Like some yuppie bad boy guaranteed to break hearts and take no prisoners.

He's a total player, she reminded herself sternly, a sort she'd had more than enough exposure to over the past several years, thank you very much. And at the end of the day, he wasn't even her type, with his clean-cut businessman look. She liked guys with an edge, guys with long hair and tattoos.

"What's with the suit?"

"Client meeting. Management flew in from the east coast, and those guys still tend to equate work casual with west coast flakiness."

"Hmm. You look like a Bank of America escapee." Actually, hot was how he looked, but the last thing Tyler's ego needed was yet another woman drooling all over him.

Besides, clothes could hide a multitude of sins. He probably had a decent set of love handles hidden under the fabric of his dress shirt. She led him over to Reggie's couch and offered him a seat. "I just got here so I still need to print out a copy of the updated schedule."

"Look, I don't mean to be a jerk," he said, glancing at his watch, "but I'm kind of in a hurry."

"Got your latest shipment from Bimbos 'R Us?" she teased, trying to convince herself she was absolutely *not* jealous.

He laughed good-naturedly. "No, I'm having dinner with the lawyer across the street again."

Later she'd analyze and agonize over why she cared. Right now she seized on the first smart-ass remark that popped into her head. "Ooh, three whole dates with the same girl? Better be careful or the male slut club will revoke your membership."

He raised his eyebrow and tapped his watch meaningfully.

She stood, eager for the excuse to get away from him. What was it about him? No matter how cool and collected she tried to be, he inevitably made her feel like a flustered teenager, alternately trying to gain his approval or goad him into an argument. "Help yourself to anything you find in the fridge."

The sound of a cabinet door opening and shutting followed by the hum of the faucet echoed down the hall as she walked into the office and snapped on the light.

As she reached for the computer, an eerie chill washed through her, distracting her from the Tyler-induced butterflies in her stomach. A stack of bills sat on the top edge of the desk, just to the left of center. She could have sworn she left them on the top right-hand corner, like Reggie always did.

She flipped on the computer and took a look around while she waited for it to boot up.

From what she could tell, none of the books on the shelves was disturbed. All of Reggie's office equipment, anything that might have attracted a thief, was all accounted for.

She went into the bedroom. Discarded clothes from Natalie's last-minute cleanout of Reggie's suitcase still lay in a pile on the bed. Her Manolo slides were in the precise spot where Natalie had kicked them off last week after she'd borrowed them.

Moving closer to the dresser, she squinted at the carefully organized items on Reggie's dresser. Perfume bottles, jewelry case, and framed photos were all perfectly arranged, with none of the clutter of carelessly strewn knickknacks, pocket change, and scraps of paper that decorated Natalie's own dresser.

But something was odd. Different from the last time she'd been in here, but so subtle she immediately dismissed it as paranoia.

She couldn't dismiss the creepy feeling that someone had been here, someone had touched Reggie's things and replaced them, but not quite precisely enough. Reggie had mentioned in her e-mail that she hadn't heard from the stalker in two weeks. But maybe she'd spoken too soon.

She went back to the office and in a few short keystrokes accessed and printed Reggie's schedule for the upcoming trip to L.A., along with their travel itinerary.

She walked back out into the living room and handed Tyler the schedule. "Is anything wrong?" he asked when he saw her frown.

"No," she said distractedly, rubbing her hands up and down her arms to ward off the chill that had suddenly engulfed her. "I have the weirdest feeling, like someone's been in here."

Tyler looked around and she waited for him to tell her she was crazy. But he only asked if anything was missing.

"No, but things have been moved." She frowned, thinking of the bills on the desk. "At least, I think so. It's just a sense I get, you know? Like a premonition or something." She watched him look over the printout. "I hope you don't mind that I'll be joining you in L.A. Reggie said she wanted me there."

That wasn't precisely true, but Natalie had managed to convince Reggie that she needed her there as a fashion consultant on the photo shoot.

"Who else can you trust to make sure they don't put you in anything unflattering?" she'd said.

Tyler unbuttoned his shirt cuffs and pushed the sleeves up ropy forearms dusted with a sprinkling of blond hair. Hair that would rasp against her fingertips as she traced every muscle and tendon . . .

Natalie's throat went bone dry. Desperate for a diet soda, she retreated for the kitchen. Her stomach seized as she caught something strange in the corner of her eye.

Rex, Reggie's prized ficus, was in its usual place in the corner next to her kitchen table. But his green, glossy leaves were scattered all over the floor. Branches were torn off as though in a fit of rage.

Her soda slipped from nerveless fingers as she hurried over for a closer look. The main stalk had been twisted off near the base and now lay forlornly against the side of the pot.

Pooling at the roots was a shallow puddle of blood.

Her screech brought Tyler skidding across the slate floor.

He wrapped his arms around her waist and caught her as her knees buckled.

"What?" His voice was frantic in her ear.

"He killed Rex!"

"Huh?"

His arm was still around her waist, and through her terror she became aware of his hard, lean body pressing against her back. What do you know, no potbelly after all.

But this was no time to succumb to inappropriate lust. "Rex, Reggie's ficus, the one she's been nursing for the past five years. The stalker ripped him apart and there's blood all over it."

She felt him gasp as he spotted the carnage. "Jesus." Tyler knelt down, careful not to get any sticky red liquid on his suit pants. He leaned closer and sniffed. "I think it's just paint." He stood and pulled her into a soothing embrace.

Relief coursed through her at the fact it wasn't blood, but only briefly. Someone had broken into Reggie's apartment.

Even though it wasn't her own stuff that had been pawed through, she felt violated on her sister's behalf, and couldn't imagine how Reggie was going to take the news.

Another wave of panic shot through her belly. Turning, she burrowed her face in Tyler's chest. The silk of his tie rasped against her cheek, and she inhaled the scent of his faint sandalwood cologne and underneath his own musky, enticing scent.

"It's okay," he soothed, his hands moving in strong, calming strokes down her back. "When was the last time you were here?"

"Last night. I brought in the mail and watered Rex before I did some work on the computer." Little by little her panic was subsiding; his big, warm hands helped to dissipate the chill that had settled deep in her bones. "Poor Reggie. Why won't this guy leave her alone?"

"Just be glad you didn't interrupt him."

Another shudder racked her body at the thought of catching the deranged fan on her own. Tyler squeezed her harder and pressed a kiss to her forehead.

She tilted her head back. Even in her three-inch heels, she had to tilt way back to look into his face. The bright overhead lights of the kitchen picked up white blond highlights in his hair, and she wondered inanely if they were natural. They must be, she decided. As well groomed as he was, she couldn't imagine Tyler sitting quietly with a head full of foil wraps. A faint shadow of beard dusted his jaw, and she noticed that some of his whiskers were dark red.

He stared down at her, his blue eyes soft with concern. Her gaze dipped to his firm, full lips, and she was suddenly, achingly curious to find out how good they would taste.

Flustered, she stepped back, stumbling a little on her spike heel. "We better call the police."

He dropped his hands, and she wasn't sure, but she thought maybe they lingered for a few extra seconds on her hips.

Fifteen minutes later, two uniforms were there to take their statement. ". . . and then I found Rex, my sister's plant, ripped apart with paint all over it."

While the first officer did a walk-through of the apartment, she and Tyler gave them a quick rundown on the stalker and the harassing activity to date.

"But you say he's never broken into the house before?" the officer asked.

Natalie shook her head. "Not that we know of."

"And the alarm didn't go off?" His eyes did a quick survey of the room. "This looks like a sophisticated system. It should have gone off."

"The only time it went off was when I didn't turn it off in time," she admitted.

The officer's dark eyes narrowed on Natalie's face. "You say you've been watching the place while your sister's out of town?"

She nodded.

"Any chance you forgot to set the alarm after you left yesterday?"

"No," she denied vehemently. "I'm extremely careful to always set it before I leave."

"Sometimes you leave in a rush, you forget things."

Before Natalie could deny carelessness, Tyler broke in. "Officer, if she set the alarm, she set the alarm. Natalie doesn't forget stuff like that."

The patrolman looked like he wanted to argue, but thought better of it. He flipped his notebook closed. "We'll have someone over to dust for prints. And since this is likely connected to your sister's stalker, the detective assigned to the case will call you both in the next few days and will come by to interview the neighbors."

"Do we need to stick around, or can we leave?"

Right. The date with the lawyer. Wasn't Tyler lucky that he could so easily deal with a break-in, a hysterical sister, and still have the energy to go bone his latest conquest.

The officer said they could leave if they wanted.

She sighed, suddenly exhausted as the final drops of fear-based adrenaline evaporated from her bloodstream. "Should we call Reggie?"

Tyler was silent a moment, considering, then shook his head. "Let's wait and see what the police have to say tomorrow. Nothing she can do about it from Seattle. For now, let's go. You shouldn't stay here. Tyler grabbed her arm and she let him lead her out the door, even though she didn't particularly relish the idea of going home, alone, to her none-too-secure flat within spitting distance of the Tenderloin. "Come on, we can finish going over everything back at my place."

He led her down the block and ushered her into his silver BMW. She'd never admit it, but Natalie loved this car, with its smooth leather seats and dashboard that reminded her of a cockpit. "Did you know the BMW is one of the top five most popular cars with gay males?"

He shot her a quelling look and reached for his cell phone. "Hi, Christine."

What a prince, calling her to tell her he'd be late. Natalie stared out the window and tried not to eavesdrop.

"I'm sorry for the short notice, but I'm going to have to cancel tonight."

Now that got her attention. She listened with interest as he explained that something had come up with work, and no, he couldn't meet her later.

Sounded like a brush-off to her, which was strange coming from a guy who, less than an hour ago, had seemed so eager to get on with this evening's plans.

"You can go over the schedule yourself and call me with any changes," she said when he hung up. "You didn't have to cancel your plans."

"It's okay," he said shortly. "I have some ideas I want to talk to you regarding your idea for pitching Reggie to women's magazines like *Glamour* and *Marie Claire*, and besides"—he cleared his throat uncomfortably—"you're pretty shaken up about the break-in, and I don't think you should be alone."

He didn't sound exactly resentful, but he also didn't sound overjoyed at the prospect of spending the evening with her. Besides, since he hadn't said anything since she'd initially proposed getting Reggie in some younger skewing publications, she was pretty sure of what he thought of her idea. She didn't need him feeling sorry for her. "You don't have to babysit me," she snapped. "I have plenty of people to call if I don't want to be alone."

He didn't bother answering and he guided his car through the heavy evening traffic back to his loft. He unlocked the door, tossed his keys on the entry table, and shrugged out of his suit jacket. She hung up her own coat and headed automatically for the office.

His voice caught her before she started downstairs. "I'm going to change clothes," he nodded his head toward the bedroom, an open loft at the top of a steep spiral staircase. "Why don't you open a bottle of wine, and then we can fix some dinner?"

"I thought we were working," she said uneasily.

"I'm starving," he said matter-of-factly. Then, with a sly smile she'd never seen on his face, he said, "And somehow I think we'll get along better if we both loosen up a little."

What the hell was going on? Then again, after the afternoon she'd had, a glass of wine sounded heavenly. Who was she to argue?

"Open whatever you like," he called.

She didn't know much about wine, other than that she liked it. Her usual method of purchase was to see what was on special at Safeway. Judging from Tyler's collection, he didn't shop at Safeway.

After she'd poured herself a generous glass of Australian Shiraz, she took the opportunity to snoop through his considerable CD collection. Probably the usual preppy boy mix of Dave Matthews, U2, a little Van Halen mixed in for nostalgia, and John Mayer for when he wanted to charm the ladies' pants off.

Much to her surprise, she found a wide assortment of alternative rock including the Foo Fighters and harder stuff like Nine Inch Nails and Tool. Maybe Tyler had some anger issues to work out under that Ken-doll exterior. She slid a Foo Fighters CD into the Bose surround sound.

He emerged from the loft a few minutes later dressed in a pair of jeans so old they were bleached almost white in places and the hems were frayed around his big bare feet. "I hope you don't mind." He gestured to his equally well-worn T-shirt. "I was dying to get out of that monkey suit and figured that since we weren't going anywhere . . ." his voice trailed off.

She didn't think he could look any better than he did in his *GQ* wear. But instead of looking like a slob, he looked rumpled and sexy, and more human than she'd ever seen him. Though not tight, the soft cotton of the shirt draped against his chest, clearly delineating the muscles she'd felt shifting against her earlier.

This was Tyler, she reminded herself. The guy who's barely civil to you on good days and treats you like you're mentally challenged most of the time. Drooling over him was a very, very bad idea. He was an asshole, for starters. Which for some sick reason she always found irresistible in a guy. But she couldn't justify slavering over a guy who so obviously thought she was a complete idiot. Even if he had defended her to the cops . . .

This was only happening because it had been a long, lonely six months since she'd had any action beyond a little heavy petting.

And it had been even longer since she'd experienced anything particularly noteworthy.

She took a fortifying gulp of wine, its warmth coursing through her veins. She'd bet anything Tyler really sucked in bed. Guys that good looking always did.

Oblivious to her internal vilification of his character and bedroom skills, Tyler poured himself a glass of wine, clinking it briefly against hers. "Cheers." He gave her another one of those weird looks and turned back to the refrigerator. "Let's see what we can rustle up here."

She watched uneasily as he pulled out a package of chicken and assorted bunches of vegetables. Okay, that didn't look too bad. He placed a cutting board and knife in front of her, along with the broccoli and bell peppers. "Here, julienne these."

That was a cut, she knew. But for the life of her, she couldn't remember more than that.

Tyler gave her a look, but this time it was more teasing than condescending. "That means cut it into little matchsticks. And you want to have your own cooking show," he scoffed.

She didn't bother to tell him that her idea was dead in the water, based on her last meeting with Max. If she had to listen to Tyler tell her "I told you so," she very well might commit hari-kari with his paring knife. "Every week I'll have a different chef co-host. That's the whole point," she said loftily. She picked up her knife and started in on the vegetables, giving it her best guess as to the size.

Meanwhile, Tyler sliced the chicken into thin strips and put on rice to boil.

No way was she consuming all those carbs, but she didn't want to be rude.

He tossed the chicken into a pan coated with, in her opinion, way too much oil.

"You know you can save tons of calories using a cooking spray."

He shot her a quelling look over his shoulder. "Why don't you just drink your wine and leave the cooking up to me?"

Mellow warmth surged through her, and it occurred to her that maybe she should slow down on the wine since she hadn't eaten anything since her small dry salad at lunch.

Her stomach growled as Tyler added something garlicky and spicy to the sauté pan. She filched a broccoli spear before he grabbed the cutting board and swept everything into the pan.

An awkward silence fell as he leaned his elbows onto the opposite side of the island. For several moments, the sounds of sizzling vegetables and chicken filled the room.

Finally, he said, "Like I said, I really liked your idea about targeting more than the usual cooking publications."

She jerked back so hard she almost fell off her stool. While he hadn't slammed the idea when she'd presented it, he's said so little she'd been convinced he, like Max, was just humoring her because she was Reggie's sister.

"It's a good idea. I haven't been targeting the women's magazines because I don't know the space as well, but that's no excuse for ignoring a good opportunity." He paused, watching his wine as he swirled the glass on the countertop. "I want you to come up with a couple different article pitches I can send out."

"You really think it's a good idea?"

He smiled, his eyes crinkling boyishly around the corners. "I wouldn't ask you to work on it if I didn't."

He turned away, opened a can, and poured what looked like a bunch of heavy cream into the pan.

"What is that?" she asked in horror.

"Coconut milk. I'm making curry."

"That's pure fat. I can't eat that."

"Why the hell not? It's not like you couldn't stand to gain a pound or ten."

She drained her second glass of wine and poured a third. "I have to stay thin for the camera."

"And when's the last time that was an issue?" He closed his eyes as she winced. "I'm sorry, that was rude."

She stayed mute as he dished up two huge plates of rice and the chicken mixture and plunked down on the bar stool next to her. Shoving the food around her plate, she tried to muster up more offended dignity at his slight, but in the end failed miserably. "You're right. I haven't had any decent work in two years. My career was over when I moved up here, but it's been hard to admit that I'm such a failure."

He gave her a pat on the shoulder. She reminded herself it was purely meant for comfort and there was absolutely no reason to be squirming around on her bar stool the way she was. "Maybe you're meant for greater things than hawking douche and underarm deodorant."

Hah. "Easy for you to say, with your successful business, gajillion-dollar loft, and nice car. All I have is a degree in English lit that's never been used and a short list of tampon commercials to populate my résumé."

Chuckling, he said, "You're a lot smarter than you give yourself credit for." He stopped, frowning at her hand as it guided her fork in serpentine patterns through her rice and curry. "Will you just eat some fucking food, for Christ's sake? I think we've just established it's no longer necessary to keep yourself starved to Calista Flockhart proportions."

She wasn't sure what shocked her more: that Tyler sounded on the verge of losing his ever present cool over her eating habits, or that he had actually called her smart. She forked in a mouthful of rice and curry without a thought for its fat and carb count. She let out an involuntary moan as the richness of coconut milk and spicy curry exploded in her mouth. Swallowing, she scooped up another bite, this one as orgasmic as the last.

Taking a sip of wine, she sighed in satisfaction. "That is so good."

She had no idea how it happened, but suddenly she was up on the breakfast bar as Tyler's mouth devoured hers as eagerly as she'd devoured the curry.

Shoving the plates aside, he grabbed her ass and pulled her tight against him, urging her legs to wrap around his waist.

His fist tangled in her hair, and hungry sounds escaped his throat as his tongue stroked hers in a rhythm that left her breathless and panting.

She clawed at the fabric of his T-shirt, hands shaking as her head filled with his scent, his taste. Desire shot straight to her core, settling in a deep throb between her thighs so fierce it was nearly painful. How could she heed the voice in her head that warned this was a very bad idea, when with just one kiss he had her so turned on she was ready to come, right there, rubbing against the rock-hard bulge of his crotch?

"Christ, I've been wanting to do this for so long," he muttered. His hands launched into action and their shirts ended up somewhere across the kitchen, leaving them half naked under the bright lights of the kitchen.

Thank god she'd splurged on a self-tanner application and Brazilian wax earlier that week.

Then all thoughts of beauty treatments evaporated. His hands were everywhere, splaying over the skin of her back and shoving down into the waistband of her jeans to press into the pliant flesh of her ass. Using his mouth, he tugged her bra strap down her shoulder, nuzzling the cup aside so he could tongue a tight brown nipple into his mouth.

She moaned as he bit down, holding the tight bud in his teeth and lashing with hot strokes of his tongue. His hand fumbled with the snap of her jeans, and the hiss of her zipper filled the room.

He shoved his hand inside the fly, pulling aside the crotch of her G-string to press his fingers against her wet heat. A shaky groan vibrated against her breast as he stroked her smooth, embarrassingly wet flesh.

Dragging his mouth up to hers, he whispered, "God, you're even hotter than I imagined."

Later she'd remember all the reasons why having sex with Tyler was a colossally bad idea. But right now any protest she might have mustered died at his admission that he'd been imagining her in any capacity.

He quickly got rid of her boots and tugged her jeans and thong down so they dangled off one leg. She ripped open the button fly of his jeans and shoved them off his hips.

Tyler went commando. Who would have guessed?

His cock pulsed and jumped eagerly in her palm. Of course he would have a big dick to go along with his movie-star looks. No wonder he was so arrogant.

She stroked him once, twice before he pushed her hand away.

Grasping himself in one hand, the other urging her hips closer to the edge of the bar, he guided the thick head of his cock between her juicy pussy lips.

But instead of the rough, urgent thrust she expected, he cupped her face almost tenderly, watching her as he sank inch by slow inch until he was buried all the way inside.

A soft, shuddery moan worked its way up her throat as he filled her. She could hardly believe she was here, with Tyler, and he was inside her, clutching her to him like he never wanted to let go.

He licked and sucked sweetly at her lips, breathing hard as he let her adjust to his size. Finally, he moved, two short, shallow thrusts that made her belly tighten and her toes curl.

His eyes squeezed shut, and a bead of perspiration trickled down the side of his face. "I can't wait," he whispered almost apologetically.

His hands gripped her ass, holding her as he fucked her hard now, ramming deep as she clutched frantically at his hips.

"That's it," he groaned, "take me deep, so deep."

Dimly, she realized she was moaning like a porn queen, the noise amplified as the sound echoed off the loft's high ceilings. But short of gagging herself, she didn't think she could stop.

He filled her to bursting, his cock huge and hot, rubbing against millions of tiny nerve endings inside and out.

A loud roar erupted in her head, pounding in time to his thrusts as everything inside her coiled tight. Her mouth opened wide on a strangled cry as her orgasm ripped through her with such intensity she almost blacked out.

Vaguely she heard him erupt in a string of curses as he came, spurting hotly inside her as his whole body trembled and shook.

Little by little she came back to herself, to the harsh reality that she was sprawled, mostly naked and well fucked on the cold granite of Tyler's breakfast bar, a bright recessed light

shining down on her like a spotlight. Just when she resolved
to make her escape to go wallow in a sea of confused embarrassment, he jerked her off the bar and into his arms, lifting
her with no apparent effort.

"Now that I've gotten you all dirty," he said, "let's go get
you cleaned up."

Hot water cascaded down Natalie's back, her moans echoing and bouncing off the shower's marble tiles as Tyler ran
his soapy fingers up and down her torso. His cock bobbed
between them, brushing against her stomach as he took his
time lathering up her tits. After their first, nearly frantic mat-
ing in his kitchen, now his movements were slow, almost
leisurely as he familiarized himself with every patch of skin
on her bare body.

"Your tits are so sweet and perfect," he whispered, bending to take a hard nipple into his mouth. His fingers teased
and pinched at the other, making her pussy flutter and clench
in response. He slid down to his knees, his face level with her
stomach. He scattered soft, sucking kisses across her belly
and lower, until his mouth hovered her mound.

Turning her so she leaned against the back wall, he hooked
one knee over his shoulder as her hands reached out for balance. Steam swirled around them, fragrant with soap and her
arousal, clouding her view of Tyler as he knelt before her.
The steam cleared, and her thighs tightened with embarrassment as he stared at her, spread wide to his gaze. "I've been
dying to taste you for months now," he breathed. "You have
the most gorgeous cunt," he whispered, "like a perfect, juicy
peach." One finger teasingly traced her hairless labia. He
looked up, a naughty grin glinting in his eyes. "Make that a
nectarine." His laugh wafted over her ridiculously sensitive
flesh, making her belly tense as he leaned forward and closed
his mouth over her.

Her fingers tangled in his thick wet hair as he sucked and
licked at her pussy, whispering between caresses how beauti-

ful she was, how good she tasted, how much he wanted to fuck her sweet, tight, cunt after she came against his face.

Natalie's breath came in short pants, his words turning her on almost as much as the hot wet caress of his mouth. No one had ever spoken to her like this. The things Tyler was saying were so dirty, but so eloquent and personal. As though he really *had* spent months and months fantasizing about all the things he was doing right now.

His lips pulled gently at her clit as his fingers traced the entrance of her body, teasingly denying her the penetration she craved. A high keening started in her throat as he sucked, drawing rhythmically on her clit in a way that had her digging her heel into his back and clutching his face harder against her. "I wanted to do this before," he said, sucking and releasing until she was suspended on a razor's edge of sensation. "But the second I touched you, felt how smooth and wet you were, I had to get my cock in you."

"Please," she moaned, her head rolling back and forth against the tile.

"Please what?" he said, deliberately pausing and looking up at her with an expression that made her want to kill him. Just as soon as he finished making her come.

"Slide your fingers inside me," she didn't know where the words came from, but they continued to flow as he obeyed her without hesitation. "And suck me, like you were before. Yeah," she murmured as he took up his previous rhythm. "Harder." She rocked against his fingers, groaning as he increased his pace. Red streaks appeared in her vision as her whole body seized, shaking as waves of orgasm ripped through her body.

She would have collapsed had Tyler not stood up and supported her with his weight against the wall. He kissed her, his tongue musky with her taste as his cock prodded against her belly. He turned off the water, his mouth never breaking contact as he guided her out of the shower to lean against the mirrored vanity.

To her amazement, the first tendrils of renewed arousal crept up her spine, fueled by the hot taste of his mouth and the slide of his wet skin against hers. Pulling her mouth free, she licked her way down the warm, salty cords of his neck, nuzzled away the blond curls of chest hair so she could close her teeth over his nipple. His muscles tensed as though hit with an electric current. She closed her hand around his cock, savoring the sound of his moan as she pumped him. He was so big, so thick, and her pussy clenched in anticipation of having him inside her again. But first she wanted to show him she could give as well as she got.

With her hand still wrapped firmly around his dick, she turned him so his ass rested against the edge of the counter and slid to her knees. Tiny droplets of water trickled down the flat of his lower abdomen, daring her tongue to capture them. His whole body tensed at each feather light contact, and Natalie shivered as the soft hair dusting his thighs teased her nipples.

Openmouthed, she explored every inch of his abs and thighs, savoring the way he swore and moaned as his cock swelled even bigger against her fist. She nipped and kissed her way up his inner thighs, not stopping until she felt the firm, tight weight of his balls against her lips. His fingers tangled in her hair at the first lash of her tongue, and when she gently sucked one into her mouth his strangled curse echoed off the ceiling.

She kept him there on the edge as her thumb circled the plump head of his cock and her lips and tongue played with his balls. "Please," he finally groaned. "Jesus, Natalie, please."

She sat back on her heels, marveling at the sheer beauty of his erect penis. "Please what?" she threw his taunt back at him.

His blue eyes glittered in the dim misty light of the bathroom as he stared down at her. "Suck my cock."

"You mean like this?" She barely closed her lips over the tip of him, swirling her tongue around the silky smooth head, flicking it against the bundle of nerves on the underside.

His hand fisted in her hair, the subtle pressure an incredible turn-on as she continued to torment him, taking just the head of his cock between her lips. "Or do you want it like this?" she asked before taking him deep into her mouth until he pressed against the back of her throat. She released him, millimeter by torturous millimeter, her pussy flooding with renewed desire as she felt him throb against her lips. "Maybe you want it like this," she said, closing her lips over the head and pumping him firmly with her fist. His breath came in harsh pants, and she felt the subtle trembling in his legs, as though he struggled not to fuck her mouth with no restraint whatsoever. "Or maybe you want this," her fingers slid down over his balls and further back to tease the crack of his ass. "I know some guys like it when—"

He yanked her to her feet. "Fucking little tease," he said, the harsh tone in his voice sending heat coursing through her body. Holding her almost roughly, he positioned her so she was bent at the waist, hands braced on the cool, smooth countertop.

"You want to know how I like it?" He kicked her feet apart and grasped his cock in one hand, guiding himself to the hot, slick entrance of her sex. "This is how I like it," he panted, shoving himself inside, so deep and so hard the force of it lifted her up onto her toes. "I like it when I can feel you, snug and wet around my dick."

From this angle he felt huge, stretching her wide as his cock rasped against nerve endings she never knew she had. Her palms slid along the slick surface of the counter, searching for purchase as his slamming thrusts propelled her forward. "I like fucking you deep and hard." His hands closed over her hips, steadying her. "I like it like this, when I can watch my cock sink all the way inside you, and I can see your face and know you're about to come."

Natalie looked up, startled by the sheer carnality of their reflection. Her face was flushed bright pink, her lips swollen, blurred, and parted around her pants and moans. With his lips pulled tight, teeth bared, muscles rippling and flexing as he pounded into her, Tyler looked like some kind of Viking warlord, and she the hapless wench to be claimed.

The musky scent of their sex hung in the steamy air, the moist sounds of sex bounced off the smooth walls. A now familiar tightness built between her legs, and she rocked back to meet each drive of his hips. Her breath hitched as his name broke past her lips, and she ground her ass against him as her whole body shattered with release.

Tyler held himself deep, reaching one hand around to palm her and draw out the last waves of her orgasm. Within seconds he joined her, pumping in quick, shallow thrusts. With a shout, he surged deep one last time as his cock jerked and pulsed inside her. He pulled her tight against him and she could feel the rise and fall of his chest, the pounding of his heart against her back. Turning her to face him, he bent and kissed her.

This kiss had none of the passion of the previous ones they shared. It was soft, tender. She would have called it sweet had they not been naked and plastered together. It was the kind of kiss two lovers shared, full of warmth and deep emotion. And it felt so good that for a split second Natalie almost let herself believe Tyler really cared.

But she knew better than to waste her time on useless fantasies. Thrusting her tongue against his lips, she turned their kiss in an entirely different direction, reminding them both what this night was really about.

Later, she lay staring at the ceiling of his loft bedroom as images of the past several hours played in her mind, at turns incredibly arousing and embarrassing.

So much for her theory that Tyler was bad in bed. He'd proved himself to be more than adequately skilled, not only in bed, but in the kitchen and the shower as well.

He'd come four times in the past six hours. She didn't know any man over the age of thirty capable of that.

As for herself, she'd lost count after the first seven or so.

Tyler softly snored beside her in a well-earned, exhausted sleep, an arm and a leg thrown over her body.

As much as she would have liked to have stayed right where she was, she had no illusions that she'd wake up to flowers and a romantic breakfast in bed.

Tyler had love 'em and leave 'em practically tattooed on his long, pink, perfectly proportioned cock. And despite his graphic descriptions of all the things he'd been wanting to do for her for months, she didn't flatter herself that he meant anything by them.

However, if she was ever in the mood for phone sex, she knew exactly whom to call. He had one of the most deliciously filthy mouths she'd ever heard on a man.

She eased out from under his arm and leg, freezing when he muttered something. Her breathing resumed when he flopped on his back with an even louder snore.

Thank God he had at least one flaw.

Shivering as her feet hit the cold slate floor of his room, she swore softly when she remembered that all of her clothes were scattered around his kitchen and living room.

She felt her way over to the spiral staircase, praying as she descended that she wouldn't slip in the dark and break her neck.

Afraid she'd wake him if she turned on a light, she fumbled around for her clothes, distressed when she came up short of her bra.

Of all the things to leave in his apartment, it was among the worst. Knowing Tyler, though, he was probably so used to women flinging their clothes off with abandon, yet another bra would hardly faze him. The painful thought of the many women who had come before—and the many women who would come after—was enough to make her abandon her search for her lingerie before Tyler woke up.

Too, bad. The peach demi-cup edged in French lace matched her thong, and it irked her to break up the set.

Chapter Fourteen

R eggie's fingers were nerveless around her phone as Natalie told her about the break-in and the demise of Rex.

"But there was nothing, no other note or anything?"

"Here's the number for the detective who's handling the case," Natalie rattled off a number. "He can give you all the details, but right now it doesn't sound like they know much of anything."

A lump settled in her throat. Stupid to cry for a dead plant, but still. "I'll have Gabe call him." Right now she was afraid she'd fail at any attempt at rational conversation.

They'd wrapped the shoot in Seattle and were packing up their hotel room when Natalie had called. They hadn't talked any more about Malcolm's offer, but Reggie knew Gabe's decision was essentially made.

Now he looked at her with dark, concerned eyes. He swore viciously when she told him the news.

"This shouldn't affect your decision either way," she said shortly.

"The hell it won't! Obviously our guy was just laying low for a little while." He paced around the room, fingers dragging through his close-cropped hair. "I want to know how the fuck he got into your apartment without the alarm going off."

"I don't know," she said, flinging a handful of underwear

into her suitcase. "Maybe he was able to bypass it. No system is foolproof."

She could tell by the coiled tension in his body that he was struggling mightily to restrain his temper. "Impossible, unless he's some kind of expert at bypassing sophisticated alarm systems. More likely your sister forgot to reset it when she left."

She opened her mouth to defend Natalie, but even though Natalie had recently stepped up to the plate with a vengeance, her attention to detail often left much to be desired.

Silently, Reggie handed Gabe the number for the detective at the SFPD.

He fired a rapid series of questions at the officer, obviously not getting any answers he liked.

"No signs of a break-in, no prints that can't be accounted for." He sighed angrily and sat down on the edge of the bed. "Looks like you're gonna be stuck with me for a while." But his attempt at a smile was a lame one.

Just two days ago she'd wished for another incident so she'd have an excuse to pressure Gabe into staying with her. Now she felt sick at the idea that someone had violated her home and potentially put her sister in danger. What if Natalie had been there when the stalker broke in? Bile burned at the back of Reggie's throat.

And she felt guilty that Gabe was sacrificing a critical career opportunity when she knew very well she could find a replacement capable of keeping her safe.

If Gabe wouldn't make the right decision, she'd have to do it for him. He was meeting with Malcolm the day after tomorrow. If he didn't take the job, she had no choice but to fire him.

"I don't see why we have to be here so early," Gabe grumbled as they shuffled onto the set for Reggie's *Men's Only* photo shoot.

"They need to do wardrobe fittings and makeup," she

replied patiently. Someone had woken up on the wrong side of the bed this morning. It wasn't like she was psyched to be up and about at the ungodly hour of six-thirty A.M.

And as if things between her and Gabe hadn't been strained enough for the past two days, he'd been quietly simmering since last night when she'd told him her photo shoot was for *Men's Only*.

"You can't do this," he'd shouted across their suite at the Beverly Wilshire.

She'd been shocked at his reaction. "I don't know why you're bringing this up now. It's been on the schedule from the beginning."

Okay, so it had been listed as "photo shoot, Roderick Publishing group studio," not under the name of the magazine. He'd only realized it was for the popular men's magazine known for it's racy—albeit, fully clothed—photo spreads when Reggie had mentioned the publication by name.

"It's a great opportunity to get attract more male viewers."

Exasperated, he'd finished stripping off his clothes and stormed off to shower, muttering, "If you don't have a problem with guys spanking it all over your pictures, I don't know why I should."

They'd traveled in tense silence, Reggie casting anxious and resentful glances at Gabe's set jaw as he white knuckled the steering wheel.

Within moments of arrival, she had what felt like five hundred people fussing over her, lifting her hair, tilting her chin up to blinding spotlights, standing her up and spinning her around as they commented on every feature and flaw as though she couldn't hear them.

"We'll want to minimize the butt."

"Hair definitely needs help with volume."

"Make sure her eyes don't disappear into her face."

"Can you make her look like she has cheekbones?"

Over the din the creative editor went over the concept for the shoot.

Not surprisingly, they'd designed a set to look like a kitchen, complete with oven, mixing bowls, and several high-grade utensils.

The stylist held up several sample outfits, consisting mainly of frilly aprons and matching G-strings.

Why had she ever let Natalie and Tyler talk her into this?

A ruckus erupted as the door swung open and several crew members, still reeling from Gabe's military-style briefing on the need for set security, rushed to intercept the intruder.

"I'm supposed to be here," a female voice protested. Speak of the devil. "Hey, Gabe, can you tell them to let me in?" she heard Natalie call.

Natalie might have been partly to blame for her current predicament, but Reggie was glad to see a familiar and friendly face.

"I thought you wouldn't be here till later."

Natalie grabbed her in a quick hug and pulled up a seat next to the makeup chair. "I flew in last night. I thought you might need me."

The tension knotting her shoulders eased infinitesimally. That was Natalie for you. She could be the biggest flake in the world and carelessly inconsiderate, but when Reggie really needed her, somehow Natalie sensed it without even needing to be told.

"What's with crabby pants over there?" Natalie pointed her chin in Gabe's direction. "He looks like he's about to turn green and bust through his clothes."

Reggie grinned at big, tough Gabe being described as "crabby pants." Her expression immediately sobered as she saw him sweep the room with an icy glare. "He's not happy about this," she said, blinking to avoid losing an eye to the mascara brush.

"You should make her eyes smokier," Natalie commented to the makeup artist, ignoring the vicious look she received in return. "Is he concerned about your safety?"

"He thinks I should reevaluate the kind of publicity I

seek." The makeup Nazi huffed in annoyance as her lip brush went astray. Reggie obediently shut up as what felt like the twentieth coat of lip gloss was applied and blotted on her lips before speaking again. "Especially considering recent events."

The makeup artist stood back and eyed her critically, whisking on yet another dusting of blush and highlight powder before she was apparently satisfied. "We'll do your body once we pick out the outfits."

"Body?"

The makeup artist gave her a look that shouted "Duh!" "With those outfits, you'll need some touch-ups. And if you need to shave, I have extra razors in my case."

"I shaved my legs last night," she said.

Eyebrows raised, Natalie shot a meaningful look at the array of panties hanging from the clothing rack.

"Everything else is well trimmed too," she muttered, grateful that her regular waxes meant she wouldn't have to resort to shaving her bikini line in a public bathroom.

As the hairdresser laced her hair liberally with gel and rolled it in hot rollers, the stylist held up several outfits for Reggie's approval.

Reggie saw the see-through lace bra with strategically placed strawberries and choked on her latte.

Thankfully, Natalie stepped in. "No, no way. Reggie has great abs, so you should have her in something like this." Natalie snatched up a little half shirt in a stretchy gingham fabric, like something a slutty farm girl would wear. She pulled out a pair of Daisy Duke–style cutoffs to match.

The stylist nodded in agreement. Reggie sighed. At least it wasn't a thong.

Gabe paced the set like a caged animal. He knew he was bothering the crew, at turns pissing them off and scaring them, but he didn't give a shit.

For four torturous hours he'd been forced to watch his girlfriend dress up in a series of progressively sexier outfits.

A fantasy come true under most circumstances, but not with an audience of twenty. And not when she was being photographed so millions of readers could ogle her lusciously curved ass, currently showcased in a pair of bikini panties with lace ruffles on the butt.

The last time he'd seen panties like that, they'd been on his three-year-old niece. Now he felt like some kind of pervert for getting turned on by seeing Reggie in them.

"You gonna be okay, buddy?"

He barely restrained himself from turning and slamming Tyler in the face. It was partly his fault Reggie was putting herself on display for the enjoyment of sex-starved males everywhere.

Tyler had arrived about an hour and a half ago and had spent the first few moments exchanging vicious whispers with Natalie. Something about not calling to let him know she'd changed her travel plans.

Gabe had been too distracted by Reggie in the Daisy Dukes to listen carefully.

He clenched and unclenched his fists, rotated his neck, and took several deep breaths, trying yet again to clamp down on his unreasonable jealousy.

This was why he didn't get involved. He got too possessive, too territorial, to the point where the thought of another guy even looking at his woman made him want to put his fist through a wall. "If the photographer tells her to make love to the camera one more time, I'm gonna kill him."

Tyler chuckled. "Whatever he said, it worked with that strawberry. I wouldn't have thought Reggie had it in her."

Gabe's ruff started to prickle until he realized it was friendly admiration, not lasciviousness in Tyler's voice.

He let out a shaky sigh as he recalled the shot. The photographer had had her dip a strawberry in fudge sauce and suck it off, little by little. As her ripe, glossy lips closed over the berry, she'd looked right at Gabe, her eyes telling him she was remembering all the fun they'd had with chocolate strawberries in Santa Fe.

He'd had to sit down and cross his legs to avoid embarrassing himself.

The creative director called for a break. Natalie brought Reggie some water, and the two conversed quietly for several minutes.

Natalie turned, an angry gleam in her eyes as she made a beeline for the two men, and Tyler immediately stiffened. But apparently Tyler wasn't Natalie's target.

"How can you leave my sister?" she demanded with a sharp poke to the center of Gabe's chest.

Gabe shook his head, in no mood to explain the situation right now. "I'm not going anywhere. That's all you need to know."

"Then why did Reggie tell me to get someone named Malcolm's number from you so I could hire a new security person?"

Without another word, Gabe stormed over to where Reggie stood, sipping her water as she waited for the crew to set up the next shot. This was too damned much. He knew exactly what she was trying to do: Take the decision out of his hands.

As if he could leave her now.

Ignoring her protests, he grabbed her by the arm and propelled her out the door.

Natalie stared wide-eyed as Gabe hauled her sister out of the studio with all the finesse of a Neanderthal on steroids. "I'll go see what's wrong," she said to the room in general, grateful for the excuse to get away from Tyler.

Tyler's hand shot out and gripped her arm before she could slip away. Jesus, what was up with all the manhandling? Even though she had to admit that it was totally hot.

"She's fine. They need to talk." He pulled her farther in to a shadowy corner. "And so do we."

"What about?" she asked, striving for nonchalant but sounding more like Minnie Mouse.

He backed her against the wall and put his hands on either side of her head, effectively boxing her in. "Why did you leave without saying anything the other night?"

She stiffened and pressed into the wall, but unfortunately couldn't disappear into it. "We were done. I wanted to go home." Which wasn't precisely true. Actually, she'd wanted to stay snuggled in Tyler's big California king with him snoring beside her and have him wake up with a big, sleepy smile in the morning at the sight of her.

But she'd indulged in that unrealistic hope far too many times and been burned in the past, thank you very much. The cab ride home may have been dark and lonely, but it was far more dignified than the walk of shame illuminated by morning's harsh glare.

"You should have said something. I would have given you a ride home."

She rolled her eyes. "Please, you would have given me cab fare and told me not to let the door smack me on the ass on my way out." He looked so offended that she laughed. "Like that's never happened."

She'd hit a bull's-eye, judging from the red slashes that appeared on his high cheekbones. Smiling gently, she gave him a condescending pat on the cheek. "It's okay, Tyler, Reggie won't fire you for fucking her flaky little sister."

He grabbed her hand and wouldn't let go even when she tugged. Instead, he laced his fingers through hers and drew their clasped hands down his chest. "You think I'm mad because I'm afraid of getting fired?" He looked so confused, hurt even, that for a moment she believed he was actually upset.

But she knew better than to fall for his concerned façade. She knew Tyler's type all too well and wouldn't be doing herself any favors by holding out any hope that he wanted anything more than a quick lay.

Swallowing hard, she whispered, "You're a PR guy. You need to spin this. You think you have to act all gentlemanly and let me down easy. You don't have to act all offended that I left. I know you don't have any real interest in me." She struggled to keep her composure as she voiced the truths she'd spent the past two days drilling into her psyche. Deliberately hardening her voice, she said, "We fucked. It was fun. It's finished."

He leaned in and kissed her, oblivious to anyone who might see him. Immediately Natalie felt her knees turn to water and her center turn into liquid magma.

When he pulled away, his lips were swollen and smeared with her lip gloss as his eyes shot blue flames. "I wish it were that simple. Most of the time you piss me off, and I really wish I could just fuck you and not give it another thought. But I think about you all the time." He ran a frustrated hand through his thick blond hair. "The truth is, I like you, Natalie, more than I ever expected to. You're funny and smart—not to mention beautiful. When you're not around I find myself wishing you were there to argue with." His voice dropped to a husky whisper. "And for the past two days, I can't think of anything but how good you tasted, how it felt to have you tight and wet around my cock."

She gasped, on fire with lust and embarrassment even though no one else could hear. He kissed her again, tongue stroking hotly against hers. Was it possible to orgasm from making out?

Sadly, he pulled away before she could find out.

He pushed away, discreetly adjusting the fly of his trousers. "After we're done here, you're going to come back to my hotel and we're going to have a long talk. Among other things." Reaching for the catering tray, he shoved half a turkey sandwich toward her mouth. "Eat this. You'll need the energy."

Reeling from his words and the warm way he was looking at her, Natalie obediently chewed and swallowed, not even bothering to pick off the cheese.

*   *   *

"Why did you tell Natalie I'm quitting?"

Reggie didn't back down from Gabe's glower, even though he was using every body language trick in the book to intimidate her. She glared back at him, hands on hips and feet braced wide, forgetting for a moment that she was clad in a white and pink lace-trimmed bra, pink skirt that barely covered her butt, and pink panties with white lace ruffles across the back. Chin tilted up pugnaciously, she cried, "Because you are. And I don't appreciate you pushing me around."

A vein began to pulse in his broad forehead. He opened his mouth to speak, then closed it when one of the editorial assistants walked by with an alarmed look. Gabe quickly scanned the hallway and pulled her by the forearm into the unisex bathroom located two doors down.

"I'm not quitting," he yelled, his voice echoing off the tiled floor and ceiling.

"Then I'm firing you," she yelled back. "I won't let you make a decision you regret, then turn around and blame me for ruining your career."

"The hell you will. I'll make my own goddamn choices here, and I'm not putting the woman I love in danger so I can make a better career move."

She didn't know who was more stunned by what he'd just said.

For a second his mouth worked open and closed as though trying to recall the outburst. He closed his eyes and thrust his fingers into his hair. In a shaky voice, he said, "That didn't exactly come out the way I planned."

"Did you mean that?" Legs suddenly wobbly in her high-heeled slides, Reggie leaned back against the cold tile wall, bracing her hands beside her. The icy porcelain felt good against her suddenly red-hot skin.

He wiped a big hand down his face and sighed. "Yeah, I meant it."

"Would it kill you to sound happier about it?"

He gave an irritated grunt and shook his head. "This was a complication I didn't anticipate," he admitted.

"Well, I didn't want to fall in love with you either," she snapped.

"One thing's for sure, I'm not quitting, and you're sure as hell not firing me."

She held her hands up, fingers spread. "Be reasonable. There's no reason for you to stay with me when I can easily hire—"

He slammed his mouth down on hers, effectively cutting her off. She made a lame attempt to push him away, but within seconds her hands were clawing at his shirt as she sucked eagerly at his lips and tongue.

"I can't leave you," he whispered as his tongue trailed hotly down her neck. His mouth slid down to her exposed cleavage, raining hot kisses along the lacy border of her bra. "I don't give a shit what you say." He spun her around to face the wall and ran his hands up under her nothing of a skirt. "You're mine, and I don't trust anyone else to take care of you."

Through his pants she could feel the massive bulge of his erection throbbing against her ass. She moaned and ground back against him, knowing this argument wasn't settled, but physically incapable of pursuing it now.

One big, hard hand slid inside the ridiculous panties and cupped one cheek, and he groaned against her shoulder. "It makes me crazy, knowing every man in America gets to see you in these sexy little outfits."

She gasped as he tugged the panties down her thighs. Something had to be wrong with her to be this turned on by his rough treatment. But as his fingers sank into the drenched folds of her sex, she couldn't deny her response.

Panting breath and mingled groans echoed off the tile walls as Gabe unfastened his pants and unceremoniously shoved himself inside her.

He held her hips and thrust deep. She tipped forward,

bracing herself with her palms as he began a fast, jarring rhythm. From this angle his cock felt impossibly huge, impossibly hard as he drove inside her.

She bucked back against him, moaning, desperate to take him deeper, harder.

Pressing against her back, he rested his cheek against hers. His hot breath bathed the side of her face as his sweat-slicked skin grazed hers. "Say it, Reggie," he murmured, sounding almost desperate now. "Tell me you love me."

"I love you," she moaned. "I don't want to, but I love you."

He came with a harsh cry, jerking and shaking against her as his cock throbbed and surged inside her. His orgasm set off her own, and she pulsed hard around him, kneading his shaft as she came.

Through the roaring of her climax, she heard his harsh whisper. "I love you, too, Reggie. God, I fucking love you."

He nuzzled against her cheek for a few more seconds before easing from her body.

Vaguely, she heard the toilet flush as he rid himself of the condom he'd produced from nowhere.

Somehow Reggie found the courage to look in the mirror.

"I think you'll need a touch-up," Gabe said lightly, but his face reflected over her shoulder was grave.

He was right. Her many coats of lip gloss were now smeared across her face and his. Her hair still looked okay, though, since the activity had only added to the sexy, tousled look the hairstylist had spent over an hour perfecting.

And her face was so red she didn't think she'd need blush for the rest of her life.

Handing him a paper towel, she washed her hands and wiped at the pink streaks on her jaw while he did the same. "We're not finished with this discussion," she said, struggling for a businesslike tone. "Don't think you can distract me with sex."

He didn't reply and silently handed her the frilly panties.

*   *   *

What the fuck was wrong with him? Clearly, he was completely insane, incapable of good judgment when he got within two feet of her.

Gabe walked Reggie down the hall, discreetly checking his fly before they entered the studio.

Like they wouldn't take one look at Reggie's face and know exactly what they'd been up to. But she handled the situation with admirable grace, ignoring the speculative looks and settling in the makeup chair like nothing had happened. "I smeared my lip gloss," she said matter-of-factly.

Natalie looked up as he closed the door, her brow furrowed in concern. Understandable, since he'd practically dragged Reggie out by her hair.

Maybe he *should* quit. How could he protect Reggie when all he could think about was getting into her pants? The scary part was that even as he'd been tearing off those ridiculous hard-on–inducing panties, he'd known he should stop. But he'd gotten to a point where he didn't give a shit. Didn't care about Reggie's stalker, didn't care about his professional reputation, didn't care about anything but sinking hard and deep inside her, staking his claim in the most primal way he could.

And blurting out that he loved her. He didn't even want to go there right now.

But he couldn't deny the fierce bolt of joy at the memory of her whispering that she loved him as she came around his cock.

What a fuckin' mess.

Natalie was walking toward him, biting her cheeks as though trying to hold back laughter. Her gaze kept flashing toward his crotch.

He resisted the urge to check his zipper again as heat flooded his face. Could she tell he was still semihard? He shifted his weight uncomfortably.

"What?" he snapped.

Placing a hand on his shoulder, she stood on tiptoes to whisper in his ear. "You need to clean up."

He wiped at his cheeks. "Do I still have that lip gunk on me?"

"No," she giggled, flicking another glance down his front. "You, um, got some body makeup on you I think."

He frowned down at the front of his shirt, seeing nothing.

"Lower," she whispered.

Sure enough, there were flesh-colored streaks all over the front of his pants.

She dug in her bag and produced what looked like a giant wet wipe. "You should get that off, makeup can stain really bad."

"Why the fuck would they put makeup on her ass?" he muttered, swiping at the crotch of his pants.

Great. The makeup was gone, but it looked like he'd pissed himself.

And Reggie, oblivious to it all, sat chatting and laughing in the makeup chair.

One of the stylist's assistants walked up to her with an envelope in her hand. "This came for you while you were . . . out," she said with a sly wink.

"Thanks," Reggie responded with a wink of her own.

An overwhelming sense of blackness shook Gabe as she tore open the seal.

His gut was screaming bloody murder again. He didn't know how he knew it, but whatever was in that envelope was Bad with a capital B. He hurried across the room, and his suspicions were confirmed when Reggie dropped the contents of the envelope with a shocked gasp.

"Give me a pair of tweezers," he barked at the makeup artist, who fumbled in her toolbox and found the pair of purple slant tips.

Gingerly, he picked it up by the edge and placed it on the counter in front of Reggie. As she gazed down, all the color leeched from her face, turning her rosy complexion white and chalky under the many layers of makeup.

"Son of a motherfucking bitch," Gabe muttered, unable to keep the violent tangle of emotions in check.

Before him lay an eight-by-ten photo of him and Reggie taken in Santa Fe.

He remembered the exact moment. They had walked out of an art gallery on Canyon Road, and Reggie had been marveling at the collection of horse sculptures made from grass and plaster of Paris. Gabe had been marveling at how hot she looked and had grabbed her and gave her a fierce, tongue-thrusting kiss.

At the time, he hadn't given a rat's ass who might be watching his public display of affection. The picture conveyed the mood perfectly, the barely leashed passion of the couple, the way his fingers splayed across her hip in a grip that was both affectionate and possessive.

It would have been a beautiful portrait of a couple in the first giddy stages of love, if not for the deep scratches across the surface, and the word WHORE written in what looked like red nail polish across Reggie's image.

"How did this get here?" His voice sounded gravelly and strained to his own ears.

The assistant who had delivered it looked nearly as white as Reggie. "The receptionist called. It came from a messenger service."

Struggling to regain some semblance of composure, Gabe curtly ordered the assistant to find out where the messenger came from and who ordered the delivery.

He knew the efforts would be futile. Whoever it was could easily have used a fake name and paid with cash.

"Was there anything else in the package?" he asked Reggie softly. She'd recovered some of her color and gave him a shaky smile.

"I don't know," she replied, reaching for the envelope before Gabe stopped her.

"Fingerprints," he said in response to her questioning look. Though he was willing to bet his left nut that when the analysis was done, the only identifiable prints would belong to the messenger, Reggie, the receptionist, and the assistant.

Using the tweezers, he carefully pulled a single sheet of paper from the envelope.

"I see he's finished with his magazine collage phase," Reggie observed wryly.

That was one thing he liked about Reggie. She never succumbed to hysterics, even when she was perfectly justified.

Gabe placed the note on top of the defaced photo, leaning over Reggie's shoulder to read.

> *You slut. I thought you were different, but you're not. I didn't believe you'd let that gorilla thug touch you, but you're nothing but a filthy slut. I would have loved you, Reggie. Now you have to be punished.*

"It's okay," Gabe whispered. "I'm not going to let him get to you." Even as he said it, the words knotted in his throat. How could he possibly promise that? He, who'd let his anger and jealousy overwhelm his good sense to the point he hadn't been paying attention when the package was delivered. So distracted by Reggie that he hadn't noticed someone following them in Santa Fe, possibly photographing their every move. Worse, his involvement with Reggie was making the stalker jealous, more aggressive. More dangerous.

The stalker was quickly evolving from a frightening nuisance to a physical threat. And because Gabe couldn't control his feelings for her, he'd put her in even more danger.

Her small white hand covered his and squeezed. "Don't. This isn't your fault."

Gabe sighed raggedly, wincing as the pressure of frustrated tears pressed the back of his eyes. Christ, he loved her. Trying to comfort him when someone was threatening to hurt her in God knew what vile fashion. "Reggie, you can't deny I've made things worse," he whispered. "Maybe it's better if you hire someone else, give the stalker the impression we've cooled things off. I can't have you hurt."

She laced her fingers more tightly through his, and he realized then that he was shaking with the effort to contain the force of emotions roaring through him.

He wanted to rage, throw chairs at walls, strap on an arsenal "Punisher" style, and hunt down the man who would dare threaten the woman he loved. He wanted to bundle Reggie up and haul her off to an impenetrable fortress in the mountains where he could keep her locked up and safe from the world.

Instead, he swallowed his anger, focusing on her melting brown eyes, her soft hand curled so trustingly around his. "You can't leave me," she whispered. "You love me, remember?"

Chapter Fifteen

Somehow Reggie got through the rest of the day. A police officer arrived and questioned the assistant, Reggie, and Gabe and took the photo and note as evidence. Gabe also contacted the detective in San Francisco to make sure he was in touch with the LAPD.

It shocked Reggie how easy it was to get back into the groove of the photo shoot, given the morning's events. The stalker's message had shaken her to her core, and she didn't think she was capable of pasting on a sultry smile for the cameras.

Except every time she looked she saw Gabe watching her with that tormented intensity of his. All at once she could feel his hands on her sweaty skin, feel him grinding deep inside her, whispering how much he loved her.

Each time the thought popped into her head, the photographer would shout, "Yes! That's the look I want!"

Maybe she was turning into a nympho, when even threats of physical harm couldn't dissuade her body from throbbing with lust every time she so much as looked at Gabe.

Later that evening, she and Gabe met Natalie and Tyler for dinner to discuss how to manage a major public appearance she had scheduled for the following night.

"I can't cancel every public appearance, Gabe," she said as she sipped at her Kirin. They were at a trendy sushi place in

West Hollywood. She'd been skeptical when Natalie suggested taking them to one of her "favorite L.A. restaurants," fully expecting the menu to contain nothing but an assortment of lettuces and corresponding fat-free dressings.

Then again, Reggie remembered reading somewhere that sashimi was widely hailed by many stars as a favorite diet food.

Gabe drank iced tea, coldly refusing Tyler's suggestion of a beer with his patented "I'm on the job and don't have time to dick around" look. "The guy knows your every move. He says he wants to punish you, and you want to go to an unsecured venue where anyone can get close. It's a bad idea." He sat back in his chair, as though the matter was closed.

Reggie expected Tyler to defend her case, but he rubbed his jaw pensively and looked at Natalie as though waiting for her opinion.

Weird. Since when did Tyler give a crap what Natalie thought, Reggie thought crabbily. She took another sip of her beer. Clearly, the stress of the day was catching up.

The waiter came over and Natalie started to order, but Reggie jumped in, too hungry to risk letting her dinner get messed up by Natalie's finicky food habits. After she requested her nigiri combo and miso soup, she nudged Gabe, who ordered a mountain of sushi and a plate of chicken teriyaki.

Tyler graciously motioned for Natalie to order. "I'll have the sashimi appetizer and a salad, no dressing."

Tyler glared at her for a split second, then smiled up to the waiter. "She'll also have an order of unagi, a California roll, and a spicy tuna hand roll. And a regular beer. I'll have the nigiri combo with tempura, and bring out edamame and gyoza for the table."

"I can't eat all that," Natalie said through clenched teeth. "I'll blow up like Jabba the Hutt."

"You ordered one ounce of fish and lettuce," Tyler snapped. "You can't live on that."

Reggie was fascinated, momentarily distracted from her personal safety issues by the interchange between her sister and Tyler.

As far as she knew, Tyler only tolerated Natalie because she was Reggie's sister.

Now Natalie, who meticulously controlled every morsel of food she ingested, had allowed someone else to order for her. And when the appetizers arrived, she actually ate a pork-filled, oil-sautéed potsticker.

"You're going to regret this when I get huge," Natalie muttered to Tyler around the dumpling. "Especially when I already ate a sandwich today. With mayonnaise!"

"You ate a sandwich?" Reggie said, stunned. "You don't eat bread."

"Half a sandwich," Tyler corrected, expertly wielding the chopsticks to proffer up another dumpling.

Reggie nearly fell off her chair.

Gabe busily chewed his own dumpling, clearly unconcerned by the bizarre interaction occurring across the table.

"Are you a secret chubby chaser?" Natalie said, giving Tyler a look that was positively gooney.

As though she and Gabe didn't exist, Tyler slid his arm across the back of her sister's chair and nuzzled his nose into the caramel-streaked hair covering her ear. Whatever he whispered made her emit a squealing giggle and slap him playfully on the shoulder.

Reggie cleared her throat pointedly. "So, Tyler, what do we do about tomorrow? Tickets have been on sale for months."

Tyler sat up straight, but didn't remove his arm from Natalie's chair. "I agree with Gabe," he said reluctantly. He held up his hand when Reggie opened her mouth to protest. "It's not safe. People get close to you when you sign their books—what if someone sneaks a weapon in?" He looked to Gabe for confirmation.

"Why can't we do security checks at the door?" Natalie

asked as she nibbled on another soybean pod. "Frisk people and stuff."

Tyler shook his head, leaning back as the waitress swapped empty appetizer plates for their entrées. "We're talking tomorrow. That doesn't give the bookstore enough time to hire a real security force. I'm assuming we'd want something better than the usual rent-a-cops."

Gabe nodded in agreement.

Reggie chewed sullenly at a piece of yellowtail sushi. "I'm willing to take the risk, so I don't see why it's a problem." She reached out and slid her hand along Gabe's thigh, reassured by the heat and muscled strength seeping through the fabric of his pants. "I know you'll protect me."

Gabe shook his head wearily. "But you're the only one I can protect. What about Natalie?"

Reggie noticed that Tyler's hand instinctively tightened over her sister's shoulder.

"What if this guy goes after the people close to you if he can't get to you?"

"He did kill Rex," Natalie pointed out around a mouthful of Ahi tuna.

Guilt and worry turned Reggie's sushi into a big rice cement ball in her gut. When had she become so selfish? It had never occurred to her that the people around her were in danger too. She would never forgive herself if anything happened to Natalie, or God forbid, Gabe, just because she was too afraid of disappointing fans and getting bad publicity.

"You're right," she said quietly. "I'm being stupid." She pushed her sushi over to Gabe, who obligingly went to work on her uneaten portion. To Tyler, she said, "How do we do this without angering the event organizers?"

It would be a major headache for the store to have to refund tickets and preordered books. Not to mention that it would reflect badly on Tyler when he tried to book future clients.

"I have an idea," Natalie interjected. "The sketchiest part is the book signing, right? That's the only time strangers get to actually approach you." At Reggie's nod, she continued, "The rest of the time you're on a stage. So what if we got a few more rent-a-cops to surround the podium area and you just presigned all of the books? Only the book signing is canceled, but fans still get your autograph, and the store keeps money from ticket and book sales."

Reggie wondered if she'd stumbled into some bizarro parallel universe when Tyler told Natalie she was the biggest creative genius he'd ever met.

It took more prodding to convince Gabe, but he'd finally, albeit reluctantly, agreed to their amended security plan.

"Think of it as a professional challenge," Reggie had joked. "When's the last time on this job you've had to really be on your toes?"

Gabe was only slightly mollified by the five additional security guards that flanked the demo stage. They all struck him as lazy and unobservant. One had even complained that he'd have to stand for the entire forty-five minutes of Reggie's presentation.

The way he saw it, he was on his own.

Even more irritating was Reggie's seemingly cavalier attitude about the whole thing, and he told her so.

"What do you want me to do?" she said as she directed the cooking assistants where to place her ingredients. "Curl up in a cave until this guy gets caught or gives up for real?"

"Sounds good to me." He ignored her glare. "You strike me as remarkably cheery for a woman who has a guy out there who wants to punish her."

"But I can also look on the bright side," she said with a grin. "Since the local press covered the incident yesterday, tickets for this event sold out, and they expect to move every single copy of my book." She tied an apron around her trim waist.

The sellout crowd was starting to file in. Mostly women,

as usual, but a larger than average number of younger men were in the mix. Guys who had seen the gossip and wanted to see whether Reggie was actually hot enough to merit her own stalker.

Judging from the looks she received, every man in the room thought she was.

Gabe's hands fisted at his sides as he fought the urge to wrap her up in his suit coat, hiding her luscious curves from fifty pairs of leering eyes. "If I didn't know you better," he said through clenched teeth, "I'd almost think you were grateful for the stalker and all the extra publicity he's gotten you."

Reggie, who was busy fixing her makeup, slowly lowered her lipstick and deliberately rubbed her lips together. "That was a really shitty thing to say." She snapped her purse shut. "And I'm going to try really hard to forget it."

Shame filled him, bringing heated color to his face. Fuck. This was why he sucked at relationships. Invariably he got upset and said things he didn't mean. "I'm sorry," he said softly. "I'm worried about you. You know that. And sometimes I don't think you take your safety seriously enough."

Her cold expression barely softened. "You can't blame me for trying to make the best of a crappy situation, Gabe. That's the kind of person I am. If I see an opportunity, I'll take it. Even if it means putting a positive spin on having a psycho follow me."

Before he could reply, the store manager motioned her that it was time to begin. As though a curtain came over her, her tense façade melted away, giving way to the bubbly smile millions of fans knew and loved.

Her rapid, effortless transformation gave him a slightly queasy feeling.

Reggie was a much better actress than he realized.

An hour later, Gabe stood within easy arm's reach of Reggie as she chatted with the store events manager. The crowd was dispersing quickly, and if they were disappointed that they couldn't get their books signed personally, they didn't show it.

Was their guy here? Gabe had scanned the crowd a hundred times looking for any sign that might point him in the right direction. An overly intense stare. Even a fake-looking beard or head of hair that could indicate a disguise.

He'd asked Reggie to keep an eye out for anyone she might recognize with no luck.

Then again, the stalker seemed to get off on contacting Reggie when she least expected it, when her whereabouts were supposed to be secret. This event had been scheduled and publicized for weeks. It would be too obvious for him to show up here.

His eyes locked on to someone approaching Reggie from behind—a man, about five-foot ten with a medium build and enough product in his dirty blond hair to present a fire hazard. His mouth was set in tight lines and his hand was outstretched, reaching for her arm.

A nanosecond later, Gabe had the guy's forearm in a vice grip behind his back and was grinding his face into the demo table.

"What the hell?" the guy yelled, his voice muffled as Gabe squashed his face into the Formica.

"Keep your hands off her," Gabe roared, Reggie's frantic voice barely registering over the pounding in his ears. Something about her tone penetrated the red haze before he snapped the guy's arm and he eased up, but just barely.

"I know him; you can let him go." Reggie placed one hand against Gabe's back, the other on the hand that still viciously gripped the other guy's arm. "Let him go, Gabe."

He did so reluctantly enough to convey the message that if the guy so much as breathed wrong, Gabe wouldn't hesitate to inflict more damage.

The guy shot Reggie a look of outrage, but apparently had enough sense to keep his mouth shut.

"Craig Ferguson, meet Gabe Bankovic." Neither offered a hand.

Turning to Gabe, she said in a falsely bright tone, "Craig is my ex-boyfriend, who you've heard about"—she swung around to Craig—"and Gabe is my bodyguard and . . ." Her voice trailed off and he heard her mumble something under her breath.

"Bodyguard?" Craig sounded surprised. Obviously he hadn't been keeping up on his ex's press clippings lately. "Since when do you need a bodyguard?"

"I've had some . . . unusual fan activity recently," Reggie replied.

"Hey, if you didn't like the stuff I sent—"

Gabe leaned forward menacingly. He didn't think Craig was their guy, but the way he came off, so arrogant and trying to play himself off as a badass, really pissed him off. Not to mention the fact that the guy was apparently so much of a pussy he couldn't handle it when his girlfriend's success rivaled his own.

"Hey"—Craig held up his hands and scrambled back—"I'm kidding!" He shot Reggie an indignant look. "How'd you hook up with Cro-Magnon man?"

Reggie gave him the short version of the stalker and his increasingly violent threats. Craig made appropriately sympathetic noises.

"Sorry to hear about your trouble. I was in town and wanted to say hi. Word around the network is that your new show is going to be a huge hit, and I wanted to say congratulations." Craig said the last part in the tone of someone who is sincerely happy for someone else's success, while simultaneously burning with envy that it is not his own.

Reggie smiled warmly up at Craig, impulsively drawing him close for a hug. Gabe ignored the tight knot in his belly as he watched the other man return the embrace.

It wasn't that he was jealous or threatened in any way by the little wuss. He just didn't like the idea that this man at one point had access to every silky inch of Reggie's body.

He wondered idly if Reggie would feel the same unpleasant burn the next time she saw Marly Chase on a magazine cover.

Reggie thanked Craig and excused herself to go speak with the event organizer, who looked very pleased with tonight's turnout.

Craig shook his head, a reluctant grin sliding across his face. "A stalker. If I know Reggie, she's turned this whole thing into a massive PR opportunity, hasn't she?" Without waiting for Gabe to answer, he said, "She looks all sweet and genuine, but underneath she knows how to turn almost any situation to her advantage." Though his assessment wasn't entirely complimentary, his tone was admiring.

"She doesn't strike me as manipulative," Gabe said.

"That's the beauty. She's also smart enough to keep it from the rest of us. Snaked her first show right out from under me, and I didn't even see it coming." Craig shook his head. "That's not fair of me to say. She has great appeal, and fans love her, there's no denying that. But she's a very savvy businesswoman." He shook his head and laughed ruefully. "Hell, I wouldn't put it past her to make the whole stalker thing up, or at least blow it out of proportion if she thought it could help her."

Craig's words nibbled at the back of Gabe's brain, feeding the little kernel of doubt Malcolm had planted last week about why certain aspects of this situation didn't add up.

He mentally shook himself. He was letting the remarks of an insecure dickhead feed into his own baggage.

Just then Reggie caught his eye from across the room. The sweet, tentative smile she sent him was softly uncertain and it almost brought him to his knees. His own lips curled in response. His gut, which he'd ignored for the past year, told him there was no way he'd be dumb enough to fall for the shrewd manipulator Craig had described.

Reggie was exactly what she appeared: sweet, smart, genuine, and driven. He had to trust himself on that. It scared the hell out of him to admit it, but he loved her too much not to.

Chapter Sixteen

"This doesn't make any sense." Gabe's warm hand rested on Reggie's shoulder as he read the latest e-mail sent by the stalker.

Fort the past week, he'd sent at least one a day. But instead of threats of violence, the e-mails were almost friendly in tone. Today's included an attachment, another picture of a lingerie-clad model with Reggie's face Photoshopped into it. Since they'd returned to San Francisco three days ago, it had gotten to the point where Reggie was afraid to turn on her computer for fear of what revolting thing she might receive.

"This guy should have revealed himself by now," Gabe continued, his hot breath dusting her ear.

Reggie turned away from the computer screen to face him, her breath catching a little at the sexy, rumpled picture he presented. His T-shirt and jeans were worn soft, and his dark eyes were heavy with sleep. It was after one A.M., and he'd been dozing on the couch when Reggie had called him into the office.

"Revealed himself?"

Gabe squatted down so he was at eye level with her and rested his hands on her thighs. "Stalkers aren't known for their discretion. Your guy obviously thinks he has some claim on you, some relationship, that he has the right to be jealous or threaten you because you're with me. Even if they keep their identity secret at the beginning, most stalkers will eventually try to make personal contact, because in his mind, you'll welcome that."

"You don't call that personal contact?" Reggie pointed her thumb over her shoulder, where the doctored photo was vibrantly displayed on her flat panel.

"It's unusual for him to remain anonymous this long." He straightened up, scratching his chin as though in deep thought. "I keep feeling like I'm missing something important, like the answer's right in front of me."

Reggie stretched and sighed. "I don't think we're going to find him tonight, and I'm beat."

He smiled distractedly and asked about her book.

"If I have a few more days like today, I should be able to hand in the last round of revisions before Thanksgiving." Thank God. The mere thought of sending off the final chapters made her shoulders lift. "It's easier to get work done when I'm home."

She moved easily into his arms for a kiss, tasting distraction on his lips.

"Do you mind if I poke around in your e-mail a little bit?"

She debated for a minute, scrambling to remember if there was anything embarrassing he might find. Then she shrugged. He might find some things about himself, but nothing she hadn't told him to his face. Other than that, it was mostly business and mundane daily correspondence.

Noticing her hesitation, he said, "Don't worry. I'll limit my snooping to the past few months," he said. "I want to take a look at who's writing you, maybe see if there are similarities in the language, anything suggestive you might have missed if you weren't expecting it from someone."

She nodded, leaning into his chest for one last squeeze before bed. "I also set up an account for Natalie on there too. It's all business-related stuff, but maybe there's something in there."

* * *

Gabe wiped the grit from his eyes, futilely trying to blink back moisture into his screen-scorched eyeballs. He'd searched through Reggie's e-mails, but once again came up blank. But he'd gone ahead and sent copies of the stalker's most recent e-mails to Malcolm for analysis, along with e-mails from Tyler, Max, and a handful of other male contacts he didn't recognize. He also gave Malcolm access to Natalie's account to see if there was a clue as to how the stalker was getting such detailed information on Reggie's schedule.

He hadn't heard anything yet on the previous e-mails, as Malcolm's hacking team was tied up tracking down a credit card fraud ring.

Other than getting more info on the e-mails, Gabe was not in a hurry to talk to his old friend anytime soon. Though he hadn't said it, Gabe had clearly heard the words, "You're a dumbass," in his friend's voice when he'd told Malcolm about his decision to stay with Reggie.

Still, Malcolm hadn't pulled any punches. "This is a bad decision, and I won't tell you otherwise," Malcolm had said curtly. "I have twenty guys I can call to do what you're doing. There's no reason you should be wasting your time when your skills could be put to much better use."

"I couldn't forgive myself if anything happened to her." Gabe had practically choked on the admission. "I can't quit till we find this guy."

"Yeah, you made a commitment and I respect that, but be careful you're not thinking with your little head."

Malcolm's blunt assessment still sat like a sack of rocks in his stomach. He could only hope that once the guy was caught and this was all over, Malcolm would still be willing to hire him back.

He put the finishing touches on his latest masterpiece, once again thanking his good fortune for those graphic design classes he'd taken a couple of years ago. At the time he'd hoped to incorporate them into his work, saving money on promotional materials for himself and his clients.

In the end, his design skills were remedial at best, but he could doctor up a photo like nobody's business. All it took was a high-speed Internet connection and an extensive collection of pornography was at his fingertips. Add in a little Photoshop, and Reggie became the star of any number of twisted fantasies.

If only he could share them with her. But now was not the time. For now he had to content himself with sending her the tamer photos. He knew better than to frighten her with what he really had in mind.

He was particularly proud of his latest work. The woman even looked like Reggie, with her big doe eyes and full mouth. Her body was similar, too—perky breasts, flat belly, and a full, lush ass. A masked man stood over her wielding an abnormally large dildo.

Maybe he wouldn't have to edit in Reggie's face. Which would be nice because the woman was wincing in pain, blobs of mascara smudged around her eyes, lipstick smeared across her chin as though she'd had a particularly hard time of it.

He copied the file to his flash stick for safekeeping.

He hoped the tokens he'd sent so far were driving the gorilla to distraction.

Bile curdled in his throat, searing his insides as it did every time he thought of that animal pawing at Reggie.

It hurt him, what he had to do to Reggie. Sometimes it nearly brought him to tears, to know that the perfect life he had planned for them—the creative genius and his muse—was not to be.

But she'd been unfaithful and was continuing to be so. Just today he'd seen her on the street, grinning up at the gorilla like a dirty slut as he pawed her perfect ass in the middle of the street.

But the gorilla would be gone soon.

He had to be patient. After enough time passed and Reggie let her guard down, he could finally make his move.

Grinning hugely at the camera, Reggie swept her arm to encompass the magnificent view behind her. "Welcome to *Simply Delicious, USA*. I'm Reggie Caldwell, and today I can't wait to show you around my hometown of San Francisco!"

She didn't have to fake a second of her enthusiastic intro. How could she be anything but deliriously happy? She was home, finally, and today was a perfect Bay Area fall day. Clear and sunny, their vantage in North Beach offered breathtaking views of the bay, the Golden Gate Bridge, and the verdant green of the Marin headlands.

Best of all, ever-watchful Gabe stood discreetly behind the cameraman giving her a look that said he couldn't wait to take her home and rip off her clothes.

She breezed through the establishing shots, winning an enthusiastic thumbs-up from Carrie. "Great energy, Reggie. Carry that over into tomorrow's segment."

Even though she was more than ready to finish up with location shoots and get back to some semblance of a normal life, she was excited for tomorrow's shoot. Unbeknownst to Gabe, she had a surprise planned.

Several weeks ago, she'd talked to Carrie about changing the San Francisco show topic. Originally, she was going to visit three of Chinatown's most renowned chefs. But Gabe and his reminiscing about his Croatian grandmother's cooking had given her a truly unique idea.

The Tadisch Grill was a landmark restaurant in San Francisco. Open since 1849, it was the oldest restaurant in the city. Although it served primarily traditional American seafood, the restaurant had its roots as a coffee and sandwich stand started by two Croatian immigrants. Since then, it had been run by a succession of Croatian families.

He didn't know it, but he was going to join her on air and help them create a traditional Croatian feast, complete with the Prsurate he so loved.

As the crew started the process of packing up, she walked over to Gabe and caught him around the waist. She buried her face into the open neck of his shirt, the spicy, masculine scent of him sending a burst of warmth between her thighs.

Reaching a hand around his neck, she tugged his head down until his ear was level to her mouth. "I want to take you home and lick you all over," she whispered, giggling as ruddy color flooded his face.

She snuck a glance at her watch. Oh yeah, they definitely had time to sneak in a quickie before she got back to work on her latest round of revisions.

Gabe slid his hand under her jacket, tracing a path of heat up her spine.

The shrill cry of her cell phone erupted from her pocket. Oops. She hadn't realized she'd left it on. "Good thing . . ." she scanned the caller ID screen, "Tyler didn't call five minutes ago."

Stepping back from Gabe with an apologetic grin, she lifted the phone to her ear.

"I have great news," Tyler boomed.

"You and Natalie are moving in together," she teased. After their dinner in L.A., Natalie had filled in the details on the sudden change in her relationship with Tyler. Reggie had been nervous at first, not sure if it was a smart move for either one of them. But Natalie's giddy happiness and blooming self-confidence—not to mention the way Tyler looked at her sister like she was the most perfect creation he'd ever seen—quickly put Reggie's mind at ease.

Tyler choked out a flustered reply. "Wha—no, well, not now, but maybe . . ." He cleared his throat as Reggie stifled a laugh at her usually cool, glib publicist's loss of composure. "The network wants you to do their live holiday special."

She nearly dropped the phone. "You're kidding." Every

year the Cuisine Network aired an hour-long, live Christmas Eve special with their top hosts. Even better, once the live broadcast was over, the show was syndicated to network affiliates and shown on regular network television.

All of the hosts participating were Cuisine Network veterans, and most had at least three different series to boast of. It was almost unheard of for a relatively new talent, with just a few seasons of one show under her belt, to be invited to participate.

Dazed with excitement, she asked Tyler to e-mail her all the details and call her later. She was simply too excited to absorb any pertinent information.

The Cuisine Network wanted her to be a star. They were banking on her to be as huge a draw as their other big-name hosts. This was it. She was finally going to make up for all the years she struggled to make ends meet as a personal chef, all the years she felt like a loser and wondered if she'd been insane to give up a steady, lucrative career in accounting to pursue her passion for food. Even her mother, who thought her show was barely a rung above a cable access program, would have to admit that an appearance on network television connoted some measure of success.

Almost immediately her breath accelerated and her heart began to pound. Was this what an anxiety attack felt like?

What if she screwed up? What if the other chefs looked down at her for her self-taught credentials and comparatively simple food preparation? What if she messed up the entire show by spilling on herself or someone else during the live broadcast?

"Reggie." Gabe wrapped a steadying arm around her. "Are you okay? You're white. Did something happen? Is someone hurt?" He started to pull her over to a folding chair, but she shook her head and took a steadying, head-clearing, heart-slowing breath.

Leaning into him to steady herself, she said, "No, it's great news, actually." She went on to explain that one of the original chefs had to cancel and the network wanted her to fill his spot.

His eyebrows drew into a thick, dark line and familiar tense lines bracketed his sensual lips. Of course he wouldn't be as excited as she, as he had no idea what this meant. "This is a great opportunity," she said quickly, ticking off the list of celebrity chefs participating in the live Christmas Eve broadcast.

But the more information she gave, the more cold and closed Gabe's expression grew. Until he appeared the same man who had walked into her apartment nearly two months ago—aloof, indifferent, uncaring.

Raw panic snaked down her spine. What had she done now? "Why are you so upset? I thought you'd be happy for me." She hated the whiny note that crept into her voice.

Her body felt cold where he'd removed his supporting arm. "I am happy for you," he said quietly. "What I'm not so happy about is canceling the reservations for our Christmas trip I just made."

Oh, crap. Her stomach dropping somewhere around her ankles, Reggie raised a placating hand. "I'm sorry, I forgot, but we never confirmed those plans and—"

He barked a humorless laugh. "Right. I'll remember from now on verbal commitments don't count unless they're programmed into your Palm Pilot, and even then they're negotiable."

"That's unfair," she protested feebly, but deep down she knew he was right. He'd watched her cancel personal plans right and left this week as she worked to finish her book and did phone interviews to promote the upcoming season of *Simply Delicious*.

But what choice had she had? Her book was on a deadline, and both Tyler and Natalie had worked their asses off to get the interviews scheduled.

Then she looked at Gabe, his face set in tense lines of resignation. That awful look that said he was disappointed not just in her for casually dismissing their plans, but in himself for expecting anything better from her.

"You'll come to New York with me," she said, her voice cracking. "We'll spend a few extra days in Manhattan."

"And I'll see you in between filming and publicity events," he said quietly.

She didn't bother to deny it.

"I'm sorry," she said, staring into his face for some sign of softness, forgiveness, patience.

"I understand," he said.

She feared he understood too much.

Gabe paced Reggie's living room like a caged tiger. This was but one of the practical problems that came with getting personally involved with a client: no escape.

With the freaky pervert still at large, he couldn't possibly leave her alone. A solitary, head-clearing run or beer at the bar around the corner was out of the question.

Sometimes working on his own really sucked the big one.

Reggie had tried to cheer them both up on the walk back to her place, brightly listing all of the fun things they could do in and around New York at Christmastime.

He'd managed some semienthusiastic grunts.

She'd looked at him with big, sad brown eyes, chewing on that plump lower lip of hers. "Try to understand," she'd said for about the fifteenth time.

"I do," he'd responded every time.

"Then stop looking at me like that."

He'd schooled his face into an impassive mask, but that only seemed to upset her more.

Truth was, he did understand. Completely. Her career was on a slingshot trajectory, and if she could hang on and capitalize on all the opportunities thrown her way, she'd be set.

For a while anyway.

Then she would have to go into career maintenance mode,

make sure her face was out there enough, get involved in other ventures to expand her "brand."

In the short time he'd worked with her and around others making careers out of food television, he'd learned plenty about how this business worked. How demanding, competitive, and thankless it could be.

For those who wanted to achieve great success, they had to work at it, one hundred percent of the time.

And Reggie wanted that success. He didn't fault her for it. He knew how hard she'd worked to achieve this level of fame. Though hailed as Cuisine Network's "overnight success," he knew how much she'd struggled for the first five years, scraping by, listening to the harsh doubts of family and friends. She deserved every bit of fame and fortune she received.

And he was acting like a chick, pouting because she had to cancel plans they hadn't even really confirmed.

How many times had he done that to women when he was in the forces? Granted, when a mission came up, he'd had no choice but to go. At the time, if a woman had uttered a single word of complaint, it was grounds for immediate dumping.

Shit. He of all people should understand how work commitments get in the way of romance.

Funny how things worked out. For his entire adult life, marriage and family had loomed amorphously off in the horizon, like someplace he wanted to get to someday, but was in no particular hurry to do so. It wasn't that he had commitment issues, as many of his past girlfriends had accused, it was simply that he hadn't met a woman he could imagine spending forever with.

Until now. A woman so busy and committed to her own career, she probably wouldn't be able to pencil in a wedding for the next five years. But, he acknowledged, he loved Reggie enough to wait twice that long.

He had no choice but to suck it up and apologize, and after that, wait patiently on the sidelines for whatever scraps of time she could devote to him.

Something niggled at his consciousness—an interview he'd read of an entrepreneur who'd started several successful businesses from the ground up. His advice to other aspiring entrepreneurs? "Don't do it, unless you literally can't imagine being happy doing anything else."

Right now, loving Reggie felt about like that. Part of him wondered if he was setting himself up for misery, even as he faced the terrifying knowledge that he'd never be happy without her.

He started down the hallway to her office, interrupted halfway by his cell phone.

Malcolm.

Gabe greeted him curtly, eager to get off the phone and apologize to Reggie before his sulk had the chance to inflict too much damage.

But Malcolm's next words had his immediate attention. "I've got news on the e-mails. You're not going to like it."

Reggie's office door swung open so hard it smashed into the wall, making her jump in surprise. Spinning in her chair, she saw Gabe looming in the doorway, and one look told her his mood hadn't improved since they'd come home.

If anything, it was worse. His jaw was tight, an angry tendon pulsing near his ear. His dark eyes were icy obsidian chips, chilling her.

Her own temper boiled in response. What right did he have to be so angry with her? Didn't he understand how important the holiday special was to her? If he really loved her, wouldn't he be happy for her success?

She never would have guessed he could be so selfish. A creeping, sick feeling of doubt consumed her as she wondered whether she'd actually fallen in love with the real man or a heroic fantasy lover she'd created in her head.

She opened her mouth to tell him off, but his flat, almost toneless voice pierced the air.

"I know about the e-mails."

Relief flooded her. He wasn't mad at her! He was mad at whoever sent them. Then that sick feeling doubled in force as she wondered which of her friends or acquaintances had stooped to sending her creepy and threatening communications over the past two months. "Who—" she licked her lips nervously, almost afraid to hear the answer—"Who is it?"

His harsh grin didn't reach his eyes. In fact, he wasn't grinning at all, but snarling whitely against his tan skin. "Like you don't know."

Shaking her head mutely, she watched as he advanced. Instinctively, she pushed her chair back on its rollers, halting with a thud as she came up against her desk.

He was big and tough and burly and intimidating, and right now, Gabe looked downright scary. Every sinew coiled with rage. The muscles of his arms and shoulders actually strained against the cotton broadcloth of his shirt, and a vein pounded so fiercely in his neck she feared he was at risk for an aneurysm.

Most frightening of all was that his fury appeared to be inexplicably aimed at *her*.

"What I can't figure out," he spat the words as though they were poisonous, "is why you would bother hiring me in the first place."

What was he talking about? "Natalie made me hire you," she stuttered.

"Did you think I would give more validity to your story?" His Southern drawl thickened, and for once she didn't find it sexy. He reached her chair and leaned over her, effectively pinning her in with his arms braced on either side of the desk. "Hiring me cost you a lot of money." His cold whisper sent a shiver through her core. "But I suppose you'd do anything to buy publicity."

Struck speechless, Reggie could only stare. He'd lost his mind. That was the only explanation. He said he had intense emotions. Maybe that was his code way of saying emotionally unstable. As in schizophrenic. Or manic-depressive. Or otherwise certifiable.

"And I bet when the two of you got tired of this whole stalker thing, Natalie could oh so conveniently dig up my past and you could ride the scandal of having hired a brutal thug as your personal security guard."

"What do you mean, stalker *thing*?"

"I talked to Malcolm. The jig is up," he growled. "I should have known when you weren't even scared, when all you could talk about was all the press and the boost to your sales." His eyes raked her with such caustic contempt, she thought she smelled her skin burn. "But you swung your sweet little ass in my face and I fell for every single bit of it."

The soundtrack from *Psycho* rang in her head. "I have no idea what you're talking about," she choked around the lump of anxiety clogging her throat.

"I know everything, Reggie. I know you faked the whole thing."

It was so ludicrous, so patently ridiculous, for a moment the words didn't even register. Then reality slowly sunk in.

Gabe, the man she'd fallen in love with, who claimed to be in love with her, was accusing her of faking being stalked to gain more publicity. Whatever Malcolm had told him had convinced him, and based on his cold expression, he didn't doubt his friend for a minute.

"I don't know what you think you know," she said, her voice shaking, "but I would never lie about something like this just to get attention."

He straightened up to his full imposing height and pointed an accusing finger at her computer screen. "Then explain how every single e-mail you've received in the last week was generated from this computer."

"We didn't get back until three days ago!"

"Natalie should have covered her tracks a little better," he snapped. "What about Tyler? Was he in on it too?"

"You're crazy."

"Am I? Then how come Malcolm can trace every other

e-mail to the exact Internet cafés in the exact cities where you were working on the road?"

Her heart stopped, then throbbed painfully in her chest. The stalker had been closer more often than she'd even realized, and they'd had no idea. Which meant he could be anywhere, anytime, undetected. Was he somehow able to get into her apartment when she wasn't here to send e-mails? God, her brain couldn't even wrap itself around that right now.

"I don't know, Gabe. Maybe he's some kind of computer wiz, and this is a way to get your experts"—she couldn't resist adding sarcastic air quotes—"off his trail."

Massive arms folded across his chest, the hard lines of his face so cold and imposing, he was almost unrecognizable as the passionate lover who'd just this morning whispered he loved her as he buried himself in her. "Or maybe," he replied, his voice once again void of any emotion, "the most obvious answer is the correct one. Except for the initial mailing, every single communication is easily traced back to you."

"What about the phone call?" Reggie said, desperately reaching for any shred of evidence that might help him realize the sheer insanity of his accusations. "How could I have faked that?"

"Easy," he scoffed. "You or your sister easily could have put some sap of an intern or production assistant up to playing a tape." He reached over her shoulder for her computer mouse so quickly she flinched.

"Don't worry," he sneered, "I don't stoop to beating women."

The sound of the mouse click echoed like a gunshot in the room, and she craned her neck to see what he was doing. "Adobe Photoshop. How convenient."

"I got it for designing my personal chef menus," she protested. This was unreal. Obviously, he thought she'd used it to doctor up her own obscene photos! Her stomach felt like she'd eaten about ten pounds of rotten meat.

He leaned over her once again, and now she could see

through the icy blackness of his eyes underneath to the raging storm of grief, pain, and betrayal. "I wanted to believe in you so bad." Tears burned in her eyes at the slight quiver in his voice. "If you had just told me the truth, I could have overlooked everything.

"But what really kills me," he said almost casually, as though she hadn't said anything, "is that you were stupid enough to admit your scheme in an e-mail to Natalie." He made a scolding sound. "Really, you should know better in this day and age to leave any kind of electronic trail."

What on earth was he talking about?

"You're a great little actress, Reggie, I'll give you that, and your fake look of confusion is almost convincing." He ground his palms against his eyes for a moment. "Or who knows. Maybe you were so sure I'd never figure it out that you don't even remember what I'm talking about."

He clicked on her screen once more, this time logging into Natalie's e-mail account and quickly pulling up a message. One Reggie had sent from Santa Fe.

He read her message back to her:

"With things so quiet, I don't have an excuse to keep Gabe around. If only my little stalker friend would send one of his special messages, maybe Gabe would forget all about this other job offer.

Galvanized by rage, Reggie practically exploded from her desk chair. "That is your big piece of evidence? A sarcastic e-mail I wrote to my sister when I thought you were going to leave?" This was too much. She knew he had trust and intimacy issues, but this was ridiculous. "If I was so intent on keeping you around, why would I encourage you to take Malcolm's offer? Why would I tell Natalie to start calling other security firms?"

"I don't know, Reggie, and I really don't care."

He started to turn away.

"How can you do this?" she demanded, her voice cracking. "How can you tell me that you love me and think I'd be capable of this?"

"I fell in love with a lie. I was just too stupid to see it."

Reggie stood, shaking, as Gabe walked slowly to the door. He'd almost made it to the front door before she caught him. "Gabe, don't." She grabbed his arm, her heart bursting in her chest. "If you just listen you'll see there's another explanation."

His eyes killed her, cold once again, looking through her as though she were dead. "I'll have Marjorie send you a final invoice."

Chapter Seventeen

Two hours later, Gabe found himself at his sister's apartment. After he left Reggie's he'd started walking aimlessly, with no idea where he was going. Eventually he ended up here, at the flat his sister and brother-in-law kept in Pacific Heights.

Ironically, it was less than half a mile away from Reggie's place.

Brian, a partner at a venture capital firm, had made an assload of money before the Internet went bust, and he and Adrienne spent most of the time in their huge house in Woodside. But they kept the three-bedroom apartment in the city for the times they craved a more cosmopolitan pace.

Back when he was still in the military, he'd often stayed here when he was on leave, and in the year he'd worked for Malcolm, he'd used it when he was in San Francisco on business.

He fumbled for the spare key he always kept on his keychain and let himself in, breathing a slow sigh of relief when it appeared Adrienne and Brian weren't in residence.

Not that he didn't love his sister, or even his brother-in-law, for that matter. But right now he couldn't face their probing questions. Fortunately, he'd kept several changes of clothes and a full array of toiletries here, since he hadn't had the presence of mind to pack up his stuff before he left Reggie's apartment.

An image invaded his brain, one of Reggie smiling shyly as she shoved aside a pile of underwear to make room for his boxers and socks.

Slumping down in an overstuffed armchair, Gabe fought the onslaught of tears threatening to choke him. Ridiculous that the memory of his boxer briefs nestled against her delicate, lacy panties made him want to bawl like a baby.

God had he ever fucked up.

Once again he'd thrown his career away over a woman. He'd been taken in and let his emotions get involved; now he was suffering the consequences.

He scrambled to hold on to the icy numbness that had settled in as he wandered aimlessly around the city. He didn't want to feel, didn't want to face the fact that he'd fallen, fallen completely, stupidly, balls out in love with a liar.

She'd *lied* to him.

Even now part of him struggled to find a way not to believe it.

But what choice did he have?

The evidence was all there, in black and white, no matter that his heart screamed that she couldn't be that big a liar.

Hadn't he learned the hard way not to be led by his heart or other interested organs? He was a hothead, he knew that, knew he had to be more careful than most to evaluate a situation coolly, calmly, rationally.

And though it felt like swallowing glass to admit it, the evidence Malcolm presented had only one rational conclusion.

If he hadn't been so blinded by lust, he would have seen it sooner. The pattern of escalation was all off. The timing of incidents was just too perfect. And the way the stalker seemed to know just enough, but not too much, about Reggie's whereabouts stunk of Natalie's involvement.

What if there's someone else, someone who could get the information, someone you never suspected?

No. He could drive himself crazy tilting at windmills, but Malcolm had presented the facts in indisputable detail. Gabe knew his friend was one of the best at gathering intelligence, and Gabe knew he wouldn't have come to the conclusion that Reggie and her sister were behind everything if he hadn't been completely certain. Even so, Gabe had protested, questioned every piece of evidence his friend had presented, desperately searching for another explanation.

In the end, Malcolm had informed him with deep regret that there was no other viable explanation.

He didn't know how long he sat there in the fading November light, staring at the ceiling as tears burned like acid down his cheeks.

"Reggie, you have to calm down," Natalie frantically met Tyler's anxious gaze.

Cupping her hand over the receiver, she whispered, "She's hysterical. I can't figure out what's going on. Something really bad is happening." Tears welled as all she heard from the other end were Reggie's garbled sobs. "She never gets like this, not even when the stalker killed Rex."

As Tyler pressed a soft kiss to her forehead and left the office to give her privacy, Natalie felt her breathing accelerate dangerously and scolded herself to keep it together. She might have been the more dramatic of the two, but it would do Reggie no good at all if Natalie lost her shit too.

By focusing really, really hard, Natalie was able to make out about one word in five. "He's gone," "left," "liar," "e-mails." Nothing made any sense.

It didn't sound like anyone had died, and the stalker hadn't attacked or injured her in any way. From what Natalie could understand, this had something to do with Gabe. The only course of action was to listen patiently and make appropriate noises to assure Reggie that she was listening, even if she couldn't understand a damn thing through Reggie's uncharacteristic hysteria.

Finally, after about ten minutes, the sobs had faded to hic-cupping gulps, and Reggie seemed capable of stringing more than two intelligible words together at a time.

As she finally pieced together what had happened, Natalie felt her blood begin to boil. "He thinks we faked it?" Tyler shuffled back into the office, setting a diet soda in front of her with an inquiring look.

"Yes," Reggie gasped. For a second, Natalie feared her sis-ter would dissolve again. But Reggie took a deep, fortifying breath and blew her nose. "To get publicity. He thinks we took the initial mailing and decided to run with it. He said if the stalker was real, he would have escalated by now and tried to approach me in person or attack me or something." Reggie's wet swallow was audible through the phone. "Like he wanted me to be hurt or something."

Natalie slumped back into her chair, hating the sensation of helplessness that gripped her. Reggie was always the strong one. Whether struggling with a new career, facing a bad breakup, or dealing with their mother's incessant criti-cism, Reggie seemed to have an unending capacity to pick herself up, dust herself off, and get on with her life.

But now she sounded . . . broken.

A trickle of panic crept up her spine as she realized their roles had reversed. For her entire life she'd relied on Reggie to help her out of any number of tight spots, had always known that when she got in a jam, big sister would bail her out, no matter how much Natalie acted like an ungrateful bitch.

As she listened to her sister on the other line, struggling not to fall apart and failing miserably, Natalie realized what a huge burden she'd placed on Reggie's shoulders for all these years.

"It's okay, Reg," Natalie said in a soothing, nurturing tone she'd never known she possessed, "I'm coming over and we'll figure out how to get through this."

* * *

By the time Natalie arrived with shopping bags full of Ben and Jerry's, Mallomars, and red wine, Reggie had momentarily set aside her grief and was indulging in a fit of raging, healthy temper.

"Can you fucking believe him?" she cried as she opened the door at Natalie's knock.

Natalie's eyes widened at the abruptness of her greeting or at her unusual use of profanity, or perhaps both.

Reggie didn't fucking care. It felt good to say that word, even in her head. And other words too. Like asshole. Or better yet, fucking asshole.

"Why would anyone make up a stalker?" she ranted as Natalie rummaged around in her kitchen and returned bearing two pints of ice cream, a spoon stuck in each. She passed Reggie the Chubby Hubby and set chocolate low-fat yogurt down for herself. Natalie made another trip, returning with an open bottle of cabernet, two tumblers, and the Mallomars.

Reggie poured almost half the bottle into her glass and gulped it like soda. She chased it with a bite of ice cream, but the rich vanilla mixed with chocolate-covered pretzels congealed on her tongue, nearly making her gag.

But the wine, she discovered, went down silky smooth.

Her rage continued through the first glass, egged on by Natalie as they called Gabe every foul name they could think of and labeled him a paranoid nut job.

But midway through the next glass she started to get maudlin, and by the third she was close to weeping and berating herself for ever thinking she and Gabe could have worked. "It's better this way," she said sullenly, "him ending it before I could mess it up."

She shook off Natalie's protests. "I can't have a boyfriend right now. I have too many obli . . . obla . . ." Her wine-thick tongue tripped over the word and she gave up. "I have too much to do. And Gabe, it's like he sucks up all my energy. He never would have been cool with waiting around until I had time to spend with him. So it's good this way," she said with drunken optimism, determined to see a bright side if it killed her. "Now I can be pissed at him because it's his fault, and I won't have to blame myself later for screwing things up with the guy I wanted to marry."

Natalie leaned over and caught her in a tight hug. Reggie buried her face in her slender shoulder. "I'm so sorry, Reg." The heartfelt sympathy in her sister's voice was enough to send her right back into the pit of despair.

"How could he think I would lie like that?" she sobbed. "What kind of person does he think I am?"

That was the real kicker. That even after she'd opened herself up to him, let him see the hopes and fears that really drove her, he turned around and twisted it all against her in his mind until somehow she was the villain. A woman capable of deceit, the kind of woman who would use anyone and any situation to get ahead.

Her insides shattered into a million tiny fragments.

She sent Natalie back to Tyler's shortly after, assuring her she'd be fine and needed to be alone. Natalie protested, reminding her that the stalker was still out there somewhere.

Emotionally wasted, Reggie couldn't summon the least smidgeon of fear. "I changed the alarm code. I'll be fine."

Besides, maybe the pervert will break in and put me out of my misery.

After Natalie left, Reggie flipped on the TV in a vain attempt to drown out the lonely echo in her head and worked her way steadily through another bottle of wine. If only Gabe would listen, really listen to her, he would see that he was wrong, she was incapable of the things he'd accused.

Before she knew it, the phone was in her hand and her last sober brain cell was screaming at her that drunk dialing was never a good idea. Ignoring it, she summoned up her considerable liquor courage and entered the number for Gabe's emergency cell.

"This is Bankovic," he muttered as though she'd woken

him out of a deep sleep or he'd had indulged in a few cocktails himself.

"Is everything all right?" his voice cracked over the line,
startling her out of her frozen silence.

"Gabe, it's me," she whispered feebly. "I just want to talk
to you."

"Are you in immediate physical danger?"

Goosebumps formed on her bare arms at his icy tone.
"No," she whispered, barely audible.

"Don't contact me again."

Chapter Eighteen

Reggie jumped as Max snapped his fingers in front of her nose. "Sorry. I spaced out for a minute."

Max sighed, shuffling and restacking the notes scattered around her coffee table. "It's fine. We're almost done here, anyway."

They were going through the list of potential show topics for the upcoming season. Even though she wasn't scheduled to start shooting again until March, she didn't mind getting ahead of the game.

Besides, since she'd handed in final revisions on her book and wrapped shooting on *Simply Delicious, USA* nearly a month ago, she needed something to fill the hours.

Anything to keep her mind off of him.

Which was why she'd invited Max over to review show ideas even though she was leaving for New York tomorrow for the Cuisine Network's Live Christmas bash.

Sure, she still had to test her recipe for the live Christmas Eve special, wrap presents and deliver them to Natalie for distribution since she was missing Christmas, and pack.

But who needed to sleep?

Or go to bed at all, when most nights she lay awake, staring at the ceiling, feeling hollow as a jack-o'-lantern. Like someone had scraped out her insides with an ice cream scoop.

She walked Max to the door, taken aback when he pulled

her into an awkward embrace. Max wasn't generally the most touchy-feely guy. Still, it felt nice to be held by a man, even if he was her gay producer. She leaned into him, wrinkling her nose at the scent of expensive, potent cologne. Gabe had always smelled perfect, like dryer sheets and soap.

She sniffed harder, driving the memory of Gabe's scent from her brain.

"You need to take better care of yourself, Reggie," Max admonished.

Smiling feebly, she stepped out of his arms. "I'm fine. And now that the stalker seems to have relented, it's one less thing I have to stress about."

As though to mock her, since Gabe ripped her apart she hadn't heard one word from the pervert. Zip. Nada. Zilch. As though he was playing into Gabe's assertion that it was all some big scam.

"And I'm saving a boatload of money not paying for full-time security." *That's it, Reggie, always look on the bright side, no matter how dim.* It was true, though. Over Natalie's protests, she'd refused to hire another full-time security person, but had given in when Natalie insisted that she at least have someone escort her to public appearances.

Otherwise, she made do with friends walking her home and having her neighbors be on the lookout for any weirdos.

Max reached for the doorknob.

"Wait," she cried, rushing to enter the security code for her alarm. That was one procedure she hadn't abandoned: setting the alarm every time she entered her apartment, whether she was alone or not. Even though the stalker had laid off, she wasn't completely foolish.

"Sorry. Wouldn't want to summon the cavalry," Max said in an odd, breathless tone. "Especially now that your goon has abandoned you."

Turning, she got the oddest sensation that Max had been staring at her ass. But now his eyes were pinned firmly, innocently on her face.

Abandoned. What a perfect word choice. She wished Max Merry Christmas and locked the door behind him.

"This is really how you want to spend Christmas?"

Gabe tilted his head against the back of the overstuffed armchair and met Adrienne's irritated gaze. He took a sip from his fourth—or was it fifth?—scotch. Who cared. He wasn't working today, anyway. The CEO he'd been hired to protect, a friend of Brian's, was safe at home and well guarded by his domestic security staff.

"You'd rather sit here by yourself, drinking yourself into a stupor, than come with us to Brian's sister's house."

Gabe took another sip of scotch, pretending to consider the two options. Spend Christmas Eve by himself getting plowed, or go to his brother-in-law's sister's house where he'd have to act civilized and make small talk with someone else's family.

No contest.

"Yep, I'll be fine. I even have a Hungry Man turkey dinner waiting in the freezer. Besides," he said, flicking on the fifty-two-inch plasma TV mounted on the wall, "it's too late now, anyway."

"Really, we'll wait if you want to come."

Even though Brian waited at the door with her coat, Adrienne didn't seem inclined to leave. She stared down at him, like if she held his gaze long enough, her powers of mind control would convince him to get his ass out of the chair and into the shower.

"Hi everyone, I'm Reggie Caldwell. Welcome to *Simply Delicious*."

Adrienne gasped and Gabe instinctively lifted the remote, thumb frozen over the channel up button.

Caught red fingered.

"You're pathetic, you know that?" Adrienne said, her voice full of sympathy.

Didn't he know it. Crying in his scotch while he watched on TV the woman who'd pulverized his heart.

He felt the comforting warmth of his sister's hand on his shoulder as she stood next to the chair, both riveted by Reggie's face on the screen.

"She looks so nice on TV," Adrienne murmured. "And the way you talked about her . . . it's hard to believe she'd do what you said."

His thumb punched down hard on the remote, not letting up until the screen flashed the speed and noise of motocross racing on ESPN. "Not the first time I've made a bad decision," he said curtly.

Leaning down to kiss him on the cheek, Adrienne said good-bye and left him to his wallowing.

Inexorably, the satellite box tuned back to the Cuisine Network, just in time for the live Christmas Eve celebrity bash.

His throat swelled like he'd swallowed a softball when he saw her, wholesome good looks emphasized by her tight leaf green sweater.

I can't believe she's capable of the things you said. Christ, when he looked at her, he couldn't believe it either. Didn't want to.

He grabbed the bottle of single malt from the end table, this time not even bothering with ice or a glass. It was the liquor that made his eyes sting and his throat hitch, not the sight of Reggie, her lush lips spread in a smile that didn't quite reach her eyes.

Not Reggie, who, when he focused through the alcohol haze, looked thinner than he remembered, her rounded cheekbones sharpened into high relief, her collarbone standing out above the V-neck of her sweater.

For a split second, he allowed concern to ooze through. Shit, if she looked that thin on TV, what did she look like in person? And now that he looked closer, he could see the tired, unhappy lines that bracketed her mouth, even as she struggled to keep up her bright, cheerful mask.

Panic clogged his throat, the way it had more than once

over the past month. Panic that he'd been completely, horribly wrong.

He was actually reaching for his cell phone when she chortled at another chef's comment. Any soft emotions he might have nurtured fled. He took another sullen gulp of the scotch. *Look at her. Smiling, laughing.* He was kidding himself thinking she'd suffered for a second over their split. She was exactly where she wanted to be, and he was an idiot if he wasted any time worrying about her.

A week after the live Cuisine Network Christmas Eve special aired, Reggie was back in San Francisco. A mere month and a half ago, she'd envisioned spending New Year's Eve having wild, hedonistic sex on the beach with Gabe. Instead, she was in rainy San Francisco, alone and dateless. At least she was working instead of sitting at home crying her way through another bottle of cabernet.

"And now we put the finishing touch on the filet mignon with Gorgonzola Madeira sauce." She discreetly scratched behind her ear as she sprinkled parsley across the plate. The headset mic itched like crazy, but she had to wear it if she wanted to be heard above the crowd gathered for the Save the Bay Fund's annual New Year's Eve Gala.

Reggie was just one of several local celebrities putting in an appearance tonight. Having nothing better to do, she'd offered at the last minute to do a cooking demo and had also donated a private cooking lesson and a chance to attend a taping of *Simply Delicious* to the silent auction.

She smiled aimlessly out into the crowd, unable to distinguish any faces with the spotlight beating down into her face. Max was here somewhere. And Natalie was out there, she knew, draped in a sexy turquoise spaghetti strap BCBG gown. Along with her favorite accessory—a smoking-hot, tuxedo-clad Tyler.

Waving one last time at the crowd, Reggie absently wiped her hands on her chef's smock. Normally she would have been as excited as Natalie to dress up and go all out on hair and makeup, but this year she was glad she had an excuse not to.

Frumpy smock, check. Basic black pants and sensible shoes, check. The blah ordinariness of her outfit more than matched her incessantly bleak mood.

She stepped down from the stage, discreetly trailed by the female security guard she'd hired for the evening. Working her way through the throng, she found herself suddenly blocked by a wall of hard, male chest.

And suddenly she wished passionately that she was wearing a slinky cocktail dress, sexy stilettos, and a fresh coat of lip gloss when she looked up to see that the chest belonged to none other than Gabe.

God, he looked good. Mile-wide shoulders encased in black gabardine, a lock of dark hair spilling over his forehead.

Pain sliced through her, so sharp she couldn't speak for several seconds. She stared up at him like an idiot, swallowing convulsively as her throat went as dry as Death Valley.

"Gabe," she finally managed in a feeble croak, barely audible above the low roar of the crowd.

She met his dark gaze and felt like she was dying, crumbling inside as she simultaneously fought the urge to heave herself into his arms and never let go or knee him in the groin for making her feel so hideous.

His lips were set in tight lines, and his eyes were full of grief and torment. *He missed her too.*

Tell me you're sorry, she thought frantically, trying to telepathically project her thoughts to his brain. *I'll forgive you, I'll take you back no questions asked. All you have to say is you miss me and you're sorry.*

Instead, he blinked, and when his eyes opened they were flat, black, revealing nothing. He nodded curtly and made to move past her.

"Wait," she grabbed frantically at his arm, withering inside as he pulled it gently but deliberately from her grasp.

"I'm working." He tipped his chin in the direction of a

paunchy, tux-clad man with salt-and-pepper hair a few feet to his right.

"Yeah, me too," she said stupidly, then stepped aside.

"Is everything all right, Ms. Caldwell?" Jill, the bodyguard she'd hired for the night, was at her left elbow. Unlike Gabe, who seemed to suck all the oxygen out of any room he entered, Jill was so quiet and unassuming, Reggie forgot for a moment that she was right next to her.

And had no doubt witnessed Gabe's humiliating brush-off.

Was everything all right? Let's see. She was starting the year off with a lacerated heart, a bruised ego, and, oh yeah, a crazed fan who, although he hadn't made any moves lately, might very well be waiting for the opportunity to "punish" her.

But on the bright side, she'd lost at least ten pounds in the last month, and even her mother told her how thin she'd looked on the live Christmas special.

Assuring Jill she was fine, she set off to find Natalie and Tyler. She had to get out of here. As though caught in a tractor beam, her gaze kept landing on Gabe. Now that she knew he was here, she couldn't seem to lose track of him no matter how hard she tried.

He seemed to have no problem ignoring her.

Reggie was sure that if she looked down at her smock, she'd actually see blood bubbling out of the left side of her chest.

"Reggie, that was fabulous." Max dashed up, wrapped an arm around her waist, and pressed a sloppy kiss to her cheek. Jeez, a few glasses of champagne and he was loving on everybody.

Jill stiffened at her side.

"It's okay," Reggie reassured her and performed a quick introduction.

"Was that Gabe the gorilla I saw you with?" Max asked, lips pursing as though his champagne had just turned to cat's piss.

Reggie nodded tiredly. "I can't believe how much it hurt to see him."

She took Max's dark look for one of sympathy, then excused herself to renew her search for Natalie, who had also spotted Gabe, and from the looks of it was ripping him a new one as Tyler physically held her back.

". . . and I'm going to tell your client that you suck," Natalie sputtered, flushed with anger and liquor courage, "that you fuck your clients and quit on them when they need you, because you're a paranoid psycho who can't see the truth when it's in front of him."

Gabe, of course, remained impassive, looking somewhere past Natalie's shoulder as he ignored her rant. When she finally paused to take a breath, he seized the opportunity to escape.

As he turned, his gaze locked momentarily with Reggie's, and for a split second she saw something—anger, hurt, disgust. Then the icy curtain dropped once again and he turned away without a word.

"I'm going home," Reggie announced. Natalie, still fuming, muttered something about what she'd like to do to Gabe's genitalia. But when she focused on Reggie, her gaze immediately softened.

"Are you sure? It's not even midnight yet, and the party's just getting started."

Oh great. She could stick around and watch everyone kiss each other Happy New Year and get all drunk and romantic while the man she loved by turns ignored her or looked at her like she was something he'd scraped off the bottom of his shoe.

Sounded fabulous.

Reggie shook her head. "I'm exhausted and . . ." *Every time I look at Gabe I feel like someone is sticking a red-hot meat skewer through my heart.*

Natalie nodded, reading her thoughts perfectly. "I'll come with you and spend the night." She looked up at Tyler who, to give him credit, admirably covered his disappointment with a resigned smile.

Touched by the show of sibling support, Reggie nevertheless refused. "Don't let me ruin two nights," she said. "I'll be fine. Jill will see me home safe. Besides, I think I need to be alone."

Once she got home, Reggie set the alarm, poured herself a generous glass of cabernet, settled into bed, and switched on the TV.

After forty-five minutes of channel surfing, she was both wired and disgusted with the fact that even with five hundred channels available, there was nothing to watch. She finally settled on a retrospective about the worst celebrity breakups of the year.

Perfect.

An idea struck her and she went into her office to retrieve her laptop, stopping on the way to refill her wine.

Within minutes she had an outline for a show, and possibly a new book: *Best Breakup Recipes.*

Cynical? Maybe. But she bet come Valentine's Day, a lot of viewers would be relieved not to have to watch yet another special on what to make your schmoopie poopie to ensure you got laid.

Suddenly, inexplicably, the hairs on her neck stood up. And that funny, tickly, *creepy* sensation gripped her stomach. Muting the television, she carefully moved the laptop to the bedside table and swung her feet to the floor.

She crept to her bedroom door, open just a crack, and peered down the dark hallway.

There. Again. The sound that must have gotten her attention last time. A soft creak of the floorboards, a scuffing sound like a shoe across her rug.

Someone is in my apartment!

Someone who knows how to bypass the alarm.

She shut the door firmly but softly, not wanting to alert the intruder that she knew of his presence. The click of the knob button lock rang like a gunshot.

Oh God, why hadn't she called the locksmith to install a deadbolt on the door like Gabe instructed months ago?

Terrified, she backed away from the door, giving a sigh of relief when she saw the phone handset on its cradle charging. Without thinking, she dialed.

Unable to face the loneliness of his sister's unoccupied apartment, after Gabe dropped off the CEO and his wife, he'd opted to hit one of the hip Marina bars and get himself good and shit-faced.

He couldn't decide what was worse, sitting home alone wallowing in pathetic loserdom as he drowned himself in single malt, or sitting on the outskirts of what looked like a giant sorority-fraternity mixer with slightly older students.

Cursing himself for not choosing a small dive, not that there was such a thing in this neighborhood, Gabe ignored yet another sidelong glance from yet another designer-clad cupcake showing ample but tasteful amounts of skin.

Part of him wished he could take her home, mindlessly bang her until images of Reggie, with her too-thin face and big, sad eyes, melted from his brain for a few precious minutes.

The bartender finally slid his drink in front of him and Gabe winced as icy scotch seared his throat. Oh, Reggie. It had nearly killed him, seeing her tonight. It took everything he had not to sink to his knees, bury his head against her stomach, and beg her to take him back.

He wanted to kiss the frown off her soft, delectable mouth and make love to her until the sadness in her eyes was replaced with the elemental joy of sexual satisfaction.

And feed her, for Christ's sake. She looked like she hadn't had a decent meal in weeks.

But he'd resisted. Actually, he surprised himself with his own resolve. A sign he was getting stronger, and that someday he'd be able to think about her without feeling like Freddy Krueger was clawing out his intestines.

His phone buzzed in his pocket and he pulled it out. Shit, couldn't she just leave him alone?

Finally, the damn thing went quiet as Reggie was sent to voice mail, only to immediately start ringing again.

Though a voice screamed that turning off his emergency phone was a major breach of professional conduct, he didn't trust himself and what he might do if he kept seeing her name on the caller ID. Besides, Reggie wasn't even a client anymore.

But just as he was about to flip the switch, a strange, uneasy feeling seized him. Gabe tried to pass it off as scotch in his empty stomach.

But as the phone rang for the third time, the agitation ate at him, chewing at his insides like an alien trying to break free. The same feeling he'd struggled with for weeks now, beaten into submission but never completely vanquished.

The feeling that he was completely wrong about Reggie.

Again, his brain kicked in, cataloging all the evidence against her in cold, analytical scrutiny.

His gut instinct that he'd had so little faith in recently kicked up a fierce ruckus. Something was wrong, it screamed. Something was really, really wrong.

And what if you're just making excuses to go see her because deep down you want her so much you don't even care if she's a liar.

What's the harm in checking on her? his gut argued. *What are you afraid of? Afraid you're so weak you won't be able to resist her charms and you'll fall into bed with her again.*

An idea, he admitted, that sounded pretty fuckin' good at two A.M. on a lonely New Year's.

What if you do? Do you want to risk being vulnerable again? Being that raw, that exposed?

What if something happens to her? Can you live with yourself?

And with that, his gut rested, and won, its case.

He threw several bills on the bar and pushed his way through the crowd, every instinct fiber of his being screaming to get to Reggie.

* * *

"Pickuppickuppickuppickup," she whispered frantically.

How could he not be answering his emergency line?

After four rings she was dropped into voice mail. She hung up and redialed immediately. Maybe he was somewhere loud and didn't hear the phone in time.

Still no answer.

Was he ignoring her?

She started to leave a message anyway. "Gabe, it's me—I—there's someone here—" Her bedroom door burst open, literally hanging off the hinges as a male body plowed through it.

Reggie gave a sharp scream and dropped the phone, scrambling back over the bed when she saw the vicious-looking chef's knife he held.

He lunged at her, and by the light of the bedside lamp she finally got a good look at his face.

"Max!" she gasped.

She had no time to wrap her mind around it as he approached, slowly but steadily, the razor-sharp blade glinting in the dim light.

"Why—why are you doing this?"

"You were mine, Reggie, always mine. I made you what you are. I gave you your show. And how do you repay me?"

Her heart seized as he brandished the knife near her nose.

"You let the network steal you away, steal my ideas like I'm some two-bit nothing."

"They bought the rights—you agreed—"

"And I could have lived with that, Reggie," Max continued as though she hadn't spoken, "but then you let him touch you. Whored yourself all over the country while I waited for you, waited for you to come back to me."

She froze, staring at the blade dancing in front of her as though she were a cobra and he a snake charmer.

"Want to know the funny thing? I was almost ready to forgive you. And then I saw you tonight." His face pulled in an expression of fierce disgust. "The way you look at him, still panting after him like a dirty bitch in heat. You have to be punished, Reggie."

He lifted his left hand, revealing a coil of rope.

Her brain seized as she tried to absorb the fact that Max, friendly, benign, *gay* Max was behind the strange notes, the threats, and the break-ins.

One thing she knew with brutal certainty: She couldn't let him tie her up.

"You don't want to do this, Max," she said, backing away across the bed, awkwardly shuffling on her knees. "I'm your friend, why would you want to hurt me?"

"Oh, darling Reggie," his evil grin sent chills through her very core, "you are so lovely, but so stupid. Not only do I *want* to do this, you have absolutely no idea how much I will *enjoy* doing this."

Nausea rose in Reggie's throat as she watched Max advance, knife in one hand, rope in another. Suddenly, he lunged, and without thinking, Reggie hurled herself onto the floor, slamming her knee into the bed frame; pain jolted up her arm as she caught her weight with her wrist. Scrambling to her feet, she aimed for the door in a staggering run.

A hand twisted in the hair at her nape and jerked hard, nearly pulling her off of her feet. Sobbing as she whirled around, she thrashed against his grip, numb to the pain of him pulling her hair out by the roots.

Through the echo of blood pounding in her head, she heard his vicious curses and her own harsh sobbing. In the corner of her eye she saw a glint of steel arching above her.

With one last, desperate twist, she jerked her head from his grasp and threw her arms up in front of her. Icy heat sliced through her left forearm, followed by an oozing liquid warmth.

He froze, as though shocked that he'd actually cut her. Adrenaline surging, she lunged for the door and sped down the hall, his footsteps thundering behind her.

His weight hit her full force as she raced for the front door, knocking her face-first against the hardwood floor. He scrambled for her hands, struggling to grip her wrists in one hand as he tied them with the other.

Did he still have the knife? She couldn't tell.

Bucking like a crazed bull underneath him, somehow she managed to twist onto her back and brace a foot against his chest. Using every ounce of strength in her body, she nailed him in the chest with her heel, toppling him over on his butt as he gasped for air.

"Help me!" she screamed as she ran for the kitchen, Max blocking the front door. "Help me," she yelled again, grasping the first weapon she found: her sturdy cast-iron frying pan.

Gabe ran down the block, his pace picking up as he became more and more convinced that something had happened to Reggie.

Fuck it. Even if nothing had happened to Reggie, he was pretty sure he didn't give a shit whether she'd faked the whole stalker thing or not.

He loved her that much. What that said about his professional character, he didn't care to think.

Not letting up his pace, he pulled out his cell phone and dialed in his voice mail code to listen to Reggie's message. A cold fist of fear squeezed his spine at the sound of her voice.

Gabe? It's me I—there's someone here—then the sound of a scuffle, the static-filled thump scrape of the phone being dropped, followed by Reggie's sharp, high scream.

He hung up, dialed 911, and broke into a sprint.

Ohchristohchristohchrist. Please let me get to her in time.

He hauled ass down Lombard, ignoring the curses of drunken partiers staggering out of bars and the blaring horn of the cab that nearly took him out.

Guilt and self-loathing choked him, but he forced it down. Later, he would beat himself up. Now, he had to get to Reggie.

Max recovered quickly and within seconds cornered Reggie in the kitchen. "Put it down, Reggie." He motioned the knife at the frying pan. "If you go quietly, I'll make it easier on you. I promise."

Rage, white hot and blinding, surged through her, consuming, for the moment, her near-paralyzing fear. How dare he? How dare this man take her trust, her friendship, and twist it to the point where he thought he had the right to do this to her.

With a cry like a banshee, she lunged straight at him, barely feeling the sharp blade as it sliced across her ribs. Gripping the heavy cast-iron handle with both hands, she did her best imitation of Barry Bonds on steroids and imagined knocking Max's head over the wall and into the bay.

Max slumped to the floor with an unnaturally loud thud. It was only when she heard the frantic male voice calling her name that she realized the thud was the sound of her door being kicked open.

"Reggie." Gabe skidded into the kitchen, quickly realized she wasn't the one out cold on the floor, and grabbed her in his arms.

Her head felt like it was stuffed with cotton. The cast-iron pan slid from her grasp, its sharp clang muffled as though under water.

Gabe was cradling her face in his hands, muttering something, kissing her face, looking like he was about to cry. She wanted to lean into his chest and go to sleep, but something reminded her that she needed to be mad at him.

Her arm hurt. Bad. And her side felt like someone had scraped her with a red-hot iron.

"I'm sorry, honey. I'm so sorry. You're going to be okay now, I promise I'll never leave you alone again." He was hugging her tight, burying his head in her hair as his body shook against her.

Now she remembered.

She pushed back, vaguely surprised to see tears streaking down his face. "You didn't answer your phone."

As sirens echoed outside her window, she slid into a dead faint.

Chapter Nineteen

The next several hours passed in a blur. The police arrived, quickly followed by an ambulance.

Reggie quickly regained consciousness, but she was so dazed from shock it was up to Gabe to fill them in on what happened as the paramedics examined the wounds on her arm and side.

Jesus Christ. Max.

The one guy they'd all dismissed out of hand.

Now Max was being loaded up on a stretcher, too, groggily indignant to find himself handcuffed and muttering something about a lawyer.

Gabe did his best to block him out, a hairsbreadth away from leaping across the room and choking him to death in full view of the cops.

"Are you all right, sir?" one of the paramedics asked. Looking down, he saw that streaks of blood marred the otherwise pristine white of his shirt.

Reggie's blood.

He barely made it to the bathroom before puking up the watery remains of his scotch.

The police needed to ask him more questions, so by the time he got to the hospital, Reggie was already in surgery to repair a damaged tendon in her left forearm.

Natalie and Tyler were in the waiting room, slumped

against each other exhausted, until Gabe walked in the room.

Natalie sprang to her feet and ran at him swinging, connecting her small fist into his jaw with surprising force.

"You asshole," she cried, hitting him again, this time in the stomach.

He didn't even bother to block her blows.

Thankfully, Tyler managed to grab her before she did any lasting damage. Not that he didn't deserve a broken nose or worse.

"You thought she was lying, and it almost got her killed," Natalie raged, but allowed Tyler to pull her into his arms.

"I'm sorry" was all Gabe said, knowing it was useless to defend himself.

The doctor came out and summoned Natalie into the treatment room.

You didn't answer your phone. Reggie's soft accusation echoed in his head, flaying him from the inside out. She'd called him for help, and he'd had himself so convinced of her perfidy that he'd ignored her.

When Natalie emerged and coldly informed him that Reggie wanted to talk to him, Gabe was shocked.

Tears burned his eyes and nose when he saw her, looking so helpless, her left arm wrapped up in thick, bulky layers of gauze and an IV protruding from her right.

Her face was ashen against the dark mass of hair against the pillow. Even her bright pink lips were leeched of color, and dark circles framed her tired eyes.

Even though he knew he didn't deserve to, he took the seat next to the bed and clasped her right hand, careful not to jostle the IV drip.

His heart exploded into a million tiny pieces when she feebly tried to tug her hand from his grip.

But he resisted, bringing her hand instead to his lips, closing his eyes and blocking out her look of hurt and betrayal. This was the last time he would ever touch her, and he wasn't above taking advantage of her weakened, pain-medicated state to savor it.

He breathed in, pressing his lips to her skin, imagining he could detect the warm cinnamon and skin scent he loved so much through the sharp antiseptic smell of the hospital.

Swallowing hard, he opened his eyes and finally dropped her hand.

"Why did you come tonight?" she whispered. "Did you get my message and finally believe me?"

"I was on my way before I even listened. I realized I needed to trust how I felt about you. Deep down I knew you hadn't made it all up."

"Too bad you couldn't have trusted yourself—and me—sooner." She was silent for a moment, eyelids drooping tiredly. "I want you to go now, Gabe."

His breath hitched on a sob as her eyes drifted closed. Bending down, he pressed his lips to her forehead, ignoring the way she stiffened. "I love you, Reggie Caldwell."

"Has she called you back?" Malcolm asked after he'd finished giving Gabe the details about the biotech company in Palo Alto where Gabe would be performing a security evaluation over the next week.

"No," Gabe replied shortly. He didn't tell Malcolm that in the past week he'd called Reggie twice and sent four e-mails. "But I talked to her sister again, who surprisingly didn't try to tear me a new asshole."

When he'd asked Natalie how Reggie was, she'd informed him that Reggie was miserable, as would be expected of a woman who was accused of being a liar by the man she loved before being attacked by a business associate she'd trusted. All in a very civil manner. But maybe that was because Natalie had her own guilt to work through after realizing that, through her own carelessness and her quest to develop her own TV show, she had inadvertently fed Max all of the information he needed not only to follow Reggie around the country, but to bypass her alarm system and break into her computer.

"I still can't believe we never caught on to this guy," Malcolm said. Gabe couldn't even take pleasure in the way Malcolm easily slipped back into "we" speak when he talked about work, now that Malcolm had hired him back as a full-time consultant. "He didn't even cover his tracks all that well."

Contrary to everyone's assumptions, Max was not gay. Judging by the vast amounts of pornography found on his computer—all doctored so Reggie's face replaced that of the models—he was heterosexual with a bondage S&M fetish. While following Reggie, he'd been able to easily cover his tracks with a series of business trips. He'd been smart about it too. He'd never flown into the exact city where Reggie was shooting; instead, he'd rented cars and sometimes drove several hours to get to her. Natalie, having had no reason to be suspicious of Max, had not only unwittingly fed him information about her schedule, but had freely used the security code for Reggie's alarm, as well as the password on her computer, never suspecting that Max was carefully watching over her shoulder.

"I'm sorry, man," Malcolm said, "if my bad intel permanently fucked this up for you."

"I had a choice not to listen," Gabe replied. That was the real crux of the matter. Evidence to the contrary or no, he should have listened to his instincts, which told him Reggie wasn't a liar, rather than giving in to his own fears of being taken for a ride by another celebrity client. He'd made the choice to ignore his gut and make the "logical" conclusion. He couldn't fault Reggie for never wanting to see him again.

But even though she'd made her wishes clear, he was determined to see her one last time. Not to offer excuses or explanations—he knew better than that. But to apologize to her face and tell her he loved her when her brain wasn't fogged with pain and vicodin.

* * *

Reggie stretched and flexed the fingers of her left hand. After three weeks, the doctors were sure her arm would make a full recovery, but she still got a stiff, tingling feeling every once in a while.

"Do you need an ibuprofen?" Natalie asked.

Reggie shook her head, marveling at the mother hen that had seemingly invaded her sister's body. Since the attack, Natalie had spent practically every waking hour with her, helping her get dressed and ready in the morning, making sure the kitchen was stocked.

After taking care of her sister for so many years, Reggie found the role reversal disconcerting. "I'm fine," she grumbled, "just a little stiff."

"Maybe you should take a break," Natalie said for like the hundredth time. Reggie was going through the galleys and reviewing the artwork for her new book.

Reggie rolled her eyes. "It's not like this is strenuous. Besides, what else am I going to do?"

As far as Reggie was concerned, that was the worst, most grating part of her current situation. What else *was* she going to do? Now that Max was in jail awaiting trial, *Simply Delicious* was on indefinite hiatus. There was even some question of scrapping the show altogether, for fear that it would be forever tainted.

As for *Simply Delicious, USA*, it was surrounded by its own scandal as details of Max's activities were reiterated all over the news. And even without the black mark, the network wouldn't commit to another season until they got the ratings for the first few episodes.

The irony of her situation was not lost on her. After doing everything in her power to make sure nothing threatened her career, now she was stuck in limbo, waiting for the network to call her with their decision.

Which left Reggie with something she hadn't had in over a year and a half: a wide open expanse of idle time.

A really bad state, considering that the second her mind wasn't occupied, it focused unerringly on Gabe. And mostly on that moment in the hospital when he kissed her hand and told her he loved her in a voice that sounded ripped from the bottom of his soul.

Most of the time she could convince herself it was all a drug-induced hallucination. Because if she let herself acknowledge the reality . . . She'd already cried enough in the last month to last four lifetimes.

So desperate was she for something to do, she'd asked Natalie to start booking private cooking lessons again.

Flipping another page, she made another note for her editor before the phone interrupted her.

"That might be Tyler," Natalie said as she jumped up.

Reggie tried to stifle her sneer. God, she hated the nasty attitude she couldn't seem to shake. The last two months had stripped her of her usual joy and optimism, leaving her uncharacteristically sullen and cynical. She should be happy for her sister.

It wasn't Natalie's fault she was wildly in love with a great guy, whereas Reggie's heart still felt like it had gone through a meat grinder.

Natalie held the handset out to her. "It's him."

As she'd done the four other times he'd called this week, Reggie silently shook her head.

"Are you sure?"

The question took her aback. Was she sure? How could she be sure when she wanted with her whole being to be able to feel nothing for Gabe? When not answering his call literally felt like it might kill her?

Mercifully, the phone stopped ringing.

"Maybe you should talk to him," Natalie said quietly, placing a glass of sparkling water next to Reggie's elbow as she sat.

"Are you insane? You were as angry at him as I was when he accused us of making the whole thing up."

Natalie held her hand up as though to staunch the tirade. "I know," she acknowledged. "But," she shook her head, "I know he's sorry and he really loves you. Call me crazy, but maybe he deserves another chance."

"How could I ever forgive him for what he did?"

"You forgave me." Natalie's voice cracked at that.

Reggie's own eyes filled in response. No matter how Reggie tried to convince her that none of it was her fault, Natalie couldn't stop blaming herself. "First of all, you didn't mean for anything to happen. Second of all, you're my sister and I love you, so even if it was somehow your fault—which it's not—I have to forgive you."

"If I deserve it, so does he," Natalie said stubbornly, continuing when she saw Reggie about to interrupt, "I know it was unfair and unreasonable, but he had his own twisted logic for believing Malcolm's conclusions."

"I can't believe you're defending him."

"I'm not saying he doesn't have his issues, but avoiding him isn't making you any happier."

No, she definitely wasn't any happier, Reggie thought two days later as she trudged up Vallejo Street. She noted sourly that the early February weather in San Francisco perfectly matched her mood—cold, damp, and utterly depressing.

Ducking her head against the cold breeze, she cursed her lack of gloves. The plastic handles of shopping bags dug into her icy fingers. She prayed feeling would come back by the time she started cooking, or she was liable to lose a finger on the cutting board.

She should have taken a cab, but for some stupid reason she'd thought the five-block walk from Whole Foods would be invigorating.

Instead, her left arm throbbed, her fingers threatened to permanently cramp into claws, and the ball of her right foot ached inside her high-heeled boot.

It was her own damn fault, she acknowledged as she

checked the address and confirmed that the gorgeous Victorian was indeed her destination. She was the one who'd told Natalie to start booking her private clients. She was the one who wanted to keep busy.

Now she was stuck teaching some guy how to cook dinner for his girlfriend so he could give her a really special Valentine's Day.

So romantic it made her want to puke.

She pressed the buzzer and was quickly greeted by a static-muffled voice. "Come on up, it's open."

Nice. He didn't even bother to open the door and help her with the groceries. Forget the romantic dinner. This guy needed a crash course in basic courtesy.

She pushed open the door and found herself at the foot of a steep staircase dimly lit by small alabaster sconces. Halfway up the stairs she realized something littered the cream runner that ran their length. Bending closer to see in the feeble light, she realized they were rose petals.

She paused, and an uneasy sensation creeped up her spine. God help me . . . No. Max was in jail. Natalie was on speed dial and knew exactly where to send the police if Reggie called.

Resentful of the lingering paranoia she feared would always be with her, Reggie charged the rest of the way up the stairs. No doubt the guy was using this as a practice session to set the scene for his big night.

Chapter Twenty

Gabe listened to Reggie's footsteps approaching and wiped his sweaty palms against his slacks.

Jesus, he'd had terrorists pointing semiautomatic rifles at him and hadn't been this nervous.

His eyes performed another quick scan of the room. In addition to the rose petals on the stairs, the living room boasted three bouquets of peonies, Reggie's favorite flower, as Natalie informed him. And damn hard to get this time of year.

Thank God for his sister, both for obtaining the flowers and assuring him that the apartment was his for the rest of the week.

A bottle of 1992 Silver Oak Cabernet was decanting on the table. All he needed was the girl.

"Hello," she called, and his gut twisted at the sound of her voice. "Should I just put these in the kitch—" The grocery bags slid from her fingers. An onion spilled out and rolled across the hardwood floor.

"What's going on?" She took a small step back as he approached. "Natalie," she whispered and whirled toward the stairs.

Gabe reached her in two strides and caught her by the arm. "Don't go. Please don't go."

She froze but didn't pull away, which he took as a good sign. He watched her gaze take in the details of the room.

"Why are you doing this?" She struggled to keep her voice flat, uninterested. "Why the big, elaborate setup?"

He closed his eyes and blew out a breath, wishing for once he was the kind of guy who could deliver a smooth line, charm his way out of trouble. "You wouldn't talk to me, and I had to see you." Sliding his hand down the leather sleeve of her jacket, he tangled his fingers in her icy ones.

She was shaking even harder than he was.

"So you and Natalie made up some BS about trying to impress your girlfriend?"

He risked one step closer, inhaling her spicy cinnamon scent. "It wasn't all BS. I'll cook you dinner for the rest of your life if you give me a second chance." He paused, squeezing his eyes shut. "I love you, Reggie. You have to know that."

She turned to look at him, finally, nose red and eyes glassy. "So what? I'm supposed to forgive you? You love me again, and it's all supposed to be okay?"

"I never stopped loving you." His voice was getting louder, but he didn't give a shit. Spinning her around, he gripped her shoulders and stared down into her beautiful, sweet face. "That night when I saw that you called—"

"You didn't answer your phone."

Gabe swallowed past the lump in his throat. Those five words would haunt him forever. "I was on my way to your apartment anyway. I didn't care if you made the whole thing up. I didn't care if you cared more about your career than you ever would about me."

She planted her fists on her hips and tilted her chin back. "That's supposed to make me feel better? You believed I was a liar but were willing to forgive me."

"That's not what I meant. I realized you couldn't have faked it, but even if you had, I would have forgiven you." He pressed the heels of his palms to his eyes. He hadn't exactly expected her to fall into his arms, but this was even harder than he'd imagined.

He jerked her into his arms, felt her shuddering against him as she fought tears. "And then when I knew he was hurting you, I wanted to die."

Reggie wanted to push him away, and she also wanted to throw her arms around him. Instead, she clutched at the front of his shirt, burying her face against his hard chest. She was sobbing now, unable to stop.

"Why can't I just hate you?" she wailed.

His lips trailed down her cheek, and he sniffed and swallowed hard, crying now too. He took her mouth and she tasted salty tears mixed with his unique masculine flavor.

I have to get out of here.

Avoiding him isn't making you any happier.

What if something happens and he decides I'm not trustworthy?

What if you walk away now and you have to live the rest of your life knowing you gave up the man of your dreams?

Her lips parted under his for the first soft, tentative flick of his tongue. Nothing had ever tasted better.

She prided herself on seizing every opportunity that came her way.

She'd never forgive herself if she didn't do the same now, didn't take the chance. For love. For happiness. For joy.

And fifty years or so of really amazing sex.

Shrugging out of her jacket, she coiled her arms around his neck and pressed close. He groaned, a low sound of relief that rumbled through his chest and down into her core. "I love you," she murmured between kisses, "but you're not even close to being off the hook."

He went wild then, fingers yanking her sweater up over her head as he pushed her back onto the couch. She didn't let go as she toppled over, yanking him down on top of her. "I can't make any promises this time," he said, voice muffled as his mouth slid, open and wet, down her throat. "Later—I'll start making it up to you later."

Buttons flew as they fought to pull his shirt off. Her bra

sprang open with a flick of his fingers. And then they were skin to skin, shaking and squirming against each other, and it felt so good it brought on another rush of tears.

"I was afraid I'd never get to touch you again," he whispered, as though reading her thoughts, bending his head to rain frantic kisses over the plump rise of her breasts. He sucked her nipple into his mouth like he would die if he didn't taste her, touch her.

Her eyes flew open, shocked at the immediate, almost painful burst of pleasure pulsing in her groin. "Wait," she murmured, suddenly aware that she was half naked and about to have sex on—whose couch? "Where are we?"

"Sister's place," he muttered around a mouthful of nipple. "Not coming home."

His dark hair brushed against her skin, soft, tickly, contrasting the hard suction of his mouth. He released her nipple with a pop, pushing away to strip off her boots, pants, and thong.

Then he was naked, too, so turned on she could smell it coming off him in musky waves. Uttering a harsh cry, he wrapped her legs around his hips and sank hard and deep inside her.

"I love you," he said, eyes black and fierce as he held her gaze. His big hands gripped her ass, tilting her up to take him deeper, harder, until she could feel him at the base of her spine.

I love you too. But she couldn't speak, clutching him to her as she rocked against him. God, she'd forgotten how good he felt inside her, huge and hard and powerful. She'd been so close to never feeling this again.

Sweat beaded and slicked their skin as he invaded her, surrounded her, overwhelmed her. She held him close and gave as good as she got.

"Tell me," he groaned. "Tell me you love me."

"I love you," she gasped as her orgasm took hold.

His face tightened, strained, and he shook and jerked

against her. Gripping his butt, she ground herself hard against his twitching cock, milking him hard as she came.

Later, bundled in robes, they sat at the kitchen table drinking wine and eating the dinner they'd finally prepared.

"Steak's overdone," Gabe grinned around a huge mouthful.

"You'll get the hang of it," Reggie said as she speared a limp, overcooked stalk of asparagus. She raised an eyebrow and pointed her fork menacingly. "You better."

Cooking dinner on his own was only the beginning of paying his dues, but he'd do whatever it took.

"What are you grinning about?" she laughed, her own smile stretching across the bottom half of her face.

Smiling, he pulled her off her chair and into his lap. "Damn, you make me happy, woman," he drawled. "You have from the beginning. But I was too afraid to trust it. I'm sorry, Reggie. Sorry I didn't trust the way I feel about you."

"As long as you do from now on," she warned, snuggling into his chest.

"So how long do we have?"

She tilted her chin up and gave him a puzzled look.

"Until you have to start traveling all over hell and gone to promote your book, or your show, or whatever." He felt her stiffen defensively. "Not that I mind," he quickly clarified.

"I don't know. Everything's completely up in the air." She lifted her hand to brush her hair back and the wide sleeve of her robe slid up her arm.

Gabe winced when he caught sight of the angry red scar slashing across her pale skin. For the rest of his life he'd never be able to look at that scar without guilt.

Pressing a kiss to the still raw-looking line, he said, "I'm sure they won't have you sidelined long."

She shifted on his lap, the soft squirm of her ass almost making him forget what they were talking about.

She noticed, and squirmed harder. "I don't care." She

pursed that luscious mouth. "That's not true. I do care. I don't want to lose my show." Smiling up at him, she said, "But I want to have a life too. With you." She slid her hand down and tugged at the knot of his robe. "And as many dirty weekends in Hawaii as we can squeeze in."

Turn the page for a sizzling excerpt from
OPERATION G-SPOT,
coming soon from Aphrodisia!

Chapter One

"**O**h my gosh, yes! Right there, Colin!"
They were doing it again, screwing like rabbits on speed.

In an attempt to shut out the sound of her brother and his girlfriend, Joyce, going at it in the neighboring bedroom, Liz Hart covered her ears and hummed into the darkness. The nonstop thump, thump, thump of a headboard slamming against a wall and the unmistakable moans and groans of hot, heavy sex refused to be blocked.

Liz uncovered her ears and let free a moan of her own, this one all about misery.

Karma had a real fucking funny sense of humor. The last year she'd gotten her daily laugh by sharing every screaming, quaking detail of her sex life with Colin. He had a major hang-up when it came to hearing about his little sister's exploits. Liz might understand that if she were actually little, or rather young.

She was twenty-four, old enough to be knocked up a half dozen times and divorced just as many. She didn't have kids, a husband—ex, or otherwise—or even a potential lover. And that was the reason karma was so funny.

For all she teased Colin by bragging about her many sexual conquests, 95 percent of what she told him was make-believe. 95 percent of what she told him was a lie. 95 percent of the time she didn't care. Listening to the ceaseless heavy panting and encroaching sounds of orgasm, the residual five percent reared its head. And damnit was it ugly. Make that jealous.

Just once Liz wanted to move past the fear she carried her mother's promiscuous genes, which made the woman put physical pleasure before anything else, including her daughter, and enjoy sex for the gratifying experience it should be. Just once she wanted to be the bold, sexually confident woman she pretended at. Just once she wanted to be the one screaming, moaning, and soaking the bed with a bona fide orgasm and not one she faked in order to end yet another unsatisfying encounter.

As if on cue, Joyce's emphatic cry rang out from the next room. "Ooh . . . don't st-op. I'm going to . . . come!"

Rolling her eyes, Liz sat up in bed and switched on the nightstand lamp. She couldn't handle playing the part of eavesdropping voyeur a second longer. Since it was after one A.M., she couldn't pick up the phone and call someone either. Not that there was anyone she would call on this particular matter. Imagine the response she would get if she phoned Diane, her friend and co-waitress, and whined she was envious of Joyce's orgasm because Liz had never had one of her own. Like almost everyone else, Diane knew her as the flamboyant, brash-acting, sex maniac she impersonated to avoid the psychoanalysis (a.k.a. bullshit) that would accompany the truth.

The phone wasn't an option for venting her orgasm envy. Thank God for the Internet.

Six weeks ago, following what should have been an assured climax with a man reputed for his bedroom skills—a night that once again ended orgasm-less—Liz had become desperate and searched for support online. It turned out that she wasn't the only healthy, twenty-something woman whose mind overruled her body's desire. There were at least two other women who suffered similar ailments.

Fiona lived states away in Michigan, but was still in the same time zone. The headstrong lawyer would either be asleep or have her legs wrapped around her latest attempt at orgasm. In Seattle, Kristi was three hours behind Atlanta time. The sex toy designer could be home . . . and more likely testing out her latest pleasure gadget.

Unlike Liz, neither Fiona nor Kristi had a problem getting off with the aid of battery-operated plastic. It was when a man entered the equation that their G-spots performed a disappearing act. Liz clearly had no G-spot, period. She'd tried over a dozen of Kristi's guaranteed-to-get-you-off products and not one managed to do the job.

Sighing, Liz climbed from bed and pulled a T-shirt over her nude body. She ran a hand through her straight, cropped black hair as she padded barefoot to the desk in the corner of her bedroom, fired up her laptop, and connected to the Internet.

A fresh series of moans came from the bedroom next door, and she grimaced.

Oh, gawd. Not again.

A year ago, she'd moved into her brother's place to keep him from feeling alone following his messy divorce from Satan in a deceptively sugary sweet package. Now that Colin had Joyce—a genuinely sugary sweet package—in his life and, subsequently, someone to share his large house with, Liz seriously needed to think about getting back into a place of her own. Until then . . . *Please let Kristi be online.*

Opening up the instant messenger program, she logged into *Operation G-Spot*, the group the women had created for private chats, and buzzed Kristi.

Liz: Tell me you're there.
Kristi: No can do. I'm in the South Pacific, bare-assed and bent over a lounge chair, while the local orgasm gods fight over who gets to tongue me to climax next.
Liz: As long as you're fantasizing, mind if I join you on that chair? Sure as hell would be better than being here. Yet

again, I have the pleasure of falling asleep to the sounds of huffing and puffing and my brother getting his rocks off.

Kristi: Colin's having another sex marathon overnighter?

Liz: Yes! And I'm sooo jealous.

Kristi: Ditto. Have you considered Fi's advice to give the sure thing another try? You said he had you wet before your brother walked in on the two of you.

Liz: Pull-eaze tell me you're joking. Dusty had me wet for a few seconds, but he couldn't finish the job. Besides, as I've told you a gazillion times, the guy's a conceited ass-hole. If he were the last man alive, I wouldn't spread my legs for him again.

Kristi: Mmm . . . maybe I should come to Atlanta and give him a try. Way you described him a few weeks ago, he sounds deserving of that conceit—totally dee-lish and hung like an elephant. Not that I have a prob with a teeny weenie, but a big one on a man who knows how to use it sounds damned promising.

Liz: Yeah, promising in a 'never going to accomplish the impossible' sort of way. Hey, I gotta go. I just remembered I'm working the breakfast shift. TTYL.

Kristi: Bye, GLGS.

Liz snorted at the acronym as she closed the messenger program out. She didn't need "good luck getting some." She needed good luck getting off. And not with Dusty either.

Damn Kristi for bringing up Colin's longtime friend, Dusty Marr. The woman could generally be counted on for encouragement and a bad joke or two, just enough to improve Liz's mood. Tonight Kristi hadn't improved her mood a bit, but forced her to lie about working the breakfast shift so she could end the conversation about a guy she would just as soon dropped off the planet.

On top of having a cock that even Liz had to admit was impressive, Dusty was tall, built, blond, and, a month and a half ago, had managed the improbable. Unlike any man or machine before him, his smooth moves had vanquished Liz's fear of turning into her mother long enough to have her wet and eager to fuck. Before they could move past oral gratification, Colin had come home, found them getting nasty on the living room floor, and burst the hedonistic bubble. After taking things to her bedroom, Liz had tried to clear her mind and get back into the heat of the moment to no avail.

And she couldn't be happier for that.

She'd decided to sleep with Dusty because his reputation claimed him a sure thing. The moment she'd stopped thinking with her pheromones, she remembered that he was a lot more than a sure thing. He was an arrogant, shallow dickhead who put sex above all else, screwing a different woman every night of the week without care for whom his actions might hurt. In other words, he was the male equivalent of her mother.

She wasn't doing Dusty again. No way. No how. No matter if thinking of his talented tongue pushing into her nether lips had her sex shockingly moist.

Suppressing the urge to rub her hand between her tingling thighs, Liz stood and returned to the bed. She tugged the T-shirt over her head to reveal tented nipples. Her wetness and the aroused state of her nipples were side effects of the rain-cooled, September night air snaking in the slightly ajar bedroom window. The cold could make a person wet. Tonight it could, because she refused to believe thoughts of Dusty and his sexual prowess were behind her stimulated body.

"What do you say I rub your balls for luck?"

Dusty Marr halted the slide of his pool stick mid-draw to quirk an appreciative eyebrow at the leggy blonde reclining against the pool table. Decked out in a snug black cat suit with a daringly scoop-necked bodice and matching stilettos, the carnal tilt of her smile and the heat in her emerald eyes told him exactly which balls she had in mind. Not the ones on the table, but those stirring to life along with his dick.

He hadn't had sex in weeks, since the night Liz Hart, his best friend's younger sister, had shocked the hell out of him by challenging him to a game of pool where oral sex was the stake. A decade his junior, he'd first met her as a loudmouth sixteen-year-old. Jail bait personified, she'd already been endowed with all the right assets to have his testosterone spiking, as well as an overt loathing of him that said he would never get his hands on her. Despite the fact that her dislike of him remained intact, eight years later he'd gotten his hands, and his mouth, on her. Her moans of pleasure said she'd loved every minute of it, too. That is, right up until the moment she'd started trembling with the first signs of climax, only to stop short, tell him he sucked in the sack and ordered him out of her brother's house.

Despite the recent hiatus, Dusty was no stranger to sex. He loved every aspect of it—from the feel of a woman's soft curves and the breathy gasps and sighs of her coming undone to the knowledge it was the one thing in life he was truly good at and no one he'd ever slept with could believe otherwise.

No one but Liz.

He wasn't about to let his ego or his dick suffer from the accusations of one questionably sane woman.

Dusty signaled to his pool opponent to continue without him. With a wicked smile, he turned to the blonde. He opened his mouth to tell her she was welcome to rub far more than his balls; the slender woman with olive skin and closely cropped ebony hair sitting at the bar fifty feet away stopped him from saying a word.

The place was fairly dark and equally smoky. Still, there was no mistaking her identity. Liz. Shit.

What was she doing here?

Outside of that night several weeks ago, she never came to his bar. Not only was *Dusty's Backroom* located in a small town nearly a half hour from her Atlanta home, it was a country bar. Liz was as rock and roll as a person could get.

Stranger than her presence, was her attire. She was a jeans and T-shirt kind of gal, a woman who didn't bother with makeup and didn't need to. Only, tonight she had bothered with makeup, and the jeans and T-shirt were nowhere to be found. A dress the same electric blue shade as her eyes molded to her curves, managing to cover her from throat to elbow to knee and somehow still look sinful as hell, maybe because he remembered exactly how she looked out of that dress. Tall, toned, and slippery when wet.

His cock hardened further, pressing against the fly of his jeans. She hadn't climaxed for him, but that she'd been dripping wet right up until she'd ended things was no exaggeration.

"Dusty?" a husky feminine voice questioned.

He turned back, realizing it was the blonde who'd spoken. Had they slept together, or how did she know his name?

Movement from the corner of his eye had him looking back at Liz. His gut tightened. She had company. Dusty knew those who frequented his bar. Between his gauzy pink shirt and painted nails, which lent serious question to his sexuality, and spiked black with blond-streaked hair, the guy didn't look like a local, or someone Liz's brother would approve of. For Colin's sake, he would get rid of the jerk.

"Give me a few minutes," he told the blonde. "I need to take care of something." For an instant she looked agitated, but then her smile returned. Leaning in so that her plentiful tits couldn't help but press against him, she rubbed her knuckles along his whiskered cheek. "As I recall, you're well worth the wait."

Obviously they had slept together, Dusty thought as he started toward the bar. That the blonde was not only back for more, but willing to wait for him without asking why proved how inaccurate Liz was in calling him a bad lover. If there was a bad lover between them, it was she . . . and so it seemed her frilly new friend was trying to find out firsthand.

In a move as old as dirt, the guy slid his arm around her

shoulders, then coasted his hand down her side to caress the outer swell of a breast. The hand continued to rub, inching slowly inward. Disgust swept through Dusty, mirroring the look in Liz's eyes. He expected her temper to take flight and for her to punch the unsuspecting schmuck. She didn't move a muscle, but plastered on a smile an idiot could tell was fake.

She might be okay with getting felt up by a creep in front of dozens of prying eyes, but Colin sure as hell wouldn't approve. For her brother, Dusty would save her ass.

Reaching her, he took her free hand and tugged her from the barstool, dislodging the other man's arm. She was a tall woman, inches beneath his six-foot-one frame. In three-inch spiked heels, her mouth was nearly even with his. She must have done some thickening trick with her ruby red lipstick because, as he pulled her into his side, he noticed her lips were plumper than ever. Plump and glistening, they brought to mind the way her mouth had looked wrapped around his dick.

The woman might be a nutcase, to kick him out the way she had, but he remembered now that she wasn't bad at sex. At least the oral variety. Those full, gifted lips gave head like no other before her.

He rubbed his thump in the valley of her palm. "Elizabeth." Dressed the way she was, her full, more feminine name sounded appropriate. "I was wondering when you'd get here."

The feigned smile left her lips and icy blue eyes bored into his. She yanked at her hand. "What the fuck do you want, Marr?"

Dusty smirked. Now there was the Liz he knew. He let free her hand to give her ass a gentle swat. "Such a bitchy tease. You know what that does to me, babe."

"No, *babe*," she retorted, drawing out the bogus endearment. "I'm afraid I don't."

"That's my Elizabeth, always fishing for a reminder."

Kissing her was bound to lose him a night of carnal bliss with the blonde. Dusty glanced back to the pool table where the woman waited in all her leggy glory. She looked like the type who could get her legs behind her ears without any trouble at all. Liz would owe him for the loss, big time.

He looked back at Liz. His attention returned to her lush mouth, and his cock jerked. Though he hadn't planned on getting naked with her again, several excellent ways she might repay him—each of which had to do with leaving a ruby red ring around his shaft—popped into his head.

"Open up," he ordered, giving her ass another swat.

Her mouth opened, likely to tell him off. Before she could speak, he pulled her snug to him and sank his tongue past her lips. Her gasp pushed into his mouth as a blast of hot air, a sultry puff at odds with the biting pinch of her short nails into his arms.

Call him a sadist, but he loved that bite and the way she brought her knee up, attempting to leave a permanent mark on the family jewels. Loved even more the way she couldn't stop her hot little sigh as he sucked at the softness of her inner cheeks. He brought his tongue over her teeth, across her gums and twined it with her own stubbornly still one, consuming her taste—a mixture of dark imported beer and white hot, fiery female.

The nip of Liz's nails gentled as he tilted his hips into hers and rubbed his erection against her mound. A second, far breathier sigh slid between their joined mouths and she shifted her pelvis in a restless way that applied pressure to his constrained dick so forcefully it bordered on pain. Her tongue shot to life, no longer denying her passionate nature, but stroking against his with wild urgency. Meeting that urgency head on, by stripping her naked and banging her on the hardwood dance floor, held real appeal. Any other place and time he might have done it. Here, in his bar, he didn't dare.

He might talk sex here, might even regularly meet a lover at

the bar, but he would never risk his authority with his employees by doing a woman while on the job. Hell, he'd already risked too much with his current behavior.

Dusty lifted his mouth from Liz's to find her looking at
him, nostrils flaring and breath coming in warm, sexy, shallow pants. The points of her aroused nipples stabbed at her
dress, taunting his mouth to pull them inside and suck.

"Bastard." She hissed the word, bringing his attention
from her tits to the narrowed set of her eyes and making him
question his decision not to screw her here and now.

Had ticked-off women always had this rampant effect on
his libido, or did the mad urge to plow into her despite their
surroundings have to do with her ordering him out when
she'd been on the verge of orgasm? Was her behavior that
night the real reason he'd gone so long without sex?

He'd told himself the recent dry spell had to do with a hec-
tic work schedule and not lack of desire. Maybe that wasn't
the case. Maybe her accusation of him as a bad lover had
messed with his ego and, in turn, his head.

"Looks like you're busy, so I guess I'll see you around,"
Frilly-guy said from somewhere to Dusty's left.

Liz glanced over and mumbled a good-bye. Leveling her
gaze on Dusty, she swiped the back of her hand across her
mouth. "Do you want to die?"

Only if they were talking about the little death, and then,
yeah, for better or worse, he was rock hard and more than
ready. "Man like that only has one thing on his mind."

She went wide-eyed. "Ohmigawd! You think he was trying
to get in my pants? And here I thought he wanted to hook up
some afternoon for tea and cookies." Dismissing the innocent
act, she grabbed her beer bottle from the bar and pushed past
him. "I came here to find a guy to fuck, so if you don't
mind . . ."

Grabbing hold of her arm, he spun her back. "Does Colin
know why you're here?"

She looked incredulous. "Maybe you've suddenly decided

to care if my brother approves of my behavior around men, but I could give a crap less."

It wasn't her behavior around men in general, Dusty told himself, but that around strangers who could be after her for God only knew what reasons. Right. As if his own intentions hadn't taken a far from noble turn. "He worries about you."

"Yeah, well, he shouldn't. I'm a big girl."

She sure as hell was.

He should let her remark slide and her arm go, before he made himself look like a complete hypocrite. Blame it on the celibacy streak, but temptation was too great to resist. He sent his gaze the length of her, lingering on her small but firm breasts and then lower to her crotch.

Was she wet for him after the kiss?

Dusty inhaled, half expecting the musky scent of her arousal to cut through the mixed aroma of cigarettes, perfume, and greasy food. Returning to her eyes, he let the lust reflect in his voice. "As if I could forget."

For a fleeting moment, desire kindled in Liz's eyes, deepening the already intense shade of blue. Then she pulled her arm free of his hold and planted a hand at her hip. "Let me clear something up for you, Marr. When I said I came here to find a guy to fuck, I didn't mean you. I'm looking for someone who doesn't need a 10-step program to find a woman's G-spot."

The barb pricked deeper than he cared to acknowledge. He pushed out a laugh. "Babe, I had your G-spot pegged in seconds. Or did you forget you were about to come before you pulled the Jekyll and Hyde routine and tossed me out on my ass?"

"I'm not your *babe,* and you're damned lucky you got as far as you did. Now, unless you came over here for some reason other than to piss me off, I suggest you get back to your flavor-of-the-night. As good as you think you are, I seriously doubt Blondie's going to wait forever."

Dusty glanced at the pool tables and found the blonde

standing where he'd left her. He should be thrilled the woman had stuck around after witnessing him doing the tongue-mambo with Liz. Another night he would have been. Tonight he could only see the desperation in the move. The blonde would be no challenge for his sexual confidence. Whether his recent dry spell had to do with Liz's cutting accusation, he suddenly found he needed that challenge.

Smirking at Liz, he teased, "Watching, were you? Getting jealous?"

She snorted and turned on her heel, flashing a tight ass he knew she owed to daily jogs. An ass, he also knew, that felt more than a little fine filling his hands. "Good-bye, Marr. Be careful not to trip over your ego on the way back to the pool table. An obstacle that big's liable to cause serious damage."